# VIRAL BOUND

Written by
## Dan Waltz

DW Publishing

www.danwaltz.com

## ACKNOWLEDGEMENTS

Thanks to the many people involved in this project including my wife, Candis, for giving me the space and understanding I needed to complete such a task. To my family and friends for their encouragement and support that allows me to "Follow my Dreams" that much easier. Special thanks to Rose & Tyler Kenny for their military experience and expertise. Also to Dan Cheff for his expert shooting, and research. Special thanks to my two editors, Tony Root and Jan Waltz who helped make this book legible enough for you to read.

-

Original FX Makeup by Joelene Brzezinski, as I appeared in the 2011 film, "Zombie Apocalypse; Redemption."

-

Thanks also to the following songs and verses for their words and inspiration...
• For What It's Worth - Buffalo Springfield and Stephen Stills
• Ecclesiastes 3:1-8 - The King James Bible
• Maroon 5
• Turn! Turn! Turn! - The Byrds and Pete Seeger
• Signs - Five Man Electric Band and Les Emmerson

## DEDICATION

This novel is dedicated to my grandmother, Louise Case, diagnosed with colon cancer in 2009. She lived a full and happy life, right up to the end. 1920-2012. Thank you Grandma, for all your love and support over the years. R.I.P.

# PROLOGUE

"There is an appointed time for everything. And there is a time for every event under heaven: A time to give birth, and a time to die; a time to plant and a time to uproot what is planted. A time to kill and a time to heal; a time to tear down and a time to build up. A time to weep, and a time to laugh; a time to mourn, and a time to dance. A time to throw stones, and a time to gather stones; a time to embrace, and a time to shun embracing. A time to search, and a time to give up as lost; a time to keep, and a time to throw away. A time to tear apart, and a time to sew together; a time to be silent, and a time to speak. A time to love, and a time to hate; a time for war, and a time for peace."

~ Ecclesiastes 3:1-8 KJV

"I'm terribly sorry, Steve, but I'm afraid that you have cancer." A doctor, dressed in typical doctor garb right down to the white jacket and stethoscope wrapped around his neck, broke the bad news to Steve as he stared him dead in the eye. The doctor was stone-faced as hell, as if he had delivered the same news to thousands of patients hundreds of times before. Or was it hundreds of patients thousands of times before? Whichever the case may be, it was then that Steve's living nightmare began.

Steve, feeling faint, passed out in the hallway of Atlanta General Hospital. His body fell limp and sank to the floor, hitting his head hard against the brick wall and then again on the tiled floor. His mullet-styled hair mopped up most of the blood that trickled from the gash in the back of his head. It also helped hide the pool forming beneath him and the seriousness of the fall.

**Facebook Page:**
A CURE for CANCER FOUND!
• Like - 650700

**Twitter:** Breaking news! "A cure for cancer has been found!" More, as the story develops.

**Facebook:** Sue Beck
"So I don't need to quit smoking after all:)?"
• Like · 1020 people

**Facebook:** Bob Hickey
"Honestly, what the hell took you so long?"
• Like · 4800 people

**Facebook:** Janet Arnez
"Thank you sweet Jesus. Mother will be saved!" • Like - 18

**Facebook:** Tim Thompson
"My father suffers from prostate cancer. You have no idea what this means to me. Thank you." • Like - 178 people

**Facebook:** Cindy McKinley
"A little too late for my mother. She died of lung cancer last week." • Like - 0

**Twitter:** Matt Calhound
"So where do we get this amazing drug?"

**Facebook:** <u>Sabrina Catcher</u>
"Cure for cancer, really? Where were you a month ago when my mother died?"
• Like - 0


<u>"A Cure for CANCER found!"</u>  This was the most popular headline that read on newspapers and blogs across the country, as well as the world. On January 01, 2012, the day that would go down in history as the day that "the world as it once was" changed for everyone.

Thousands of blog posts and nonstop tweets on Twitter were a daily occurrence. A page on Facebook with the same title instantly received thousands of posts and "Likes" every hour.

Thousands of people were posting what kind of cancer that they or a loved one has or once had, and how thankful they were for such spectacular news. But some posts weren't so grateful at all. Some wallowed in resentment, bemoaning "too little, too late." Obviously their loved ones had already passed away from this dreaded disease. Some posts were filled with sarcasm as if it were too good to be true. Most posts were filled with questions, asking how, when, or where cancer patients could get this miracle drug. Every question seemed ignored and went unanswered, buried in a sea of comments.

No one seemed to know anything about the supposed cure or even how word about it had gotten out in the first place. National NEWS kept reporting the same story over and over again, as if there were no other news to report. The ticker scrolled at the bottom of the screen, repeating, "A cure for cancer found, more on tonight's special newscast" – a newscast that eventually was canceled due to a lack of information.

Answers could not be found anywhere, and the creators of Facebook and Twitter weren't revealing who was behind the original posts about the cure. They, possibly the only ones who would know, who started this chaos.

Some suspected the claims about the cure were false, blaming ugly rumors and foul play. "How dare people get others' hopes up like that," some cried. "They're playing with people's minds, for God's sake."

But many still believed the cure had been found. The religious thanked their gods, while the atheistic simply thanked their lucky stars for a dream-come-true.

It was, in fact, true, wasn't it? No one would post anything like that if it weren't, would they?

Was there really a cure for cancer? That was the multi-billion-dollar question. As for Dr. Scott Selmer, he believed with all his heart the cure had really been found.

**Facebook:** McOzy Maryland Cozwell
"I lost my 7-year-old daughter to leukemia last year. Thanks, but no thanks." • Like 0

**Facebook:** Donald Wakefield
"If you were interested in the public good, you would post the cure, not the discovery. Otherwise, I think you're selling it. Someone you love will die needlessly because of the delay."
• Like 89

**Facebook:** Crazy Larry
"Now I can do all the things bad for me." • Like 66

**Facebook:** Sharon Smith
"Why now? Are your patents expiring? I've always been a skeptic about the entire healthcare field." • Like 19

**Facebook:** The Ribbon Cutters
"Cancer is a necessary evil." • Like 0

**Facebook:** Dirk Williams
"Hurray! I can finally eat what I want, drink what want, and almost smoke what I want. Two out three ain't bad." • Like 4320

**Facebook:** California Sunshine
"I am so thankful that there is finally something that stopped/cured cancer. I have lost family members to it, and because I lived in Los Angeles for 32 years, I often wondered if the air that I breathed would be the end of me. Now let's fix the AIDS problem!" • Like 1244

**Facebook:** CandyApples Candi Appleton
"Thank God and all the doctors for everyday miracles; now if they could find a cure for war!" • Like 1333

**Facebook:** George Currier
"If it had only come a year sooner, I would not have lost five

good friends. I know several others maimed from chemo and radiation, drastically limiting their quality of life." • Like 974

**Facebook:** Adam Sales
"Everything related to cancer treatments are one big lie ... always has been; it's always been about PROFIT. Make money off DISEASE." • Like 3203

**Twitter:** Glenn Bradshaw
"It's about damn time! I can hardly pee."

**Twitter:** Timothy Sutton
"Does anyone know how this whole thing got started?"

**Facebook:** Tom Glenwood
"Why isn't anyone answering any of the questions? Hello? Is anyone there?" • Like 209

**Facebook:** Dr. Frank Steinbek
"Only time will tell if the cure itself causes yet another medical affliction caused by man." • Like 678

**Twitter:** MAChound
"So where do we get this amazing drug? Anybody?" • Like 5677

Dr. Scott Selmer was a family man with his first grandchild on the way. He was a 10-year veteran of modern medicine, specializing in virology. He graduated with highest honors, at the top of his class. With those credentials and more, plus a little help from some powerful friends of the family, he quickly worked his way up the food chain and landed a cushy job overseeing a small lab at a subsidiary of one of the largest pharmaceutical companies in the world.

The lab, based in South America, was where researchers developed medications to help people around the world live more painless and happier lives. What would the world be without painkillers and Prozac?

Some would have considered Selmer a hero for taking away all the pain and suffering humankind once knew, all with one little pill. The world owed Selmer a great deal of gratitude for all of his award-winning hard work, dedication, and accomplishments over the years.

Selmer had grave concerns over the latest news, though – news that had spread like wildfire, only faster. The same news that headlined every newspaper and magazine on the planet. The news about "The Cure for Cancer." He had concerns for his job, for one, and his family, for another. But more importantly, he had grave concerns for the future of the United States and what a cure like this could do to his country.

Selmer truly believed that a cure for cancer would bring an end to life, as everyone knew it. He believed that the economy would tank, believe it or not, worse than it already had. The job market could not possibly accommodate the approximately 1,500 more people per day who, without this cure, would have – should have – died from some type of cancer or another. The unemployment system was not prepared to provide for them either.

If that wasn't bad enough, what about the millions of physicians, scientists, nurses, morticians, lab, and pharmaceutical employees who would lose their jobs? The list would go on and on. What would they do for work? There would be hospitals, pharmacies, labs, funeral parlors, and research facilities closing down across America and all over the world. Cemeteries would not have the funds to maintain their grounds. Funeral homes would have to look for creative ways to stay afloat by possibly opening their beautiful parlors to wedding ceremonies and banquets when fewer people were dying, and they assuredly would. Who would want to get married and buried at the same place?

After all, cancer accounts for the majority of deaths in the United States and abroad. Flower shops and nurseries would probably close their doors. Most of their business went to the dead. Prescription drugs would skyrocket in price as the pharmaceutical companies attempted to stay in business, which would send health insurance premiums through the roof. And, let's not forget about the trickle down effect. With so many more people out of work, few would be spending money at stores, let alone buying new cars and appliances. There would be layoffs and closings beyond anyone's imagination.

Mass panic would ensue. And who would be able to pay for this magical drug? Who would pay for patients who simply couldn't afford it? Would the government foot the bill and raise taxes? What about coverage? Insurance? Medicaid?

Or would society just let the unprivileged die while others, possibly sharing the same hospital room, were cured of this terrible disease simply because one had money and the other did not?

While collapsing the economy, could this also cause riots? What about natural resources? Would there be enough food? Enough gas? Enough oil? With fewer people dying and more people living longer, could the Earth provide enough resources to go around, and, if so, for how long? Scientists have estimated that the Earth can only provide for about 12 billion people. The population was already at 7 billion. Without cancer, how much time would it take to reach or exceed 12?

Most people were too blinded by the news of the cure to worry about any repercussions, but not Dr. Scott Selmer.

Could all this really happen? Yes? No? Maybe? Who the hell knows? In Selmer's eyes, it most definitely and assuredly would.

Selmer was not the type to just sit back and watch things happen. He didn't ascend to the top of his profession just by sitting back and watching what others accomplished. Sure, he had help, but he was also very good at what he did. He had a family to think about and a grandchild on the way. Their future was at stake. He had to do something about it.

And something about it he certainly did.

•••

# CHAPTER 1

A young man in his early 30s got ready to leave a country bar at 2:30 in the morning. The man stretched his neck as far as he could as he tried exiting the car with a final kiss. Falling backward out of the backseat of the car, he heard giggles as his bare ass smacked hard against the black pavement. He felt no pain, even though sharp gravel pitted his buttocks and the palms of his hands when he landed. He stumbled to his feet, brushed his ass off, sending gravel in both directions before he pulled up his pants, zipped up his fly, and staggered across the maintenance-deprived parking lot. He then mounted his sunburst-yellow crotch rocket.

The young man fumbled with his keys, dropping them once, no, twice on the pavement before successfully guiding the right key into the ignition and starting the bike. He shoved his helmet on over his ears, fastened the strap under his chin, and gripped the clutch. He revved the engine twice before taking off like there was no tomorrow. He had no clue just how true that cliché was at the time.

Steve, the man on the bike, left drunk but no drunker than usual, as he'd made this trip many times in worse condition. He frequented this dive several times each week to take advantage of the cheap beer and the trashy women who hung out there. A mint 1974 GTO was parked in Steve's garage, restored by himself, but he chose the bike so he didn't have to take the bimbos home at the end of the night.

While at the bar, Steve usually got what he came for, and it was usually in the back seat of the girl's car or out in the field behind the Dumpsters. He didn't care where, and the girls were usually too far wasted to know any better.

The bar, considered a dive by most, was located out in the country about 15 miles west of the nearest town, Bear Creek. Its surroundings were nothing but farmland, mainly cornfields, beans, and acres upon acres of woods. For the most part, the biker's biggest hazard at this time of night were animals crossing in front of him, mainly deer, fox, coons, and an occasional skunk. Oh, how he would regret the nights the skunks appeared, but so far he'd been pretty lucky. He'd only had a couple of near misses and one or two skunks in his many years of visiting this fine establishment.

Steve traveled east toward town. He usually slowed down as he passed through town, but not this time. This time, his mind was preoccupied with earlier events. A brief smile appeared on his face as images of Sarah in the backseat of her car flashed through his mind. This was the first time with Sarah and, for all he knew, probably the last.

Sarah wasn't a regular at the bar, yet no other had the effect on him that she had. *"This girl was dangerous,"* he thought. He could get too into her. His heart could be broken, and he constantly fought to prevent that. His walls went up and quickly wiped her from his mind, replacing images of her with clutter and worry. He was running a little late, much later than usual.

Steve was worried about getting home and getting some rest before work the next morning. For Steve, it was already the next morning, and he had to be at the garage where he worked as a mechanic in just a few hours. He leaned into the handlebars and jumped on the gas.

Steve was not just an average mechanic. He was quite exceptional. He could have made a decent living in a different town. But here in Bear Creek, out in the middle of Nowheresville, where the average income was well below the poverty level, he barely scraped by and pretty much spent every dime he made and then some. Unfortunately, he pissed away most of what he made in booze.

Steve approached the small town at about 90 mph, and when the speed limit changed from rural 55 mph to city 25 mph, his speedometer hardly fluttered. He didn't lay off the gas, and he didn't pull in the clutch. He just turned off his headlights and sailed straight through. In fact, he rode so fast that he didn't even notice cutting off another driver at the curve. He was clean out of sight when that car lost control, jumped the curb, and slammed head-on into a nearby building. It was a crash that could be heard for miles if people were actually awake at that hour. Steve, on the other hand, with his helmet on and the radio blasting in his ears, didn't hear a sound.

●●●

# CHAPTER 2

NZ—NZ—NZ—NZ, the audible alarm sounded. Lights glared, sirens pierced the air, and the sweet smell of burning antifreeze quickly filled the air shortly after the car crashed into a solid-brick building.

Rescue workers wasted no time extracting a young girl from the completely totaled wreckage and transported her to the nearest emergency room. The car, a maroon 1997 Chevy Monte Carlo, lay empty, sticking halfway in and halfway out of a privately owned laboratory. The girl, for the moment dubbed Jane Doe, as emergency crews found no identification on her, was alive but barely. For the type of injuries she suffered, an airlift was necessary, if she had any chance of living at all. The local hospital quickly called for a helicopter to transfer her to the metropolitan hospital an hour away by air.

Emergency services wasted no time getting to the scene of the accident, as the municipal offices were just a little more than a mile away. The sound of the accident had been heard from there, as well as the 24-hour donut shop just down the road. The electricity at the popular police hangout flickered off and then back on again from the car deflecting off a power pole right before striking the brick building.

Hitting the pole had slowed the car, possibly saving the young girl's life. The brick building she'd hit still had power, but it was quickly cut when the emergency workers arrived, in fear of fire breaking out. Some of the wall sockets and switches had already begun smoking.

The privately owned laboratory inside the building was equipped with both silent and audible alarms for break-ins or fires. The ceiling's sprinkler system was already dispersing water, sensing the steam and smoke pouring from the car's hood and from the arcing electrical wires in the damaged wall.

The owner of the laboratory arrived shortly after the ambulance had departed with the unconscious girl. The professor quickly scurried around the demolished car, assessing the damage with the beam from his mini-Maglight that he kept in his lab coat pocket. He peered inside the car as he shuffled by.

"Oh my god," the professor said as he cringed, looking at the blood splattered in all directions. The car appeared to have a faulty airbag that failed to do what it was designed to do. The windshield was smashed from both directions, from the driver's head hitting it from the inside and from the bombardment of bricks crashing down upon it on the outside. There was no doubt in the professor's mind that whoever had been driving this car probably wouldn't make it to the hospital alive.

Steam still rose up from the car's hood and fogged the main room of the lab, making it a bit of a challenge to see and difficult to breathe. Squinting, the professor looked around, following the beam of the flashlight. Battery-powered emergency lights above the doors helped a bit but were mainly just illuminating the exits. Water sprayed down from the sprinklers above, drenching the professor as he carefully walked through the room. Shards of glass glistened everywhere the professor looked as the beam of light fell upon them. Shattered test tubes and beakers and overturned tables filled the flashlight's path.

The beam of light abruptly stopped when the professor spotted something that disturbed him greatly. The lab cages, which lined the exterior wall, were knocked down, some crushed and bent to hell as bricks had rained down upon them. Others had traveled a great distance, airborne from the impact, and slammed hard against the wall on the opposite side of the room, taking out anything in their path. The professor found cage after cage, most in complete shambles, tossed about as if caught in a cyclone.

Inside each cage the professor found dead mouse after dead mouse, and dead lab rat after dead lab rat. His heart broke and sank deep in his chest when he thought of the months of hard work and research that had just been lost. He had been only weeks away from finishing many of the projects in progress. Then he came across a few more cages that lay mangled on the floor. They appeared to be intertwined with one another. Tags on the cages indicated their level of importance and of potential danger. These were the highest, and among the worst, in that order. One had a dead lab rat lying just outside what was left of its wire frame. The rat appeared to be partially eaten, presumably by one of the two rats that were housed in the two adjacent cages, which lay empty on the floor. The professor quickly became nervous, edgy, and extremely anxious after confirming the tags on the cages, and the tag piercing the partially eaten rat's ear.

The professor started rambling to himself, "Oh no, no. This can't be." He looked in all directions and constantly backed into things, knocking them to the floor as he tried to make his way out of the dark lab as quickly as he could. He stared down at the floor and spotted what appeared to be a microscope and its accompanying slides and cultured trays used for growing cells. Steam or smoke was rising from some of the trays and from the slides spread across the floor. A beaker, filled with who-knows-what, was tipped over on the table, dripping its contents onto the items below and causing some unknown chemical to flee airborne. The wide-eyed professor quickly grabbed a handkerchief from his lab coat, covered his nose and mouth, and continued to evacuate the room as quickly as he could. He started shaking and sweating profusely. For the first time, the thought of being sent to prison for not reporting some of his findings to the Centers for Disease Control, entered his mind. Confused and not knowing what to do, he stumbled his way into his office.

The professor grabbed his laptop and travel bag from the closet. He quickly filled the bag with a few items from his desk and from one of the tables, being very careful not to take the handkerchief away from his face. He then grabbed a small box from the mini-refrigerator and stuck it in his travel bag as well. The box contained samples that he didn't care for the authorities to see.

The professor made his way to exit the building, avoiding the officials talking in the next room. The only way out without being seen was the way he had come in. He squeezed back through the hole in the wall next to the car, stumbling over loose debris and glass. A shard of broken glass from the car's headlamp snagged the hem of his lab coat as he passed. He tugged on the coat, tearing it on the sharp glass. He glanced briefly at the car's license plate, making a mental note of its number as he left.

The professor loaded his bag into his car and drove around the block to an alleyway. He pulled up alongside a Dumpster and took the small box from his bag and tossed it in before leaving for who-knows-where.

•••

## CHAPTER 3

Steve pulled his bike up the drive and parked it in his garage next to the GTO. He stroked the car's fender as he walked by as if it was his pride and joy, and it was. All the blood, sweat, and tears shed in laboring over the car to restore it to mint condition had certainly paid off. It was truly something to see.

He quickly stripped off his clothes, jumped in the shower, and headed off to bed right after, without a care in the world. Steve was grinning from ear to ear as he reminisced about the events of the evening. He couldn't keep his mind off her.

Steve fell fast asleep shortly after his head hit the pillow, not even waiting for his hair to dry. Minutes later, he was awakened by a low-flying helicopter. The rotor blades pounded the cool morning air, vibrating the windows of Steve's home. He cursed, rolled over, squeezed his pillow down over his aching head, and quickly fell back to sleep. Another half-hour passed and he was awakened once again by the window rattling above his head. It was the same helicopter flying the return trip. Little did Steve know that it was a medical helicopter, and its only cargo was the driver of the car he had cut off, not much more than an hour earlier.

Two hours later, Steve was startled once again, but this time by his alarm clock. It was time for work. Steve slammed his hand on the snooze button, rolled over, and was off to sleep again only to be awakened nine minutes later when his alarm sounded again. Once again, Steve hit the snooze.

"Damn it! What a frickin' night," Steve said as the alarm sounded for the fourth time. He threw off his pillow, kicked down his sheets and sat up on the edge of the bed, hanging his head wearily. He thought about calling in sick. This thought soon evaporated from his mind when nature started calling. He stumbled out of bed, buck- naked and with clear signs of a hangover.

Steve walked out from the bathroom a minute later, sporting a lit cigarette drooping from his lips. He grabbed the daily newspaper from his porch and the TV remote from the table, and flipped the TV set on to catch some local news. He listened as he made his way back to the bathroom to get ready for work. His subconscious mind was hard at work as most of his actions were done without a thought and with his eyes closed. Like most people, he was caught up in his morning routine.

Now standing in his boxers, he dragged a comb through his hair while watching the morning news. This was when he first learned of a near-fatal accident downtown in the wee hours of the morning.

"That's funny, I didn't see anything on the road last night, and I drove right through there," he thought aloud. Steve clicked off the set with the remote, slid into his pants, and stepped into his shoes, all in one smooth move. He then struggled to pull his shirt over his head, refusing to let go of his cigarette. He grabbed his helmet off the dresser and hurried to his bike.

He tried to push his helmet on over his head, but he failed to complete the task. The pressure of his hangover was far too great, so he fastened the helmet to the side of the bike and drove off like a bat out of hell. He clipped the curb at the end of the drive, sending the bike airborne a few feet before coming to rest. The tires screeched when they hit the pavement. Steve would be fashionably late once again, just one of many bad habits that he possessed.

•••

# CHAPTER 4

"Did anyone get a hold of the owner of this place?" the chief asked at the scene of the accident.

"Yes, sir," an officer answered. "I talked to him a few minutes ago on the phone. He was already en route. The alarm company had already notified him, sir."

"He only lives a couple miles down the road? Where the hell is he then?"

"Sir?" a voice from another officer spoke.

"Yes, lieutenant?"

"Wasn't he just here? I thought I saw someone walking around in the lab a few minutes ago in a white lab coat. That wasn't him?"

"That might have been a crime-scene officer," the chief

replied. "You saw someone walking around and you didn't stop him?"

"Sir, he was headed this way. I thought he was coming to see us."

The officers took off in the direction of the lab. One branched off and looked inside the office.

"Sir, there are things missing in here."

"Missing? What the hell?" asked the chief.

"There was a laptop here, sir, sitting right here on the desk, and now it's gone."

"Are you sure, lieutenant?"

"Yes, sir. Absolutely, sir," the lieutenant said. "It was the same model as mine."

"Maybe it was just a looter, sir," another officer spoke from the other side of the building.

"A looter? In Bear Creek?"

"There are looters everywhere, sir."

The chief walked over to the smashed car and looked it over. Something caught his eye. "Possibly, I guess, but this looter was wearing a white lab coat, and I'll bet you anything that it was the professor," the chief said as he peeled a piece of torn fabric from the front end of the car. He paused and stared at the officer who'd seen the professor earlier.

"Find out why he left and what he took with him," the chief said. "And find out why he didn't come and talk to us before leaving." The chief paused. "Something's not right here. Find him and bring him to me!"

The police, puzzled by the professor's disappearance, taped off the lab as if it were a crime scene, in hopes of deterring anyone else from coming in and snooping around. The lab housed many kinds of drugs and very expensive equipment that should not be left unattended. Since locking up the building wasn't an option due to the gaping hole left in the wall after the car had been towed away, the chief ordered one of the officers to remain at the scene until the professor could be located.

Four more hours had passed, and there was still no sign of the professor. The officer in the patrol car at the accident scene was getting antsy and wanting to go home, tired of waiting and waving away gawkers. *Where could the professor have gone? And why did he leave in the first place?* These were just a couple of the unanswered questions that filled the officer's mind. He needed answers and needed them now so he could go home to his wife and kids. His shift was about to end, and the chief ordered the building to be boarded up. The officer knew he would have to wait for that to be completed before he could leave. Overtime once again.

The bill for securing the building and the overtime would be sent to the lab. That was one bill that would probably never be paid, as the professor was now hundreds of miles away, sitting comfortably in the cockpit of his private plane headed to who-knows-where.

The building was finally boarded up two hours after the officer's shift was supposed to have ended, and he was finally able to go home to his family. Dinner would be cold once again. He made one more walk around, checking all the doors and windows of the lab before climbing back into his squad car.

Just before he turned the key to start the engine, he heard and felt two large staccato thumps. The car rocked back and forth.

•••

# CHAPTER 5

At the service station, Steve worked under a 1999 Chevy Caprice performing the standard grease job and oil change, while the news played on the flat screen, mounted high on the nearby wall. It hung opposite a row of chairs for their waiting patrons, entertaining them while they waited for their cars to be repaired.

Once again, the news repeated the same accident story as before, only this time asking for anyone who saw anything or knew the whereabouts of Professor Simon Campbell, the owner of the lab, to call the local police department. The contact number for the police station continuously scrolled across the bottom of the screen. No one had reported seeing anything as yet, but the newscast did mention that police had found the laboratory's security DVR, as two cameras were mounted on the outside of the building.

Robert, Steve's boss, noticed Steve under the Caprice, holding his head in pain. "You all right Steve? Hit your head?" he asked.

"Fine, just fine, Bob. Kind of a late night last night and a bit of a headache, that's all," Steve replied.

"Hangover, huh? Visiting that sleazy bar again, I see."

Steve shrugged and ignored the comment. Bob knew Steve well enough after working together for more than eight years that his question really didn't need answering.

"Hey, you must have seen that accident last night then," Bob said.

"No, actually not, Bob. Seems like I should have, though. I drove right through there about the same time that they are saying it happened. Must have just missed it, I guess."

Nothing more was said, even though Bob appeared to be a bit troubled. Bob walked over to Steve's motorcycle parked in the corner of the garage. He looked it over as if he were looking for some damage. Seeing none, he looked back at Steve and shrugged.

•••

## CHAPTER 6

Twenty-four hours had passed since the accident and there was still no sign of the professor. A warrant was issued, and the lab's DVR was confiscated for review. The outside cameras on the building primarily covered the back door and the small parking area along the side of the building. It also covered a very small section of the road that passed in front of the building and the intersection that the car passed through. Unfortunately, the cameras were also on a timer, which kept them panning the parking lot, the street, and then back again. The Monte Carlo was only pictured for a split second, right before it jumped curb. There were no obvious signs of anything else.

"Anything on the tape, sergeant?" the lieutenant asked as he walked into the room where the sergeant was reviewing the file.

"No, sir. I went through the whole thing three times. You barely see the car just before it jumps the curb. There's nothing there to speak of, sir."

"Damn, that's too bad. I was really hoping for something other than a girl losing control of her car," the lieutenant said.

"Alcohol involved?"

"I would assume, but we haven't heard back from the hospital yet. The girl was pretty messed up. She'll be lucky if she makes it."

"Unfortunately, it will probably take an autopsy to find out, sir."

"Yeah, you're probably right. Thanks for looking, sergeant."

"Sir?"

"Yes, sergeant? What's on your mind?"

"Well, sir, what if she doesn't make it?"

"Unless someone comes forward, we'll probably have to close the case. I'm afraid we have nothing to go on here. A deer could have run out in front of her for all we know."

"Roger that, sir."

•••

# CHAPTER 7

About a half-mile up the road from the lab, a flatbed truck hauling a load of used tires swerved off the road. It narrowly missed a large crow pecking away at a dead rat lying in the middle of the street. The rat was freshly killed, a fallen victim to a car less than an hour ago. The crow seemed to be enjoying his meal and refused to leave it unless he really had to, like at the very last second as a vehicle approached, its driver swerving and scared half to death.

The truck ended up off the road, fishtailing in the loose gravel in the driver's efforts to bring the truck back onto the pavement without losing his load. Unfortunately, he wasn't that lucky, and used tires bounced off the flatbed left and right and rolled in all directions. Two of the tires headed downhill toward town, picking up speed as if they had a mind of their own. Others wobbled to their not-so-far-off destinations. The two tires that went racing down the road eventually came to an abrupt halt, but only after hitting the rear end of a squad car.

"What the hell?" were the only words that came to mind for the confused officer sitting behind the steering wheel. He turned to look over his shoulder and saw two tires wobbling in the middle of the street. Something told him that his shift was not quite over yet, after all.

The officer stepped out of the squad car and watched the two tires make their final wobble before coming to a rest.

"What the hell is going on?" he said, scratching his head as he looked down the street in the direction from where the tires had come.

Moments earlier, up the road, the crow flew off to a nearby tree, narrowly escaping being run over by one of the two runaway tires, one of which bounced off the dead rat the crow had just been standing on. A little bit of the rat's blood was thrown from the tire with each revolution it made as it rolled down the hill.

Soon the rat was joined by two of the crow's closest friends who chose to share this little snack. The driver of the truck who'd just lost his load soon interrupted the crows' tasty meal. He came stomping over, venting his frustration at the birds. A few choice words and some gravel kicked their way was all it took for the remaining crows to skedaddle up in the tree themselves, cawing all the way. One crow refused to leave the food behind and peeled the rat's carcass off the road with his claws, taking his meal to go. The bird soon dropped the carcass after carrying it only a couple hundred feet. The rat landed just off the shoulder of the road next to a sidewalk in front of a small white house.

Moments later, the front door of the house opened and a little old lady, probably in her mid- to late 70s, appeared in the doorway. She opened the door and out came a usually well-behaved golden retriever on a short leash.

The old lady usually took her dog for a walk at the same time every day. This day was no different, except the normally well-behaved dog was not behaving very well at all.

The retriever literally pulled the old lady down the front porch steps and dragged her down the drive. Once past the drive, the dog continued to drag her onto the sidewalk, where he then made a beeline right to the dead rat's carcass as if he had seen the darned thing fall from the sky.

The golden retriever snatched the dead rodent in his mouth before the lady could do anything about it. She was too busy trying to catch her breath, and she had no idea the rat had even been there. The lady told the dog to "drop it" in a firm voice umpteen times. It was a voice not expected to come out of such a little lady. Regardless, the dog refused to listen. He just shied away and chomped down harder. The blood from the rat filled the dog's chops and dripped down his chin. It was clear by the dog's expression that the rodent tasted pretty good to him. The rat's blood ran down his long tongue to the back of his throat with every chomp. Years of Kibbles and Bits and Dog Chow never tasted this good to the canine, and it would be hard for the dog to ever go back to his old diet.

Without thinking, the old lady grabbed the tail of the rat, which was protruding from the dog's mouth, and she pulled. She tugged on it with all her might. The dog just pulled back, unwilling to loosen his grip. She yanked at the tail, and the dog yanked back, his hind feet digging into the soft ground. The lady yanked at the rat once more, and the dog retaliated with another tug of his own. He shook his head from side to side, this time with a low, playful growl.

Suddenly, with a final tug, the carcass came apart and the old lady fell back on her duff in the soft grass. The tug of war was now over. The dog wolfed down his half of the carcass in not much more than a gulp, thinking his owner would be back for more. The lady, now sitting on the lawn, held in her hands a very-bloodied tail attached to the blood-dripping buttock and rear legs of what once had been a white rat.

Blood dripped onto her clothes. She threw the remains to the ground as if it had tried to bite her and pulled the dog away, while wiping her bloodied hands on the grass.

Today's walk was over before it began.

•••

## CHAPTER 8

In an alleyway behind the lab, another large, grungy-looking white rat struggled through the same small crack the now-dead rat had exited a short time ago. The mortar had fallen out between the cinder blocks from the impact of the car on the opposite side of the building.

The rat left behind a streak of blood on the sidewalls of the jagged hole. Patches of rat hair stuck to the brick. The rat looked like it had crawled through a war zone, with missing hair and deep cuts along both sides of its body.

The look on the rat's face after squeezing out from the hole was like that of a prisoner just released from solitary confinement. Freedom. The rat squinted in the bright sunlight and stretched his long, skinny body. He sniffed the clean air above, then twitched his nose and sniffed the ground below. Instincts set in as he hugged close to the building and scrounged around for something good to eat. He found a few morsels here and there, but it wasn't enough. It's never enough. Ever since the professor gave him that shot, he always hungered for food.

A French fry, rolled in dirt, discarded by a passing car, tasted pretty good to the rat, but not as good as a hamburger would have. He craved meat more than anything.

It wasn't long before the rat stumbled across a drunken wino, sound asleep between a Dumpster and the adjacent building's brick wall. The rat sniffed the bottom of the sot's boot, worked his way along the man's leg, and then cautiously approached the brown paper sack the man held in his hand. The rat sniffed the base of the bag, which held a bottle of the drunk's favorite cheap wine. The rat jumped back, startled by a slight movement of the paper bag. The rat then cautiously followed the shape of the bottle up to the neck, which led directly to the wino's hand. The rat sniffed the hand, licked his chops, and bit down on the guy's little finger, which was sticking out a hole in the man's worn-out glove.

The bite drew blood, and lots of it. This startled the drunk, waking him from his stupor, but he was in no condition to feel much pain. Nevertheless, he jerked his hand away. He slowly focused his eyes and found himself face-to-face with a very large, ugly, white rat. He quickly backhanded the rat away, hitting it with the hand holding the bottle and sending the rat crashing against the Dumpster with a loud echoing thud. The crash didn't seem to faze the rat at all. It slid down the side of the Dumpster and fell to the ground, flat on its rump. The rat wasted no time getting back to its feet. It shook off the impact and charged the old man. The rat bit him again, this time on the shin exposed by the drunk's torn coveralls.

The man kicked at the rat, sending it back to the Dumpster again and again, but each time the rat just shook off each blow with no long-term effect. The drunk finally had enough time to stumble to his feet. He turned and awkwardly staggered away from the apparently rabid animal at an awkward pace, leaving a small trail of blood behind. The rat followed, pausing at each blood droplet. It lapped up each drop of blood as it worked its way down the alley, as if it were playing connect-the-dots in hopes of finding the drunken man at the end of the trail.

The old man stumbled down the road, falling, tripping over his own feet, but he wasted no time getting back up and moving on, even if he were on his knees temporarily. The fear of that crazed rat drove him forward but kept him looking back over his shoulder, making him stumble even more. Seeing nothing following for a short while, he headed down another alley and found a new cozy place to sleep off his stupor. He sat down on a short step at the back door of a business and dressed his wounds with napkins he found in the trash. Leaning back against a wall, with one eye partially open, he nervously awaited sleep. He hoped the rat would never find him again. A short time later, he succumbed to the booze in his system and fell fast asleep in the back doorway of an old family-owned bookstore named Orville's Books.

Yet another animal soon woke the drunk. It startled the old man as he kicked his way back into the corner of the doorway. This time, it was only a half-starved alley cat licking at the man's wounds through the blood-soaked napkins. The drunk soon realized that it wasn't the rat and warmed up to the animal. He stroked the cat's soft fur and fell back asleep once again with the cat purring in his arms.

The old drunk, bound to get no sleep, was awakened yet a third time. This time, he was roused by the bookstore's owner, himself, Mr. Orville. He arrived to open his shop like he did every day. He woke the drunk with a slight kick to the sleeping man's boot. The man moaned and rolled over to the side. He then received a harder kick. This got his attention. Mr. Orville then set him straight and sent him on his merry way. Mr. Orville then unlocked the door and cracked it open, and the alley cat pushed his way through.

"Hey!" Mr. Orville cried out. "Get out of here, cat!" He reached down and picked up the mangy cat by the scruff of its neck and looked it over. "Wow, you don't look so hot, buddy."

The cat, in a paralyzing grip, just stared back with a dazed look in his runny eyes. The storeowner set the cat down on the floor and knelt beside it. He began to stroke the cat's whiskers back with his index finger, not once, but twice. The cat seemed to enjoy it, so Mr. Orville stroked the whiskers back a third time. This time, without hesitation the cat sank its teeth deep into Mr. Orville's forefinger as it passed near the cat's mouth.

The bite was deep and drew a lot of blood. Mr.

Orville backhanded the cat and got to his feet. He then kicked the cat out the back door, cursing and holding his injured hand.

"With my luck, the damned thing probably has rabies," he mumbled to himself as he made his way to the bathroom to wash his wound. He returned with his finger wrapped in a ball of toilet paper. He then went on with his daily routine.

Mr. Orville first unlocked the front door and turned on the lights. He then flipped the sign from "Closed" to "Open," and stepped behind the counter to count the drawer.

"Open for business," he said to himself, shaking the pain from his finger.

An hour later, a customer found Mr. Orville passed out and not breathing, lying behind the counter. His clothes were soaked with sweat. His index finger festered with oozing pus, bruised black and blue, and swelled three times its normal size. It was practically bursting out of its own skin.

The female customer who found him was a registered nurse in her late 30s. She quickly checked for vital signs as she reached in her purse for her cell phone to call for help. When she wasn't looking, the apparently dead storeowner awoke and grabbed her arm, pulling himself up and biting a chunk of flesh from the woman's cheek. The nurse threw a hand to her face and wailed in pain. Blood poured down her cheek onto her shoulder and arm. She struggled to free herself, but Mr. Orville's grip was too strong. He pulled her to the floor as he moved in for another bite. The third bite, to her neck, was fatal. It sheared her jugular vein and blood spurted in all directions like a fountain until all blood pressure was lost. The storeowner spent the next few minutes feeding on the nurse's flesh as if he hadn't eaten in months.

A strip of bells hung from the ceiling near the front door rang out as the door to the bookstore pushed open. Another customer entered the store. Mr. Orville paused a moment when he heard the chiming bells but quickly returned to the meal at hand. The customer, a young boy, looked at the children's books for awhile until he heard some disgusting noises coming from behind the counter. Curious at what could possibly be making such crude sounds, the young boy peeked around the counter for a look. Shocked at what he saw, the boy fled the store screaming bloody murder at the top of his lungs.

The boy ran for help and didn't stop until he found it. Mr. Orville tried getting up to follow, but he slipped on the pool of blood on the floor and continued with his meal instead. The boy was long gone before the old man could get to his feet.

Minutes later, two police officers arrived at the bookstore, finding what appeared to be a blood bath. Blood was just about everywhere they looked; the floor, the walls, the ceiling, and even the books were spattered with it. Hunks of torn flesh from what was left of the dismembered nurse were found behind the counter. One officer found parts of the woman, coincidentally, in the horror/fiction aisle with the book "Hannibal" peering down from the shelf with a big smile on Lecter's face. The officers looked around some more, weapons drawn in disbelief, wondering who or what could possibly do such a horrible thing.

One officer pulled a handkerchief from his pocket to cover his nose and mouth, while the other dropped to his knees and uncontrollably vomited all over the hardwood floors. Chunks of coffee-saturated donuts mixed in with the officer's own bile, splashed across the floor in a sloppy, slippery mess.

Mr. Orville was nowhere to be found and presumed no longer in the store, as a trail of blood led the police out the back door and through the alley.

As the police officers followed the blood trail, they came across another dead body – dead, with chucks of flesh missing and its neck torn wide open. This victim was just a 9-year-old girl, her mother sitting in the alley holding the child in her bloodied arms, crying out for help and pointing in the direction Mr. Orville went after making a snack out of her little girl. The police officers radioed for help.

•••

# CHAPTER 9

Jane Doe passed away less than a day after the car accident. She died at the hospital before the surgeons could do anything for her. She arrived with a very high fever, and even though the nurses had her on ice, they were unable to bring her temperature down. The doctors reported that the girl's temperature had reached in excess of 112 degrees and that she basically barbecued her own brain from the inside out.

Her body was marked with the infamous toe tag and sent down to the basement morgue. No autopsy was ordered, as everyone knew what had happened and no family members could be found because she had no identification and no one had come forward to claim the body. "Death caused by a multitude of injuries from ramming a Monte Carlo head-on into a brick wall" was a good enough explanation for everyone involved, including the mortician. *Why add unnecessary work?* the mortician thought. *No sense in spending tax dollars on someone we can't identify who died for reasons that were so blatantly obvious.*

Maybe an autopsy would have come to quite a different conclusion, though. Maybe it could have prevented what happened next. The mortician might have noticed the rat bites up and down the girl's left leg and chose to investigate further. He might have run extensive blood tests to find out what was lurking inside the girl's body.

Instead, as the mortician was filling out the paperwork for the local funeral parlor for pickup, Jane Doe's body slowly began to twitch on the gurney. Her arms and legs started moving, and before the mortician knew anything was happening, Jane Doe was sitting upright on the gurney no more than four feet behind him.

The girl stared at the back of the mortician's head with her milky eyes and let out an eerie moan. The moan startled the mortician, but before he could turn all the way around to look, Jane Doe was already upon him with her teeth sunk deep into his shoulder. Blood spurted in all directions, splattering the stainless-steel table, the walls, and the floor. The mortician tried to fight her off, but it was too late; he'd lost too much blood too quickly and was on the verge of passing out. Jane Doe must have nicked the mortician's jugular. The girl continued to feast upon him, eating him alive as he lay dying on the floor.

Down the hallway, a third-shift nurse stepped out of the elevator, humming a song by Maroon 5. She walked past the glass doors and entered the morgue. She walked in on Jane Doe and interrupted her meal. The nurse dropped the surgical tray she carried containing stainless-steel utensils and a fresh cup of coffee. Not knowing what to do next, the nurse screamed at the top of her lungs. She couldn't believe what she was seeing and was fully unaware that she had just dumped a scorching-hot cup of coffee down the front of her scrubs.

Jane Doe got to her feet and turned to face the nurse. The young nurse turned and fled down the hall as hot coffee ran down her legs. She skidded to a stop in front of the elevator doors. The nurse frantically hit the buttons but didn't wait for the doors to open, as the afflicted girl from the morgue shambled closer and closer, dragging her broken limbs behind.

The mortician's blood was dripping from Jane Doe's mouth, down her chin, and onto the tiled floor. It mixed in with her own blood from her mangled body as it smeared grossly across the floor. With one arm extended and the other limp by her side, she moaned in the nurse's direction. The nurse ran from her and quickly found a place to hide. She froze in place, petrified with fear.

If only the nurse had kept running, she'd have easily outrun the mangled girl and made it to the stairs. There would be no way for Jane Doe to follow; she couldn't have climbed them in her condition. She would have been safe for sure. Instead, she hunkered down and tried to slow her breathing as best she could. She couldn't stop shaking, though. Her teeth chattered like a jackhammer. She was letting her nerves get the best of her. If she didn't settle down, she was going to get herself killed.

Luckily for the nurse, the elevator doors opened wide just as Jane Doe passed in front of them. The girl lugged her broken body inside, and the doors slid shut, trapping her inside. Jane Doe leaned motionless against the elevator wall for a moment, not knowing what to do. She had nowhere to go, at least until someone else pushed a button signaling the elevator for a pickup on another floor.

On the sixth floor, a male nurse pushed the button and awaited the elevator's arrival. He had a male patient on a gurney, headed for surgery. The elevator rose to the challenge and started its journey upward.

Meanwhile, the morgue nurse finally caught her breath but was still shaking uncontrollably. She had no clue where Jane Doe was. For all she knew, the girl could be standing right around the corner. The nurse's mind raced, playing tricks on her with every sound she heard or imagined.

•••

# CHAPTER 10

Back in town, two police officers followed a blood trail out of the alley. As they turned the corner, they noticed a dozen or so people gathered in the park in the center of town. Concerned, they cautiously approached to make sure that everything was all right. They thought Mr. Orville may have headed in that direction and hoped they could apprehend him there.

More people continued to join the group, at least doubling its size in a matter of minutes. A feeling of uncertainty fell over the officers as they approached the growing crowd.

As they got closer, they noticed similarities in the people that were a bit out of the norm. The group appeared as if they were lost, bewildered, possibly even drunk. Partiers, the officers immediately suspected. Soon they heard moans coming from the crowd, growing louder and louder as the officers approached.

"What do you think?" one officer asked the other.

"Maybe protesters?"

"Protesters? Really? I can't believe they would even consider 'Occupying' this hick town."

"Look, there are some gathered in front of the bank over there," one officer sarcastically stated as he pointed to the bank on the other side of the park.

The other officer chuckled. "We could only wish they were protestors. This doesn't look good. Maybe we should call for backup?"

"Hate to say it, Harry, but I'm your backup. Looks like we're it."

The crowd seemed to be shambling around, aimlessly bumping into one another. Some even appeared to be sniffing the air like dogs as the officers approached.

Bear Creek was usually a pretty quiet town, with the exception of a couple of times when the Hell's Angels rode in for a day or two. This wasn't any Hell's Angels group, though. The ground didn't shake for days on end, and there weren't any signs of bikes anywhere. The officers continued to approach with caution. At 50 yards away, the officers looked at each other blankly. Both of them reached for their batons at the same time as if reading each other's minds. They were now close enough to be noticed by a few in the group; some instantly started stumbling in their direction.

"Hold it right there," one of the cops hollered out while holding a hand up, but they kept coming, staggering one step at a time. "They're all drunk, all right."

Some had their arms stretched out, reaching, while others had arms limp at their sides. Some were even dragging a leg all the way. They all were moaning, reaching, and swaying in all directions. Again, one of the officers shouted out for the crowd to stand down, and again he got absolutely no response, at least not the response he was wanting. His voice attracted the attention of more individuals from the crowd, and they headed in the officers' direction. One officer pulled his side arm and fired a warning shot over the group's heads. The shot was loud and echoed its way through the alleys of the town. It also attracted even more apparently drunk people to the group. They started coming out of the shadows, from behind trees, around cars, and from doorways. Now, even more were meandering in the officers' direction.

"Way to go, hotshot. Now they're all headed this way. We're in trouble here!"

One of the cops quickly reached for his mic; the other drew his side arm. Before long, it looked as if half the population of Bear Creek was in Central Park, moaning, hissing, and shambling in their direction.

The cops began backpedaling at a pretty fast clip, thinking this could end badly. The crowd kept coming, and the first among the crowd were almost upon them. Now they could see every bloody, grotesque detail of the oncoming crowd. Moans, growls, and bloody saliva dripped from their chins, staining their clothes from head to toe. They wouldn't stop. The officers were about to be trampled by a slow-moving stampede if they didn't come up with a solution quick.

"Where's our backup?" one cop asked, while leaning into the radio attached to his shoulder. "We're in trouble here!" Both cops are now retreating, shuffling backward, back to the alley they came from earlier, and backing right into, and coming face-to-face with, the mom they met earlier in the alley, the one who'd been holding her dead daughter. The daughter wasn't dead after all, but was walking with her mother side-by-side. They both had the same milky, glazed, dead look in their eyes, and both moaned, almost growled in sync with each other. Like mother, like daughter.

"We're trapped!" one of the officers exclaimed.

"Wait, not yet." The other cop started firing, taking the girl and her mother out first. His partner could not believe what he'd just seen. *Did my partner just gun down a mother and her child?* They were the first threat, after all, and had to be first to go in order to survive the oncoming mob, which was slowly closing in on them.

But the bullets had little effect on them. The officer fired two rounds at the mother's chest, then shot again. It knocked her back and down to the ground, but she kept getting up, reaching for them, moaning, hissing. The little girl was now almost upon them. A quick baton blow to the little girl's head, crushing her skull, sent her to the ground for good, and the officer learned that a shot to the head was probably the only way to take these people down. He confirmed his theory by sending a shot through the mother's skull.

"Headshots only!" the officer yelled to his partner.

They both fired a few headshots, dropping the front line of the group before they retreated back into the alley.

"For God's sake, I think we've just encountered something unbelievable," one officer said to the other. "Zombies?"

Static sounded over their radios as the dispatcher keyed her mic. "We hear gunshots. What seems to be the problem, officers?" she inquired.

"No problem here, ma'am. Everything's under control now," the officer stated sarcastically into the mic, totally out of breath. "We're just being chased by a flash mob of zombies, that's all, ma'am."

"Zombies. Funny," the dispatcher replied. "We don't have time for your practical jokes, Officer Wills. Our switchboard is lighting up like crazy and the hospital is being flooded with bite victims, but I'll be happy to pass on any sarcasm you have to the chief. If you don't mind, there's a lot of crazies I have to attend to, real emergencies, you know." She clicked off the mic. "Damn him and his stupid jokes," she said quietly, hoping no one would hear her.

"You do just that ma'am, and while you're at it, tell him to get over to Orville's Books on Lincoln Avenue ASAP! We have a serious problem here, and he better not come alone! Wills out!"

•••

# CHAPTER 11

The old elevator crept slowly upward. The stretched cables let out a moaning growl. The cargo inside waited and staggered to keep afoot, when the elevator finally came to an abrupt stop on the sixth floor of Atlanta General Hospital. The door slid open and the male nurse struggled to roll his patient, resting on a gurney, all the way to the back. While doing so, he accidentally backed right into Jane Doe. Jane stumbled and fell backward against the control panel on the opposite wall, letting out a soft moan. The elevator door closed and they started their descent.

"Excuse me, miss," the nurse said. "I'm so sorry, I didn't see you th..." Startled by Jane Doe's appearance, the male nurse was unable to finish his apology. "Are you all right, miss?" he asked, as he scanned Jane's injuries from her legs up. When his eyes finally met hers, he gasped and noticed how milky-white they were. He then stared at her blood-covered mouth, chin, and clothing.

The infected girl attacked the nurse instantly, catching him off guard and pinning him between the gurney and the wall. There was nowhere for the nurse to turn. Sharing the elevator with a gurney trapped him in very tight quarters. He pushed with his arms and legs and tried desperately to fight back. He tried everything to get out of Jane's way, but to no avail. It was like fighting a rabid dog in a cage with his bare hands. There was just no space to move, so eventually he was bitten on the hand, several times on the arm, and on one shoulder at the base of his neck. He lost a lot blood, fast.

The male nurse felt weak in the knees and dropped to the floor. Jane Doe then turned and bit a chunk of flesh out of the leg of the sedated patient lying on the gurney. She chewed on the mouthful of meat, blood dripping down her chin and onto the floor. She savored every bit, growling like a dog with a bone.

The elevator jerked to a stop, throwing her to her knees, and the door slid open. Jane Doe dragged herself out before the door closed, leaving the bleeding nurse and his patient behind. She crawled to the wall and pulled herself up and shambled on into an empty post-op room, still chewing on the hunk of flesh. She appeared lost, bumping into things and pivoting like a human pinball as if she were looking for a way out of the same room she had just entered.

Meanwhile, in the elevator, the nurse bled to death on the floor beneath the gurney. Shortly after, his legs began twitching, then his arms. His eyes popped open, looking like sour milk, pupils almost completely gone. He got to his feet shortly before the door opened onto another floor. He attacked the first person he saw, then another and another. The patient on the gurney rose and attacked anyone in sight as well.

One by one, floor by floor, patients, nurses, and doctors were bitten, died, and reanimated, only to infect more. Visitors to the hospital were not immune. They too got bitten and became temporary patients themselves, only to become one of the growing mob of undead monsters a short time after. Soon, entire floors were filled with the infected, leaving only a few survivors to fend for their lives, to run, to hide. Years of playing hide-and-seek as kids never came close to preparing them for the hide-and-seek game they were playing now. This was for real, all playfulness aside.

The remaining unaffected hospital staff quickly followed regulations and went on lockdown. No one goes in and no one goes out, trapping the virus inside so it wouldn't spread any further. The problem was, it also trapped the survivors, who were in the building with the infected, with no place to go.

The virus soon spread to every floor of Atlanta General, all 16 of them.

•••

## CHAPTER 12

"Any sign of the professor?" Chief Malone asked Sergeant Hull, a five-year veteran of the force, as he walked into the police station.

"No, sir. No one has seen or heard from him in town. I asked around at Starbucks this morning. The workers say he usually comes in by 7:15 every morning for his favorite mocha. No show."

"We need to find him. Check around some more, will ya? We just can't leave that building like that. Who knows what weird stuff he's been working on lately. Hate to have young Frankenstein starve to death in the basement, if you know what I mean."

"Yeah, will do, Chief. If he's out there, we'll find him.

I would think the lab rats – at least the ones that survived the wreck – are probably getting pretty darned hungry by now," Hull answered. He walked to the door but hesitated at the doorway before leaving. "Hey, Chief?"

"Yes, Sarge?"

"Are the rumors true?" He paused. "Atlanta General?"

"I'm hearing the same as you, Sarge. Let's hope not."

Chief Malone and Sergeant Hull's radios both sounded at the same time. "Officers in trouble, requesting backup," Hull's radio announced. "Mob downtown at the corner of Fifth and Main."

"The chief is requested to be at Orville's Books for assistance ASAP," broadcasted through the chief's radio. "Bring backup. Out."

John grabbed his radio. "Chief Malone and Sergeant Hull en route."

They both raced to their cars and ran hot, Hull leaving the lot first, smoking his tires on his way out. The chief followed close behind, clipping the curb with his back tire, spilling his coffee. They both arrived at the mob scene in less than two minutes, as it was only a mile down the road. When they arrived, they couldn't believe their eyes.

•••

# CHAPTER 13

SMS: Johnny, are you all right? I heard the news. Please text back. I'm worried.

SMS: Johnny, please respond.

SMS: Dammit Johnny! What's going on?

SMS: We're screwed. The CDC is never going to let us out.

SMS: David, ones headed your way, HIDE!

MMS: Picture message showing a zom eating a nurse. Shared to Facebook. Caption: She was my team leader.

SMS: I just uploaded a video to YouTube. You have to see this. Link.

The video was filmed with an iPhone from inside the hospital. It showed the reanimation of a dead woman and her attacking the very doctor who just pronounced her dead moments before. It received more than a thousand hits within minutes of being uploaded and was quickly shared on countless Facebook pages and Twitter feeds.

It wasn't long before more videos were uploaded and ads were placed on them. They were quickly monetized for click-through rates. People were profiting quite heavily from this terrible event. Soon, the videos were broadcast over many TV newscasts. Broadcasting these graphic events was illegal under FCC laws, but the networks weren't too concerned. They had the "play it now, apologize later," type of attitude working in their minds, all hungry for top ratings.

SMS: Honey, we're trapped in here. They won't let us out. It doesn't look good. Tell the kids I love them.

SMS: Stop talking like that. You're going to be fine. Hide and wait. Everything will be fine.

SMS: I don't think you understand, honey.

SMS: Just hide, will you. Don't be a hero.

SMS: Judy, I'm going to be late for dinner. Don't wait up and don't worry.

SMS: Hi mom. Listen, something's come up. Can you go to my house and let my dog out? It's going to be a long night. Thanks.

SMS: We're screwed!

SMS: What the hell is going on here. Why are these doors locked? Let me out of here!

SMS: We are under lockdown.
SMS: I just saw one of those things. He just limped by. WOW.

SMS: What do we do?

SMS: We're all going to die!

SMS: Promise me that if I get infected, that you will do it. Promise.

SMS: You're going to be fine. We'll get out.

SMS: There's one at the ICU nursing station. Stay clear.

SMS: I'm all right.

SMS: They locked their kids in a locker. I can't believe it.

SMS: He got him!

SMS: Help me.

SMS: Text only, please. I turned my sound off. I don't want to be heard.

The hospital's outbreak was quickly revealed to the outside world via landline and cell phone, but word soon spread mostly by posts on social networks such as Twitter, Facebook, and Google+.

Text messaging was most commonly used by those still hiding inside the hospital to communicate with close friends, family, and coworkers, some of whom were likewise trapped inside. Most of the messages said nothing more than "I'm scared," or asked, "r u ok?" or "Where r u?" Some texts between coworkers were filled with warnings of "one," meaning the walking dead, possibly coming in their direction. A few texts of reassurance were sent saying, "everything is going to be ok," but not many and no one believed it. Some simply said "We r FUCKED!" which was a universal expression that needed no explanation. It was probably how most of them really felt after they learned that the CDC was involved, and there was no way out of the hospital.

Texting worked best, as the people who were trapped inside the hospital were too afraid to speak out in fear of being heard, and ultimately found. The survivors feared for their lives, running from room to room, hiding when and where they could. Some hid alone, trapped under furniture, while others hid in small groups, trapped in closets. Parents stuffed their screaming kids in lockers, locking them inside and running away, thinking the children would be safe from the walkers in there.

The children kicked their feet and pounded their tiny fists against the locker doors from the inside. They wanted out. They wanted their moms and dads, but their parents were nowhere to be seen. The noise and their screams only attracted the undead, so the parents had to abandon the area or become victims themselves. The zombies gathered around the noise, clawing and hissing at the lockers. They tried hard to get in. They couldn't see what was inside, but they sure could smell and hear them. The smell of the children through the louvered doors was sweeter than a pot roast simmering in a crockpot for hours. They knew fresh flesh awaited them on the other side; they just didn't know how to get to it. This, of course, frightened the kids more and more as the zoms banged back, slapping their bloody palms up against the lockers. Some kids clammed right up, sank to the floor, and hid their faces between their knees. Others panicked, throwing temper tantrums inside their confined spaces, some dying from hyperventilation. Some just continued to yell, screaming at the top of their lungs for dear old, and possibly doomed, mom and dad.

A few survivors chose to hide up in the ceiling, crawling their way through the air ducts. Some of the staff chose to arm themselves with surgical tools, bed rails, and fire extinguishers. They grabbed anything and everything they could find that brought them a little security and comfort. They soon found that whatever they had was nothing next to what they were up against.

A few doctors and nurses refused to take up the makeshift weaponry. Instead, they chose to uphold their oath to "heal not harm." They were the first to be overtaken by the dead. Some were eaten alive, while others thought they had escaped with only a bite or scratch. They eventually would also die, slowly and painfully. It began with a severe headache with fever, eventually boiling their brains, only to turn into one of the undead, throwing away their medical oath after all.

News was broadcast on radio and television and was soon printed in newspapers across the globe. People couldn't believe what they were hearing and instantly thought of Orson Wells' "War of the Worlds" broadcast.

The web was also used, informing virtually everyone with wireless, broadband, or dial-up service of the epidemic, but no one knew exactly what it was, where it came from, or why it was happening. More importantly, they didn't know what to do about it. They just knew that the staff of Atlanta General, and most of the patients, were trapped inside with the infected, with no way out.

The National Guard was called in soon after the CDC got word, and carried out a chain of events that came "straight from the book." They started with the chaining of all of the exit doors from the outside and then boarded up all of the ground-level windows, sealing what they could with plastic. They heavily guarded the rest of the building and assigned snipers to watch any uncovered windows. They had strict orders: absolutely no one goes into the hospital, and absolutely no one comes out, period. They set up a staging area and started planning their attack.

When the CDC is involved with a virus on the loose, the process generally goes by the book, depending on the severity of the virus. It was a bit early in the game, but they knew this particular affliction was not to be fooled with, and needed to be stopped before it got out of hand, sparing no expense and with every life being expendable.

The CDC had been in direct communication with one of the doctors inside the hospital. He had personally witnessed many attacks, killings, and reanimations. The doctor actually watched the reanimation of his own patient, a patient who had been bitten by one of the walking dead. He had checked the patient's vitals himself, and the victim was, in fact, dead by all accounts. The doctor pronounced the patient dead at 11:42 a.m. By noon, before the nurse even had a chance to take the body down to the morgue, the doctor watched the same patient shamble down the hallway and take on a few victims of his own. He didn't know what to think or how this could even be possible. How could someone be dead one minute and walking around the next? He also wondered how long he or any of the other survivors had before they were all infected; he bet not long.

The doctor estimated that 80 percent of the hospital's staff and 90 percent of its patients had now been in contact with at least one of these … these things … these monsters, for a lack of a better term. There were no words to describe them. Most of the staff had been bitten and had died of high fever, frying their own brains, and had already reanimated into creatures like something from a George Romero zombie flick. The only difference that the doctor could see was that this was actually happening before his eyes, not on the silver screen.

The National Guard was in full charge of the situation now and had given the orders to do whatever necessary to dissolve this as quickly and cleanly as possible – and to do it before the press had a field day with it and panic spread across the country.

The press was ordered to stay back and wasn't allowed any closer than a half-mile from the scene. Absolutely no footage was to be broadcast of the people involved, dead or alive, with no exceptions. This, of course, was too late as reporters had shown up at the scene well before the Guard arrived. The reporters just didn't know what to report when they got there. As usual, they reported anything and everything they got their hands on, just to claim that "you saw it here first" on their network.

Most of the news was inaccurate and wildly reported, apparently without concern for the damage that kind of news could bring. Videos appeared from cell phones from inside the hospital, which were far too graphic for the local news, but some stations took the risk and showed them anyway, hoping to have the first footage and boost their ratings. An apology to the Federal Communications Commission would be in order afterward. Little did they know that most of the videos were already uploaded to YouTube and were already generating thousands of hits, showing up on blogs and social media worldwide. Many Internet gurus were making a killing on the videos, as they monetized their click-through strategies on related ads.

People all over the world were glued to this fascinating story, still early in its development, and were hungry for any and all information that they could get their hands on. The U.S. government threatened to block the Internet if these videos weren't taken down immediately. But everyone knew it was an idle threat. The president wouldn't dare jeopardize his re-election prospects.

•••

# CHAPTER 14

The local hospital in Bear Creek received news of the goings-on at Atlanta General and of local patient Jane Doe. The outbreak there sounded very similar to a multitude of cases the Bear Creek authorities themselves have been seeing all morning long.

Bites, mostly human, some animal, and lots of them have been reported repeatedly throughout the morning. The local emergency room had been swamped with walk-ins, ranging from bites and scratches to high fevers. Those patients were now under close surveillance, and under guard.

The patients were guarded, not to protect the patients themselves, but to protect the hospital staff and the family members who came to visit. The stories that these patients brought with them were terrifying and very similar to the stories coming out of the hospital in Atlanta.

The local police and the FBI suspected Jane Doe was the start of the outbreak in Atlanta and that the small lab she'd crashed her car into may have had something to do with it. The FBI took over the case and ordered a thorough search of the damaged facility. They ordered a background check on Professor Simon Campbell and obtained access to all his accounts, including his banking, schooling, licensing, and also his e-mail and social media accounts. There wasn't much to which, with a little time, they couldn't gain access.

The FBI quickly learned a lot about the professor. They learned that he was retired from the CDC after 38 years of service. He graduated at the top of his class at Brooklyn University with his doctorate earned at Cornell University in New York. While working for the CDC, he also had his own practice on the side, presumably just for fun and for the passion he had for the field of medicine. Still, his lab showed very few records of what he actually did there. Little did the authorities know that most of the records were on his laptop and a backup hard drive that Campbell took with him from the scene of the accident.

What the FBI did find, though, was that the professor performed a lot of reverse-engineering for pharmaceutical companies. Copycat products. Companies brought out products very similar to those from competitors, simply by changing or swapping one ingredient for another and then slapping their own label on it, calling it their own. Obviously a great deal of money could be made in the practice, as

Campbell's bank account had grown enormously over a period of just a few years. The FBI also found a series of suspicious direct messages on his Twitter account. They were from missionaries in Brazil asking, almost begging, for his assistance. The professor had very little contact with these people but what the authorities found was enough for them to investigate further. The Twitter messages read as follows:

**DM:** You don't know me and by the time you receive this message I may have already passed.

**DM:** The vial and tissue sample I sent you needs testing. It contains a very, very bad virus; one that I'm infected with.

**DM:** I was bitten by something that appeared to be a corpse wearing a lab coat. I won't go into detail, but the ID said he was Dr. Scott Selmer.

**DM:** I am part of a group of nine. We're missionaries in South America and ran across this corpse covered with birds feeding on it.

**DM:** The corpse wasn't really a corpse at all, as it rose from the dead and bit me on the arm. It also took a good chunk out of my wife's cheek.

**DM:** It bit Sam when he tried pulling this guy off us. It acted like it was on Bath Salts. It's dead now. Had to crush its skull to do it.

**DM:** Nothing else worked, he just kept attacking. He wouldn't stop until five us were bitten or scratched.

**DM:** We are God-fearing Christians, but there was no other way. We had to kill it before it killed us.

**DM:** We all have severe fevers now, at least the ones who are still alive. I watched Sam die and turn into one of these monsters.

**DM:** Sam and Virginia, who also died, attacked the others. Now we are all either dead or have been bitten.

**DM:** We had to kill our brothers and sisters. God forgive us. Professor, please, I beg you to find out what's in this blood.

**DM:** The blood you have is my own. The tissue sample is off the corpse that bit me.

**DM:** I can't believe it's just Bath Salts. With your background I don't need to tell you what could happen if this spreads any farther.

**DM:** Don't bother DM'ing back, as I'm sure we will no longer be here by the time you read this. I'm burning up with fever as I type.

**DM:** Good luck, professor, God bless and Godspeed.

•••

# CHAPTER 15

SMS: What's happening? I see a lot of military down there. What's taken them so long to get us out of here?

SMS: Hang in there. It looks like something's going on down there now. Hopefully they'll do something soon. Here comes one of those things my way. Taking cover.

SMS: Please be careful!

The National Guard was ordered to storm Atlanta General Hospital and do what's needed to be done before the virus got out and spread far and wide. The CDC wanted the virus contained to this hospital and to this hospital only. It simply couldn't be allowed to get out and spread any further; that was just not an option. They were totally unaware of the current events developing at Bear Creek at the same time. All eyes and ears were on Atlanta, including Bear Creek's.

The commanders went over the floor plans of the hospital and made plans for their attack. And an attack is exactly what it would be.

It wasn't long before tear gas was shot through the windows of several floors while soldiers lined up at a couple of the entrances. Specific chains were unlocked and replaced by soldiers as Guard units rushed in, outfitted with HAZMAT gear. Their guns were at the ready and they fired at anything and everything that moved, infected or not. They didn't take any chances, nor did they take the time to ask any questions.

The staccato blasts of M-4s and small arms could be heard for miles around. They sparked the interest of news reporters, whose networks simply announced, "Gunshots heard from Atlanta Hospital. More at eleven." The reporters were too far away to see firsthand what was going on. A news helicopter tried its best to sneak in. The air space around the hospital was also off limits. Pilots had been threatened that they'd be blown out of the sky if they didn't comply. Footage was shot from where they were, showing the first wisps of smoke rising from the building.

Inside the hospital, screams of people begging not to be shot could be heard echoing through the corridors. A woman in a nurse's uniform raised her hands and pleaded for mercy.

"We're not infected," she cried as she motioned to a

little boy tucked under the table. "Please don't shoot. Get us out of here!" The approaching soldier looked down beneath the table and examined the boy and then the woman from afar, and for a while it appeared that the soldier was considering helping them. At long last, he motioned to the boy to get out from under the table. The nurse helped him, thanking the soldier over and over. The soldier paused, somewhat hesitant, wondering how the hell he would get them out of the hospital safely. Then six shots rang out from behind him. The soldier turned to face one of his comrades with the smoking barrel of his M-4 pointed his way. Turning back, he saw the nurse and the little boy lying dead against the wall. Not a single sign of remorse could be seen from the shooter's face.

"We have our orders, soldier!" the gunman barked.

The other shook his head and muttered, "thanks."

Glass shattered throughout the building as survivors desperately sought out ways to escape. Most were easily picked off by snipers positioned outside. Some did manage to jump from windows on higher floors, floors the snipers weren't as concerned about, knowing the jump would be a fatal one anyway.

Fire broke out in many locations throughout the building. Smoke could now be seen for miles. No one knew if the guards set the fires with charges or if the fires simply started by accident, but the hospital burned to the ground that day, with everyone but the National Guard trapped inside.

The fire department watched billows of smoke rise from

blocks away. They too weren't allowed past the barriers and were stranded back with the news crews.

No one but the CDC understood why no efforts were made to save anyone inside the hospital. The Guard did as ordered, no questions asked, and the government considered it a job well done. Many soldiers would be awarded for their heroic efforts.

In a news conference shortly after, a government spokesman claimed that the fires were not intentionally set at all, and all efforts were made to rescue as many victims as they could and apologized for their failed attempts. Not too many people believed that story and presumed it was just another government cover-up.

A small radical group protested during the clean-up efforts but its outcry didn't amount to much at all, as public attention was soon directed from Atlanta to a small town about 100 miles east of the hospital, where the same or a similar epidemic was believed to have broken out. It was none other than Bear Creek.

•••

## CHAPTER 16

The two crows met up with the first in the large oak tree, not 50 yards from the truck that had been hauling old tires. The tree overlooked a small swamp, home to many wild animals, including the muskrat, beaver, frogs, and quite a few species of birds. All three crows began making their calls, as they usually do just before they gather. Their calls brought the attention of a pair of red-winged blackbirds nesting in the cattails below.

Soon the crows were bombarded by the pesky smaller birds. They began to dive-bomb them in hopes of driving them away from their nests. This, to an onlooker, would appear to be a suicidal act, as the crows were at least five or six times the size of their attackers, but the blackbirds continued to instinctively protect their nest. They poked and prodded the large birds until they left their branch and fled. The attack didn't end there either. The blackbirds continued their efforts, diving, darting, poking, and prodding, until they drew blood. They kept at it until they drove the crows miles from the blackbirds' nests. They knew if they didn't, their young would be in constant danger. It was very common for crows to steal young or even eggs from others birds' nests just for tasty treats.

The blackbirds were relentless, and the crows finally knew that their only chance for escape was to put as much distance between themselves and the blackbirds' nesting area. Unfortunately, during the chase one of the crows flew into some high-tension power lines. The lines arced and sparked, electrocuting the poor bird. The crow fell lifeless to the ground. The dead crow's body was soon to be eaten, or partially eaten, by a stray cat out mousing in the nearby field. Raccoons, coyotes, field mice, or whatever other scavenger that passed through that night would gladly finish the rest, leaving only bones. Nature sure has a way of cleaning up its own mess. Nothing seems to go to waste, not even road kill.

When the chase was finally over, the blackbirds arrived back at their nest and fed their young with the food they found along the way. Their young were big and getting ready to fledge. They were ready to make it on their own. Free as a bird. In fact, one of the chicks left the nest later that evening and was soon reacquainted with the other two the following day.

In the days that followed, the blackbirds would

mingle with others nesting nearby. They traveled for long distances in flocks. Before they knew it, they had traveled thousands of miles, mingling with many other flocks, making many friends and even a few enemies along the way.

•••

# CHAPTER 17

The news of the epidemic was spreading rapidly through Bear Creek and, thanks to the Internet, made its way around the world in no time at all. News reporters were already on location, setting up their camera angles while avoiding the dead. They streamed live video from their vans via satellite to their newsrooms. They got as much footage as they could before the Guard pushed its way in and the news crews out, just as it did in Atlanta.

Bear Creek was a bit different, though. The National Guard didn't have just a single building to contain but the whole town, and the residents had grave concerns about how the soldiers were going to handle it. Blogs, Facebook, and constant tweets of this disaster cluttered the Internet, and everyone who had access was tuned in.

Panic spread across Bear Creek as the rumors of the Guard coming ran rampant throughout the town. People plainly didn't know what to do. Some just sat in their homes and cried, while others packed their belongings and readied themselves for the worst. Some even armed themselves, ready to fight back if need be.

Bear Creek's local hospital heard the rumors and paid close attention to what had happened at Atlanta General. They refused to follow the standard lockdown procedures as Atlanta had. They certainly didn't want to end up like their friends and colleagues there.

Most of the doctors and nurses had friends and family working at Atlanta General and didn't believe anything the government was saying about the incident. They tended to believe what they heard from the inside, from the horrible text messages and stories from their friends and families while it was happening.

Instead of locking down the hospital, most chose to leave the premises, going home to their own families and leaving most of the infected strapped to their beds behind locked doors. Some of the doctors and nurses refused to leave some of their uninfected patients and took those who could travel with them. Visiting family members were encouraged to take their loved ones home as long as they had no contact with the infected. If their loved ones had potentially come in contact with the infected, the families were encouraged to leave the patients behind in locked rooms. This was hard for some to do, and some families had to be physically pulled away from loved ones. Some grabbed bed rails, refusing to go.

As the medical staff left, so did some of the infected, as they literally followed them out the front door and into town. The town itself was rapidly filling with the walking dead. The 'unaware' were being bitten just in passing, some by strangers, others by friends, and many others by their own family members. Some were even being bitten or scratched by their family pets in play, not realizing that they too could be infected, but as carriers only, showing no signs of the disease.

Getting out of Dodge was on most everyone's minds, as they quickly packed their belongings to head out of town as soon as possible. They didn't want to be around when the Guard arrived. Some chose to stay anyway, refusing to leave their homes, and barricaded themselves in, hoping to ride out the virus and hoping the National Guard would pass them by.

Local stores were mobbed with people who were stealing anything and everything they could get their hands on. All the necessities were gone first, as people stocked up as much as they possibly could, filling grocery carts to their limits, pushing one while pulling another.

Fights broke out over the most mundane things, like the last loaf of bread on the shelf, and eggs, more of which were broken than not. Of course, booze and tobacco products rated near the top of the list. Bottled water, toilet paper, and personal hygiene products were among the first items to go, along with flashlights, portable radios, and batteries. For some reason, they became more important now than they were in everyday life. People underestimate the importance of simple things until those things no longer can be found. Nevertheless, people still did everything they could to try to maintain a little normalcy, despite all the ugliness surrounding them.

Gunshots rang out across the town from people trying to protect themselves and their property. People were stealing things from homes they presumed to be vacant, some would-be thieves surprised to be staring down the barrel of a shotgun upon entering, realizing some of these houses had not been abandoned after all. People were just in hiding with barricaded doors and boarded-up windows. Most every curtain was drawn tight. The town was in a chaotic state, and a lot of innocent lives were lost in a matter of just a few hours of panic.

The center of town looked like a riot scene. No one really knew who was infected with this awful disease and who was not, so people just started shooting, looting, and cracking heads. No one could trust anyone else, and everyone feared for their lives.

The doctors and nurses of the Bear Creek hospital fled, racing to their cars, locking all the doors, and rolling up the windows as soon as they got in. If they were lucky enough to get in, that is. Some didn't make it, being tackled just short of their goal, while others, the lucky ones, drove away, taking a few undead with them by running them over or giving them a ride as they glommed onto anything they could get a hold of.

Sarah, an RN, and her patient, a 7-year-old girl with a broken arm, were two of the lucky ones to escape without a scratch. Sarah quickly drove her Cavalier out of the parking area and instinctively headed toward home on the other side of town. She quickly learned that wasn't the right direction to take.

"What's your name, little one?" Sarah asked as she nervously drove down the road. The young patient just stared out the side window in shock and said nothing.

"It's going to be all right, honey," Sarah continued, looking for some reassurance herself.

Sarah drove through the middle of town. People were everywhere, fighting, running, clubbing, throwing rocks, swinging bats, and shambling around. She stopped the car and took in the scene, covering the child's eyes with her arms so she couldn't see the brutal attacks. This was the kind of scene Bear Creek residents would usually only see on the news, with people in some far-flung third-world country, violently trying to overthrow their government, but this was happening right here in their small town, no politics involved. She couldn't believe her own eyes.

Minutes later, her car was inundated by an overwhelming crowd. She had no idea what to do next or where to go. She tried hard to control her emotions but failed, letting out a little scream as bloody palm prints smeared across her window.

She rolled the car forward, bumping people out of her way, not knowing what else to do. She was completely surrounded and didn't want to hurt anyone, but she didn't want to stay there either.

"Move! Please get out of the way!" she yelled, but the

crowed ignored her pleas. They rocked the car back and forth, as bloody palms slapped hard against the windows on both sides. She apologized with every thump she felt as she moved the car forward. "I'm sorry, so sorry." She tried hard to stay strong in front of her young passenger, but she couldn't help but to succumb to tears.

As a nurse, she knew the damage she must have inflicted on the mob with her car. She cringed every time she hit someone. Seeing a break in the crowd, Sarah gave the car more gas. It rolled faster, bumping away the last couple of zombies standing in front of the car. One folded at the waist over the hood, legs straddling both sides of one of the front tires. It wasn't long when his hands lost grip and gave way. His bloody body slid down off the hood and under the car. The car bounced high in the air twice, once when the front tire cleared him, then again with the rear tire. Sarah and the little girl bounced in their seats. Sarah reached for the seatbelt and strapped the girl in.

Out of nowhere, an older man ran up to the car from behind, pleading to let him in. He slapped the palm of his hand on the trunk of the car, then the roof, as he gained ground.

"I'm not infected, ma'am, I swear! Please, please ma'am, let me in! I beg you, please," he pleaded with his rough voice. The car moved faster and pulled away. The old man couldn't keep up and quickly fell behind. But Sarah felt she owed the man an explanation and slowed the car. The old man caught up again.

*What if he is lying and is infected?* Sarah thought to

herself. *He would attack us both.*

"I can't, I can't. I'm sorry," she cried, then paused. "She's injured," she added, nodding at the girl in the passenger seat while keeping both hands, white knuckled, on the steering wheel. "I can't, I'm sorry." With tears streaming down her face, she recalled images from years ago of her diseased grandfather reaching for her as she reached back for him. He had tried to help her up a very steep embankment that she had just fallen down when she was just a child. At the time, she had probably been the same age as the little girl sitting next to her. The little girl, herself, was now pleading to let the old man in. Sarah looked in the side mirror for the old man, then at her rearview mirror. He fell back 20, maybe 30, feet and looked winded, white as a ghost. He couldn't keep the pace. The undead would catch up to him soon. Sarah stared at him a moment longer. He had a striking resemblance of her grandpa at that distance.

*He's someone's grandpa, too. I know. I just know it*, she thought.

The infected were getting closer. Sarah slammed on the brakes, and the little girl rocked forward but the seatbelt kept her in place. Sarah unlocked the back door. "Get in!" she yelled out her half-open window. The old man's eyes lit up, and a relieved grin spread across his face. He looked back at the zombies closing in on him, and for a moment he forgot that he was an 80-year-old man and began to run like he was 20. He reached the car in no time at all. Jumping in quickly, he slammed the door behind him. The little girl flinched at the sound of the door.

Sarah locked the doors and rolled her window up. She closely examined the man in the rearview mirror. Seeing no visible cuts or bites on the old man, she sighed in relief.

"Thank you," he said as he tried to catch his breath. "Thank you ... Thank you so much ... They almost had me."

Just then, more slapping noises hit the back of the car, startling the old man. It was loud, almost deafening. The car rocked back and forth as bodies pushed up against it. Sarah panicked but did nothing. She held the little girl sitting next to her. The old man freaked out, as all he could see were palms, bloody palms pressed up against the windows, slapping hard and pushing, trying to get in. The moans, the sickening sound of the muffled, gurgling moans, and the moist, slapping noise on the car were almost unbearable.

Sarah wrapped her other arm around her own head, trying to muffle the sound. Just then, a bright yellow motorcycle pulled up alongside, its rider taking out a couple of the infected with a baseball bat. He soon would be overtaken by the mob of zoms if he didn't move out quickly. Laying on his horn to get Sarah's attention, he signaled for the car to follow him and recklessly took off, swinging the bat as he rode, as if he were playing cricket with the zombies' heads being the ball.

"Excuse me, miss," said the old man, trying to gain Sarah's attention. "That man on the bike wants us to follow him. Miss?"

Sarah looked out the window and barely saw the back end of the bike. She slammed the gas pedal to the floorboards, running down a few of the undead and bouncing off others like an arcade pinball machine. She was following the biker to who-knew-where. All she knew was that anywhere was better than where they were.

Both vehicles escaped down a side street less than a mile up the road. The end of the street was blocked with more of the undead. The biker stopped, looked back at the car, and then back at the shambling dead again. He did a double take as if he recognized the girl behind the wheel of the car.

"Damn," he said quietly to himself. Looking beyond the car to the undead they left behind, who were now rounding the corner and closing in, he said aloud to himself, "We're trapped." He dismounted the bike and ran over to a service bay door on one of the adjacent abandoned buildings. It was locked. He pulled harder, but it was no use. He tried the door next to it. No good. The mob was getting closer from both directions. Then gunshots erupted.

Men with guns picked off the undead one by one. They were on the rooftop, above the bay door. The service bay door suddenly opened. More shots were fired. The biker took out the closest zom with his baseball bat, then ran inside, while Sarah pulled her car through the open bay door. The door was pulled shut. Safety, blessed safety.

Once inside, the biker, Sarah, the child, and the old man were pleasantly greeted. They all were now looking down two gun barrels, not the warmest of greetings by far, but it beat the alternative.

"Who the hell are you?" asked one of the two men

inside, pointing his gun at the biker. He appeared to be the leader.

"Name here is Steve, thank you." Steve grabbed the end of the barrel and pushed it aside. "Would you mind getting that out of my face, please? Seriously, if you wanted us dead you would have just left us out there."

The gunman lowered the muzzle but still held his gun at the ready. At least it was temporarily out of Steve's face.

"My name is David. Over there, Marcus." The gunman pointed to the other man holding a rifle. "Anyone infected?" Dave asked, while eying the child with her arm in a sling. "What about the little girl?"

"She's fine," Sarah grunted. "She just has a broken arm. I'm a nurse. I assure you, she is not infected. Now, will you put that damn gun down before it goes off?"

"Nurse? RN?" Dave asked. Sarah nodded. "Come with me." He grabbed her arm and dragged her to the stairway.

"What about the old man? What's his story? He looks half-dead," Marcus bellowed. The old man slowly pulled himself out the back seat of the car.

"Easy, old man. You armed?"

"He's OK," Sarah replied. "He's just a little shaken up. And no, he's not armed." She paused and yanked her arm from Dave's grip. "Get your frickin' hands off me!" she demanded.

"Upstairs, now!" Dave ordered, taking hold of her arm again.

"Where are you taking me, asshole?" There was a

moment of silence, and she looked in Dave's eyes. "Oh no you don't, that is not going to happen, I can tell you that right now," Sarah replied.

"Don't flatter yourself, chick. I'm married and you're not all that... My wife needs your help upstairs. Would you mind taking a look at her?"

Sarah pulled away and faced him. "Is she hurt?"

"Just take a look, will ya?"

Sarah took off up the stairs, her feet hitting every other step, leaving the little girl behind with Steve and the old man.

"Dave!" Steve yelled to get Dave's attention. "You touch her again and you're a dead man. Am I clear?"

Dave just looked at him and extended his hand holding the shotgun. "Do you want this? My wife is upstairs. She's pregnant. I just want her to get looked at. She's been through a lot."

"We all have. We aren't your enemy; they are," Steve said, pointing to the door. "What's your story? I don't recognize either of you. It's a small town, you know."

"Traveling."

"Traveling? I can think of a lot better places to vacation."

"Linda, my wife, she has relatives on the other side of town," Dave said. "We were coming to visit and got cut off."

"You normally travel with guns? Is it really hunting season?"

"Sporting goods store down the street. We took advantage of it when things went down."

"Any left?" Steve asked.

"'Fraid not. We were lucky to get these."

"Marcus? Don't tell me, he's your brother?" Steve nodded in the African- American's direction.

Dave chuckled, "Brothers from different mothers, I'd say," trying to be funny. "My best friend."

"OK. So what's your plan?"

"Plan? We don't have a plan," Dave said. "We haven't been here long. Wife needed to rest and our car is out of commission."

"Don't tell me that's your car up the road, beat to hell."

"That'd be the one," Dave said. "We were surrounded with nowhere to go except through them. After hitting a parked car, I had no choice but to stay and run over as many as I could. I knew the car wouldn't go far. It was like a demolition derby without the cars. I must have run over a couple dozen of them before the car stopped running. We made it this far on foot. Marcus went back out alone to get the guns. I wouldn't leave my wife."

"I see," Steve said. "Well, we can't stay here. The Guard will be here shortly. So what do we have?"

"Well, let's see. A pregnant wife, a nurse, an old man…"

"The name's Eli. Stop calling me 'old man.'"

"Sorry. So we also have Eli, a little girl, two guns, some supplies, you, me, Marcus, a Cavalier, and a bike," answered Dave. "It will be tight."

"Tight? We need wheels. Something that can handle

things," Steve replied.

"Things?"

"A load, terrain. Something that won't fall to pieces if we run into a zombie or two."

Sarah came down from upstairs. Dave met her at the bottom. "Well?"

"She's fine, just nerves getting the best of her. She's really happy that I'm here now. Glad someone is." She made it past Dave and walked over to the little girl.

"Sarah," he said. She stopped and looked back. "Thanks."

Sarah said nothing and turned away to tend to the little girl and the old man.

•••

# CHAPTER 18

## THE 'TURN INTO BLOG

-

U r not going to believe what I'm seeing here, folks. Thank u for stopping into my blog, by the way. It's a little different format today, as I'm here sitting in the car with my mom, dad, and baby sister. We r stuck in the biggest traffic jam in Bear Creek's history. It's a parking lot out here! Seems we all tried 2 leave Dodge at the same time. I'm writing this blog from my iPhone, so please excuse any typos. I'm not going 2 take the time to fix mistakes as I want to type as fast as I can to keep u informed for as long as I can. I will keep blogging as long as I have batteries and internet access.

This is truly something to c.

Wait a minute. What in the hell is going on? No, that did not just happen. Folks, just seconds ago, a man stepped out of his vehicle to get a better view of what's ahead. He wasn't out there 10 seconds when a flash mob of zombies came circling around a moving van and attacked him. Took him right to the ground. OMG, he didn't have a chance.

Oh no, now people are panicking. They're driving their cars into one another, pushing, bumping, crashing, in their efforts to get away from the mob. It's like an all out crash'em up, smash'em up derby out here.

It only made things worse. We're not going anywhere now. We're totally boxed in by a bunch of idiots with broken-down cars.

My sister just announced that she has to use the bathroom. Mom told her she'd have to hold it.

People, stay away from the X-way; find another route. What the hell is that guy doing? He just dragged someone out of the front seat of a car. No, no. He shot him. He literally shot him for bumping into his car. It was a nice car, in all respects, but really; shoot someone for that?

Oh man, he's not moving now. Someone needs to help him. Blood is pooling beneath him. Isn't someone going to help him? No one's moving. The guy's lying there in the street bleeding to death, and no one has the balls to go help him. Wait a minute, there is someone going to help. That figures, it had to be a girl to show some compassion, big kudos to her.

Oh no, the flash mob just passed by our car. "Nobody move. Don't make a sound," Dad said. We've all ducked down in our seats now. My sister stated again her need for a bathroom and is now crying.

"Shhhhhh. honey, it will be alright. Just a little longer, that's all," my mom whispered, trying to comfort her. It wasn't working. I grabbed hold of her and covered her mouth, muffling her cries.

The zoms are headed for the girl, I think. I don't know it's too hard to c now. I'm sitting too low in the seat and there's just too many zoms to look through. No wait, there she is. My mom instinctively pounded on the window and started yelling to her. Warning her that they are coming.

"What are you doing? Stop! Be quiet!" yelled Dad.

"We have to warn her!" my mother replied back.

"She can't hear you for Christ's sake," my father spouted in a whisper tone, gritting his teeth.

I think it's too late. Rubbernecking the best I can, I can't c her anymore.

I tried to get Dad's attention. He ordered back, "Will you all just please be quiet!"

"Dad," I whispered again.

"What is it, son?"

"I think they heard us. They're turning around and coming for us. Look."

"Crap, are you kidding me?"

Sure enough, it wasn't long and we had bloodied hands, slapping hard against our windows. The weight of the zoms pressing against the car made it rock back and forth. We all ducked low, and hid under blankets and coats, whatever we could find. My sister was crying again. Actually, I don't think she ever stopped, and I think my mom is too.

Peeking through the blanket I was hiding under, all I could see was gore. Bloody palm prints smeared across the windows the full length of the car. Morbid faces peering in. The slapping, the repetitive slapping of moist hands hitting glass, like a wet mop hitting the floor. The car rocked back and forth, back and forth, and the moans. The moans were awful. They have to stop!

We had to roll our windows up tight. They were cracked open an inch to get a little fresh air, but not now. The zombies' fingers were slithering in and grabbing hold. Dad rolled his up, pinching a couple of fingers in between the glass and the frame. The zom pulled back. Without any sign of pain, his fingers ripped at the knuckles, leaving them behind in the window.

It's hot in here. We're covered with blankets and coats; it's really warm. 93 degrees outside means it's well above 110 in here. We're cooking ourselves to death. It's hard to breathe; hot, whatever temperature that is, and what's that smell? I know our antiperspirants had to be failing hours ago, but geez. This is bad.

"Honey," my mom whispered to Dad.

"Yeah?"

"Can you close the vents? The stench!"

"They are closed, dear."

Oh man, I think it's my sister. "I think she crapped her pants, and I have to take a piss really bad myself." My dad handed me a Coke bottle. Really? I have to pee in front of everyone into a Coke bottle? I don't think I can do that. This is not the time for a nervous bladder. I tried, not even a drip and I have to go; my kidneys are hurting. They're making my sister strip down. Dad wants her soiled panties out of the car. Not sure how he plans to do that but he's going to try. My mom said she needs to go really bad, too, but she can wait. Wait? Wait for what! The zoms don't appear to be going anywhere and neither are we.

My little sister wadded her panties up in a ball and handed them to Mom. She sensibly sticks them inside a plastic shopping bag and ties it shut. Dad reached for the bag. At that time, there weren't as many zoms as there had been by his window. Dad turned the key to aux position, hit the button and the window crept partway down with a slight jerk. He hit the button again and the window came down more, too far. He quickly corrected it and it moved all the way closed again.

"Dammit!" he cried out, wishing now that his car had standard manual window cranks. He tried the button again and settled for whatever opening the window fell to. It was not enough for the bag to easily fit through, so he forced it through with his fingers and quickly jerked his hand back and rolled the window back up. The plastic bag dropped to the road and was quickly swarmed by zoms like flies to butter. The car still smelled like shit hours after.

•••

Day 2: I would have started yesterday's post with Day 1, but I really didn't know we would still be here.

We're hot, sweaty, smelly, and very hungry. Does anyone deliver pizza to cars? If so, we would surely be interested. The zombies moved on sometime in the night, leaving only a few stragglers left shambling back and forth, like in delirium. I let my phone charge most of the night, so I should be good for a while.  Dad would run the engine to keep the car battery up and cool us down with the air every once in a while. I wish he could just leave it running. Then I think of all the cars next to us, in front of us, and behind us, that may not even have a/c at all, and I wondered how they were faring. The car in front of us hasn't run since a couple hours after we got here. I think they ran out of gas or something. I haven't seen any heads pop up in that car for many hours, either. I hope they are all right.

Dad is acting funny this morning. He says he doesn't feel well. Who does? Mom's concerned but that's just the way she is. She worries about everything.

I've managed to successfully fill and empty my Coke bottle urinal out the window several times now. My nervous bladder syndrome seems to be cured. Dad, well, it's been about 24 hours and he hasn't had to borrow the Coke bottle urinal yet, but he hasn't had anything to drink, either. Maybe that's why he doesn't feel well. Maybe he's dehydrated. Hell, we all should be dehydrated by now. We need water and food desperately, and a way out of here. We're open for suggestions, if anyone has any.

Early this morning, when the outside temps were cool, cool meaning below 90, Dad claimed he was hot, burning up, he said. Mom checked his forehead with the back of her hand and sure enough, he felt warm. Fever warm. Maybe he is getting sick.

Mom noticed a bloodstain building on the sheet that Dad hid under. She freaked, "Are you all right, dear?" she asked, nodding to his crotch area.

My dad looked down and jerked his hand away. "Yeah, fine. What the …!"

It looked like he'd peed himself in the night. But there was blood in his urine. I guess that's why he hasn't asked me for the Coke bottle. He must have a urinary tract infection or a kidney stone or something. That would explain the fever, wouldn't it? What do I know? I'm only 16 years old.

Mom pulled the sheet away from Dad, exposing his hand and soaked jeans. Both were soaked with blood. It wasn't urine after all. Two of his fingers were all festered up, bleeding and full of pus. "You're cut. How did you do that?"

My dad looked down at his fingers, shocked. "I'm not sure," he said, but you could tell something was up. My dad doesn't lie; he just wasn't good at it.

"You mean to tell me that you don't remember doing this?" Mom again, getting a little upset.

"Ok, I felt a pinch when I threw that bag out the window."

"A pinch, what's a pinch, you mean a bite? Did you get bit?"

"I didn't think so. I looked right after it happened and I didn't see any blood. It was fine."

"Fine? You call this fine!" OK, now mom's yelling.

I asked mom to calm down. She was upsetting sis, but she didn't listen. She kept right on him.

More words were exchanged, mostly bad; words I'd

rather not share here. I run a family blog. She started bringing up the past a lot, and how unhappy she was, and how my dad wasn't ever there for her, for us, when we needed him. I pleaded again to Mom to stop, but she kept right on going, running my father to the ground. Kicking him when he was down. Dad was hurting. First, I thought just mentally but, no, his fever had gotten worse over the last couple of hours. Mom was to a point where she didn't know what to do and wasn't talking anymore. And then ...

"Get out!" she screamed out of the middle of nowhere. I couldn't believe what I was hearing. She was ordering my dad to get out of the car.

"No, Mommm," I cried out and so did my sister.

"You're not going to hurt us anymore. You're going to turn into one of them, them things and you're going to hurt us. You're going to kill us all and I can't let you do that. Now go!" She pushed him, urging him to leave.

Sis was bawling her eyes out. Mom yelled at her to stop. Sis and I yelled back at Mom, even louder, to STOP. Dad was non- responsive now. He just sat there with his chin resting on his chest, moaning.

It was complete pandemonium in the car. Everyone screaming, yelling at one another, for what seemed like hours, but I'm sure it was mere minutes. Then silence. Complete fuckin' silence. Sorry, I forgot, "Family Blog." But my family was falling apart right now, right here in front of me, and it upsets me. Sorry.

No one was saying a word. I'm not sure which is worse. Only faint sniffles could be heard, and soft moans coming from Dad.

I told Mom that we have to get Dad help, but she said there was nothing we could do, that there was no cure. Still, we argued back and forth about it, arguing until we were blue in the face.

Speaking of blue in the face, Dad's color wasn't good. He was kind of turning blue and pale; very pale like he's lost all pigment in his skin. I think he's dying.

Batteries are getting low. What's wrong with this thing? It used to last all day. I have to run and charge up. Be back.

-

Me again, with only a two-hour charge on my battery. Dad got a lot worse. As soon as it was safe enough, Mom reached over and opened Dad's door; she pushed him out. He went without resisting, without even saying goodbye. He just rolled off the seat and onto the pavement. Mom said it was because he knew it was the right thing to do. I just think he was too weak to fight back. Either way, there he was, lying on the street just outside the driver's door. He was curled up in a ball waiting to die. I think they call it fetal position, something to do with the position of the fetus in the mother's womb, I guess. I still can see him breathing. I'm sad. My sister just hides under the blanket; Mom's just not talking. She stares out the windshield as if she were a thousand miles away. Wouldn't that be great, to be a thousand miles from here. Then again, maybe it's like this there, too.

A zombie shambled by a minute ago. I thought he was going to eat Dad. I tried to distract it by tapping on the window but it was more interested in Dad lying on the street, as if he knew I was pretty much protected by the car. It probably tried countless times with hundreds of cars and had failed each time. I assume even the simplest minds can be beaten into submission. "You bastard, leave my dad alone!" I cried, as the zombie bent down to my dad's level. Down on his knees, the zombie sniffed the air and growled like a wild beast, or maybe he was just sniffing Dad; I couldn't tell. He got back to his feet and left. He left without taking a single bite. He didn't eat my dad. We still can get him the help he needs. Then Mom reminded me again that there was no helping him. I just watched on, teary-eyed. I could no longer see Dad breathing. He must have died.

I looked again a minute later and Dad was sitting up. He was leaning up against the front tire, knees in the air, elbow resting on them.

"Mom?" I tried to get Mom's attention. "Dad moved, Mom. He's leaning up against the front tire. Do you think the fever broke and he's alright?"

Mom half smiled, "No, son. He's not your dad anymore," she replied.

I looked back at Dad but at this angle he was very hard to c. All I could c before was just a part of him and his legs. I couldn't even c that anymore. He must be gone. I looked around the front of the car. I saw nothing. Then I heard two hands slapping hard against the window beside me. It startled me and I jumped, but I didn't dare look. Then curiosity got the best of me and I turned around. In between both palms was Dad's face staring in at me with milked over eyes and shoelace strings of saliva hanging from his mouth, dripping slowly to the ground. I jumped back and grabbed my sister. I covered her eyes. Dad, or what used to be our dad, started beating on the glass. He beat the window hard. I thought it was going to break. His earlier moans have now turned into vicious growls. He wanted in, in a bad way. He wanted to kill us. He wanted so badly to come in and eat us.

Mom screamed and turned her head. She covered herself up with a sheet. She couldn't watch. It was too painful. She begged us to do the same. My sis climbed into the front seat and under the covers with Mom. I stayed in the center of the back seat away from the windows. Mom threw me part of the sheet. We all huddled close for hours.

DAY 3: Dad finally wandered off sometime in the night. Probably went looking for food. We're all starved, and since that's what he lived for now, he had to find something, because he wasn't going to get any here. My mind was made up, three days with no food or water in 90+ degree temps was taking its toll. I'm leaving today while Mom sleeps. She'll never know. I'm going to get help.

•••

"We have to find this family. We have to help them," Sarah said while reading over Dave's shoulder as he browsed the Internet for information. "There's more. Scroll down." Dave refused to scroll down any further. Instead, he clicked over to another blog.

"Hey, asshole, I was reading that," Sarah barked.

"Sarah, there's nothing we can do for them," Dave said. "They could be anywhere, and besides, those posts were

111

hours, if not days, old. They could be dead already and we would be wasting our time and risking our lives trying to find them. Now move on, already."

Sarah brought her arm back, ready to slap Dave across the face when Steve grabbed it in mid-swing. "Dave's right, Sarah. Sorry." She relaxed her arm after a moment of gazing into Steve's eyes.

"How do you know he's right? You have no idea what this is about."

"Dave's usually right. Now's not the time to second-guess him."

"I can't figure you out, Steve," she said as she turned and walked away.

"It's not hard," Steve replied under his breath. "What was that all about? Never mind, don't answer that. I just hope you were right. Whatcha got? Find anything on this crazy virus yet?"

Dave quickly bounced back to that kid's blog and scanned the dates and times of the posts. The last post, which Sarah didn't read, was posted just 18 minutes before. It also mentioned that they were just off the on ramp, off Highway 15, which Dave took mental note of. He clicked the track pad back and directed his attention toward Steve.

"No, just something on some blogs that I found about birds falling out of the sky. It's really weird stuff. I found the link on Twitter. It looked interesting, so I followed it."

"What is it?" Steve asked. Dave stood up from the milk crate he was sitting on and pointed to the Netbook on the adjacent milk crate so Steve could sit and read for himself.

"Weird? Weirder than what's going on here? It can't be any weirder than this," Steve remarked before reading.

"That's for sure. It's just a different weird. Something's not right, Steve."

"What do you mean, Dave? What's up?"

"They're saying that birds have been falling from the sky in droves in several states and countries. Not just birds. Fish, crabs, and starfish are washing up on shorelines dead in masses as well; dolphins in Florida, too."

"Droves? Masses? Give me some real numbers, Dave. Speak English, man."

"Birds by the thousands, Steve, all dead, lab tested with no explanations. People are out there cleaning up the messes themselves. Thousands of dead birds have fallen to the ground in people's yards and on streets. Kids are playing around them in playgrounds. Look, here's a kid picking them up and throwing them to see if they will fly." Steve and Dave were mesmerized by a YouTube video of two kids tossing dead birds back and forth to each other.

"That's just not right. Where are their parents?" Steve inquired. "No cause, you say? Birds don't just fall out of the sky dead for no reason at all, Dave."

"Just speculation, Steve. Something to do with fireworks or possibly the secret governmental program that just leaked out over the Internet. I found it on Google news, believe it or not. It's called 'Bye, Bye Blackbird' or 'Bye, Bye Birdie,' or something like that. Something the government secretly uses to control the animal populations." Dave continued to explain the program to Steve.

"That's seriously messed up, and our tax dollars pay for such programs. Wow! We've got to get out of here, Dave. Pack it up. Let's go."

"Wait, you have to look at this."

"What do you have there?"

"It's another link on Twitter. It just popped up a few minutes ago. Another YouTube video. Look. People in HAZMAT suits sweeping the birds off the streets and picking them up with gloves and putting them in sealed bags."

"Yeah, so?"

"They just got done saying that there's no danger, Steve. If the birds were safe to clean up, what's with the suits?"

"Good point. Do you think it's related to what's going on here?"

"Probably just a coincidence, but maybe. Who knows? Here's another blog on it here." Dave clicked yet another bookmark to a blog he had found earlier.

## Welcome to my Daily Grind (Blog)

A new story appeared on the news today. Did you see it? It appeared to be unrelated to the ugly events that are still out of control, but it was just as mystifying. At least it was for me, an avid bird watcher.

Thousands of dead fish washed to shore near Maryland. Tens of thousands of dead crabs wash up in Europe. Birds have been falling from the sky in droves, with little to no explanation in several U.S. states, including Kentucky, Missouri, and Arkansas. More were reported falling in southern California, New Mexico, Michigan, and Arizona. Flocks of blackbirds were reported flying in very unusual patterns across the U.S. and Canada. Same thing has happened in Italy, Sweden, and Australia.

Fish and wildlife officials blame these unusual mass deaths on area fireworks from nearby celebrations and trauma, of course, but no one seems to buy it. I don't either. Fireworks occur several times a year and this has never happened before. Why is it happening now?

Dead birds have been picked up off the streets and sent to labs in two different states. No sound conclusion found from either one. They are sticking to the fireworks story. Oh, and trauma. Well, of course there was trauma, they fell from the sky and hit buildings, cars, and even people as they fell to their deaths. There's speculation of bad weather, wind shear, tornados, or even that hail in the area may have knocked them out of the sky, yet the closest storm was over 100 miles away from any of the occurrences. And what about the fish? Who can explain that?

A government report leaked out on the Internet explaining the government's way of animal control. It has the code name of "Bye, Bye Blackbird," and used a company in Kentucky to produce the chemicals for it. The same company is believed to have developed the insecticide DDT, which almost killed off the bald eagle population in the 1940s. The same company may have produced the chemical called "Agent Orange" to control plant life over in Vietnam. We all know the ending to that story: there isn't one. People are still paying the price for that mistake. My uncle just died from the effects of it more than 30 years later. To this day, they continue to produce many chemicals for agriculture even after the past mistakes. Could it be that they produced a bad batch again and it's killing off the wildlife? Or was this just part of the government's Bye, Bye Blackbird program gone wrong? The company who produces the chemicals, who I might add is government-subsidized, refused to comment. Maybe it's yet another government cover-up, but maybe not. Whatever it was, it was happening all over the world, with more and more birds falling each and every day.

Until next time, people. If there is one!

P.S. Don't forget your hardhats if you venture outside.

"Geez, what the heck is going on?" Steve asked himself before Dave clicked on another bookmark to another blog he'd read earlier.

"Here's another." Dave pointed to the screen.

**From the daily Blog of WTF**

Dead birds are reported blanketing the streets, yards, and parks across the States. Citizens, young and old, are out cleaning up the mess themselves, throwing the dead birds in their own trash, some burying them in their own backyards. Many people are just throwing them over the fence, leaving them for the neighbors to pick up. There's so many, they don't know what to do with them.

Landfills are now getting filled with dead birds, which are attracting more and more scavenger birds to the dumps. There are plenty for all to get their fill. Families found it difficult to keep their dogs and cats away from them, sweeping them from the walkways, streets, and drives and raking them from the yards into heaping piles.

The government assured the people that it was perfectly safe and to go on with their daily routines. Still, people wait for answers as to why the birds fell in the first place. In the matter of a couple of days, the news no longer reported the topic. It's like it never happened. At least until a few days later when people in HAZMAT gear, shot via cell phone video, appeared on YouTube picking up the birds.

My question of the day would be... If the dead birds were in fact safe, then what's with the HAZMAT gear?

Thanks for reading The Blog of WTF!


"There's link after link with the same related story. One after another," said Dave.

"I've read enough," Steve said. "I think we have the gist of what's going on. Come on, let's pack. We have to get out of here before the Guard rolls in."

"The president is supposed to be on in about 15 minutes to address the nation. It's something we need to listen to, Steve."

"Yeah, I suppose you're right, but we have to leave right after that, all right? The Guard will be here anytime, and when they get here, we need to be gone."

"Roger that, Steve."

## CHAPTER 19

## BREAKING DEVELOPMENTS
## THE BIRD CRISIS

-

The president addresses the nation.

-

An alert sounded on every television set and radio across America from the Emergency Alert System. This was one of the few times it wasn't a test, and only a test, or a local weather alert.

This time it was really used for what it was intended for. Also, all Internet service providers were interrupted and diverted to the live broadcast so anyone online at the time would automatically be bounced to the live video feed of the president. Most cell phones received a link to click on via a text message so their users too could see the video live via their smartphone. It was the first time in history this function had been activated.

Shortly after a piercing tone, the president of the United States appeared on the screen of Dave's tiny Netbook. Steve and Dave looked on.

The President began to speak...

"Good evening." The president stood behind a podium in front of the American flag with blue drapes hung in the background. "I'm here tonight with grave concerns. As you all are probably aware by now, America has been under attack by a deadly virus, a virus that has spread across the country at an extraordinarily fast pace. This is a virus that seems like something that would only be seen on television or on the big screen. Alfred Hitchcock's 'The Birds' quickly came to my mind after my briefing.

"We had thought that we had a grip on this, well, before it fully got started. Obviously, that's not the case.

"We have a lot to learn about this virus, but this is what we do know so far. This virus is nothing to be fooled with. Its main focus is to survive and spread. The way it spreads is through fluid transfers, meaning through bites, saliva, open cuts, and sexual intercourse. It is not an airborne virus, at least not yet. There is always a chance it could mutate to become airborne. Let's pray it doesn't.

"If you have been bitten, by all means, report to

officials for treatment. Do your friends and family a favor and keep your distance from them. If you have not been bitten, stay away for anyone who has been infected in any way. We have learned that this virus can spread through animals, as well. I repeat, animals can indeed get infected with this virus, but they seem to show no signs of the effect afterward. They become carriers only, as far as we know, and we freely admit we have more to learn.

"We have learned, however, how this virus has spread so far and so fast. It has spread through birds – flocks of birds.

"The birds that have fallen in recent days have been tested and appear to be clean of every virus known to mankind. This virus, however, is new and unknown; we are still learning about it and will be for months to come. We have retested the birds for this strain of the virus, and they have, in fact, tested positive and it was the cause of their untimely deaths and the spread of the virus across the country. Our initial thoughts were that this virus was isolated. It's proven to us since that it is not.

"The birds' brains were much too small to handle such a virus and caused them to plummet to their deaths when they overexerted themselves, mainly when they flocked together. They do not reanimate like humans, but rather just die off in flight with the virus intact, in hopes someone or something will come in contact with them, one way or another. This, of course, would complete the cycle and spread the virus to as many hosts as possible.

"Friends, citizens of the United States and abroad, this is not limited to just you and me. It also includes animals, wild animals, livestock, and yes, maybe even your own pets and the neighborhood strays. They could simply get the virus by picking up an infected bird, tasting or eating it. Do not, I repeat, do not under any circumstances come in contact with any of these animals. It will be difficult, if not impossible, for you to tell if your animals are carriers of the virus, which is why I urge you, if you are a pet owner, to think of yourself and your family. If there is any possibility that your dog, cat, goat, or pig could have been in contact with one or more of these birds or any other animal that has, I urge you to give your pet up to the authorities to be quarantined until an antidote is found. There will be drop-off centers established near each major city. Do not set your pet or livestock free in fear of this disease. That will only make things worse for everyone. If you can't make it to one of the drop-off centers, a member of the Guard can take your animals there for you. I urge you to avoid at all cost any contact with infected animals, including the fallen birds.

"There have also been reports from all over the world of dead fish, crabs, starfish, and even dolphins washing up to shore. Although they have not been tested, we can only assume they have met the same fate as the birds. Keep away from anyone or anything that you know may have come in contact with any suspected animal, dead or alive, without proper protection. Anyone who has come in contact, even if you have no symptoms of the virus, needs to report to the local authorities. They will guide you to the proper places to go for treatment.

"Symptoms are as follows: heavy sweating, vomiting,

burning of the eyes and stomach, migraine headache, and extreme fever. If you have any of these symptoms, you must report to the authorities at once. Without proper treatment, you will suffer and die. Soon after, you will reanimate into what people are referring to as "The Walking Dead." Transformation has been clocked at anywhere from a couple of minutes to a couple of days."

The president appeared confused on the screen for a moment. He seemed to be distracted by someone or something off-camera. The camera zoomed slightly out and panned over, catching the secretary of defense and the president exchanging hushed words. The president covered his lapel mic with his hand and in a very muffled, almost inaudible voice, the nationwide audience faintly heard, "Sorry, Mr. President, I don't mean to cut you off short. There's no time to explain, but it's imperative that we leave, sir. Now." The camera returned to focus only on the president himself.

"If at all possible, hunker down inside your homes," he said. "Let no one in. Leave your homes only for emergencies. Like all other adversities we've faced in the past, we will prevail. We will get a handle on this. We will survive. God be with you."

The green light on the top of the camera turned red. They were off the air.

"What is the meaning of this?" the president demanded as he turned away from the camera and television sets throughout the nation returned to regular programming.

"Sorry, sir. It's in our best interest to make sure you

are secure. It's the White House and the Capitol, sir."

"Go on."

"Well, sir, we've learned that the grounds have been breached. We have to get you in the air. Now!"

"Breached? By whom?"

"The infected, sir. We must go."

"My family?"

"Already on board Marine 1."

"Marine 1?"

"High Point, sir."

"Mt. Weather? What is going on? Is this worse than I've been informed?"

"Yes, sir, and getting worse by the minute."

The Secret Service led the president through rooms and down several hallways. They came across a long hall and ran down it without hesitation. As they arrived at the other end, gunfire erupted. The hallway, which was blocked by CIA agents firing on a seemingly endless stream of the undead, had not been a good choice. The walkers were pushing their way through the doorway. This passageway to the roof was cut off.

"Plan B," one of the agents cried out, and the team immediately turned the president around. A Secret Service agent got on the radio. "Junkyard Dog in trouble, Junkyard Dog in trouble. Plan B, I repeat, switching to Plan B."

"Plan B?" the president asked.

"The tunnels, sir."

Just then they heard the whine of Marine 1's rotor blades. It was lifting off the roof, leaving the president behind. "The first lady and family safely up and on course," the pilot announced over the Secret Service radio frequency.

"You'll be briefed on the rail, sir. We really have no time to talk right now."

The president and some of the remaining cabinet members, along with a few members of the CIA and Secret Service, rushed the president through the White House and into the tunnels below, as the staccato blasts of small arms and M-4s rang through the halls.

"Tell me something. Is that what the world is facing?" asked the president.

"Sir?"

"Those … those things back there." The president looked over this shoulder to see if they were being followed. "That's not what I've seen on any of the footage I've been briefed on."

"Sorry, sir, but yes. They seem much more tolerable on camera, don't they?"

"Tolerable? They're downright disgusting and ready to rip you to pieces given the chance. I want a full news crew standing by awaiting my arrival."

"Without a press conference, sir?"

"Yes, without a press conference. No one will feed me these lines. I don't want anyone's propaganda. People need to be informed. They need to know the truth so they can protect themselves."

"Sir, with all due respect, most people already know."

"Are there any places in the U.S. that have not reported sightings of the infected?" the president inquired.

"Hawaii, sir. That's the only state in the union that has not reported any walkers."

"Thank God."

"Safe zone, sir?"

"No, that's where I vacation," the president responded.

"Roger that," the CIA agent chuckled. "It's only a matter of time. Someone who's been infected could be stepping off a plane or a ship right now – a carrier who doesn't even know it."

"Screen them."

"We can't, sir. We would have to know what it is first, and we'd have to do a blood test before letting them through. What about the birds, sir? Birds have been seen migrating between San Francisco and throughout South America. I'm sure some could have headed toward Hawaii."

The president, thinking aloud, said, "There is no way an infected bird could possibly make that flight."

"You might be right, sir, but I should remind you it only takes one, riding the thermals and possibly resting on ships. It's not only possible, sir, it's very probable. Birds from all over the world make longer flights during migration every year."

"Notify Hawaii. Tell them what's coming. Don't hold back. They need to know what they are up against."

"They've been warned, sir."

"Why do I feel I'm always the last to know what's going on?" asked the president.

"You're pretty busy, sir. By the way, how's that coffee

bill coming?"

"What, the one about the labels warning people of it being too hot to touch? Good, almost passed. Why do you ask?"

"I spilled coffee on myself this morning, scorched my leg. That bill should save this country a lot of pain and agony."

•••

## CHAPTER 20

"I knew it. I knew those damn birds had something to do with it. They're everywhere you look. This is bad, man, really fuckin' bad," Dave said.

"Yeah, 'bad' is kind of an understatement. We've got to get out of here, Dave," Steve replied.

"They're also saying not to eat any fish or wild game because it might be a carrier. Well, what about everything else? Who knows where these birds have fallen. What about the water supply? Crops? Could they get contaminated from birds dying in the fields? Or, what about where they shit, man? Is that a factor, too?"

"Could be, Dave. We will assume it is."

"Another thing I thought was really strange.

Remember a few days ago when all headlines read happy news; news about some cure for cancer? What the hell happened to that? Now we hear absolutely nothing about it."

"Very true, Dave, but we all know bad news sells more than good and spreads a lot faster. Maybe when this is all over we'll learn more about that. Until then, the only cancer I'm concerned about is the walking dead ones outside."

"Hi guys, what's up?" Sarah walked into a room of blank faces. Dave looked at Steve. Steve returned the look. Dave prodded Steve to take the floor.

"I'm afraid it's bad news, Sarah."

"More bad news? What now?"

The guys, mainly Steve, filled Sarah in on the latest news.

"So does this mean these walking corpses are everywhere now? Not just here?" Sarah asked.

"Possibly, and if not now, soon," Steve expounded.

"Oh my gosh. What are we going to do? Where do we go?"

"Write down as many places as you can remember where all these dead birds and fish have been found. We'll try to avoid those areas, as well as large cities where they'll be the most populated. For now, let's just head for the hills and decide what to do then."

"In what?" Sarah asked, looking at her poor car sitting nearby. It had sustained a lot of damage from the zombies, and she knew it wouldn't handle everyone inside for very long.

Just then they felt a rumble under their feet.

"What the hell? Did you feel that?" Dave asked.

"Yeah, I still do," said Steve.

"Earthquake?" Dave asked.

"Here? I don't think so. Maybe worse," Steve remarked.

"Worse? What could be worse?" asked Sarah.

"The Guard?" Steve ran for the stairs and up onto the roof. The others followed. "They're here. Look, over there." Steve pointed off to the right.

Sure enough, an army caravan was driving into town and extended beyond the horizon. Countless Humvees, and trucks hauling heavy equipment were making their way into town, rattling the ground as they passed by. "No way," Marcus said, eyes glued to a pair of binoculars. "What the hell? Tanks! What's with the tanks, man?"

"They're here to do to us what they did to the hospital in Atlanta," said Steve.

"What do you think of that, Steve?" Marcus pointed to a black cloud rising near the end of the caravan.

"Toss me the specs," Steve asked, as he motioned and reached. Marcus tossed the binoculars over to Steve. "It's not smoke."

"It's not? Well what is it then?"

"Birds. A huge flock of blackbirds flying in formation."

"They're *murmuring*," said Dave.

"Expert on birds now, Dave?" Steve teased.

"Funny. Make fun of my bird-watching skills.

131

Hilarious."

"Sorry, Dave, I didn't mean anything by it. What's murmuring?"

"That." Dave pointed to the black cloud dancing in the sky. "It's simply a large flock of birds flying in formation. They're known to travel farther in groups like that. It has something to do with the wind resistance, and keeping together like that takes less energy or something."

"I don't see how they do it without crashing into each other," Steve said. "Amazing."

Suddenly they heard the rat-tat-tat of M-4s. The caravan must have run into trouble.

"They're headed to the hospital downtown, aren't they?" Dave asked.

"Probably, but they won't stop there, not once they get the taste of what's ahead." More rapid fire echoed through the town. "In fact, it sounds like they're getting their fill right now," said Steve

"They're going to seal off the town. You watch. This town will be wiped off the map, just like Raccoon City in 'Resident Evil,'" Marcus stated.

"Sorry, I'm not sticking around for that," Steve remarked.

Steve, Dave, and Marcus bee-lined down the stairs where Sarah quickly cut them off.

"Excuse me, but I have a valid question on the floor. Are we just leaving it there?"

"What? What question?" asked Dave.

"What are we leaving in?" Sarah said. "My car is not

going to hold us all."

"The garage where I work is about eight or nine blocks from here. There's an old Jeep pickup out back that I've been working on. It's not much to look at, but it runs like a top and it's rugged. Between that, your car, and my bike, we'll get by," replied Steve.

"What about the car you were telling me about? The GTO. Can I see that?" Sarah questioned.

"Are you crazy? No way! When this is all over, I will be back to get my GTO. It's not leaving the safety of my garage. Besides, we have to hide out for a while. That could mean very rugged terrain. We need the truck."

"You two seem to have had a history," stated Marcus, eyeing Sarah nonchalantly.

"Not much of one," Steve said shaking his head, pretending it wasn't a big deal. "You guys hang tight here. Finish packing up and be ready. I'm going to get the truck."

"Taking the bike? I'm going with you. You'll need help," said Dave.

"No. You stay here with your wife. The bike attracts too much attention. I'm going on foot, alone."

"Are you nuts? There are zombies everywhere out there, and now the military. If it's anything like Atlanta, they'll just shoot you."

"That's why I have to go alone. I can stay low and out of sight."

"Call if you're in trouble, and I'll be right there," Dave stated reluctantly.

"Will do, but the cell will be off. I don't want it to go

off accidentally while I'm sneaking around. Give me an hour. If I'm not back, start your back-up plan."

"Back-up plan?"

"Yeah. You have an hour to create one, Dave."

While Sarah and the others argued about Steve going alone, Steve slowly opened the service door, peeked outside, and slipped out without anyone noticing.

The alley, for the most part, was fairly clear with the exception of a couple walkers that Steve felt he could easily avoid or outrun if he had to.

Steve wasn't gone long when he learned that being on foot for eight or nine blocks was going to be a bit more challenging than he thought. He stealthily made his way down the alley, ducking down between cars, mailboxes and rubbish cans, and hid inside doorways. He managed to make it to the end of the alley unseen.

Staying low to the ground, Steve peered around the corner building. Zombies were everywhere. They seemed to be multiplying like flies on shit. He waited and watched every move the zombies made, hoping to learn as much as he could about them and possibly use it to his advantage, instead of just running from them all the time.

*If I could just find their weaknesses*, he thought to himself. Then he heard someone kick a pop can from behind. It rolled down the sidewalk, down the curb, and into the street.

"Way to go, asshole. I told you to stay put," Steve said, expecting to find Dave or Marcus coming up from behind. "You want everyone to hear you or what?" he whispered over his shoulder.

Steve looked over his shoulder. "Whoa, shit!" He noticed it wasn't Dave or Marcus after all. A shambler approached from the rear and was upon him. Steve gripped his baseball bat with both hands, and with one slick move he clobbered the zombie's head, sending him crashing to the ground, never to get up again. Bloody brain matter oozed out of the gash in the zombie's skull and puddled onto the sidewalk. To Steve's surprise, he'd taken out his attacker without being noticed by the others.

This built Steve's confidence, as if he really needed it. He was about as cocky as they come. His friends would say he had a little too much confidence at times. Steve would say there was no such thing as too much confidence.

Steve saw a clearing in the walkers and fearlessly made a break to cross the street, zigzagging around and between zoms, swinging his bat and clubbing a few down as he ran. He made it across the street and into a vacant property on the other side. He bolted across the lot, gaining distance from the herd of zombies now shambling in his direction. He cleared the lot and ran around a corner. It was a party store. Steve ducked inside.

Lucky for Steve, the zombies moved rather slowly, so he had a minute to catch his breath and get his bearings. Shaking his head, he realized that he might be a little farther from his shop then he had anticipated. He had to keep moving. One or two zombies were no big deal and could be easily avoided, but a herd of them was like stopping a stampede of buffalo.

•••

"Where's Steve?" Sarah asked, glancing around the garage.

"I don't know. He was standing ..." Dave paused, looking at the door. "He was standing right there, in front of that door."

"He's gone. He left, didn't he? He left all by himself. Great!" Sarah said, throwing her arms in the air.

"That was the plan, Sarah. He didn't want to be responsible for anyone else. He said he didn't want to be slowed down either, and it would be easier to keep out of sight alone. I offered to go, but he wanted nothing to do with it. It's 2:15 p.m. He has one hour. Let's get ready."

"Ready? Ready for what?" Sarah questioned.

"Steve's return, of course, with the truck," Dave replied. "Or, Plan B, whatever that is." He said that to himself. "Let's get your car packed."

"Plan B?"

•••

# CHAPTER 21

The National Guard continued to cut a path straight through town in the direction of the local hospital. They cut down everything in their path. Roadblocks were formed. Barricades and bunkers were built. A few units branched off in different directions along the way, sawing down as many zoms as they possibly could. They tried to find different areas to secure and hunker down.

The heavy equipment started tearing down bridges and overpasses as they made their way around, cutting off all the main roads leading in and out of the town. Charges were set and bridges were blown, sending shockwaves throughout the neighborhoods. The noise could be heard and felt for miles.

Gunshots could also be heard from miles away, as the soldiers attempted to clear the streets with their automatic weapons and grenades.

Bear Creek, a town much like many other small towns throughout the country, was being tattered and torn, shredded into a million little pieces and transformed into a battlefield in a matter of minutes. The National Guard had made its entrance and made perfectly clear its intentions. People feared for their lives.

Heavy equipment bulldozed the way through the streets, clearing them of all debris, while piling cars, trucks, park benches, and trash cans as if they were plowing snow. Their treads tore up the asphalt as they advanced through, crumbling it into chunks. They scooped up bodies of zombies in their steel buckets and piled them high. Before moving on, they set them afire, destroying any possibility of them spreading the virus ever again.

All the while, the zombies kept coming, more and more by the minute. Army personnel driving bulldozers were picking them off right and left with their side arms as they plowed through the streets. In the meantime, some troops fell to the swarms of the undead, overpowered by sheer numbers and not enough ammo. Enlisted soldiers in uniform soon became infected walkers.

There wasn't much left of the local police department. They did their best to answer as many distress calls as possible, but one by one they too were overtaken by the dead. "Officer down" calls were all too common until only a couple officers remained among the living.

The 911 operators stayed alert and active for as long as they could; as long as they felt useful, anyway. They were good at calming the stressed and giving peace to the restless, but unfortunately that was all that was left for them to do. Sending help was out of their hands. They vowed to stay on duty until the bitter end and barricaded themselves in. They locked all doors and boarded all the windows, settling in with nothing more than what they brought in for lunch that day and enough coffee to last for weeks.

•••

# CHAPTER 22

The party store that Steve stepped into had been heavily looted. All the windows were smashed out, and most of the inventory was gone from the shelves.

Steve grabbed a couple of candy bars laying on the floor, one broken into several pieces, the other looking as if it had been trampled by a herd of cows, but Steve didn't care. The package wasn't ripped. Food is food, after all, and he knew it would be scarce. He stuffed the candy into his pockets and grabbed a handful of chips that had been spilt on the shelf and stuffed them into his mouth. The salt his body was craving tasted so good that he had to grab another handful on his way out. He quickly got back on the path to the garage.

Steve stayed low, meandering in between buildings, trucks, signs, mailboxes, and cars. He took advantage of anything that would give him some kind of cover.

*Another block in my back pocket,* he thought to himself as he started a new one. He counted them off one block at a time. This helped keep his sanity. His mind raced.

Steve had barely entered the next block when he suddenly felt trapped. Zombies were closing in around him. There were about five in front of him to the right and a group of 10 or so to the left, not to mention a whole herd of them trailing behind. He looked around, slowed his breathing and gathered his thoughts. *What do I do? Think, dammit, think …*

Steve was mostly out of sight at the moment but didn't dare to move. He paused again to watch the way the zombies moved. He tried hard to figure them out and to possibly learn what they were thinking. Did they really think at all? Were they just acting on instinct? Did they do whatever the virus commands them to do? Nothing more? Nothing less? He studied them for as long a time as he could waste, which wasn't long at all. He had one hour to get to the station, get the Jeep and get back before his companions came looking for him. *They will come looking, won't they?*

If Steve didn't show after an hour, the others were supposed to come up with "Plan B," but he knew their Plan B would probably be to locate him, so he had to keep moving. Steve didn't want his companions, especially the women, out looking for him with all of these things, these monsters on the loose.

Steve waited for just the right moment and then made

a break for it. He rolled out of his hiding place in the backseat of an abandoned car, a place he was all too familiar with but under much different circumstances. He then ran to another vehicle and then to another. Running from car to car was going to take forever, but he didn't have much of a choice. He darted around the zoms one by one like a linebacker with the ball, striking a few down with his baseball bat as he ran past. He set his sights on a schoolyard just a couple blocks away, and he was hoping to make up some ground there in its wide-open space with plenty of room to run.

Steve cleared the zombies on the left and took out a few on the right, then sprinted behind a vacant house where he ducked inside. He looked around for anything that may come in handy and found himself in the kitchen. His chest heaved as he leaned on the kitchen table, trying to catch his breath.

He felt a strange sensation run through his veins. The hair on his arms and neck stood on end. He gripped the handle of his bat tighter, took a deep breath, and walked out the back door without looking back, until he was well clear of the house. He feared he hadn't been alone inside the house, and he didn't have the energy to stick around to find out who or what else was in there. When he finally turned to look, a shadow of a man passed by the kitchen window. Friend or foe? He didn't care; his instinct was to get out of there, so that's what he did.

To Steve's surprise, the home's backyard was clear and so were the two adjacent yards, at least as far as he could see. He traveled across a few backyards, running from tree to tree.

He saw only a few zoms along the way, but they were off in the distance and didn't pose much of a threat.

Steve traveled from yard to yard, hiding behind trees, bushes, and the occasional shed. Privacy fences helped a great deal, especially when he thought there was a chance of being seen. In yards with nowhere to hide, he would shamble around and do his best to look like a zom. No one could tell the difference at a distance, not even the zombies. They thought he was one of them. But he only did this when they were off in the distance. He took no chances when they were up close or even downwind. Steve had a strange suspicion that they could smell humans.

It wasn't as though humans smelled bad to them, just different – different from the way the zombies themselves smelled, which was seriously rank. How they could smell anything at all over their own decaying, sulfuric stink was beyond anyone's comprehension. Maybe they couldn't smell themselves, or maybe they enjoyed it. Who knew? Whatever the case, they certainly put up with their own stench without complaint. Even skunks don't like their own smell, and zombies were pretty close to them on the rating scale of "stink."

Steve tried to stay downwind from the zombies as much as he could, but downwind to some was, of course, upwind to others, and his scent, or lack thereof, was traveling and drawing a little attention not quite a block away.

Steve, now just two blocks away from the garage and behind schedule, ended up in a rather dangerous predicament. Less than a block away, a mob of hungry zombies were slowly closing in on him. He heard them well before he saw them but didn't know what direction they were coming from. The alleyways made sound direction deceiving at times. When Steve did see them, it was too late to do anything about it. They were close, and there were a lot of them.

Steve detoured down an alley to try to lose them. This was an alley he was unfamiliar with. He ran fast and hard, gaining ground with every step only to end up at the end of the alley facing a sign that read "Dead End, No Exit." *How ironic*, he thought. Steve looked around. He was completely boxed in by building after building with walls 30, 40, and some 60 feet high or more. The only way out was up or the way he came in. The way he came in was out of the question, as he could hear the moans not too far from the opening of the alley.

Steve ran to the nearest fire escape. After a few failed attempts to jump and reach it, he realized it was much too high to grab. No matter how many times he tried, he was still nearly three inches from the bottom rung.

"It's true, white men can't jump," he said to himself. Steve simply didn't have the strength to jump any higher.

Steve searched for something to climb on and came up empty-handed. He tried doors and windows but all were locked or boarded up. He looked for something to use to pry the doors open and still came up empty-handed.

"You've got to be kidding me," he said to himself as panic began to run through his veins like a freight train. His body started to shake. He wrapped his arms around his shoulders and squeezed. "I'm not going to die like this, dammit!" he said aloud. He tried using his bat as a ramrod, trying to beat the doors in, but this only made a lot of noise, echoing through the alley like a dinner bell for more zombies to home in on. Time was running out, and it was much too late to turn and run out the same way he'd come in. Confused and feeling a bit hopeless, he looked all around for an answer.

Steve could hear the constant murmurs of the mob of shamblers heading in his direction. They were rounding the corner and coming down the alley. He could almost smell them. The noise, the constant noise, cluttered his mind to no end. He cried out, squeezing his eyes tight and cupping his hands over his ears, irritated. "I can't think!" he said, bending over to his knees. A plastic water bottle came into focus as he opened his eyes, now staring down at the ground. "Garbage," he said to himself. Still irritated, he kicked the bottle away. He followed the plastic bottle with his eyes as it spun away down the alley. It came to rest no more than 15 feet from where he was standing but in the distance a garbage Dumpster came into view. Thinking nothing of it, he returned to facing the ground, and while wishing the noise of the oncoming zoms away, he tried desperately to clear his mind, hoping to make room for some answers.

"Garbage," he said to himself again. His back cracked with several pops when he slowly straightened upright. *Ahh, that felt good. I can make it there*, he thought.

He quickly ran up to the Dumpster, thinking that this couldn't be the answer, but it was all he had. He leaned his back into it to push it closer to a nearby fire escape. It was much heavier than he thought, and it wouldn't budge. He climbed on top of it and tried to judge the distance to jump to the nearest fire escape. He decided right away it was too far and that he'd never make it, or he would probably break a leg trying. Then he would be doomed for sure if he weren't already. Steve hung his head. *Guess this wasn't the answer after all.*

*They're not taking me without a fight*, he thought while shaking his bat and taking advantage of the height, preparing for a real-life version of King of the Hill and determined to take as many down with him as he could.

Then, like a door slamming in his face, all the air left his lungs and he succumbed to hopelessness. He was tired and ready to give up all hope – hope of surviving, hope of ever seeing Sarah again, and hope of getting out of the alley alive. He turned his back and hung his head. He stood there a second and waited for the first attack. There would be no fight. He looked down past the edge of the Dumpster. His eyes widened when he noticed there was no lock on the side door of the Dumpster and it was slightly ajar. Down on his knees, he hung over the edge and reached down to slide the door open. On his belly, he leaned over as far as he could and stuck his head inside to look around. He looked for something to use. *A ladder would be nice*, he thought, but it was much too dark to see anything at all. His body was blocking the only light source available.

The noise from the herd of zoms was overwhelming. The closer they got, the louder they were, and this time there was no stopping them. The front line had arrived at the Dumpster. They clawed at the steel box. Steve jumped to his feet and crushed in the skulls of the first two. They fell instantly to the ground but were immediately replaced by another and another. He swung the bat a few more times, sending several more to the ground, but there was a never-ending line. There was no way for Steve to keep up pace. He'd soon be overtaken and ripped to shreds for sure. His body would be spread throughout the herd for food with no chance to become one of them this time.

"Here goes nothing," Steve said as he dove toward the side door of the Dumpster. He climbed inside the steel tomb, sliding the door shut behind him. Palms immediately banged on the opposite side of the door, wanting in.

Steve quickly covered his nose and mouth as a gut-wrenching odor filled his sinus cavities. He stayed perfectly still for minutes and waited for the zoms to leave the door. He could hardly breathe. Within those minutes Steve's eyes had time to adjust to the darkness. He could see a little but not much, enough to find what he thought was stinking up the place. It was a small box that stunk like road kill baking in the sun on hot pavement.

The box was moist and seeping, covered with flies. It had such a disgusting odor to it, as if something was dead inside. Steve wanted it out of there in a bad way. He couldn't slide the door open to throw it out; it was too risky. So he dug a hole in the trash below the door and buried the box as deep as he could. He then piled trash on top of it all the way to the roof, blocking the door and barricading himself in. He hoped that would help cover up the acrid smell, at least enough to be able to breathe, but it didn't help at all. The air was still thick and filled with that disgusting stench. The air had no way to escape. He piled more and more trash in front the door while making more space for himself, but he still was waist-deep in trash.

Steve began digging a hole for himself. He dug deep and buried himself in the trash, hoping to cover his own scent, lessening the chance of being found by the zoms. The smell around him certainly overpowered his own scent tenfold, but he didn't want to take any chances. "Bloodhounds couldn't pick up my scent in here," he muttered.

The mob of zombies kept coming one after another, sometimes three or four abreast. It wasn't long before the alley was full. They were standing elbow-to-elbow, packed like a can of sardines.

The muffled moans that Steve heard from inside his steel coffin were haunting. He wondered if this, in fact, was going to be his tomb after all, his final resting place, never to be found again.

It was like an oven inside as the sun beat down on the steel container. The heat and the stench made it almost impossible for Steve to breathe, yet he was breathing harder and harder as his nerves were getting the best of him. *I'm going to die in here.*

With each breath, Steve held his stomach. It convulsed in and out like an oil well pumping his stomach acid up into his esophagus. He could taste the bile rising in the back of his throat, waiting for the opportune time to make its outward escape. He'd been in tight situations before, but it seemed that his claustrophobia was getting the best of him. In his mind, the walls were closing in on him like a trash compactor. He tried hard to slow his breathing, but hyperventilation kept sneaking in on him. "No, not the dry heaves," he said. But dry heaves it wouldn't be. His lunch was ready to leave the station. It took everything he had to keep it down. He didn't want to make a noise and draw more attention to the Dumpster nor did he want a new odor in the air – one that surely would be detected by the dead outside. He wanted the zoms to get bored and wander off so he could get out of this place. Time was wasting.

Steve's disappearance into the Dumpster seemed to confuse the mentally challenged zombies lurking outside. They were like bloodhounds that had lost the scented trail. They shambled back and forth, moaning, dragging their broken limbs behind. They sniffed at the air like hungry dogs and stumbled aimlessly as if they wondered why they were there in the first place. Maybe that gave them too much credit. They knew not what they did or why they did it. They just did, solely driven by their hunger to feed and spread the virus that they carried within.

Steve nervously waited in the darkness as the zombies shambled around his steel tomb. They sent chills up and down his spine every time one would brush up against the Dumpster or slap it with the palms of their bloodied hands. He had no choice but to wait it out, afraid to move and afraid to make a sound. Most of all, he was afraid of suffocating and cooking himself to death. It had to be over 100 degrees and rising inside. His clothes were soaked with sweat. He became sleepy, dehydrated, delirious, and he whispered Sarah's name just before passing out.

Time passed, how long, Steve had not a clue, but he was pretty sure his time was up. When he awoke, he found himself covered with bites all over his body. Thankfully, the bites were from insects and not from zoms. These bites were something Steve could handle. Steve remembered continuously swatting at flies right before he had passed out. *I'm not sure what's worse, being eaten alive by flies in here or by zombies outside*, he thought. What a choice to have to make.

Steve also woke up to familiar noises. He heard something faint and distant, something other than the constant moaning right outside.

"Vehicles? I hear a motor. Those idiots came to find me after all." He paused. "Oh man, how long was I out?" he asked himself. "I told them not to come looking for me." Steve, obviously delirious and upset with his friends for disobeying his orders, cussed under his breath. Yet in the back of his mind, he really expected them to show. He would probably have done the same thing. In fact, he knew that he would.

Then there were sounds that didn't quite line up with Steve's way of thinking. He heard heavy hardware, guns racking, radio chatter, and boots hitting the ground. He didn't like the sound of it at all. He wanted to peek out. Hell, he wanted to scream out, "I'm here! I'm here! Help! I'm inside the Dumpster! Help me!" But he didn't dare. He didn't want to take the chance of being shot on sight.

Steve grabbed his cell phone from his pocket, only to find that it had no signal. The steel must have blocked his cell phone service. He turned on the phone's video recorder and stuck it up through a crack in the roof. He hit the "record" button. He recorded for 10 seconds. He turned the volume all the way down and hit "play" and watched. He found it hard to believe what he was seeing. There were zombies everywhere. It was all he could see. He stuck the phone through the crack once again, this time at a little higher angle. He recorded another 10 seconds. The noise was getting louder as he heard more trucks pull up, more voices, more boots hitting the ground, and more guns racking. He watched the second video. Sure enough, in between the zoms he could see the military at the end of the alley. Soldiers were getting out of their trucks and pointing their rifles down the alley at the zombies, and at him.

"Oh shit!" he said quite loudly, but it didn't matter.

Just as the video stopped, the gunfire erupted. The army at the end of the road opened fire, cutting down the zombies with their M-4 assault rifles. The automatic fire peppered the alleyway and the Dumpster where Steve was hiding. They were hitting it lower-left-center and falling off to the upper right.

The loud staccato thuds of the bullets impacting the Dumpster were deafening. Steve turned away, covered his ears, and threw his body in the opposite direction, diving into pitch darkness. He hit the garbage hard, facedown, burying his head deep in trash. He lay flat, as low as he possibly could and pulled more trash over his body. His ears rang as more bullets hit, leaving tiny beams of light from the 1/4" size holes they left behind. He dug deeper into the garbage, away from the spray of bullets and debris but not before his back, shoulders, and neck were impaled with sharp metal shrapnel. Bullets passed through the front wall of the steel shell like it wasn't even there, spraying Steve with metal shavings. The 1/8" think steel wall posed little to no threat to the .223 rounds as they exited out the back of the dumpster as quickly as they came in, leaving yet a larger hole behind. The transfer of energy from bullet to paint chip and metal shavings left quite an impact on Steve's flesh.

The Dumpster was hit a dozen or so times before the gunfire stopped. Steve wasn't moving. Flies swarmed all around him again.

•••

# CHAPTER 23

"Did you hear that?" Sarah whispered.

"Yeah, that was close. Too close," Dave said. "We have to move. Now!"

"I'm not going anywhere," Sarah answered.

"Come on, Sarah, we have to go. We gave Steve an extra half-hour and we weren't supposed to do that. Something happened. He's gone. Now let's go before something happens to us."

"I can't just leave him behind. He saved my life."

"We aren't leaving him, Sarah. Look around. He's not here to leave. We have to go. Didn't you hear those gunshots? They're getting closer. The army is only a couple blocks away, clearing the streets and probably going door to door." Dave paused. "I don't know about you, but I don't want to be here when they come knocking. Get your things. We're leaving."

"Where are we going? I'm leaving Steve a note for when he gets back. He's alive and he will make it back. I have to let him know where we'll be," Sarah said as her eyes filled with tears. Dave didn't answer and walked away.

Sarah eventually gathered her things and the little girl and left with the rest of the gang, but not before leaving a note behind for Steve.

> *Steve:*
>
> *I'm so sorry.*
> *We had to go. The army got close. I hope you get this. We're heading east out of town. Headed for the country where there are no people. Will look for high ground, possibly near Hickory Hill. Meet us there if you can. I hope you're safe.*
> *Love,*
> *Sarah*

Sarah pinned the note next to the bottom of the stairway right above the handrail, but it didn't stay there for long. As soon as Sarah's back was turned, Marcus came bounding down the stairs and ripped it down from the wall. "What's this, a love note?" he said sarcastically.

"Hey, put that back. I just want Steve to know where we're going, that's all."

"Steve and everyone else, including the army. Afraid

not, Sarah," Marcus retorted.

Dave grabbed the note from Marcus's hands and quickly read it. "What are you trying to do, Sarah, lead the military right to us? We can't leave this." He crumpled the note and tossed it to the other side of the room where it rolled and came to rest underneath a cabinet, against the baseboard molding. "Come on, or you're staying behind."

"You bastard!" she remarked as she swung to slap him across the face.

Dave caught her arm in mid-swing and pushed it toward her gear. "Pick it up or it stays behind."

Sarah wiped tears from her eyes and began picking up her gear. Marcus offered a hand and reached to help. "I've got it!" she snapped, refusing the help. Marcus continued helping anyway.

"Sorry about your friend," Marcus said, really meaning it.

Sarah looked up at Marcus. "Thanks, but he's all right, you know. You don't know Steve."

"And you do?" he said, insinuating that maybe he did.

"A little," was all she said.

-

The Cavalier was packed like a can of sardines. It sagged low to the ground, practically scraping the pavement as it traveled southward out of town. The car followed a yellow crotch rocket while avoiding as much trouble as they possibly could. Dave rode on the bike ahead, checking the roads for debris, zoms, and any military action, all of which needed to be avoided at all costs. The car was not suitable for any kind of chase with the load it carried and the condition it was in. No bump passed without complaint.

When the street was clear, Dave would ride the bike back and signal the car to follow. Every once in a while, a zom or two would make an appearance but were quickly taken out by either Dave on the bike or Marcus in the passenger seat of the car. They were using a high-powered rifle and side arms. Each shot drew more attention to their location as zoms instinctively gathered and followed the sound.

The main roads leading out of town were congested with abandoned automobiles and makeshift roadblocks where the military had passed through. The freeways were nothing but a three-lane parking lot for as far as the eye could see. Car after car, truck after truck, were all left in the sun to bake their contents, and all had their windows rolled up tight in fear of zoms locating and pulling occupants out or climbing in with them for a warmed-up meal.

Through a pair of binoculars, one would clearly see that there were some people left inside some of those vehicles, people refusing to leave the security of their own cars or possibly already turned into zoms, trapping themselves inside and unable to figure out how to open the door or roll down the windows.

Dave and Sarah couldn't help but think that in one of those cars was the teenage boy who had been updating his blog with a detailed account of their situation. They could clearly see there were way too many stranded vehicles for them to find the boy and his family.

Most of the cars' engines had stalled from running the gas tanks dry while using as much air conditioning as the gas would allow, before the sun baked the cars' occupants to death in their expensive coffins. There was no relief from the heat, a record spell of 90-degree and higher temperatures for the past nine days. Autos easily reached in excess of 130 degrees inside, cooking people from medium-rare to medium in no time at all. Some were even looking well-done, with milky-white eyes. People were forced to leave their cars if they wanted any chance at all to survive. It was a risk very few families were willing to take. Who would go? Who could leave their loved ones behind? Most chose to stay and ride it out together, all for one and one for all. Of those who left their cars seeking help, very few survived their efforts. They became easy pickings for a mob of zoms who stood and waited nearby like vultures circling their downed prey.

Some people were bitten and climbed back into the cars for safety, afraid of being eaten alive. Some of their families chose to stay and comfort their loved ones, only to be killed, infected, or eaten by the same people they cared for.

Ultimately, people finally found out what it was like to be a dog abandoned in the car in a hot parking lot while its owner shopped for groceries.

•••

"What's he doing?" Sarah asked while slowing the car to a stop.

"He looks confused," said Marcus.

Dave stopped the bike in the middle of an intersection. He looked left, right, left again, then straight, and then back to the right again.

"He looks like he's watching a tennis match in the middle of the road," said Sarah.

Dave then looked up at the street sign and then to the roof of the corner building. He signaled to the car that he needed to get to the roof to get his bearings. He pulled up alongside a low-hanging fire escape and climbed up to check things out from above.

Dave did this quite often, and allowed himself three minutes from the time he reached the roof to the time he showed back up at the roof's edge. Any longer could mean trouble, which meant his companions in the car would have some tough choices to make: go up after him or get the hell out of Dodge, depending on the mood and situation. This was one of those times.

"It's been more than three minutes. Where the hell is he?" questioned Marcus. He stepped out of the car and looked up the fire escape. Dave's pregnant wife in the backseat of the car was trembling and in tears, being comforted by the 70-year old man sitting beside her. Marcus looked up and then back at the car again and mouthed the words, "I'll find him," to Dave's wife. Marcus got as far as the first platform when Sarah bolted out of the car, waving her arms at Marcus and trying to get him to stop. Marcus stopped the moment he saw her.

"What's up?" Marcus asked. "Kiss for luck?" he flirted.

"You can't just leave us down here with no protection, asshole," she said.

Marcus and Dave carried all the firepower that the group had. Grabbing his handgun, Marcus checked the safety and tossed it down to Sarah along with a couple of clips.

"Don't shoot yourself in the foot, pretty lady," Marcus said.

"Thanks." She paused then stated, "I'll try not to." She paused again. "Good luck, Marcus." She turned to walk back to the car.

"Sarah?" Marcus awaited Sarah's attention. Sarah turned to face him. "If I'm not back in five minutes, you guys move on, all right?" He turned and started his climb again.

Sarah nodded and returned to her car. "You bet I will," she said under her breath.

Marcus reached the rooftop and peeked over the edge. There was no sign of Dave, but he still couldn't see the entire roof, and he was sure Dave was up there somewhere. So far, he hadn't seen any signs of trouble. Everyone in the car had their eyes peeled for anything happening on the rooftop. Marcus checked his watch and climbed up on the roof and was soon out of sight. About 25 yards away, he spotted a door cracked open. Marcus ran to investigate.

Sarah looked at her watch. The time ticked on.

"How long has it been?" asked Linda.

"Not long, maybe three minutes. Don't worry, he'll find him."

Eli rubbed Linda's shoulders. Another minute crept by.

"Where are they?" asked Linda again, not really expecting an answer.

Sarah dropped her head and sighed. She rubbed the back of her neck. It was hurting from looking up for so long. As she did, she noticed movement in the rearview mirror. She looked and saw Linda in tears. Then her eyes focused passed the passengers in the back seat. Zombies were almost at her back bumper. She jammed the car into gear and sped forward.

"What, wait! What are you doing? They have another minute yet. Stop," begged Linda.

"We don't have a minute. Look behind us," Sarah said, gritting her teeth.

Eli turned and looked. "Go, go!" he shouted.

"We just can't leave them," said Linda.

"We'll come back for them." Sarah hit the gas. A herd of zoms followed close behind.

Linda rubbernecked as far as she could to see if Dave was at the top of the building looking down. "Oh David, where the hell are you?"

•••

## CHAPTER 24

Steve had passed out lying face-down in a pile of trash. When he awoke, he found himself buried up to his ears in garbage. His breathing was labored, and he must have sweated every drop of fluid from his body. He was badly dehydrated and it hurt to move. The heat and the gut-wrenching stench were too much for him. He had to do something to get out of this metal coffin and soon, before it actually became one.

Steve could feel things crawling up and down his neck, back, arms, and legs. He could only imagine what they were. He swiped them from his face and dug them out of his eye sockets, ears, and nose. He could even taste them. He spit, thinking they may still be in his mouth. Steve guessed that he was covered with maggots, and he finally vomited. *Well, that will help the smell in here*, he thought. He remembered the swarms of flies and the constant buzzing all around him before the gunfire had started and right before he'd passed out. It only made sense. Wherever there is garbage there are flies, and where there are flies there had to have been larvae at one time or another. This must have been the time. For once, Steve was so glad he couldn't see.

There must have been hundreds, if not thousands, crawling, biting, chewing, and digging in his open sores. He tried to wipe them from his mind like he did his face, but that was an impossible task as the constant stinging bites reminded him of where they were. The very thought of them crawling on him churned his stomach. He wanted to vomit again and again, but there wasn't anything left in him but dry heaves. Steve couldn't remember the last time he had a decent meal, and the leftover candy bars in his pocket had long since melted. He should have finished them when he had the chance. He ripped the packages open and licked the melted chocolate from the wrappers.

It was darker than pitch inside the Dumpster. Steve's eyes hadn't had time to readjust yet. The only available light source were the tiny beams of light coming from the bullet holes left from the gunfire and a couple small cracks in the roof.

In addition to the creepy crawlies running up and down Steve's spine, he had to deal with sharp pains from his neck to his ankles from the injuries caused by the shrapnel embedded deep in his skin – shrapnel from the bombardment of bullets hitting the Dumpster while he was inside. He was very lucky none of the bullets hit him. Looking at the bullet hole pattern on the steel wall he wondered how. His body jerked with every stinging pain as sweat beaded up and dripped into the wounds.

It was completely silent now, not a single fly buzzing. Steve wondered where they all had gone. *Thousands of flies just don't disappear for no reason*, he thought. It reminded him of the birds falling from the sky. It just doesn't happen without a good reason. *Did the flies all die from the heat? Hell, did I die from the heat? If not, how long have I been out? How long have I been dinner for these damn bugs?* He shrugged, frustrated at finding no answers to his crazy thoughts.

Steve couldn't see his hand in front of his face, let alone his watch to check the time. He reached for his cell phone in his pocket, but it was gone. It must have fallen out somewhere in the trash. He felt around for it, but it could have been anywhere and he gave up quickly. He was sure that his friends had left him behind by now. *They had better have*, he thought. He knew he'd been gone a long time. It was a lot longer than he thought, actually, and his friends hadn't come searching for him after all. If they had, maybe they just hadn't known where to look. They hadn't thought of Steve being trapped inside a Dumpster.

He heard more gunfire in the distance. Steve assumed the military was still doing street sweeps, shooting anything that moved, and he was right.

Pressing an ear to the sidewall of the Dumpster, Steve listened and heard no sounds coming from the alley now – no nearby gunshots, no shuffling of feet, no vehicles, and best of all, no moans from the undead. This was good. No, this was great. A feeling of relief fell over him but was quickly replaced with doubt. He started thinking that maybe he was deaf from the gunfire, maybe from the bullets hitting the steel Dumpster and echoing through the metal tomb, through his head and out again. His head pounded and his ears continued to ring with a high-pitched whine. *Maybe the gunshots I hear are just outside the Dumpster after all. What if I open the lid and the zombies are still there? Maybe they are just sleeping. Do zombies even sleep? What if I look out there and I'm met by the military, looking down the barrel of an M-4? Would they think I was one of ... them? Would they take me to safety?* Visions of Atlanta General entered his mind. *Are you fucking crazy? They would shoot me on sight! What if they already took Sarah and the gang? What if ...?* The heat was making the streams of what-ifs endless.

Steve barely had the strength to pull himself up from the garbage grave he'd dug, and when he finally did, a smile stretched from ear to ear when he realized he could, in fact, still hear after all. Not well, but well enough. It was just a small glimmer of hope – hope that would keep him going for another day.

He could hear paper, cardboard, tin cans, and glass crunch beneath his knees and feet and the palms of his hands as he pushed down hard against the trash. He cut his hands on jagged glass and heard himself cuss as he tried desperately to stand on uneven ground.

Steve still had a chance to get out of this tin can alive, and that was exactly what he intended to do. He stood very still with one ear pressed against the steel wall of the Dumpster, covering one of the bullet holes. Repeating all four sides, he listened intently. He then tried to look through the bullet holes, but the beams of light stung his eyeballs and he quickly shied away, rubbing them hard. He needed air, fresh air to breathe before he passed out again. The heat was just unbearable. He didn't want to fall into a trap. He slowly pushed the lid of the Dumpster up, just enough to peer out. It wasn't heavy, but it still required practically all his strength. The light was blinding at first, but the cool air rushed through his nostrils, filling his nasal cavities like standing in the frozen food aisle of a store.

He took several deep breaths. The air was cool to him, yet the air temperature was still in the low 90s. Somehow it felt refreshing. The odor, on the other hand, was not. It somehow got worse if that even seemed possible.

As Steve's eyes adjusted to the light, he soon found where all the biting flies had gone. They swarmed the decaying bodies that carpeted the alley's floor. The street, the curb, and the sidewalks were blanketed by the dead, the dead undead. It looked like a zombie massacre. He looked back inside the Dumpster for his phone now that he could see, and luck was on his side for a change. Lo and behold, it was lying there in plain sight on top of the pile of rubbish and broken glass. He gladly retrieved his phone.

Steve pulled his shirt up over his nose and mouth and then pulled himself from the oven and fell to his feet. He stretched his back, creating a couple of popping sounds. Then he sighed. While stretching, his eyes caught a glimpse of a battered sign riveted to the side of the Dumpster. It read, "cardboard only." Steve silently chuckled.

"Yeah, right," he said under his breath as he looked down at his shirt and pants. He was covered with food, blood, and maggots. The cuts on his hands and legs weren't caused from paper but from broken glass and sharp metal. He slapped at his arms and pant legs, brushing the remaining maggots and debris away.

He looked down at his watch. More than four hours had passed. He whispered to himself sadly, "Good luck, Sarah. I hope you made it out."

Steve looked at his phone and wiped the garbage from its screen. It had a signal. He started to dial Sarah's number while scanning the ground before him. The scenery made him feel sick to his stomach. He held his gut and vomited the only thing he had in his stomach: the melted candy bar he had recently eaten.

The partially digested candy bar projected from his mouth, spewing over a couple of dead zoms that were lying in the street. Steve held his stomach and dropped to his knees, clicking the "cancel" button on his phone before dialing the last number. He thought he was going to puke again.

Above all the buzzing sounds that the flies were making, Steve could hear gunfire and more trucks, and Humvees, followed by more boots hitting the pavement. They could be the same troops who'd shot up the alley earlier for all he knew, but these were close, too close for comfort. *They're coming back to check out their handiwork*, Steve presumed. *No one could have possibly survived this slaughter*, he thought. Steve couldn't be found there. If he were found he too would be shot on sight with no questions asked. No one was to be left standing, just like at Atlanta General. That would stay with him forever.

Steve looked for cover but couldn't bring himself to jump back into the Dumpster. Nor did he have time to leave the alley. Just then, the front end of a Humvee appeared at the end of the alley. Steve dove for cover in the only place readily available, right out in the open. Steve lied amongst the dead, pulling one of the dead on top of him. The Humvee pulled up and stopped. Brakes squealed. More motor sounds followed. Boots hit the ground and from the sound of them, seemed to scramble in different directions. The troops made their way through the alley, walking between the dead. They checked many of the bodies, stabbing them with the bayonets fastened to the ends of their M-4s. Nothing moved. Steve waited patiently. He slowed his breathing. A soldier was only six feet away, and Steve was sure that he was going to be stabbed. Just when the soldier finished stabbing the zom two bodies over from Steve, a whistle blew and a voice sounded over a bullhorn. "Alley all clear."

•••

## CHAPTER 25

"What the hell is going on out there?" the chief barked to whoever was listening.

"It's a war zone, sir. It appears the military has taken over, and they're destroying our town."

"Taking over the town? Under whose orders? This is my town, dammit? How come I wasn't notified?"

"I believe it was the president, sir."

"The president?"

"Yeah, him and the CDC. They want to contain the virus in a bad way, sir."

Gunfire and grenades could be heard in the background.

"Contain it! It's an extermination out there. It looks

like they are firing at anything that moves."

"Yes, sir. They are. It's martial law. They have orders to shoot anything on the streets that moves. They figure if you are outside with those … monsters … then you're probably dead already. They're not taking any chances with this, sir. They're serious."

"Who's in charge? I want him in my office ASAP."

"Sorry, Chief, that's just not possible. No one is allowed to be on the streets. You're likely to get shot or bit."

"Where are you getting your info?"

"The Web, sir. Blogs, Facebook, Twitter, and this was stuck in every door across the town." He handed the chief a flier printed on goldenrod paper. "This was stuck in our door, and one came across our fax, as well."

The chief read it.

*Citizens of Bear Creek:*

*The CDC has declared your town a high risk and has issued a state of martial law. You are ordered by the president of the United States and the CDC to stay in your homes until the ALL CLEAR has been given. As you are well aware by now, a serious virus has spread throughout your community. It's deadly and has to be contained. We cannot allow this virus to spread beyond your town's borders. If you are seen outside your home, you are risking your own life. Chances are that you will be infected. Best-case scenario, you will be shot. Worst-case scenario, both. We urge you to stay inside and lock your doors and windows. Let us do our jobs. You will be informed when it's all clear to come out.*

The chief finished reading the flier. "You've got to be kidding me, right? If this is really happening, it's got to be a joke."

"Yes, sir. I mean, no, sir. No joke. It's for real, sir."

"There will be nothing left of this town when they get done with it. You know that, right?"

"Good possibility, sir."

The chief paused. "We have to find that professor. Any news?"

"Actually, sir, we've come across some intersection tweets."

"Tweets? What the hell are tweets?"

It's Twitter, sir. It seems he's been in contact with a doctor who was doing missionary work down in South America. It seems he had found something and sent it up to the professor for tests."

"A doctor doing missionary work. Interesting. Go on."

"A doctor of veterinary medicine, sir. The doctor stopped tweeting and never answered the professor's last DMs."

"DMs? Layman's terms please, Lieutenant."

"Twitter's way to send a private message. The doctor hasn't been heard from since."

"Judging by the professor's responses, he presumed him dead or ..."

"Or what?"

"Infected, sir."

"Get me as much information as you can dig up, and get as many people as you can on this. It looks like we are stuck in this office for a while. "

"Yes, sir. Will do."

"And one more thing. Give me your undershirt."

"Sir?"

"I need a white flag, and I don't have one." The officer stripped his T-shirt off and reluctantly handed it to the chief.

"I would like to go on record, sir, and tell you that I don't think what you have in mind is a good idea."

"Noted, but I need to talk to the one in charge, and I have no other ideas at this time."

"Good luck, sir."

The chief reached inside a supply closet and grabbed a mop. He released the mop head, replacing it with the officer's undershirt. Without looking back, he walked out the front door and crossed the street to what appeared to be the National Guard command tent.

"Sir, what in the hell is going on here?" The chief walked up to the gentleman who appeared to be the one in command.

He was greeted by a couple of M-4s pointed in his direction.

"On the ground, now!" he was quickly ordered.

"I beg your pardon. I'm the chief of this ..."

The chief's voice trailed off as the commanding officer growled, "I don't care if you're Mother Theresa. On the ground. Now!"

The chief reached for his badge but was stopped by a single warning shot over his head. "If you make one more move that isn't toward the ground, Chief, the next shot I guarantee you will not hear. Do you understand me, sir?"

The chief quickly hit the ground, hands and legs spread wide. He asked to speak to the commanding officer.

"I am the commanding officer," the man barked.

"Can I ask what the hell is going on here?" the chief questioned while face-down on the pavement.

"Look around, Chief. I think it seems pretty doggone clear. Didn't you get the memo? Your town is under siege and under my command. I have direct orders from the CDC to do whatever it takes to quarantine this town. In about five minutes, no one comes in and no one alive goes out without my consent."

"Why?"

"You been living under a rock, Chief? You have a deadly virus walking around your town, and frankly, they don't want it to spread all over the damn world." The commander paused, then barked out an order. "Get him up and take him down to briefing. We could use another good man."

"Yes, sir." The grunts with the M-4s saluted in unison and helped the chief to his feet, grabbing both arms and dragging him to the adjacent tent.

•••

## CHAPTER 26

Marcus kicked the door open wide with rifle at the ready, pointed down the stairway leading to the store below. Knowing he was up against the clock, he moved quickly but silently. He reached the ground level. Boxes lined the walls and were stacked high to the ceiling, labeled with several brands of alcohol. *A liquor store*, he thought. *A fully stocked, never-looted liquor store. I'll be damned.* "Dave?" he whispered. "You down here anywhere?"

To his surprise, Dave answered. "Over here, Marcus."

"Over where? You all right?"

"Just around the corner. I knew you'd come. You wouldn't leave me."

"What is this? Was this a test, Dave?" Marcus looked

over at Dave. He was taking a long swig of whiskey.

"Look around, Marcus. We've all died and gone to heaven." Marcus, also a drinker, was wide-eyed with amazement, seeing all the crates of booze. Then he remembered the time issue. "Shit, Sarah!" he shouted.

"Sarah is going to leave us in five minutes." He looked down at his watch. "It's already been four minutes. We have to go. Now!" Marcus turned and bolted up the stairs. Dave didn't follow, at least not right away. "Dave, come on!" Marcus yelled from the roof down the stairway.

Still seeing no sign of Dave following, Marcus continued to move toward the edge of the building. He looked down to give Sarah a signal to wait, but Sarah wasn't there. The car was gone. He looked at his watch. He still had 15 seconds. "What the heck?" He looked down again, then down the road where he saw the tail end of a mob of zoms shambling after a slow-moving vehicle. "Dammit! Dave, get your ass up here now!"

Marcus looked back at the doorway as Dave stumbled through, holding his shotgun in one hand and cradling a case of whisky in the other. He staggered a few more steps in Marcus's direction when Marcus noticed movement in the shadows of the doorway behind Dave. He lifted his rifle and pointed it in Dave's direction.

"Whoa, whoa! Isn't that a little drastic, Marcus? It's just a little drink. I mean, come on, man."

Marcus fired off a round. Dave could feel the heat and heard the bullet whiz past his ear. "Shit!" Dave hit the ground, smashing the case of whiskey as a zombie fell out of the doorway behind him. Whisky poured from the corner of the case. The zombie was quickly replaced by another and yet another. Marcus fired off two more rounds, and the two remaining zoms met the same fate as the first. They piled up in the doorway.

Marcus ran to the door, kicking the dead zoms out of the way and pushing the door shut. He then piled the dead zoms in front of the door, blocking it from opening again.

"Whoa, they almost had me. Where the hell did they come from, Marcus? I didn't know they could climb steps," Dave whined. "We gotta get off this roof."

"She left us, Dave."

"Left us? My wife wouldn't leave me. She's pregnant with my child, for God's sake."

"Well, think again. They must have panicked. They're about a mile down the road being stalked by a mob of zoms."

Dave tried to pull himself to his feet but needed Marcus's help to do so. He stumbled to the edge of the roof to see for himself. The car was gone. Out of sight. "Shit," he said, swinging his body around and sliding his back down the half-brick wall. He sat on the roof and reached for a cigarette. "The bike?"

Marcus looked over the edge. "Tipped over but still intact. Should be all right."

"Good, let's go," Dave said, slurring his words. He tried to get up and reached for an arm for some help.

"Go? You're in no condition to drive a bike, you idiot."

"No shit, Sherrrrlock. You drive."

"I've never driven a bike before in my life."

Dave slid back down the wall and back on his ass and began to laugh.

• • •

# CHAPTER 27

The military gave the all clear on one alley and moved on to the next. They cleared the way, sawing zombies down everywhere they found them. This continued alley after alley, zom after zom, until the Guard felt the numbers were more manageable. When they left, so did Steve, after struggling to get out from underneath the zom he took cover under.

"Nothing but dead weight," Steve grunted, struggling to free an arm. When he finally broke free, Steve managed to make his way to the end of the "Alley of the Dead," as it would be known forever in his mind. He kept as much distance between himself and the dead zoms as he could in fear that one might reach out and touch someone, namely him. To his relief, none moved. The military did a more-than-efficient job.

Steve ducked behind the corner of the building until the military was clear out of sight. They weren't gone but a couple minutes when the main street started filling up with walkers again. The military was fooling itself about "manageable numbers." There were more zombies than the soldiers thought. Steve knew he had a very limited window of opportunity before there would be too many zoms for him to move about. He picked a target, a goal to reach, and quickly made a break for it. He moved but not without being seen by a few zoms now shambling in his direction. Their moans attracted more zombies, and soon he was being followed by another flash mob.

*Where the hell do they all keep coming from?* Steve thought to himself as he ran, trying to clear the street. Steve was soon tripped up by all of the debris left behind by the military action that had taken place. Feeling weak and unable to right himself, he stumbled and fell headfirst to the pavement, scraping skin from his arms, elbows, and knees. His cell phone flew from his pocket and bounced several times before coming to rest, smacking hard against the curb on the other side of the street. The back of the phone sprang loose and the battery was thrown clear, as well as the cover that kept it secured. Several smaller pieces scattered in different directions, and the screen instantly spider-webbed. Steve watched as pieces of his cell phone came to rest before his eyes, seemingly in slow-motion. His heart sank as if someone had just cut his lifeline. He looked to the ground while beating his bloody fist on the pavement.

Steve's cuts and scrapes quickly turned beet-red with blood. The scent of his blood was quickly filling the air. He knew there was no time to pick up the pieces, and he was pretty sure the phone wouldn't work again even if he did.

Hearing the walkers closing in on him, Steve lifted his head. He hesitated midway up. His focus wasn't on his phone anymore but on a line stretched inches away from his nose – a thin cable stretched taught for as far as he could see, a trip line set by the military, assuredly tied to explosives. A lump formed in his throat as he thought of the tragedy he could have faced.

*Oh shit*, was the first thing that entered Steve's mind. With his military background, he knew exactly what he was looking at. All he could hear were moans coming closer and closer as he stared at the thin cord. The crowd of zombies was moving in on him fast. The smell of blood in the air seemed to perk up their senses, making them vocalize and move much more fiercely. If Steve wanted any chance of escaping, he had to move now. And move now he did. He needed to gain some distance between himself and that wire before the zombies crossed it. He might be cutting it too close already.

"Now or never," Steve said to himself as he jumped to his feet, ignoring all the pain he felt throughout his body. He picked up his bat and fought off the first few zombies who were well ahead of the mob forming behind them. Running out of time, he clobbered the last of the leaders. He turned and carefully stepped over the trip wire. He had less than a 20-foot lead on the group of undead shambling toward him. It was do-or-die time. He ran as fast as his feet would carry him, increasing his lead by 10, 20, maybe even 30 more feet before the first zom reached the wire.

Steve felt the blast lift his body from the ground and push it forward as body parts of zoms rained down around him. The bodies of many zombies blew to pieces as a series of explosions went off like fireworks down the line. It killed anyone within 20 feet of that line. Some were decapitated, and some thrown as if they were rag dolls. The mixture of compression and shrapnel devices exploding side-by-side ripped arms, legs, fingers, and even heads off their bodies, tossing them easily 100 feet away. The compression blast knocked Steve off-balance. He stumbled to correct his footing as he continued to make ground between him and the remaining undead. The sound of the blast brought more zoms from a distance as they too shambled in the direction of the noise.

•••

Steve finally reached the schoolyard. He was completely exhausted from wielding his bat most of the way there. Zoms appeared from out of nowhere throughout his journey. Everywhere he turned, another zom headed in his direction. Some fell at his first strike, while others, -- fresh ones, ones who still had thick enough skulls – sometimes took several swings to bring them down. Swinging the bat that many times while running consumed a lot of energy – energy that was quickly being depleted. He needed food, drink, and rest.

Steve also needed a better weapon. He needed something that would crack heads easier, faster, and more smoothly without getting stuck, and preferably with one swing. He had an idea of such a tool and hoped that one existed nearby.

Steve swung a leg through an open window of the school building and climbed through, cranking the window shut behind him. He hoped that the school was locked and there were no other easy ways in, at least not for zoms. He didn't know if they could climb through windows, but he didn't want to take any chances. He closed all of the windows he came across. Little did he know that zoms had already entered the school.

They had gotten in while kids and teachers tried to rush out. Some didn't make it out in time. Some died during the attack and were eaten. Some had been bitten while trying to hide in lockers, closets, or under desks. Sadly, they reanimated as one of "them" and attacked others who were hiding with them.

Steve ran room-to-room, knowing that shamblers were close behind, possibly surrounding the school as he searched for something he may not even find. Each room that he entered and then left empty-handed was time wasted and ground lost. Schools aren't the best place to find weapons, after all. There had to be something, though. English classes had nothing but books and pencils, while math classrooms had protractors and rulers. He did temporarily keep a three-foot aluminum yardstick that he found. What for, he didn't know, but he didn't want to leave it behind and leave empty-handed once again. He had to have known that it probably wouldn't make a very effective weapon and would never replace his baseball bat.

Steve's mind raced as he wondered where the shop class might be. *Tools, lots of tools*, he thought. He entered an art room and found scissors of all sizes and boxes of razor blades and razor knives – sharp, but they would never take down a zom. He threw what he could in a book bag he'd found in an open locker.

Steve could now see through the windows that the shamblers were beginning to gather. They were on the playground and in parking areas. A mass of them hung around the bus garage and around one bus in particular. Looking closer, Steve saw why. The bus was rocking back and forth from zoms pushing and trying to get in. It almost appeared as if they were trying to rock it and tip it over, but this gave the zoms way too much credit. They only had the mentality to feed and only possessed the most basic of motor skills. They knew nothing else.

The bus driver locked inside the bus had his hands full with at least a half-dozen screaming kids inside with him. Little did Steve know that while he was watching the busload of kids, zombies were pouring through an open door leading into the school's gymnasium. One by one, they filtered through the halls.

A small zom shambled by the open classroom door. It looked like a little girl about nine years old. She was most likely a former student of the school, left behind. Startled at what he saw, Steve backed into a countertop. His elbow hit the arm of a large paper cutter. He pushed it back against the window, sending a sharp tingling sensation through his arm.

"Ow!" he yelled out, while grabbing his elbow and almost doubling over. He must have hit his funny bone, but Steve was not laughing.

The little walker just outside the door heard the sound and backtracked to the room she had just passed. Steve was trying to rub out the tingling pain shooting through his arm and hand. His eyes enlarged with excitement as he peered down at the cutter he had just bumped into. With a little imagination, the handle of the paper cutter was shaped like the handle of a sword. He couldn't wait to break it loose.

The little girl shambler stumbled through the door and stood perfectly still, eying Steve up and down. She let out a soft moan, followed by an evil hisssss. Steve grabbed his baseball bat but hesitated a brief second or two, not believing what he was about to do. *She's just a child*, he thought and wondered how many more kids had ended up like this one. The virus didn't discriminate based on its victims' ages. It didn't discriminate at all. Young, old, fat, skinny, black or white, it didn't matter. This was a true opportunity for all.

Steve approached the girl while swinging the bat back and forth. His swings were just like playing tee-ball as a child. He knocked the little girl's head clean off her neck with one big swing. The little girl's head splattered hard against the adjacent wall 10 or 15 feet away, leaving a good-sized dent in the drywall. The head stuck in the hole for a brief second before falling to the floor. It rolled and came to rest under a child's desk, spraying a sporadic trail of blood and brain matter along the way. The girl's body fell where it once stood, sinking in its own pool of blood. The blood puddled on the floor like a pail of spilt paint.

Steve slammed the door shut and braced it with tables, desks, and chairs. He returned to the paper cutter. This was exactly the thing he was envisioning earlier. Excited, he looked around for a screwdriver to disassemble the unit. He checked drawer after drawer only to come up empty-handed. He finally searched the teacher's desk at the head of the room. He pulled out more drawers until one revealed both flat-head and Phillips-head screwdrivers. He grabbed them both along with some pliers, which were also in the drawer. He immediately went right to work disassembling the cutter.

Steve's mechanic skills came in handy, and it showed. He had the cutter in pieces in mere seconds. He swung the blade around like a machete, getting a feel for its size and weight. "Perfect," he said with a smile. "Great balance, too." He turned to the door and saw a zom's hands smeared across the frosted glass bearing the teacher's name, Mrs. Freeman, underscored by a smeared streak of blood.

Steve slammed the blade down on one of the student's desk. The blade sank deep into the wood, cracking the tabletop in half. Steve heard a noise at his feet. It was the girl's head jarred loose from its resting point and rolling one last time, now resting against Steve's boot. The girl's milky eyes were staring up at Steve. Her mouth was open as the jaw muscles finally relaxed. He jumped back and was feeling a bit queasy, weak in the knees, and he felt his bowels instantly turn to soup. He squeezed his butt cheeks as tight as he could, almost doubling over in pain. "Bathroom! I need a bathroom now!" he said to himself. Soon, the sudden urge passed, but he knew it would return with a vengeance. He needed to find a toilet and quickly.

Like a lot classrooms in the school, this one was attached to another. They were divided by a heavy curtain, that could be pushed back out of the way like an accordion. Steve ran to the adjacent room to check the door leading to the hall. *The doors were closed. Good,* he thought. And there were no sign of zoms clawing at that door. He picked up a child's chair and threw it into the room he'd just come from. The chair crashed into the barricade he'd built and landed with a long, loud crashing noise. The sound lasted for several seconds, long enough to rile the zoms on the other side of the door. Now that they were focused on the noise, they tried harder to get in, giving Steve time to do what he had to do.

Steve opened the other door slowly and peeked out into the hallway. He looked both ways several times. He saw a couple of shamblers down the hall with their backs to him. Looking back in the opposite direction, he saw a half-dozen of them trying desperately to get through the barricaded door.

Steve couldn't wait any longer. His bowels were just about ready to give birth. He took advantage of the first opportunity he had. Unfortunately, the restroom signs pointed in the same direction as the two shamblers he'd spotted down the hallway. Steve went room to room, ducking between lockers and doorways until he reached the first bathroom. Then he noticed one of the shamblers was dragging a piece of toilet paper. He chuckled as he realized there might be shamblers inside. The girls' bathroom was first, but Steve didn't care. He couldn't wait any longer. He ducked inside. Little did he know that right when he'd snuck inside, a shambler turned and saw the back of his leg leading into the bathroom. The zombie turned and followed Steve.

Steve couldn't believe his eyes when he walked inside. The room was like a slaughterhouse. The walls were splattered and smeared with blood. It even stained the ceiling. The floor was slippery with bodily fluids: blood, urine, guts, and pieces of little children. They were scattered throughout the room. Steve felt so sick to his stomach that he had no choice but to take the first stall he came to and shut the door behind him. Inside was more carnage, so torn apart that they were unrecognizable as human beings. He quickly pushed the carcasses aside and lifted the lid.

Steve pulled his pants down and straddled the seat. Just as he did, he heard a noise – someone or something just two stalls away. Steve froze in place. His stomach cramped as he doubled over in pain again. He felt his bowels heat up to a hot liquid and tried holding it back. He didn't want to be heard and he knew it wasn't going to be quiet. He strained for as long as he could before it broke loose and came down with a continuous splash. He couldn't remember the last time he'd had this bad of a case of butt pee. It burned as he tried to slow the stream down, but it was no use. It was like pinching off a garden hose with the pressure turned all the way up. It just made it worse, jetting out even faster.

The noise from the stall two doors down grew silent but only until the stall door swung freely. Whatever it was, it was headed in Steve's direction.

Steve quietly wiped and pulled his pants up as he stood. As he was about to unlatch the door to the stall, a little girl's arms and head came sliding underneath. She looked up at Steve, showing her bloody teeth like a rabid animal. She grabbed at Steve's legs with terrible moist hisses. Steve reflexively kicked at her and then swung his blade.

*What am I doing?* Steve asked himself after decapitating yet another young zom. It was another little girl. Not quite a teenager. *This can't be happening.* But it was, and by now it was happening all over the United States and beyond, and no one knew why.

Steve carefully stepped out of the stall, surefooted, hoping not to slip on the bloody floors. He headed out of the bathroom and came face to face with another zom in the doorway. An adult this time, *thank God.* Steve didn't know if he had it in him to slaughter another child. He clobbered the zom with his blade, splitting his frontal lobe, sending the zom crashing to his feet. Steve crossed the hall running back to the art room, locking the door behind him.

He looked around some more, and quickly scurried through some of the kids' book bags that were left behind. He found a few juice cups, and snacks, mainly in the Hostess and the Little Debbie variety but he didn't care. Food is food and snacks are what Steve lived on. He packed what he found in his new go-bag, choking down a Twinkie® as he went.

Seeing a bit of a clearing outside, Steve cranked open a window and quietly stepped out of the building.

With his bat in one hand and the cutter blade in the other, he now walked taller than ever and with more confidence, as if that were even possible.

First stop, the bus garage.

•••

## CHAPTER 28

"What are we going to do?" asked Sarah.

"Just keep driving," said the old man in the back seat.

"We have to go back, we have to get Dave," cried Linda, David's wife, "I can't do this without him," she rubbed her pregnant belly and started to sob.

"Just calm down everyone. They're pretty resourceful guys, they'll figure a way to get to us." Eli said with his best effort to comfort her patting her arm.

"What if they are waiting for us?" she asked.

"Trust me ma'm, they will only wait so long."

"But,....."

The old man interrupted. "For now our safety is our main concern and they know that. Keep moving Sarah," he ordered.

"So you're giving the orders now old man?" asked Linda

"Oh come on, someone needs to make some decisions here, and my name isn't old man, it's Eli. I say we keep going as planned that's all."

"Guys?" Sarah tried to butt in. "Guys?"

"Oh is that right, well who….." Linda stopped.

"GUYS!" Sarah yelled gaining everyone's attention this time. "Look." She pointed straight ahead. Eli looked out the front and turned to look out the back and then front again.

"Ok. Now what hot shot?" Linda asked.

"Oh my, stop the car!" Eli bellowed.

Sarah slammed on the brakes and car screeched to a stop, throwing everyone in the car forward. The sound of the screaming tires was all it took for half of the mob of shambler's up ahead to turn around and start shambling in their direction.

"Great! Here they come now," cried Sarah. She threw the car in reverse and started backing the car up. She desperately searched for a place to turn around. She was not that good at driving backwards.

"What, what are you doing?" asked Linda

"What do you think I'm doing, I'm getting the hell out of here," Sarah replied.

"But there is more behind us," Linda rebutted.

"Not as many," said Eli.

The little girl sitting between the old man and Linda

pulled her legs up on the seat and buried her face between her knees and silently whimpered. Linda felt her shaking and pulled her close.

Sarah was driving the car in reverse at uncomfortable speeds for everyone. She whipped the car in between two buildings. Trash cans went flying as the back bumper crashed into them. She rammed the car in drive, before it came to a complete stop and floored it. Wheels spun wildly, spraying gravel, yelling as only rubber could yell. She drove off in the direction they came.

"Zombies straight ahead!"

•••

# CHAPTER 29

Steve stood tall like a man on a mission and was headed straight for the bus garage. He had only two things on his mind: crushing heads and saving some kids. He was fed up with the zombies always in the lead. It was time to show them a thing or two. The driver of the bus nervously watched as Steve approached.

"No, no! What the hell are you doing, fella?" the driver asked under his breath. "Go away, get back. It's suicide!" he said a little bit louder.

Steve wasn't stopping. He didn't even hesitate. He stared at his target like he was in a trance and continued to walk toward them. The driver repeatedly tried to get Steve's attention. He waved his arms and yelled as loud as he could.

Even the kids joined in, but Steve still kept coming.

As Steve approached the bus, he started cutting and clubbing zombies down one after another. The driver was in awe and at times thought Steve was a goner, especially when he could no longer see him. To his surprise, Steve always emerged from the crowd unscathed. Instead of waving Steve away, the kids now cheered him on as if he was some sort of superhero.

Steve was fearless and had taken down about a dozen zoms single-handedly. The commotion was loud and was now attracting a bigger audience. More zoms were closing in from the distance. The driver noticed them coming and tried again to get Steve's attention by banging on the windows and yelling while waving his arms. Steve was paying little attention to the pounding on the glass. He was a bit busy crushing heads. Steve sliced down the last two zoms between him and the bus before he looked up at the driver. The driver was amazed at Steve's ability, but still his face was full of fear.

The driver eagerly pointed behind Steve. He desperately tried to get Steve to look. Steve finally turned and saw his near future. There must have been 30 or 40 zombies headed his way.

"Get the kids out of here!" Steve hollered, waving his arms.

The driver slid a window open. "It won't start, fella. I've been trying."

"Pop the hood," Steve ordered as he ran to the front of the bus.

The driver, in-turn, ran to the driver's seat of the bus

while telling the kids to be quiet and sit still. Steve rounded the front of the bus. The driver gripped the lever to the hood and pulled. Steve lifted the hood, latched it, and looked underneath. The driver turned the key. Steve listened and then fiddled with a few wires.

"Try again!" he yelled.

The kids in the back of the bus were getting a little anxious as the mob of zoms closed in.

"Quiet back there!" the driver yelled. His eyes widened as he too saw how close the zoms really were. He turned the key. The engine turned over once, sputtered, and died.

"Again!" Steve yelled after adjusting the throttle by hand.

The driver turned the key again. The engine turned over and over. Steve held the throttle wide open. "Again!" he yelled. The smell of diesel fuel filled the air.

Zoms were now at the back of the bus. The engine roared. Black smoke billowed out the tail pipe. Steve revved the motor by hand a couple more times before he slammed the hood down. The zoms were now on both sides of the bus and still advancing toward him. Some slapped at the windows and reached for the kids. The kids jumped back. They were now standing in the aisles as the zoms were slapping both sides of the bus. They advanced on.

"Get in!" the driver yelled, but the zoms were already past the side door, trying to push their way in. The bus driver checked the lever to the door to make sure it was secure. Steve stepped up on the bumper of the bus and leaned back on the hood.

"Go! Go!" Steve yelled, pointing his bat forward and swinging his blade at a zom who reached over the hood for him. The blade fell on the zom's arm, cutting it clean off. It hit the hood of the bus with a loud, echoing thump-thump. He clubbed another with the bat as it rounded the opposite side. The bus slowly moved forward. Steve climbed higher up on the hood and sat down while leaning hard against the windshield.

"A little faster, please!" he yelled as politely as he could under the circumstances.

The driver was nervously driving while Steve was on the hood. He feared that Steve would slide off.

"Floor it, dammit!"

The driver stomped on the pedal until it couldn't be pressed any farther. The bus jumped forward, pressing Steve hard against the windshield. The driver didn't let off the gas until the zoms were clear out of sight.

The bus slowed to a stop, its brakes squealing. The air brakes let out their hiss. Steve slid off the hood and greeted the driver at the door. They shook hands.

"Thank you, sir. That was amazing. Come on inside."

"Sorry, I can't. I have to go," Steve said, breathing heavily. "You take the kids out of here."

"Where to?" the driver inquired.

"I don't know. Just away from here. As far away as you can, and avoid the military. They aren't on our side. They'll shoot you and the kids if you're caught."

"You're kidding me, right?"

"Afraid not. They have orders to kill anything that moves on the streets. Martial law. If you're on the streets, they're considering you dead already."

"That's absurd!"

"That's the way it is."

"Where will you go?"

"I'm headed for the hills, my friend."

"Well, that's the way we are going too, so get in. Let's go."

"I have something I must do. You go and don't stop for anything." The driver looked at Steve with a concerned grimace. "There's no time, just go. Get those kids safely out of here."

"Very well." The driver asked Steve for his name.

"Steve. The name's Steve."

"Charlie here. I've been driving bus for 37 years. Retiring next week." He paused, looking concerned again. "Are you all right, Steve?"

Steve rubbed his forehead, feeling a couple of bumps and picked at one of them with his fingernail. It looked like a large pimple. His face and arms were covered with them. White puss dripped out of the scratched openings.

"You have cuts and sores all over you. You don't look well, my friend. Are you infected? Is that why you won't come with us?"

*Strange age to have a bad case of acne. I haven't had a zit in more than ten years,* Steve thought. But that was certainly what it looked like, with big, white, rounded heads ready to pop at any time. Knowing what he'd been through,

Steve shrugged it off. "No, Charlie. I'm fine. Thanks. Just been through a lot in the last couple of hours. They're just some kind of bug bites."

"First aid kit in the bus. It'll just take a minute. Clean yourself up."

Steve looked down at his arms and noticed a couple of white spots forming there as well, but a little deeper under the skin. "Keep it for yourself, Charlie, and for the kids. You may need it. I'll be fine."

"Very well, Steve. Good luck to you." The driver nodded while shaking Steve's hand. He pulled away quickly as if he didn't want to catch anything and wiped his hand on his pants. "Thanks again."

The driver turned and climbed back aboard the bus and pushed the door shut behind him without looking back. Steve turned and walked in the direction of the garage while the yellow school bus pulled away. Steve did look back a couple of times. He was concerned about the future of those kids and wondered if they even had one.

The bus had barely hit fourth gear and was still in sight when it burst into flames, exploding into a million pieces. The explosion picked the bus up off the pavement. It came to rest on its side, not a window intact. Shattered glass flew every which way, and billows of black smoke poured from the openings where the windows once were. Flames rushed through the bus like a bullet out of a barrel. It had been struck by a military missile.

Steve fell to his knees, motionless. He looked on for a couple moments in awe. "No one could possibly have survived that. Those poor kids." He hung his head to the ground and shook it from side to side. "Why?" he asked. "Why is this happening?" After several deep breaths, Steve continued his journey to the garage, never looking back again.

With another block behind him, the auto shop where Steve worked was finally in sight. Steve couldn't believe that he'd actually made it. It had been the most exhausting six hours of his life. This was a trip that he'd estimated would take less than a half-hour.

Unfortunately, he wasn't quite there yet. Steve was in for another surprise. It seemed the military seized the garage to make repairs to its own vehicles. There were military personnel sitting out front in a very old CJ1 and a couple inside one of the bays. They didn't look like they were guarding it, per se, just sitting around chatting, smoking stogies, and carrying on. It was almost like they were having fun – just a little too relaxed of an atmosphere for Steve.

*What the hell is going on?* Steve wondered. *Is the war on zoms over? If so, I didn't get the memo and what's up with the old Jeep? They haven't used those in years.* He looked on and studied everyone's locations and movements. Every once in a while, a zombie would shamble up and the soldiers would actually make wagers on who was going to take it down and how many shots it would take. It hardly ever took more than one shot unless the soldier was shooting wrong-handed, just for the fun of it. This made Steve nervous as hell.

Steve could see a Humvee parked in the garage with one soldier bent over the hood. He could see the legs of another man sticking out from underneath, as well. From his vantage point, he couldn't see much more. There were just too many trucks obstructing his view. He had to find a way to move without the military seeing him. He didn't want them to mistake him for a zom. At this point, it really didn't matter. They were shooting anything that moved, anything that wasn't in uniform, and, in some cases, even things in uniform. Steve carefully moved in closer.

For a moment, Steve thought about scrubbing the mission. It was just too dangerous. He thought about just finding an abandoned truck on the street and hot-wiring it. Hell, he could probably find some with the keys still in them. But most were dry of gas, and he wouldn't know what condition they were in or if they would stay running at all. He knew his Jeep. He'd rebuilt it himself and knew it had a half-tank of gas and was ready to go, providing no one had siphoned it. If that was the case, he also knew where he could find more fuel. The Jeep pickup was still his best choice, so he continued on.

Steve had to make his way around the building without being seen. This was not going to be an easy task. Two soldiers sat up in a military Jeep not 40 yards away. The windshield lay flat on the hood. The two soldiers looked comfortable, sitting back in their seats and dressed in their battle dress uniforms. Their feet were propped up high on the dash. Steve ducked behind some low shrubs out of sight of the soldiers, at least temporarily.

Steve heard a sound from behind and was afraid to look, but he knew he had to. He was correct in his assumption. It was a zombie. It slowly approached from behind. It was close enough for Steve to hear a moist rattling sound deep within its throat as it moaned. Steve couldn't move. He was trapped. He was caught between getting shot by the military and being eaten by a zom. He surely would take a military bullet over being eaten alive, though.

*Why aren't they looking?* Steve asked himself. *Excuse me, I'm about to get eaten by a zom here. Will you please shoot it?* The soldiers kept on talking, laughing, drinking. *Drinking? You got to be kidding me! That better be Kool-aid!* Steve needed to make some noise to draw some attention toward the zom, but he had to do it without being seen himself. He looked around for something to throw. He grabbed a couple of rocks and tossed them toward the zom, but they didn't make enough noise. It certainly was not enough noise to overpower the soldiers' conversations and fun. Then he found a beer bottle in the shrubs where he was hiding. He waited for a quiet moment and tossed the bottle in the zom's direction. The bottle landed and smashed at its feet. The soldiers did hear that and stood to attention, side arms drawn.

"What? Oh man, not handguns!" Steve whispered. "Use your rifles, you idiots." He could barely hear the soldiers talking, but he thought he heard them betting on a headshot at 50 yards. *That would put the zombie on top of me*, Steve calculated. *Shoot the zom, dammit. Shoot him now!*

Frustration took over as Steve gritted his teeth. The zom now was no more than 30 feet away from him and moving closer. "I'm dead," he said, holding his makeshift sword on his lap while backing up deeper into the bush. *Shoot him, dammit. Shoot him! Shoot him! Shoot him! Shoot him!*

Twenty feet. Sweat beaded up on Steve's forehead and ran down his face. It stung his eyes. Fifteen feet. Steve lifted his paper-cutter sword and held it out in front of him. Ten feet. The zom moaned louder. Now he was reaching his arms out toward Steve. Steve pulled his legs in. At about five feet, a single shot rang out. To Steve, that sound was like heaven. Blood and brains burst from the back of the zom's head as it snapped backward. It then collapsed to the ground at his feet. He kicked the zom away.

"You lucky son-of-a-bitch," one soldier said to the other while handing him a twenty-spot. "Great shot, kid."

"Thank you." The soldier pocketed the cash. "You get the next one."

"The next one?" Steve whispered. Sure enough, the next one wasn't too far away and appeared to be taking the same path and shambling a little faster than the one before. It surely was excited by the sound of the shot, Steve presumed.

Steve had to move. The next time he might not be so lucky. While the soldiers had their backs turned and their heads in a cooler of beer, Steve got to his feet and made his way to the back of the shop using abandoned vehicles for protection.

The garage had its own 13-acre junkyard out back where they stored old cars and trucks for parts. No one in this town liked to buy new parts, and very few could afford them. The garage specialized in used parts. Cheap used parts. A "u-pick" junkyard, like for strawberries but this was for car parts. For an additional fee, Steve would pull the parts for customers, which was still much less expensive than buying the parts new.

Steve made his way around back, hoping not to run into any trouble from zoms and/or the military. Steve wasn't sure which one scared him more. The yard was all fenced in with a 10-foot-tall privacy fence, so he was pretty sure it wouldn't be guarded. There was also a chain-link gate where they drove, pushed, or most often towed the old or damaged cars into their final resting places. Steve's plan was to climb the fence, slip in the back room, grab the key to the gate, and head out with the Jeep pickup. Except for the barbed wire on the top of the gate, it sounded pretty simple.

In fact, it looked easier than Steve anticipated. *Finally, something going right for a change*, he thought. He didn't have to worry about the barbed wire on top of the fence after all. He simply walked through a gaping hole in the fence. It appeared that someone had it out for the military and went on a suicide mission, ramming a soldier and pinning him between a car and the fence, striking a stack of crushed cars inside the gate. If the crash didn't kill the soldier, the zombies surely did. They probably ate him alive while he was pinned down. Steve walked by the carnage, swishing flies from his face. The flies swarmed the dead body and made their way in and out of the bullet holes in the car's windshield. They feasted on the stiff inside the car as well.

Steve felt very comfortable once inside the junkyard. This was a place where he knew every nook and cranny. Anyone could name a year and model name, and Steve could tell them right where it sat, if he had one. He also could tell them if it still had tires and rims or a radio, or if the interior was worn. He knew the yard well.

Steve ran into no trouble at all making his way up to the back of the building. He looked in the window of the garage. One soldier was still there, drooped over the fender of a Humvee with his head inside the engine compartment. His M-4 leaned up against the side of the vehicle. Steve was at the wrong angle to see the other soldier inside, but he assumed the man was still there, as well. The windows were locked and so was the back door. "The gate key would have to be optional," he whispered to himself. This was an unnecessary option at that, since the Jeep pickup was equipped with a roll cage and steel tubular bumper. The Jeep key should be above the visor where he'd left it.

Steve grabbed a few gas cans that sat just outside the back door and headed straight for the Jeep. He heard a noise. *A guard?* He wondered, as he crouched down. He couldn't see anything, but he could hear someone. It sounded like it was at least two rows of cars away. "Duke?" he whispered. Steve figured it was probably just Duke, the junkyard dog, a big, mean-looking mastiff that wouldn't hurt a flea. Steve loved that dog. Duke always kept him company while he pulled parts off cars.

No one would ever go out in the yard alone while Duke was out roaming. No one except Steve and Bob, that is. Normally, dogs choose one person to be loyal to, but not Duke. Steve and Bob were equals in his eyes and the dog loved them both. Duke's home was the yard, and Duke simply being there was all the protection the yard ever needed. Up until now, that is.

Curiosity got the best of Steve. He wanted to check on Duke. He needed to know that he was okay and possibly even take Duke with him. This was no place for the dog now. Steve dropped the cans of gas off at the Jeep, sticking one in the bed and tipping the other up in the tank, letting it drain while he walked over to check on Duke.

Steve rounded the corner, but there was no sign of the dog. But the noise was still there and getting louder with every step. *Must be chewing on a bone in his pen*, he thought. As he approached Duke's kennel, Steve could hear him, crunching. "Duke," Steve whispered, hoping not to startle him when he got there. The last thing Steve needed was Duke getting all excited and making a lot noise when he saw Steve. "Duke, it's me, buddy." Steve heard more crunching sounds. He rounded the bend to see Duke lying there just inside the opened kennel gate, looking at Steve as he approached. "Hey, boy. Come here, buddy," Steve called out, slapping his jeans. Duke's head was rocking back and forth, but he didn't move. He just lay alongside his doghouse. Steve walked up closer. "Come on, buddy, let's get out of here. Want to go for a ride?" Nothing sparked a dog's interest more than those words. There was something about them that excited all dogs, but not Duke. Not this time. "Hey, what's wrong, buddy?" Steve was now close enough to touch him. He reached down to pet his head. Just then, Steve realized that Duke wasn't making that crunching sound at all. He could still hear it.

Steve glanced around the doghouse, which had been hiding half of Duke's body. He soon found what was making that noise. Tears filled Steve's eyes instantly. "No," he said quietly, but he shouldn't have spoken at all. This brought the attention of the zom making a feast out of Duke's torso, but now its attention was directed toward human flesh; toward Steve. Steve froze in place and looked to his hand for his bat or cutter blade, but neither one was there.

He felt so comfortable in his own yard that he hadn't even bothered arming himself. He'd left his weapons with the gas cans back at the Jeep. He turned and ran. The zom got to its feet and followed. Steve rounded the corner, coming face-to-face with another zombie. This one looked very familiar. It was Bob, Steve's boss. This was probably the first zombie who used to be someone Steve was close to. Steve couldn't believe what he was seeing. "Bob, it's me, Steve," he said while backing up, but Steve got no response. Bob lifted his arms and reached out for Steve. "No, Bob!" Steve faked right, then rolled left, and darted away toward the Jeep.

Steve reached the Jeep pickup and turned the key. Nothing happened. His heart sank in his chest. Then he remembered disconnecting the battery after working on it last. He popped the hood, grabbed his cutter blade, and took a look. Sure enough, the cables weren't attached. They were just dangling there. Steve picked them up and dropped them on the battery posts. They fit loosely. Steve wished he had a wrench to tighten them up, but there was no time to get one, as the two zombies shambled around the corner not 20 yards away. Steve grabbed a twig off the ground and jammed it down between the post and the clamp and broke it off, forcing a better connection on the opposite side. *That should do it*, he hoped, fingers crossed. He jumped back in the truck, zombies almost on him. The truck fired up. He jammed it in gear and off he went, splitting the two zoms down the middle and throwing them to the ground. Steve looked back at Bob. "Sorry, boss," he said as he watched him in the mirror getting back to his feet. He drove straight through the gate. The gate was no match for the modified steel tubular bumpers he'd welded on weeks ago. It swung wide, crashing up against the privacy fence as it splintered into planks.

•••

# CHAPTER 30

The commanding officer watched through a pair of field glasses as a rusty Jeep pickup sped down a back road, hightailing it out of town. He radioed ahead to a location a mile or so up the road. He provided a description and the current coordinates of the vehicle. The small group of the National Guard up ahead had very little time to prepare. Their commanding officer gave a signal when one of his soldiers had the truck in sight. Guns were drawn, and the orders were given to do whatever was necessary to stop the truck from fleeing the town. The driver might have been infected and couldn't be allowed to leave. The truck was now in the crosshairs of four M-4s and one handheld missile launcher.

"We're really going to kill an innocent man fleeing for his life?" one soldier mumbled under his breath. He held aim, waiting for just the right moment to squeeze the trigger on the launcher. He knew the M-4s's had little-to-no chance of stopping the truck at this distance. He also knew that he held the life of the driver in his hands. He had his orders. Seconds ticked by and the moment arrived. He squeezed a little tighter on the trigger. Beads of sweat broke loose from his forehead and trickled down his nose to his cheeks. He quickly wiped sweat from his burning eyes and set his aim again. The soldiers with the assault rifles began to fire, raining bullets upon the bed and the cab of the truck. The trucks body took some serious rounds, but none too serious to keep it from moving down the road. More sweat fell from the face of the man holding the missile launcher as he drew in a long, deep breath while squeezing the trigger a little tighter.

"What are you waiting for, soldier? Shoot!" the commanding officer barked out. "He's getting away, Private."

"He's fleeing, sir. He's no threat to us."

"I didn't know that was your decision to make, Private! He's a looter, a rebel. Worse, he could be infected. Shoot him! That's an order! Oh, for Christ's sake, give me that damn thing." The commanding officer reached over and grabbed the tube with his left hand and pulled it away from the private, accidentally causing the private's finger to depress the trigger all the way. The missile deployed wildly out of the heated barrel, burning the commander's hand, which he'd wrapped tightly around the barrel.

The commander quickly pulled his hand away,

throwing the missile launcher to the ground as smoke rose from the barrel. He held his burned hand close to his chest in pain as it blistered.

"Sorry, sir, it was an accident." The private shuddered as he picked the launcher up from the ground.

"Accident my ass, Private. If you would have fired, this wouldn't have happened; shit-for-brains."

The private grabbed another launcher from the crib and took aim at the truck. He now had something to prove to his commanding officer. He had to prove to him that he *could* do this and *would*, right in front of him. He breathed in, tightly gripping the trigger. He squeezed a little more as he exhaled.

The radio interrupted his concentration. "Stand down and cease fire. We're pulling out. I repeat, cease-fire and stand down. Over." The soldier holding the launcher gasped for air and tossed the launcher aside. "You're one lucky son-of-a-bitch," he muttered in the direction of the truck. The truck was clear out of sight, leaving a trail of dust behind.

The team packed their gear as quickly as they could. They paid too much attention to the task at hand and not enough to their surroundings. While they packed, a herd of zombies advanced on them, catching the troops off guard.

Faint gunshots could be heard a mile down the road where the platoon was busy packing, getting ready to move out. The commander grabbed the mic to the radio and spoke. "Baker Team, I said stand down, copy." Static filled the air as he unclicked the mic. "Baker Team, copy?"

He received no reply. Baker Team was no more. The zombies took them down fast and furiously with very little time for retaliation.

"Baker Team is not answering. Go see what's up, soldier, and don't go alone," the commanding officer ordered the nearest soldier.

"What's the deal?" the chief asked.

"Seems your town will be saved after all, chief. We just received orders to pull out."

"Change of plans?" the chief inquired.

"I just go where they tell me to. Seems your virus has spread far and wide. Your town is back in your hands again. I guess it's not our government's priority anymore."

•••

# CHAPTER 31

"What's going on, Colonel?" asked one of the soldiers.

"Sarge, look around. We're pulling out. Headed to DC. Seems things just aren't the way we left it."

"I got word that you sent some of our men to find Baker Team. They haven't returned, sir."

"Well, that's correct, and I'm sorry to hear that, soldier."

"Sir?"

"If they haven't returned by now, they probably won't. Baker Team was overtaken by a mob of walkers."

"Should I send a team, sir?"

"And what? Lose them too, and you? Are you kidding

me? Absolutely not, we've lost too many men already. Let's cut our losses and pack and pull."

"We can't just leave them, sir."

"They're zombies now, Sergeant. Most likely they're zombies who are wearing the United States Army's uniforms. Are you ready to shoot your own, Sergeant?"

"I would want someone to shoot me, sir."

"Fine, take your men and do what you need to do. We're pulling out in twenty. I hope you're not too far behind us, Sergeant." He paused but only for a second. "And Sergeant …"

"Sir?"

"Me, too. Good luck."

The corners of the sergeant's mouth curled upward. "Thank you, sir."

The sergeant signaled two soldiers to come closer and instructed them to gather what they needed for a "No-Soldier-Left-Behind" mission. The sergeant hoped it wouldn't be a "mercy" mission. The small unit soon pulled out in a couple of Humvees in search of Baker Team and their erstwhile rescuers, while the rest of the battalion packed to leave.

"Let's get movin'. I want to be on the road in twenty," barked the captain. "Let's rack 'em, pack 'em, and stack 'em, soldiers! You know the routine. Let's go!"

It wasn't long before the sergeant and his scouts found what remained of Baker Team and the search-and-rescue squad who'd previously gone after them. It appeared that the captain had been right. They found several soldiers ripped apart, with some parts missing all together. The bodies bore injuries that did not appear to have been caused by bombs or firefight, but by teeth – human bites, gouges ripped from the arms, legs, and torsos, with nothing but a bloodbath left behind.

The NSLB team was fortunate that the zoms had moved on for now and the area was relatively clear. Body bags were soon pulled from the Humvees and distributed amongst the troops. The soldiers began bagging the remains of the fallen and collecting dog tags from the dead, the real dead, not the walking dead. These were the bodies of those who hadn't reanimated into zombies because they had been used for food rather than spreading the virus – at least not spreading it in the conventional way, through reanimation.

"Bag them up and don't get anything on you, you hear?" the sergeant ordered.

"What about the small pieces? Do we bag those too, Sarge? I have an arm here and also a leg, and I'm not really sure where the toes are," the soldier said. "I didn't sign up for this shit."

When a private rolled a partially eaten body over, he heard a slight moan. The body was missing so many parts that the private was sure the moan had come from somewhere else. There was no way this man was still alive. The private looked around but saw no one else who could have made the sound.

The soldier reached into the body's front pocket to retrieve the "family letter" – the letter each soldier wrote that was to be sent home to his family after his blood had been spilt and the ultimate price paid, a letter designed to provide his family with a sense of closure.

Catching the private off guard, the corpse raised its arm, the only arm it had left, and grabbed the private by the collar and pulled him closer to the corpse's mouth. The corpse was indeed alive. Its jaws snapped like a gator trying its best to bite the private's arm, his face, or anything else it could sink its teeth into. The private tried pulling away but the corpse's grip was strong, especially for a dead man. He kicked at the mangled body, then jerked his arm back and forth like a dog playing tug-of-war, hoping the corpse would let go. But it was to no avail. It held its grip tight, tighter than a crocodile's bite down in the Mississippi boonies, where the private was from.

The private dragged the body out into the open, leaving two blood trails behind. The blood ran off the body's stumps sticking out of his ripped pants. Both legs were missing. There was nothing but blood dripping from bones.

The private yelled for help. "Shoot it! Shoot! Someone shoot this damn thing!"

The sergeant came running and butted the zombie in the head with the end of his M-4, crushing the side of the zombie's skull. The hand still held its grip. It needed to be peeled away with the captain's Gerber tool, one finger at a time. The fingers looked as if they had been stripped clean to the bone. The body lay on the street, staring up at them with milky white eyes. A sour smell filled the air.

"Geez, that was alive? Are you all right? You bit? Scratched?" the sergeant questioned.

"No, I'm fine. Thanks. Just a little shaken," replied the private. He then started to shake in his boots uncontrollably. He sat on the ground and wept.

The sergeant hollered out to all the troops, "Shoot them all in the head before touching and bagging them. This one was alive and attacked Private McGuin."

"They want us to shoot a man who's already down, and one of our own? That's crazy," whispered a private, not thinking anyone could hear.

"That's an order, Private!" barked the sergeant.

"Yes, sir!" he replied with a salute of respect. "Man, he hears everything."

The soldiers found more partial bodies scattered about. They shot them in the head as ordered, if they even had a head to shoot. They bagged them all.

"I have a live one. Injured, not dead!" a soldier yelled.

"Shoot it!" another soldier yelled out, running his way.

"Noooo! No! This one's talking. He's not one of them." More troops came running. "He's talking but not making a lot of sense. Zoms don't talk."

"He still could be infected, delirious. He may not have turned yet."

The sergeant placed the back of his hand on the wounded soldier's forehead. "No fever yet. He's in shock, I believe. Be careful. He could turn at any time. Look at all the blood. Something got him." One of the soldiers was pointing his rifle at the downed soldier's head.

The rifle was pushed away. "Looks like gunshot, sir. A

double-tap in the shoulder, it looks like. Large-caliber in the leg."

"Get him some water," the sergeant barked.

A canteen was immediately tossed in his direction. The sergeant tried to calm the soldier down and held the canteen to his mouth. The wounded soldier gulped, drinking the whole canteen. When he came up for air, the soldier finally caught his breath enough to speak with some clarity.

"Thank ... you." He gasped for air. "Shot ... not bitten ... friendly fire. Complete chaos ... sir. Bullets ... flying everywhere. They slaughtered us ... sir. Hell, we fuckin' slaughtered each other. We panicked. The whole team – gone, sir."

"Just calm down, lad. We've got you now. You're going to be all right. We need to get you to a medic and fast." The sergeant paused, then shouted, "Someone please radio for a medic. Now!"

"Aye aye, sir." Moments later, the private reported back. "Sorry, sir. They already pulled out. They're not coming back for us. They said to load him in the Humvee and bring him with us, sir."

"Damn them. We need a medic, not bandages!"

Just then, an old Cavalier drove by with Sarah behind the wheel. Eli begged her not to stop and to floor it. "Keep going! Drive on by!" he yelled. "They're going to kill us!"

A private was ordered to stop the car, so he did. He stood directly in the car's path and held a hand out in the "halt" position. No gun was drawn.

"Keep going! Don't stop. Run him down if you have

to," begged Eli from the back seat. Sarah slammed on the brakes. The car screeched to a halt. "Oh boy, we're dead," cried the old man. He began to pray. A private appeared at the side of the car and motioned her to roll her window down.

"Excuse me, miss. We mean you no harm. We have a man down over there. Do have any medical supplies with you at all? Towels, gauze, painkillers? Anything, ma'am? We're down to just bandages here."

The old man in the back seat barked out, "Why the hell should we help you? You've killed innocent people here. I saw it with my own two eyes."

"We just followed orders, sir." He paused and looked Sarah in the eye. "Ma'am?" Receiving no immediate reply he continued, this time addressing Eli. "We didn't want to do it, sir. Those orders were straight from the top and have been lifted. We're pulling out of your town as we speak. We need help if you have any of the things I asked for. A downed soldier sure could use it." The private pointed to where the injured man lay.

Sarah thought of her brother, visualizing his military funeral and wishing someone like her would have stopped and helped him in Afghanistan. Maybe he would be alive today if someone had helped.

"Ma'am, what do you ..." asked the soldier.

Seeing all the blood and gore, Sarah interrupted. "I'm an RN. I'll help." She popped the trunk and grabbed her medical bag. Still in her nurse's uniform, she may have felt she had no choice but to comply with the soldier's request.

She may have felt that she would be ordered to if she hadn't offered on her own. Nevertheless, she eagerly complied and rushed to help the fallen soldier.

The private greeted her with open arms. "This way, quickly. Thank you, ma'am."

"You be careful, Sarah. I don't trust them," shouted Eli.

•••

# CHAPTER 32

**Facebook:** Sue Micah

"I can't get ahold of my parents and I'm worried. I don't know what to do." • Like  13 people

**Facebook Comment:** George Sallone

"Hang in there, Sue, help's coming soon."

• Like 7 people

**Facebook Comment:** Sue Micah

"I hope so. I hate living this far away from them. They've never not answered my calls."

• Like  2 people

**Facebook Comment:** Scott Seagram

"What happened to all the cat pictures on Facebook? • Like 17 people

**Facebook Comment:** Sam Iman

"Really dude? Do you live under a rock or something?" • Like 11 people

**Facebook Comment:** Scott Seagram

"No, why?"

Facebook: 4 minutes ago • Like 0 people

**Facebook Comment:** Sam Iman

"Who cares about the cats? There's more important things going on right now, ass!"

• Like 0 people

**Facebook Comment:** Alex Tyley

"I let my dog out to do his business and he never came back in. I'm going out to look for him."

• Like 0 people

**Facebook Comment:** Jill Smith"Oh, Alex, so sorry. Please stay inside. Maybe he'll come back on his own. It's too dangerous out there. I love u." • Like 18 people

The military was very grateful to Sarah and gave her some of their supplies to take with her: bottled water, a couple of blankets, and enough MRE's (Meals Ready to Eat)

to last the group a few days. It was a very generous gesture indeed, especially in the situation they were in. Food was in short supply. A soldier placed everything in the trunk along with a handgun and a few hundred rounds. He tucked them inside the blankets and closed the trunk.

As he walked away, he tipped his hat to Sarah and thanked her again. He also mouthed some words to Sarah so that the sergeant couldn't hear. Unfortunately, neither could Sarah and all she heard was "blanket." She mouthed the words "Thank you" in return, unknowing what the man had been trying to tell her. It reminded her of a conversation she once tried to have in a bar when she had inadvertently agreed to something but had no idea what, just because she couldn't hear what was being said.

The group parted ways with the military with a few nods and handshakes. Eli was a bit reluctant to shake any of the soldiers' hands even after receiving the supplies.

Sarah shifted the car into drive and headed for the hills as originally planned, but not before backtracking just a bit in search of Dave and Marcus and, in the back of her mind, Steve.

While she drove, she hoped that Dave and Marcus weren't still stranded up on the rooftop, but at the same time she hoped they were still there. The air here was still pretty thick with zoms even after all the military action.

It was Eli who saw them first. He was riding shotgun for a change, while the little girl lay on the backseat resting her head on the pregnant woman's lap. Linda stroked the girl's hair and thought about how soft it was, as she daydreamed of stroking her own child's hair one day soon. She wondered if that would even happen. She wondered more about whether it *should* even happen. *What a world to bring a child into,* she thought, staring blankly out the window at the group of walkers shambling toward two men who were running out from an alley.

"Oh no, something's wrong with Dave," Sarah said after Eli pointed out the two men and recognized them as being Marcus and Dave.

Marcus' face reflected panic. He had Dave by the collar and appeared to be dragging him along. Dave staggered like a zombie behind him.

Dave lost his footing and stumbled, pulling Marcus to the ground with him, skinning their knees and elbows. Marcus got up instantly and struggled to get Dave back to his feet, while dragging both empty rifles by their straps. Dave had a hold of something in a small brown paper bag. Whatever was in that bag must have been important, because Dave never lost grip on it, protecting it from hitting the pavement.

Sarah thought that Dave must have been bitten. *Why else would he be acting the way he is? He's staggering like a zombie,* she thought to herself. *Maybe Marcus just thought he was hurt and thinks that he's saving him.* Her mind was flooded with thoughts. Then she reacted. "Marcus!" she yelled out the car window.

Marcus turned and, with the biggest grin on his face, he started tugging Dave toward the car.

"No, leave him! Save yourself. Leave him!" Sarah

yelled.

Marcus replied by shaking his head, with a strange look on his face.

"What? Leave him? Are you out of your frickin' mind? Bitch!"

Linda couldn't believe what she was hearing.

Marcus kept coming toward the car, dragging Dave all the way.

Sarah got out of the car. "Stay right there!" she yelled, pointing her finger at Marcus.

Marcus stopped dead in his tracks. "What?"

"Leave him!"

"What? No, no, no, you have it all wrong. He's just drunk."

"Drunk?"

"Yeah, I'll explain in the car." Marcus looked back over his shoulder past Dave and saw that some of the walkers were making good time and were almost upon them. "Shit!" he said as he pulled Dave harder and struggled to gain ground. Sarah ran to help. They now had Dave between them, dragging him toward the car.

"Come on, come on! Quickly! Come on," cheered Linda. They reached the car and piled in, three in the back and three in the front. The little girl rode on the old man's lap.

The car quickly became overcrowded and sank low to the ground, nearly scraping the pavement.

They debated going back for Steve's motorcycle, but the only one who knew how to ride well enough was also too drunk to stand. They decided to head for the hills and go back for the bike later.

They drove as far up into the hills as the car would allow. Once off the secondary roads, their route turned to gravel, mostly rutted like a washboard. The uneven ground battered the car's undercarriage, just about vibrating Linda's baby right out of her. They tried to travel far enough off the main dirt road as they could so the car was out of sight and stopped to set up camp.

While the group got settled, Marcus volunteered for first watch and hiked to a location where he could see everything around them. He sat on a fallen tree with his back up against another. In a very short time, he started to doze off.

Later, Marcus was awakened by distant gunshots. Startled, he grabbed his binoculars and jumped to his feet. He scanned the area near and far. The gunshots stopped, but his field glasses fell on a dusty trail. Following with his specs, he came across the source of the dust cloud.

"Well, well, well. I'll be damned. If it isn't our mystery man," said Marcus under his breath. He was looking down from a high ledge near the group's campsite. What he saw was an old Jeep pickup hightailing it out of the city, leaving a rooster tail of dust and gravel behind. "So, where have you been, Steve?" he asked aloud to himself as he watched the Jeep pass in and out of the trees. Marcus looked troubled and wasn't sure what to do next.

•••

## CHAPTER 33

Steve, afraid of being shot, still ducked his head out of sight. He drove mostly by memory as he peered above the dash every now and then, just to make sure he was still on the road. The truck fishtailed, spraying gravel from side to side as he negotiated a quick right turn down a bumpy dirt road. The road headed out of town toward the hills, toward his family's cabin that he used to visit on a regular basis. It was there that he climbed trees and fished with his father as a child, until life got in the way. After his parents' nasty divorce, the trips to the cabin became fewer and farther between. When his father passed, visits to the cabin pretty much came to a halt. Now he hardly ever had a chance to get away at all.

The gunfire had stopped minutes ago, but Steve couldn't tell. The truck shook and rattled as its tires careened over washboard road. Steve drove like a maniac, doing what he could to escape the barrage of bullets that he didn't realize had stopped several miles back.

Steve continued to drive a couple more miles to ensure that he was out of range of the gunfire. He coasted to a stop at the crest of a hill overlooking Bear Creek. The town he once knew like the back of his hand was now a stranger to him and almost unrecognizable.

Steve jumped out of the truck and took note of all the bullet holes in its body. Most of the holes were in the bed and tailgate area, one bullet narrowly missing the gas tank. Some bullets had hit vitally close to where Steve's head would have been a time or two while driving.

Steve shook his head in wonder. *Someone is looking out for me, that's for sure,* he thought. His mind was begging him not to stop. He wasn't the most religious man in the world, but he did have some spiritual beliefs.

Steve wiped his brow as he scanned what used to be a very picturesque vista of Bear Creek. It now looked more like an apocalyptic scene, a landscape filled with burning, abandoned buildings. Smoke rose in more directions than not.

"Where the hell are you, Sarah?" he whispered before climbing back into the Jeep and driving away to higher ground.

It wasn't long before Steve turned onto what looked like a deer run. Underneath all the overgrown vegetation, he could faintly see what used to be the two-track leading back to his family's cabin. This was a place he would visit just to get away, often to collect his thoughts. There was a stream there, where he had fished and camped with his father when he was a child. They used to camp there just about every weekend in the summer months. They hiked every day, and the year his father died was the same year he built a tree house in the oak out front.

The tree house had since fallen, due to the tree growth and the weather over the years. The cabin, although in need of repairs, was still standing, just not inhabitable. Steve hoped that over time that would change. Not too many people knew the cabin even existed. Steve hoped it would be relatively safe there.

Steve's father died at a very early age. Steve was only nine, and he remembered it all too well. He missed his dad, and this place was going to bring back many memories, happy ones and sad. Steve and his father had a great father-son relationship right up to the day his father succumbed to cancer. It ate him to the bone. His father always blamed good old Agent Orange. He'd brought it back from 'Nam, he claimed, and never let this thought go.

Steve was among the bitter upon hearing the recent news about a cure for cancer. Could he believe what he heard and read? He kind of did, only because that's just the way things usually worked for him: too little, too late. But in the back of his mind, he was still quite skeptical of the whole thing. It didn't really matter whether he believed it or not. He couldn't bring his father back, certainly not from the dead.

# CHAPTER 34

Meanwhile, after a week at their camp, the gang was starting to get a little edgy. Rationing food supplies had already started, even after receiving all the MREs from the soldiers. Dave was worried about his wife and unborn child, and Marcus was just plain worried, period. The secret he was carrying was weighing heavily on him, and it was starting to show with every mention of Steve's name. And Sarah mentioned Steve's name quite often.

Dave had Linda to keep him company, and Eli stayed with the little girl and vice-versa. The girl, Jamie, reminded him of the granddaughter he never had. He thought if he'd had one, he would want her to be just like Jamie. Then there was Sarah, how she secretly longed for Steve, never making it totally apparent. Little did she know that it was bluntly obvious to everyone else. Marcus had no one. Not that it should have bothered him. He'd been alone since his nasty divorce. He never wanted anyone else but his cheating wife. Now, eight long years later, he started to see things in a different light. Maybe it was the fact that he felt his world was coming to an end and the pickings were getting mighty slim. Or maybe he didn't want to die alone. Who knew? Maybe it was time to move on, and he couldn't deny an attraction to Sarah. Whatever the case, he was getting lonely, and it wasn't long before he started putting the moves on Sarah.

So far, with Steve out of the picture, Marcus' moves had been pretty well received, but for how long? How long would Steve stay out of the picture? Marcus' deviant wheels started turning the day he saw Steve hightailing it toward the mountains.

There was a cool breeze outside. Everyone was sitting around the campfire in idle conversation, just enjoying each other's company. All of a sudden, the conversation accelerated into a heated debate.

"So how long do you think?" Linda asked.

Dave answered, "How long for what, dear?"

"That it will be like this. When do you think things will start going back to normal again?"

Dave just looked at her, blankly. He didn't know what to say. He knew she was worried about the baby, and so was he. "Hopefully soon, honey," was all he could muster. "We have everything we need for now." He gave her a hug.

"Now you're sounding like Steve," Sarah said,

jumping into the conversation.

"Why is that, Sarah?" David inquired.

"He's always lived for the moment, you know, 'the here and now.' He always said that's the only time there is, and if you're doing all right, then you have nothing to complain about."

"Philosopher Steve, he's quite the guy. Too bad he didn't foresee this coming," said Marcus.

Sarah gave Marcus a nasty look. She couldn't believe Marcus just said that. "What the hell was that supposed to mean?" she asked.

"What? I didn't mean anything by it. I'm talking about the zombies and all. That's all."

Sarah grabbed Marcus' arm, which was wrapped around her and tossed it aside. She then excused herself.

"Way to go, Marcus. You have quite the way with words, my friend."

"Fuck off, Dave." Marcus stomped off toward his lookout post.

"Well on that note, I'm going to call it a night myself and leave the lovebirds alone. Goodnight, folks," said Eli. "Come on, Jamie, let's go."

Dave nodded.

"Goodnight, Eli. Goodnight, Jamie," Linda related softly.

Eli, Jamie, and Sarah turned in for the night in the comforts of their make-shift tents.

•••

The next morning, Dave and Marcus were up early

getting ready to make a supply run. Sarah was up as well. She wanted to go with them in a bad way. Dave and Marcus said no. It was the same old story, same old excuses. "You're needed at camp, Sarah." "It's too dangerous, Sarah." "We can handle it, Sarah." "Linda may need you, Sarah." Well Sarah was tired of it.

Sarah argued with the guys until she was blue in the face. "Eli would still be here," she said. "He can watch over them for a few hours. Linda will be fine. You don't understand. I can't stay here. I have to go with you. I have to find my father."

"Find your father? I thought he got bit," Dave said.

"He did. I was with him when it happened. I hid in the closet like a coward. He fought the zombie off with his bare hands. He wasn't going to let it get to me, but he was bitten in the process. I didn't know until the phone call."

"What phone call?" asked Dave.

"He told me he was all right so I left for work that night. He looked winded, but he must have hidden the bite from me. He knew what would happen next. It was a couple of hours, but he finally called me at work. He told me then what had happened and that it shouldn't be long. He was already burning up. He made me promise never to come home. I shouldn't have listened." She paused, "In fact, I didn't. I was on my way there when all hell broke loose at the hospital. I couldn't get through town. There were zombies everywhere. That's why I need to go home. I need to see him and tell him I'm sorry, tell him I love him. Maybe he's all right. I have to do something."

"OK, so let me get this straight. You want to go back on your word? Is that it?" Dave asked.

"It's not that. What if these zombies are still human? Maybe they still feel something inside and they just can't show it. What if he's still alive inside?"

"Sarah, I'm really sorry about your father. We've all lost friends and family, but if what you're saying is true, that's all the more reason to stay away."

"Fuck you!" Sarah yelled, raising an open hand to slap him. Marcus caught it and held it steady while Dave continued.

"No, listen," Dave said. "Let's just say you find your father, and he still feels things. You couldn't possibly want to put him through what would happen next."

"What do you mean?"

"Sarah, whether he could feel or not, whether he would still know who you were or not, doesn't really matter. The virus is in control of what his body does, and it's going to tell his body that it's hungry, hungry for human flesh, and he's going to want to try his damnedest to eat you. Say he did still have feelings and knew who you were. Why would you want to put him through that? No father would want to eat his own daughter. It would break him, man. Can't you see that? He's been through enough. Let him be. It's your survival that's important now, Sarah. That's what he'd want."

Sarah finally pulled her hand away from Marcus' grip and sat on the ground. She leaned back against a tree, her head held low between her knees. She was crying hard now. Marcus, seeing as opportunity, stepped forward and wrapped an arm around her and held her tight. When she finally settled down, she must have forgotten about her anger from the night before, because she even held him too.

"Thank you. Thank you both. I understand a little better what's going on now."

"I'm here for you, Sarah," said Marcus.

•••

## CHAPTER 35

Steve could hardly believe a week had gone by since he'd settled down to make camp up in the hills. He hadn't planned that long of a break; it just happened that way. It seemed the more rest he got, the more his body wanted.

The town below was getting more and more dangerous every day, and the mountains seemed like the best place to be. It was peaceful and had most everything Steve needed, at least for the time being, everything but company. So far, there wasn't a soul around. *That can be a good thing,* he thought, *but a little lonely too.* He had everything except Sarah.

Steve's relationship with Sarah had been very short. He'd met her one day, screwed her the next. Typical for him, but the impact that Sarah had on Steve was overwhelming, unlike anyone before. She was like a drug to a junkie for Steve, and he just couldn't shake her.

Sarah was also Steve's primary motivation for most of his recent trips into town. Sure, he went looking for supplies when he needed them, but most of the time he came back empty-handed. He found himself mainly going to look for Sarah. Discouraged, Steve's trips into town were getting fewer and farther between. Coming back to camp alone was sometimes unbearable.

Steve's mind was filled with worry, and he couldn't help but think of two things: zombies and the military. Either one could have easily caught his former companions.

A woman with child unable to run, a young girl with a broken arm, and an old man who could keel over from a heart attack at any minute were more than enough to slow Sarah, Dave, and Marcus down. Dave could never leave his wife and unborn child. Then there was Sarah – beautiful, caring Sarah. She would never be able to leave any of them, not even if her own life depended on it. Realistically, it was Marcus who he thought had the only real chance of surviving. With no ties to anyone, his loyalty to the others would always be in question. It was silly for Steve even to entertain the thought of the whole group surviving. The odds were stacked well against them.

Still, Steve couldn't give up hope. Not yet. Hope was what kept him going. Hope was what got him out of the Alley of Death, and hope would continue to keep him going until he was ready to give up. Until then, Sarah would remain alive if only in his mind.

"How many acres could there be to these foothills anyway?" Steve asked himself, looking back to the mountains. He exhaled. "Thousands."

Steve hoped for the best and collected his thoughts. He was far enough away from the goings-on in the city to be somewhat comfortable, but he was still a bit on edge. With every noise within earshot, Steve jumped, mentally if not always physically.

He had always lived by the seat of his pants. He lived for the day. Hell, most of the time, he lived for the moment. Whenever anyone asked him the time, he would always reply, "It's right now!"

For some reason, Steve was feeling a bit lost right about now. He thought this time he needed a plan, but a plan for what?

How could he make a plan around something no one ever dreamed would happen in a million years? Sure, there were a lot of fictional books and movies out there on the subject, and just about everyone probably had read or watched at least one in their lifetime, but this was no book or movie. This was serious and really happening right here, and as Steve would say, right now.

To make things even worse, Steve couldn't clear his thoughts if his life depended on it, which it probably did. His mind was cluttered, filled with emotion, inconsistency, and worry. Constant questions raced through his head, all of which went unanswered.

He wondered what Sarah was doing, where she was,

and if she was all right. Did the military pick her up? Did Dave and Marcus leave her behind? Did she refuse to go? Did she wait for his return? Why was this happening? And how? It was a never-ending flow of questions that were driving Steve mad.

Part of Steve thought he still should be out there searching. The more sensible part of him didn't know where else he could look. He had looked all over Bear Creek. It was such a small town, after all. Until he needed to find a particular something or someone in it, that is. Then, it might as well have been New York City.

To help clear his mind, Steve fished in a nearby stream like he had as a child with his father. He found it relaxing, and thought it would help keep his mind off Sarah. Instead, Steve found himself daydreaming about his father quite a bit. Whenever he baited the hook or cast the line, he could hear and see his father's instructions.

"Great job, Stevie. Perfect cast, son. Now let out some line, just a little. That's it, you got it, boy." His father's voice was plain as day as if he were standing beside him.

"I miss ya, Dad," Steve said. "I sure wish you were here so you could make sense of all this madness. It sure is a different world than when you left it. I wish you were here to tell me what to do. I sure could use some advice." Steve cast the line again. The bait landed perfectly between two rocks near the shore. He let it float downstream for a second or two.

"Great cast, kid. You know what you're doing, son," he heard his father say. His soft voice faded away along with his reflection in the water. It was as if the ripples from the fish Steve had just caught washed it all away.

Steve cleaned his fish and cooked his catch over an open fire, all the while hoping that the fish he had just cleaned wasn't contaminated with this nasty virus. Steve cooked everything well-done, just in case they were infected. He wasn't sure that would make a difference, but he didn't want to take the chance. So far, with five meals of fish down the hatch, he felt good. Each bite never went without hesitation, though. *It only takes one,* Steve thought before every bite he took. He hoped and prayed it wouldn't be his last bite as a human being.

Steve still felt well – still tired, but with everything that had happened, that was expected. He was a little concerned with the sores that were now covering 80 percent of his body, though. His skin was blotchy and pale, covered with what looked like a bad case of acne.

Steve wished now that he would have accepted the first-aid kit from the bus driver. It was no good to anyone now, but who would have known. Who would have thought that the military would strike a busload of kids? *They were innocent children, for God's sake,* Steve thought. In all his recent trips to the city, he hadn't seen a single emergency kit in any of the stores. Not even in the offices for their employees. They were all picked clean.

While overlooking Bear Creek below, Steve wondered if the town would ever be safe again. Or was this going to be life as they all knew it from now on? He wondered when the war on zombies would be over, if it would ever be over, and how it could be resolved. How many lives would be lost? How could anyone fix this? Could it even be fixed? He feared the worst, then quickly replaced those thoughts with more thoughts of Sarah. She was never too far from his mind, and the war would never be over until he found her.

There was a small cabin here. It was where many family vacations and weekend getaways were enjoyed. That was years ago, back when his family was together. Now it showed years of neglect, and it surely was not secure enough to sleep in. Repairs would need to be made before Steve could think of doing so.

Steve chose to sleep up in a large oak tree instead, just in case a zom wondered through at night. There were a few leftover boards up there from the tree house he and his dad had built decades before. Storms and wind had knocked most of it down.

Zoms can't climb, and they rarely look up unless attracted by noise, so Steve felt relatively safe there, uncomfortable, but safe. He draped dusty blankets from the cabin over the branches for padding and used some old rope to secure himself to the tree while he slept.

-

A small plume of smoke rose from a smoldering fire 30 feet from where Steve slept. His snores were light and easily disguised by hundreds of tree frogs singing their nightly tunes. The sky was clear of clouds but filled with streaks of smoke from the distant fires in town, which blocked most of the stars from view. It was dark, and at times a chilly breeze would hit Steve just right, coaxing him into wrapping the blankets a little tighter around him.

Steve woke abruptly from a sound sleep, feeling sore and stressed. Three and a half hours, probably the most uninterrupted sleep he'd gotten in quite some time. Anxiety rushed in as worry draped over him like a warm blanket. His first words were just an audible thought. "I have to find her." He wouldn't fully rest until he did.

He looked all around for any signs of zombies and then straight down below. The fire he had last evening was still smoldering, sending a pillar of smoke up his way. The cool breeze kept it from totally reaching him, keeping him from being asphyxiated while he'd slept.

Steve struggled to release the rope. It was tight and cutting off the circulation in his right leg. It had no feeling. The rope secured him to the tree branch while he slept, so he wouldn't roll over and fall. So far so good, but he had yet to find a way to secure the rope comfortably. He finally wiggled it loose and swung his numb leg up over the tree branch, scraping his ankle hard against the sharp-edged bark. He soon found out his leg did have feeling in it after all: the feeling of a thousand bee stings all at once.

"Shit! Damn, that hurt." He grabbed his ankle in pain while massaging the pins and needles from his leg. He tried to get the blood flowing through his veins again without losing too much from the wound on his ankle. Blood dripped from his torn skin, splattering on the fire pit below. He could hear the drops sizzle and hiss as they hit the hot ash. Steve knew the smell of fresh blood in the air was not good, and he was thankful he that he wasn't in town where it would probably draw zoms from blocks away. He hoped it wouldn't attract a stray zom wandering around in the woods. He knew the chances of that happening were getting greater and greater each day as people fled to the hills to get out of the town.

Once the pain subsided from his leg and feeling returned, he worked his way down from the tree one branch at a time. He finally jumped to the ground once he was close enough. He hit the ground with a soft thud and rolled, dispersing as much energy as he could before coming to a stop. He favored his uninjured ankle, hoping not to make the other any worse.

Steve brushed the dirt and leaves from his shoulders and legs as he stood up and scanned the area for zoms again. He then cleaned his wound as best he could and dressed it with a bandana, applying pressure to stop the bleeding by tying it tightly around his ankle. As he straightened his back, he noticed last night's fire still smoldering.

Steve quickly added a few new twigs to the fire and poked at the embers with a stick, trying to get it to ignite again. After several tries, the smoldering ash flamed up, catching some loose kindling afire. Steve's mood instantly brightened with the flames. He smiled, thinking that he saved a match for another day.

Supplies were getting thin, and he knew today was the day that he would have to make another trip into town. He dreaded it – not the task of going into town but the possibility of coming back empty-handed and, once more, alone. He stretched his legs and back and walked down to the stream where his fishing pole awaited him. *Time to catch some breakfast.* Fish became his meal of choice for breakfast, lunch and dinner.

This time while he was fishing, he thought of Sarah and looked up and down the stream, hoping she would just show up. This, of course, didn't happen, not this time, nor any of the countless other times he had hoped for in the past week.

At times, bubbles would drift by as he fished and he would fantasize that they were coming from Sarah bathing in the brook just upstream. His visions were crystal-clear and playing tricks with his mind. He could almost hear her singing while she bathed.

A faint disturbance or a nearby sound was all it took to startle Steve back to reality. It didn't take much. A bird calling in the distance or a deer breaking a twig under-hoof instantly set him off, as he was still living on edge even after a week of rest.

Steve set his fishing pole down to go and relieve himself on a nearby tree. He then quickly returned to find a good-sized rainbow trout at the end of his line.

"Someone's watching out for me again today," he said as he took the fish off the line.

It wasn't long before he had it cooking over an open fire. He had just torn off a piece to see if it was done cooking when he hesitated, again entertaining the thought of the fish possibly being contaminated with this nasty virus. He shrugged and mumbled to himself, "What the hell. What do I have to lose," before tossing it to the back of his throat. "Can't live forever. Mmm, pretty good," he said as he ripped another piece free from the bones and ate it as well.

Shortly after breakfast, Steve gathered his go-bag and emptied it out on a plastic tarp. He wrapped the items up in the tarp like a burrito and buried them in the sand. These were all the belongings he had, and he didn't want to take a chance on them being found in the Jeep while he was gone.

He parked the Jeep among the shrubs and threw tree branches and brush on it to camouflage it. At 20 feet, he could hardly tell it was there. At 10 feet, it was iffy. Steve didn't want the truck to come up missing either, so he always took the coil wire with him.

Steve had to travel light and only took the necessities with him. He needed to save room for any supplies he could find and bring back to camp.

He grabbed the empty pack, along with his blade and set off on foot for supplies. It was about an hour's walk into town, provided he didn't run into trouble, which he knew he would. He always did.

He looted a couple of empty houses on the way and grabbed whatever supplies the owners had left behind. He found signs of carnage everywhere he looked.

In one of the homes, the owners had committed suicide, and they lay in bed in each other's arms. The nightstands were covered with prescription drug bottles. Most were empty. Steve helped himself to the ones that weren't. Most of the bottles had labels representing several kinds of painkillers. They would come in handy one day, for sure.

This was all too common a scene, and it hardly fazed Steve anymore. Between suicide scenes and medicine cabinets, he had collected a good assortment of prescription drugs over time. Steve had yet to find anything that worked on his skin condition that had developed during the last week or so. Nothing had reduced the swelling, nor brought any of his natural pigment back. His skin was still as blotchy as ever, which had begun to worry him.

What fazed Steve the most were the other methods some people had used to commit suicide; methods that left horrible messes behind. Scenes of people who had shot their own families and then turned the gun on themselves were never easy to take. Women, children, and even pets all had been killed in manners that Steve would rather not recall.

As he walked through town, Steve couldn't help noticing all the notes of despair. They seemed to be plastered everywhere he looked. Letters and posters of families seeking loved ones were just blowing in the wind, literally littering his hometown. This was the town where he'd grown up, gone to school, worked, and slept. Steve loved his town and the people who lived there. Now there seemed to be nothing left. Most of his friends were missing or dead. Communities were no more.

The military was gone, but the mess it'd made remained. By the looks of things, the military obviously only rebuilt third-world countries after blowing them up, because it didn't appear that anyone was coming back to rebuild Bear Creek. This had Steve worried.

It was a pretty short stay in Steve's eyes, and in the back of his mind, he wondered why and feared the worst. The zombies were still here – more than ever. It seemed the zombies just infected more victims to replace the ones the military killed. Their numbers had at least doubled since the military departed and continued to increase daily as more and more people were infected after making their way out of their homes and cluttering the streets.

*Why would the soldiers pull out so early?* The question seemed to be stuck in Steve's mind like a song he couldn't shake. A frown appeared on his face, as if he entertained a horrible answer. Yet it was the only answer he could come up with that made any sense at all.

As Steve dodged in and out of abandoned vehicles and doorways, he couldn't help but read a few of the fliers as he walked by. They were everywhere – signs of missing people, posters of missing pets, and notes of where loved ones could be found.

"That's a good idea," Steve said to himself after reading a sign left for a family, notifying them of their loved ones' new location. He thought about how nice it would have been if the gang had thought to leave one of those notes for him. Then again, maybe they had.

Steve returned to the alley where he last saw Sarah and the gang a week or so ago. He entered the same building and searched all over for a sign but found nothing. Up on the roof? No. The doorway at ground level? No. Possibly at the bottom of the stairway? That was the first place he'd checked. It would have been the best spot, easily seen from all directions, but again, he found nothing.

Exhaustion quickly set in as Steve leaned his back against the wall and slid down to sit on the bottom step.

He looked up to the ceiling as if it were Heaven. "God, where is she?" he asked. As if his question was being answered, Steve saw a shiny spot glaring on the wall. It was a spot that looked like something may have been stuck there at one time or another. Residue left from tape was certainly a possibility, but whatever had been there was no longer. He leaned back up against the wall again and laid his blade across his knees, resting his arms and head upon it. He sat there for a moment just staring down to the floor.

Moments passed, and suddenly Steve's head popped up like a light bulb being turned on above his head. His eyes scanned the room from his lower perspective and stopped when they focused on a crumpled piece of paper lying under a cabinet across the room. Steve jumped to his feet and ran to the cabinet, hardly straightening his back, and slid to a stop as if he were sliding into second base. On his belly, he reached in as far as he could and scooped up the crumpled note.

"This is it," he said, his heart full of joy. He quickly and nervously smoothed the paper out, ironing it with the palms of his hands across his thigh. He read the note aloud.

*Steve;*

*I'm so sorry. We waited as long as we could, longer than requested. We had to go. The army got close. I hope you get this. We're headed east out of town. Headed for the country where there are fewer people. Will look for high ground. Hickory Hill was mentioned, wherever that is. Meet us there if you can. I hope you're safe.*

*Love, Sarah*

Steve read the note once more before holding it to his chest. A tear formed in his right eye, then in his left. His body trembled and soon a stream of tears started to roll down his cheeks.

"They're safe." He hoped and hoped again that they were still where she said they would be. He folded the note and jammed it into his back pocket. He wiped his eyes with his sleeves and got a grip on himself.

*Sarah's alive! I know it.* He left down the back alley in the same direction that Sarah and the gang would have taken.

A couple more blocks and Steve could hardly believe what he saw. Leaning on its side and covered with litter in a back alley was his bright-yellow crotch rocket. The moment he saw it, he knew it was his. This was the only one that he had ever seen in Bear Creek.

Shamblers were only a few yards away, though but he didn't care. He wanted his bike back in a bad way, and a couple of shamblers weren't going to stop him. He ran to it as quickly as he could, startling a flock of starlings, which created a noise that he could have done without.

The zoms heard the birds and turned his way and started moaning in his direction, moans that would surely call other walkers his way. Sure enough, they came out of the woodwork. Steve picked up his bike, and turned the key. The engine whined. It was music to his ears. He gave it some gas and popped the clutch. His back tire broke loose, screaming and smoking up the asphalt surface as Steve spun the bike around to hightail it out of there. When he had turned all the way around, he found a wall of zoms just 20 yards in front of him.

Steve pointed the bike in their direction and hit the gas, flying through the gears, and then screeched to a sliding stop right in front of them. The zoms didn't flinch. They just kept on coming and coming. Steve thought that he would have a better chance going the other way, but by the time he headed back, more zoms appeared there as well. Steve was boxed in. He realized that going straight through them would probably be suicide, but so was standing there doing nothing. He had no choice. It was do-or-die time. He looked around and then aimed the bike at a debris pile in the middle of the road. Not knowing what it was and having no time to check it out, he hoped for the best. He hoped that whatever it was, it was stable enough to support his bike and give him some lift and not crush down under his wheels. The zoms were moving in on him from both directions. The gap between was decreasing by the second. Steve gunned the throttle hard and hit the debris pile, sending him and his bike sailing over the first two rows of zoms and coming down hard on the last, taking out three with his landing. He hit the gas some more, not wanting to stick around for retaliation.

•••

Steve rode through town, assessing the damage along the way. *Wow, the military sure did a number on this town, didn't they?* he questioned in thought. He wondered again where the military went in such a hurry. Someplace more important than Bear Creek, he assumed. After seeing corpses lying in the streets wearing military BDUs and a few in full military garb shambling around made him wonder if the zombies just overtook them. Regardless, they were gone now and Steve really didn't care. They were doing a lot more damage than good, but still, there had to be a reason other than what Steve was thinking. There just had to be, Steve worried.

Steve read more posts of missing people on telephone poles and on sides of buildings. The streets were covered with them. Some would bring grown men to tears.

Anxious to get back to camp and excited about the note he'd found, Steve didn't want the trip into town to be wasted and come back empty-handed again. He still needed a few supplies, so he looted a couple more houses on the way back. This time, he hit the main drag.

Steve didn't expect to find anything good in the houses and stores on the main street. They usually were the first to be picked clean, but these looked recently abandoned, meaning the boards on the doors and windows were still intact. He found a few canned goods, toiletries, and more medical supplies, which consisted of a couple handfuls of all kinds of prescription drugs. He found more than enough items to fill his pack and carry to camp. All in all, he'd had a very productive trip.

While Steve was gathering all the prescription drugs from the bathroom of a house he'd entered, he glanced at himself in the mirror.

"Oh my gosh. What the hell?" Steve was surprised at what he saw. "Am I infected?" he asked himself with much concern.

Steve returned to camp, traveling some back roads,

hoping for signs of the gang. At the same time, he was also hoping that he didn't see anyone. His appearance worried him. If he really was infected, he didn't want to run across any of his friends. He would rather stay away.

Steve went straight to camp to wait things out. A few more days, and he'd know for sure.

•••

# CHAPTER 36

Just over a week had passed since the group last saw Steve, all but Marcus anyway. And all but Marcus presumed Steve was dead or at the very least bitten and changed into a zombie by now. Sarah still wasn't accepting it. She hadn't totally written Steve off, not yet, but her faith had started to fade just a little.

As soon as Steve was out of the picture, Marcus had started putting the moves on Sarah. Sweet talk and flirtatious conversation were becoming the norm for him, and for the most part, they had been well received. Spending late nights at the campfire with Dave and Linda, Marcus and Sarah almost looked as if they were a couple, even though there was nothing between the two. At least not admittedly. At least not yet. It wasn't but a night or so ago that Sarah was showing signs of giving up hope of ever seeing Steve again. Feeling lonely, she began cozying up to Marcus' comforts, and Marcus did his best to take full advantage of it.

Marcus kept Steve's sighting under wraps. He wanted more time with Sarah. He hoped for enough time to lock in the deal, but he didn't know how long that would take. Sarah kept her heart under lock and key. Deep down, Marcus had hoped that Steve would never again show his face, but he also knew just how resourceful that man was. *It's only a matter of time,* he thought, *before Steve comes knocking at the door.* As days went on, Sarah held onto a little bit of the past keeping a paper-thin wall up between Marcus and herself.

"Do you smell that?" asked Sarah.

"Smell what?" Dave asked.

"Smoke. I smell smoke. Do you smell it?"

"Sarah, there are fires all over the place. Look around." He nodded down to the town below.

"No, this is different. It doesn't smell like burning buildings or burning rubber."

"Then what does it smell like, Sarah? Homemade apple pie?" Dave said sarcastically.

"No, asshole, a campfire. I smell a campfire, all right?"

"Yeah, I thought I smelled it last night, too," Marcus broke in. "But I wasn't sure."

"Company? You think someone else is up here?" Dave asked Marcus.

"I bet there're a lot of people up here. Probably spread out all over the place. We're bound to run into someone sometime."

"We probably should check it out before ..." A disturbance interrupted Dave as two strangers wielding rifles walked out of the woods in their direction.

"Well, well, well. What do we have here, Jim?" one of the men said. "A few survivors?"

Both men were holding M-4 assault rifles but they didn't look military themselves. They probably took them from downed soldiers below. They pointed the rifles at Dave and Marcus and then waived them back and forth at the rest. Even though Dave knew they were outgunned, he raised his weapon anyway, and Marcus followed suit for a not-so-friendly welcome.

"Hey, assholes put your guns down," barked Dave.

"Now, now. We're not here to hurt anyone," one of the strangers said as they lowered their weapons. "We're survivors just like you, but you never know who you're going to run up against. You know what I mean. We're here to offer you our services."

"Services?" asked Marcus. "You walk into our camp waving your guns and you want to offer us a service? You're damn lucky we didn't blow your fuckin' heads off."

"You have our apologies. I admit we didn't start off on the right foot. That's clear. We are grateful it didn't come down to that."

"What is it you want?" Dave asked.

"Well, as I mentioned, we have a service that you may or may not be interested in."

"Yeah, yeah, yeah, go on. What is it?"

"You could say that we are each somewhat of a bounty hunter."

"You look more like mercenaries if you ask me," said Marcus.

"OK, back off Marcus. They mean us no harm. What do we need a bounty hunter for?" asked Dave

"Well, do you have loved ones who have turned?"

"I do," Sarah quickly spoke up.

"Sarah, no!" Dave whispered as inconspicuously as possible.

"No, wait. I want to hear what they have to say," said Sarah.

"Please hear me out." Sarah nodded her head, confirming her interest. "What we do is go into the danger zones and locate the loved ones and kill them. It's as simple as that. Humane-style. We put them out of their misery and give their families peace of mind and, more importantly, closure. No one wants to see their loved ones like that, and they don't want to be like that themselves either. What do you say?"

Sarah's eyes lit up. She knew that her dad would not want to live like a zombie, but she didn't want him to die either. But it was another thing to send a couple of mercenaries out and pay them to do the dirty work. Yet she was still interested and had to ask. "How much?"

"Sarah!" shouted Dave.

Disgusted, she looked away from him and toward the bounty hunters. "How much?" she asked again.

"$5,000 with half down, the rest paid when we bring

you back proof."

"Proof? What do you do, bring back their heads? Besides, cash has no value anymore. Look around. See any businesses open?" asked Marcus.

"Cash will always have value. Maybe not today, but things will change. And, no, we don't bring back their heads, unless that's requested. What we do is bring back a personal item that only you would recognize. We could even bring back a picture if you like."

"Picture? Hmm." Sarah struggled with her thoughts of seeing a picture of her dead father. She backed away.

"How about it, missy? I'm sure you have someone you love."

"No, no thanks, I don't have that kind of cash."

"I see. Well, here's my card. I'm sure we could work something out if you change your mind. I know you will. Hopefully the phone service will still be working. If not, we stay at the old Walker farm about 7 miles down the road. It's just past the white bridge on the left."

Sarah pocketed the card and watched the two bounty hunters walk away toward town. She wondered whose loved ones they were about to go kill.

"You're not seriously thinking about using them, are you, Sarah?" Dave inquired.

Sarah didn't answer. She just turned away and stared off at the distant fires. *There seemed to be more of them now.*

"Well, I guess that answered our question about the campfires. They must be camping nearby," Marcus assumed out loud.

That night, Sarah was awakened by a strong scent of campfire again. She woke Dave, and they both met Marcus on post. At first they thought it could be the bounty hunters, but it just didn't make sense. Why would they camp so close to home? Scout, yes, maybe out drumming up business, but actually camp? Doubtful.

One thing was for sure, they didn't want any more surprises like yesterday. Two men armed with M-4s appearing out of nowhere could have turned out badly. Admittedly, they were lucky they were still alive. Worse, the bounty hunters could have taken their supplies and left them with nothing. They decided they should investigate before it happened again, and before sunup.

•••

Dave and Marcus left camp about a half-hour before daylight. They would have left earlier but they had to take the time to argue with Sarah before they left. She wanted to go in a bad way. Dave felt it was too dangerous and she was needed at camp. Sarah felt otherwise. After a nearly 45-minute fight, Sarah finally backed down and ran to the tent, crying.

The smoke was close, so Dave knew that this shouldn't take long, and he assured everyone that they would be back soon. They left on foot through the heavy brush. The strength of the scent kept them on course, and it wasn't long before it led them into a clearing. There wasn't a soul around, but they could tell someone had been there not too long ago. They first checked out an old cabin nearby. It checked out clean. Then they came across the fire pit, which was still smoldering. Dave and Marcus had a bad feeling about that at the same time and held their guns at the ready.

"Ambush?" whispered Marcus.

"Let's hope not." They nervously looked in all directions thinking how stupid it had been for them to just walk in without scoping things out first.

"We're dead. Let's back our way out of here," said Marcus in a less-than-assuring voice. They started backing up the same way they'd come in.

"Hey guys!" came a voice from above.

Dave and Marcus freaked. They were now standing back-to-back, spinning in circles, guns at the ready. "Where is he?" Dave asked, frantically.

"Hell, I don't know."

"Guys, guys. It's me, put your guns down."

"Show yourself!" ordered Dave.

"Guys, it's me, Steve. I'm right above you."

"Steve?" Dave looked up, as did Marcus. Both pointed their guns up in the tree as if they had treed a raccoon.

"Hey now, what's with the guns, guys?"

"It is Steve!" Dave dropped his gun to his side. "Marcus?"

"Oh yeah. Yep, it's Steve all right," Marcus said, sounding oddly disappointed.

Steve climbed down from the tree and turned to face them. He held his hand out for a shake, maybe even a hug, but before he took three steps, the guys had their guns back up, aiming at Steve's head.

"Hey now!" Steve said, hands above his head. "What's

going on?"

"You tell me, Steve. You don't look good, dude. You bit?" asked Dave.

Steve's skin was pale white and blotchy all over, with very little flesh tone left. "Guys, I'm all right, I didn't get bit. What gives?"

"He's turning, Dave. I should shoot him now," said Marcus

"I'm not turning, I swear. Just let me explain," begged Steve.

"He's not going back to camp like this, Dave." Marcus was nervous as hell. Sweat poured down his face. "Say the word, Dave. I'll do it."

Steve was wide-eyed, with hands flat in front of him, begging for his life. "Dave, call your hit man off. You have to believe me."

Dave looked at Marcus, then back at Steve.

"Steve!" a voice from the brush screamed out. Sarah came sprinting out. She ran to Steve, stopping in front of Marcus. "What's going on?" she asked. "Why do you have your gun on ..." She turned to look at Steve. She took two steps back.

"Hi Sarah."

"Oh, Steve." Sarah's heart broke into a million little pieces right in front of him.

"No, Sarah, I'm not infected. I'm not bit."

Sarah looked closer at Steve, turned, and pushed Marcus' weapon down. "Really, Marcus. It's Steve, he's not going to hurt us."

Marcus lowered his gun. Sarah slowly walked closer to Steve. "Sarah, no!" Marcus said.

"What happened, Steve?" Sarah asked.

"I don't know, Sarah. I thought it was just bug bites at first, but they kept getting worse. More and more of these spots kept surfacing every day. Then ..." His voice trailed off.

"Then what?"

"Well, then I thought maybe it was the fish. I've been eating fish from the stream every day. I thought maybe they were infected, but this started before then."

Sarah was now in Steve's face examining the blotches closer.

"Not so close, Sarah, please," begged Marcus again.

All the blotches had a center core, which was hard and white. She reached out and touched one.

"Sarah, no!" Marcus yelled.

Sarah didn't listen. She grabbed hold of one of the center cores and squeezed it like a pimple, but not hard. Colors started to surface inside the circle along with a black hair. She then kissed Steve and finished with a hug. "He's all right, guys. We need to get him back to camp before they hatch."

"Hatch?" all three men asked at once.

"Well, technically, they had already hatched days ago. They are bot flies, if you must know."

"Bot flies? What the hell is a bot fly?" Dave asked with a quizzical look on his face.

"I saw those on YouTube, and they're gross," said Marcus. "But I didn't think they were around here. They're kind of rare, but so are zombies. Anything's possible, I guess. I did a paper on bot flies once when I was in school."

"It's good to see you, Steve. We have a lot of catching up to do. Come on, let's get back to camp. They're probably getting worried back there," Sarah said.

"Speaking of which, Sarah, I told you to stay at camp. You came all this way unarmed? You could have been killed," stated Marcus.

"If I wouldn't have come, you would have shot Steve," she replied, not telling him that she had a pistol tucked at the small of her back. She found it in the trunk of her car days ago, wrapped in the blankets that the soldiers had given them. It was her little secret.

"I can't argue that," said Dave, shaking his head. He shook Steve's hand. "Welcome back, buddy."

"Thanks, Dave," Steve said while looking over at Marcus. Their words were replaced with just an uncomfortable nod in both directions.

When they got back to camp, Sarah got her medical gear from her car. "We have to do this now, Steve. It's going to hurt."

"I'm ready." Steve arched his back. "Damn, that hurt."

"What?"

"It felt like someone just stabbed me in the back."

"Take off your shirt."

Steve took his shirt off and spun around.

"Oh my God. What happened to you?"

"It's long story, Sarah."

"Lie down." Sarah opened a bottle of whisky and poured it all over Steve's back.

Steve yelled in pain. "Whisky! Where the hell did you get whisky? Dammit!"

"Long story. Ask Dave sometime." She then started to apply pressure to each center core as if she was popping a zit. She squeezed until the butt end of the larva broke surface.

"Ahh! Take it easy, will you," Steve moaned.

She passed Steve the bottle. You might want to drink some. She picked and pulled at each larva like reeling in a fish. When the larva dug in, she gave it some slack. She didn't want to break it in half inside him. With as many bites as Steve had, she didn't know what damage the toxins they release would do. She wanted them whole and alive. She was shocked to see how many there were. Steve's body was covered with them. Mixed in with the larvae were shavings of metal, some buried quite deeply into his skin. Sarah pulled out as many of those as she could.

"Damn, Sarah, take it easy."

Sarah handed him a stick. "Bite down on this."

"Really?"

"Up to you, tough man. Some of these are pretty deep."

Steve grabbed the bottle of whisky and chugged it down, then pushed the stick into his mouth and bit down.

Sarah had just finished with his back and was ready to move on to another section of Steve's body. "Pants?" she said, insinuating for him to take them off.

"Oh, Sarah, you did miss me," Steve said feeling a

little tipsy from the whisky.

      SMACK!

•••

# CHAPTER 37

That evening, Dave found Sarah sitting all alone on top of the hill, staring at the town below. "Hi, Sarah. How's Steve doing?"

"He'll be fine. He's sleeping it off. His body looks like a pepperoni pizza right now. He's going to be sore, but his hangover will cover up most of that pain when he wakes up."

"I see. That bad, huh? How long before you think he's ready to move?"

"Move?"

"Yeah, we need to think about moving to higher ground."

"What about where Steve was camped? There's a cabin there. Beats the hell out of these tents," Sarah said, never taking her eyes off the town.

"Possibly. We'll see."

Sarah didn't want to go too far from town. She wanted to stay, maybe to still be able to find her father. She couldn't leave him behind. She needed to know that he was all right. She needed to know that he was being taken care of. "Maybe he is one of them now," she considered verbally. She not only considered it, but she knew it to be true. Her father probably started to turn shortly after she had walked out the door for work, leaving him there at home, lying in the bed. She never did look back, as promised. Now she lived with guilt. She pulled the bounty hunters' business card from her back pocket and read it over. She considered it once again. She had no doubt that she would do it if she had the funds.

*I'm sure we can work something out ... work something out ...* The words of the bounty hunter played over and over in her head.

Dave walked up from behind and pulled the card from her hand. He crumpled it up and threw it in the nearby fire pit.

"Don't even think about it, Sarah," he said to her sharply. "They're not right. Something about them rubs me the wrong way. They're trouble."

Sarah got to her feet. "You bastard!" she yelled, slapping him across the face.

"Whoa! What's that all about?" Steve asked while holding his head.

Dave turned, hiding his red cheek and walked away. "Ask your girlfriend, pizza face!"

272

"Hey, that's not nice, and she's not my girlfriend," Steve replied. He looked over at Sarah.

"He's thinking of packing up and leaving. I can't go, Steve."

"We have to, Sarah. There's nothing left here. We will need supplies soon. We're making one more trip into town for supplies and then we're out of here."

"I'm going with you."

"Sarah, we're all going."

"No, I mean into town. Let me go with you."

"Sarah, you need to stay here with the girls. It's dangerous down there. Sorry, but no."

"That's not fair. I want to go. My father's down there somewhere. I must go."

"I don't think so, Sarah. We can't worry about you. We need to get what we can and bug out."

Sarah sighed. "How are your sores?" she asked.

"I don't know. Fine, I guess. My head is killing me though."

"Good, because if it weren't, you'd probably be in a lot of pain."

Confused by the statement, Steve just nodded.

●●●

Dave scanned the town through a pair of binoculars. "Looks like the military has pulled out. Maybe it's safe now." He paused. "Oops, sorry. Not safe." A herd of zoms just filled his eyepiece. "Well, what the hell? There're thousands of them still down there. Where did the military go?"

"Gone, Dave," Steve replied as he approached. "Not

sure why, but they either packed and left or got taken down by the zoms. Either way, we are on our own down there."

"My guess is they had better places to be and bugged out. This is Bear Creek, after all," Dave said. "Not sure why they wanted to protect this hick town anyway. If it were me, I would have just bombed it."

Steve paused in thought. "You may be right, Dave, but I did see a few zoms wearing uniforms yesterday and quite a few soldiers dead on the ground, ripped to shreds."

"I'm sure we'll know in good time, Steve. Let's go."

Steve, Marcus, and Dave made their way to the city in the Jeep. Eli stayed behind with Jamie, Linda, and Sarah. They started packing things up while the guys were gone, getting things ready for the big move – a move to nowhere, a move to anywhere but here. The Jeep rolled to a stop in the center of town. The noise from the squeaky brakes attracted a few zoms, but not many. Not yet.

Besides the zoms, the first thing they noticed was the destruction the military had left behind. They'd pulled out, all right. The heavy equipment was gone. There was no sign of them except for a few of the fallen and the debris. The second thing they noticed was the posters. They were everywhere. "Missing!" "Found!" "Abducted!" People were searching for everything, including the family dogs, cats, and even hamsters. Everywhere they looked there were signs, which reminded Steve of a song by the Five Man Electrical Band, which he started to hum.

*And the sign says, 'long-haired freaky people need not apply'...*

274

The song faded away. Then Dave decided to join in, and they both started singing.

Marcus didn't know the song and wasn't much in the mood for singing.

*Signs, signs, everywhere there are signs.*
*Blocking out the scenery. Breaking my mind.*
*Do this! Don't do that! Can't you read the signs?*
*And the sign says, 'Anybody caught trespassing will*
*be shot on sight'*
*So I jumped on the fence and I yelled at the house,*
*Hey! What gives you the right ... to put up a fence to*
*keep me out ...*

The song trailed off.

Zombies were scarce in the immediate area, but in some others there were enough to fill a football field. They took advantage of the relative safety and decided to grab what they could where they were and head back to camp.

•••

# CHAPTER 38

It had been a couple of weeks since "the accident." That was what everyone was calling it now – the news of the car hitting the small lab in Bear Creek – the accident that released this nasty virus. It was alarming how quickly it had spread across the town, the state, and the nation. It had spread like wildfire, only faster. There had to be something more going on. Something had to have fueled the fire and helped it along. But what?

Officials from other countries were putting a lot of pressure on the United States to take care of this issue before it jumped the pond. They weren't any further along in discovering anything substantial about the virus since it began its spread. Officials conducted meeting upon meeting, all talk and very little action. The military had moved out of Bear Creek and went on to fight even bigger outbreaks. They lost a lot of soldiers, and the United States had lost a lot of cities. In two weeks' time, cities across America were taken down and overrun by the dead. The government, cozily housed in its doomsday bunkers, had some decisions to make.

•••

The gang moved from one camp to the other. Steve's camp was much more suited to their basic needs. It had fresh water for cooking, drinking, and bathing, and it was stocked with fish to eat.

The guys fixed up the cabin and hung a new door, new to them anyway. A door they had taken from a house in town. They took several, in fact. The third one was a perfect fit. The original door had been just hanging there by one screw, dangling in the wind, waiting to fall off its final hinge. They also boarded up all the cabin's windows, leaving enough cracks for a little bit of light and fresh air to sneak through. The cabin didn't look like much, but it was better than sleeping in tents and trees. They actually furnished the cabin quite nicely after a few more trips into town. Every now and then, while someone kept watch outside, they were even able to get some rest.

Sarah finally removed the sling from Jamie's arm and started her on some physical therapy. It was early but Sarah thought it was time to get her started on some light treatment. She taught Jamie what to do when she was away, so the girl could start building her muscles back.

They bathed in the stream, and Steve even got to see

one of his fantasies come true, Sarah taking a bath upstream. Of course, she was completely unaware of Steve hiding behind some bushes and peeking through the branches. Or was she? She looked in his direction more than a couple of times, giggled, and almost appeared to be teasing him.

All in all, things were the best they'd been since the outbreak. They were alive and they had each other. It almost felt like home. For them it was home, at least for now, but they were getting tired of just waiting. They had no idea what they were waiting for. Waiting for a change, hopefully for the better. Nothing seemed to be happening. It looked like this was how life was going to be from that day forward. But they'd never forget the destruction that went on and was still going on in the town below.

Every once in a while, they would have to make a quick trip into town for more supplies. There were more houses to loot there than there were up in the mountains. But there were also more people to compete with. Things were getting more dangerous by the second. Zombies weren't the biggest threat anymore. It was the survivors – the people left in the town surviving among the dead. They were strangers and unpredictable.

Being shot over a candy bar wasn't out of the question as the food supplies quickly diminished. People were running out of food left and right, unable to stock up for the long run. Unfortunately, no one knew just how long that run would be. Two weeks? Three? Maybe months. No one knew. Only the marathon runners, the ones who paced themselves and saved their reserves to the end would last.

People were hungry, desperate, and making bad decisions. No one could be trusted. With all this chaos on the streets, the zombies never lacked for food.

•••

Sarah was up early and went for an early morning stroll down by the creek. She sat on a log and stared off into the distance. This was typical for her these days, but instead of facing the town like she normally would, she faced the opposite direction, toward the sunrise. The morning was chilly and the sun warmed her face.

The sky was beautiful, vibrant, and full of color. Bright yellows and oranges bounced off the puffy clouds, filling the sky with the prettiest red tones. It looked more like a sunset than a sunrise to Sarah. Smoke rose from cities off in the distance, but for now Sarah's attention was on the sun.

"You know what that means, don't you?" asked Marcus, startling Sarah. He caught her completely off guard. She spilled her coffee on the ground.

It was Marcus' turn for morning watch and he had unintentionally snuck up on her.

"You dumb fuck. You scared the piss out of me," she said, balancing what coffee was left in her cup and trying not to spill the rest.

"Sorry, Sarah, I didn't mean to startle you. I was just watching you from over there and I thought I would come see how you were doing."

"Make some noise next time, will ya?"

Marcus moved in closer and swung an arm around her. "Sorry. How are you?"

"I'm good. It's a beautiful morning."

"Yes it is." Marcus started caressing her arm and shoulders.

Sarah pulled away. "No, Marcus, stop."

"What's wrong? You didn't mind it the other night by the campfire. It's Steve, isn't it? You have a thing for him, don't you?" Marcus grabbed for her arm but Sarah pulled back farther. She didn't answer, instead avoiding the question and trying to change the subject.

"What does it mean?" she asked.

"What does what mean?" Marcus questioned with a bit of a tone.

"When you startled me, you asked, 'do you know what that means?'"

"Oh, that." He paused. "The sky, you were looking at the sky."

"Yeah, so?"

"It's red."

"I can see it's red, Marcus."

"The old cliché, that's all. 'Red sky in morning gives sailors a warning.' If it's true, we are in for some bad weather."

"Yeah, well it sure is pretty now."

"Yes, yes you are, Sarah."

"Shouldn't you be on lookout?"

"Yeah, I need to get back." Marcus turned to walk back to his post, a vantage point where he could see the whole camp.

"Marcus," Sarah shouted. Marcus stopped in his

tracks and looked back over his shoulder. "Thank you," Sarah added. Marcus nodded, looked forward, and began walking again with a big smirk on his face.

Sarah sat back down on the log and enjoyed the beautiful sunrise. "How can that bring trouble?" she asked herself.


That afternoon, the sky darkened over the city and thunderous sounds could be heard for miles.

"Is it rain?" Steve asked.

Dave was on a hill overlooking the town with binoculars when Steve approached him from behind. "Oh, hi, Steve. I heard a plane pass over not too far from here. I thought I would take a look around. Haven't heard a plane since this whole thing started. Sure is dark over there."

"Yeah, it looks like it's raining pretty hard over the town."

"It's not rain," Dave said. He handed Steve the binoculars. Steve took a look for himself. "What the?" Steve looked puzzled. "Is that what I think it is?"

"Well, they're not butterflies, my friend."

"We have to get one," Steve said, handing the binoculars back.

"Yes, I know." Dave paused, looking back through the specs. "You ready?"

"I'll tell the others."

Minutes later, both Dave and Steve left in the Jeep. They didn't get too far down the road when they ran into the first batch of trouble.

"Zoms, slow down," Dave said. Steve hit the brakes, skidding to a stop on the loose gravel. "Wow, they're getting close. We need to warn the others."

"There's only a couple, Dave. Let's just take care of them and continue on our mission. There's no sense in alarming the others over a couple of zombies. They wouldn't let us leave, and we need to find out what's going on in the sky over the town."

"Of course, you're right." Dave readied his rifle. "Let's go," he said.

Steve laid his hand across the rifle. "Wait a minute, not the rifle. They will hear the shots back at the camp. I'll take care of this. You drive." Steve hopped out of the cab and into the truck bed, his cutter and baseball bat in hand. "Just drive up next to them and I'll do the rest."

Dave was grateful to take the wheel. He personally had never killed a zom with anything other than a gun and didn't know if he could do it. The thought of having to be that close nauseated him. Steve, on the other hand, had no problem with it and did it well.

The Jeep rolled slowly toward the oncoming zoms. There were three of them, and the truck was headed between them, two on the left and one on the right. As they rolled past the first two, the zoms were all over the truck, trying to get in at Dave. Even though Dave was pretty well protected by the closed door and rolled-up windows, he still leaned over to the center of the cab as he passed by. Dave now looked out the holes in the windshield as he drove. Steve likewise crouched down in the center of the bed behind the cab.

Steve then jumped up for a surprise attack on the zombies, cracking their heads open with a swing of his cutter blade. After taking care of the two on the left, he quickly swung around to do the same with the one on the right. When he did, he noticed a piece of paper stuck to the zom's head. On the paper he could clearly see the iconic biohazard symbol at the top and the United States flag printed at the bottom. Everything in the middle was simply unreadable due the zombie's rotted flesh soaking through it. One kick to the zombie's head allowed plenty of room for a wind-up swing of the bat, instantly decapitating the zom in one smooth swing. The head sailed off down the road, bouncing several times before rolling into the ditch. Steve then jumped off the bed of the truck and dragged the bodies off the road and into the tall weeds.

"Let's go," Steve said as he climbed back into the cab as if nothing had happened.

"You're a real piece of work, my friend. Where in hell did you learn to do that?" asked Dave as he stepped on the gas.

"Military. Served three years in special ops before honorable discharge. I've been places and seen things a hell of a lot worse than this, my friend."

Dave thought to himself, *That just can't be possible.* "Seal?"

"Sorry, Dave, can't say."

"Whatever. Glad you're on my team, whoever you are."

Steve grinned in the mirror, focusing on the road

behind them.

•••

"Did you hear that?" Sarah asked whoever was listening.

"Hear what?" answered Linda.

"I thought I heard something, that's all. It's hard to explain. Like people getting clobbered. I'll go outside and ask Marcus."

Marcus kept watch while Dave and Steve ran into town. Sarah walked up.

"We meet again. What brings you out here, my dear?"

"I heard noises."

"Noises?"

"Did Steve and Dave get down the mountain all right?"

"Yes, Sarah, just a few seconds ago actually. They got to the point and did their wave like they always do. Everything's fine. They'll be back shortly."

"Well, OK. Thanks, Marcus."

"You're welcome, my dear. I'll let you know the minute I see them return."

No response came from Sarah, except a small shoulder shrug and a nod. She walked away and returned to the cabin to join the others.

Marcus savored every step she took, watching her hips sway back and forth as she walked. "Mm, mm," he said. "Those jeans couldn't look any better."

Everyone in the cabin was busy doing what they could to throw a meal together for the night. Eli, who had enjoyed mushroom hunting with his wife before she'd passed away, and Jamie were just leaving to see what they could find in the woods. Nuts, berries, and mushrooms would all be welcome.

"Don't go too far, Eli," Sarah said as they passed through the doorway.

"Don't worry, Sarah. We'll be fine, won't we, Jamie?" he said as he wrapped his arm around Jamie's shoulder. Jamie shied away, her arm still a bit tender without her sling. She just nodded and smiled as Sarah walked by.

A blackbird landed on the roof just to the right of the doorway. Unsure of the bird's intentions, Sarah shooed it away before walking through the door. "Damn birds."

Sarah walked in on Linda while she was holding her tummy as her unborn child kicked. Linda was busy with dinner.

"Sit down before you fall down. Are you all right?" Sarah asked. "I'll handle dinner. You just take it easy."

"Thanks, Sarah. I think I will. I'm a bit lightheaded." Sarah helped her to the bed. "Can we talk? Privately?"

"Sure." Sarah looked around. "No one's here, what's on your mind?"

"This child, this world. Everything. What's not?"

"Hey, that's no way to feel. This will all be over soon. You're going to have a beautiful baby, and we'll all be back in our homes shortly. Please don't feel that way."

"Look around, Sarah. I can't bring a baby up in this world. It's not getting any better. You know that. The government's not doing a damn thing. They just made it worse. What's left? Hiding in the mountains until the food runs out?"

"The zombies need food too, Linda. They can't survive long without it either. We just have to sit tight until this blows over. You can do it, Linda. You're not alone. We'll be right here with you."

"How long do you think they can last without food?"

"Not sure, Linda. For about as long as we can, I would guess. Maybe longer, but they don't have the brains to figure things out like we do."

"Yeah ..." Linda was interrupted by a couple of nearby gunshots. Seconds later, Eli and Jamie come running into the cabin, slamming the door behind them. More gunfire erupted.

"What's going on? Are you all right?" asked Sarah.

"We're fine, Sarah. Ran into some zoms. Chased us out of the woods. Marcus is taking care of them right now," said Eli as he tried catching his breath. More shots were fired.

The gunshots echoed for miles down the rolling hills and into the streets below. Dave and Steve just looked at each other when the shots finally reached their ears.

"That sounded like a long way off," Dave remarked.

"Yes, yes it did, and it came from that direction," Steve said, pointing the piece of paper he had just picked up. He pointed up toward the mountains. Up toward camp.

Dave and Steve had just gotten to the town and hadn't even had time to look at the leaflet that the plane had dumped a short time ago. It temporarily became second behind the gunfire. Steve was already behind the wheel of the truck before Dave took three steps. Dave got in and Steve handed him the paper and floored it.

"How could you tell what direction the shots were coming from? The noise just echoed through the alleys. We can't be sure."

"No, you're right, we can't. Just call it intuition. Do you want to take the chance?"

"Oh my God," was all Dave could say. He was half-listening to Steve and reading the leaflet at the same time, paying a little more attention to the leaflet than Steve.

"What?" Steve asked, startling Dave.

Dave jumped. "Nothing, just drive."

"You tell me what it says or I'm stopping this damn truck right now!"

Dave hesitated. Steve held up on the accelerator and hovered his foot over the brake pedal.

"All right already. It says they are going to bomb Bear Creek."

Steve jumped on the brakes. The Jeep screeched to a stop, throwing Dave into the dash. The sound of rubber sliding on asphalt attracted the attention of zoms near and far. Steve ripped the paper out of Dave's hands and jumped out of the truck, not caring how close the approaching zoms were. "You drive," he said as the truck rolled ahead. Steve failed to put it in park before jumping out. Dave nervously slid behind the wheel, gaining control of the truck. In the meantime, Steve hammered a couple of zoms with his blade before getting into the passenger side and reading the pamphlet for himself. The truck pulled away, leaving a patch of rubber and a mob of zoms behind.

"What the hell was that all about?" Dave barked. "Our friends could be in trouble up there."

"Then I guess next time when I ask you something, you better answer me. I'm not much into begging."

Dave just turned his head, fuming under his breath, and looked straight ahead, worried about his wife and unborn child.

Steve continued reading and could hardly believe what the words revealed, yet it was what he had feared in the back of his mind.

When they got to the cabin, they found everyone but Marcus inside. They were all huddled together at the opposite wall. Marcus was still outside walking the grounds, watching out for more zombies.

Dave immediately ran to Linda and fell to her side. He held her tight with his head on her bulging belly.

Steve asked as soon as he walked through the door, "Is everyone all right in here?" Sarah didn't move. She was holding onto Jamie, shaking.

"Now what?" she finally spoke. "We're not safe here anymore, either?" A rhetorical question for sure. Steve didn't answer.

"We have to move higher?" Linda questioned.

"Yeah, higher," confirmed Eli, in his gravelly voice.

"No, I'm afraid not. We need to stay put until ..." Linda interrupted Steve mid-sentence.

"Until what, Steve? Until we all get eaten?" Linda

289

remarked with a questioning stare.

"Dave, Marcus and I need to talk. Eli, you're welcome to join us if you like."

"Why can't we be involved here?" asked Sarah. "Are you hiding something from us, Steve? We have a right to know everything you do, you know."

"Yeah, Sarah, you do but someone has to stay with Jamie and Linda."

"I'll stay," said Eli. "I'm too old for this, I can't make decisions to save my life, let alone save yours. I'll go with whatever you decide, and besides, the Lord will protect us. He'll show us the way." He held tight to his ragged Bible, a book that looked as if it had been carried at his side all his life, and probably had been.

"Very well, Eli, thanks. Sarah, you come with us. Eli, can you shoot?" Steve held out a gun in his direction.

"Hunted all my life. Got a deer almost every year, sometimes two."

"Great, you keep watch but stay close to the door in case Linda and Jamie need you. And, Eli ..." Steve paused to get the old man's undivided attention. Eli's head perked up in his direction. "Headshots only. Try not to waste the ammo."

"I can do that," Eli said, looking at Linda, waiting for conformation. He got a nod.

The guys and Sarah walked over to the pines and sat down on a fallen log by the fire pit. Steve pulled the flier from his rear pocket and a state map that he had pulled from the glove box of an abandoned car days ago. He read the flier aloud.

The leaflet read:

*To the people of the United States of America...*

*I'm sure you are all aware by now that America has been
under attack by a deadly plague. As of the writing of this leaflet,
no one has come forward to take responsibility, so for now we are
treating it as a plague. Terrorism has not been ruled out. I come
to you to tell you that we've exhausted all efforts to contain
and/or control this virus. It has spread too far too fast. We feared
the worst, which happened 666 years ago, known as the black
plague (Bubonic). It killed more than one third of the Earth's
population. Six hundred sixty-six is a familiar number. It's
known as "the mark of the beast." We pray at this time that this
is only coincidental.*

*The CDC has confirmed to us that as of this date, there
is no known cure for what is happening. There is no known
reversal and no known way to control the spread of this disease
except for complete annihilation.*

*These creatures that are known as zombies, because we
know no other suitable name for them, do not react to chemicals.
In fact, the only way to kill them is decapitation, a bullet to the
head, or severing the brain stem.*

*This virus has been and will continue to be the highest
priority at the CDC. They will continue to work around the
clock until a solution is found. In the meantime, we must take
drastic measures to (pardon the term) "thin the herd" if we are to
have any chance of surviving this at all. The military has tried*

street sweeps with little to no success and have lost countless lives trying. There are just too many of them and too many places for them to hide. We need to kill them in mass numbers, and we need to do this now. The only way we can do this efficiently and effectively is with bombs, all kinds, whatever we have available to us. Depending on the situation, we may even consider nuclear. Let's pray it doesn't come to that.

If you are reading this letter, then you are in danger of being within the blast zone. You have until 12:00 p.m. EST on Saturday the 28th, to clear out and get to the safety zones. Bombs will hit your town at precisely 12:30 p.m. Below you will find a diagram of the blast zone, the fallout zone, and the safety zone. It is in your best interest to do what it takes to be in the designated safety zones before the bombs hit.

Help your neighbors. Help your friends, your family, and by all means, help the elderly. We know more will die and even more will turn, but please, we have no other solution.

God be with you.
The President of the United States


"You've got to be shittin' me?"

"Afraid not, Marcus," said Steve. "Looks real, and to tell you the truth, if it's like this here, it's a hundred times worse in the bigger cities. I see no other choice, either. As soon as I saw the military bug out as quickly as they moved in, I feared this would happen."

"What are we going to do?" asked Sarah.

"We have no choice. We are here." With a stick Steve

pointed to a position on the map he had just opened up on the ground before them. "We need to be outside of here," he pointed again to the map, "by noon on Saturday."

"That's less than five days away on foot," said Dave. "It's got to be a hundred miles."

"Eighty-eight, to be precise," said Steve. "As a crow flies, that is."

"That's a lot of miles to cover in a very short time, Steve. Most of the people in the towns will be on foot; the roads will be jammed. Blocked. Most are destroyed. They'll never make it."

"Yeah, I know, Marcus. It's going to be chaos. We need to pack. This mountain will be crawling with people, followed by zoms, by tomorrow. We'll leave in the morning. Bright and early, before sunup."

That night, Steve and Sarah spent some quality time together up on the hill overlooking the city. They noticed more and more fires every day as they watched columns of smoke rise everywhere as they scanned the horizon. From a distance, it looked like the whole town was on fire. That was just days away from becoming reality. The smoke darkened the skies above, blocking the sunlight from reaching the ground, but off to the west there was the prettiest sunset in the making.

Dave walked up behind Steve and Sarah and lightly cleared his throat. He didn't want to interrupt the heavy kissing that was going on, but it was Steve's turn for watch, and Dave wanted to get back to his wife and child-to-be. Dave, now mesmerized by the sunset, let the two kiss a little longer as he stared off to the distant skies. He took in what beauty there was, as there wasn't much beauty left. While he looked off into the distance, Dave couldn't help but think about that same old cliché known by all, "Red sky at night, sailors' delight. Red sky in morning gives sailors a warning."

"I sure hope this beautiful sunset is gone by morning," he said aloud, hoping to get Steve's attention. Steve turned Dave's way with a jerk, reaching for his blade.

"Oh, geez, Dave, is there a problem?" Steve asked, disturbed.

"Sorry, bud, but it's your turn for watch," Dave said as he handed the rifle to Steve.

Steve looked at Sarah. Sarah shied away, wiping her mouth with the back of her hand. "We'll talk in the morning." Sarah nodded. Dave lent a hand to Sarah. She refused the help and got to her feet on her own.

Steve took the gun from Dave, jerking it out of his hands. "Thanks."

"Did I do something?" Dave asked.

"No, Dave, everything's cool." He paused, watching Sarah walk away. "With us anyway. Something sure is bothering her though. She won't open up and tell me what it is."

"There's a lot going on, Steve," exclaimed Dave.

"Yes there is, and I'm going to find out what," Steve said.

"Steve, we are doing way more than what anyone can expect. This pressure, constant fear, and uncertainty are a bit overwhelming. Cut her some slack, man."

"We're doing what's necessary to survive, Dave. Anything short of that risks everyone. If she has a problem, we need to know."

Dave paused, not knowing what to say to that. "Goodnight, Steve. Good luck tonight." Dave turned, not waiting for a reply, and headed back to the cabin.

•••

# CHAPTER 39

## Mt. Hope

"What are our options?" the president asked his cabinet of only the highest officials, including a few members of congress.

"Well, sir, to be honest we are quickly running out of them. We simply do not have enough troops on our own soil to handle the situation at hand. They are being spread too thin, sir. Most of the ones we had have been taken down, simply overpowered by numbers."

"The war is over, General. Get our troops home. We need them here, on our own soil."

"With all due respect, sir, that's not advisable. We are

finally in talks with the Taliban. They are finally listening to reason. If we pull the troops out now, we will lose our leverage and probably be back at war again with a vengeance, sir. Besides, it may not be enough. It would take weeks to get them all back here. If they aren't here all at once, I'm afraid that we may just be feeding the cause," the general responded.

"Then we are given no choice. Bring as many troops home as you can spare without risking leverage. We will need them here for cleanup efforts, search and rescue, and to help rebuild."

"Mr. President, you can't be serious. People are crying out for help, sir. There has to be another way," pleaded one senator.

"We are out of resources, senator, unless you have something up your sleeve that you're not telling me. We have no other choice."

The senator just shrugged and hung his head, hiding his reddening eyes.

"I didn't think so. We've either tried it and it failed, or it failed before we tried. I'm sorry, but it's been confirmed by the secretary of defense. We either do it and hope for survivors or do nothing and have a world of walking corpses."

"My family, sir?"

"Senator, get your family to safety and do it now."

"I can't reach them, sir. I lost contact two days ago when the grids went down."

"Sorry, Senator, there's nothing more I can do."

The president turned and walked into his new Oval Office two miles below the Blue Ridge Mountains. He branched off and quickly ducked into the restroom, closing the door behind him. The president could only be alone in just a couple of places, and this was one of them. He leaned over the sink and closely stared at himself in the mirror. Admiring his recently graying hair, a tear released from his reddening eyes as they welled up and rolled down his cheek. He pondered a moment over the relationship he had with the senator and his family. They were close and enjoyed many backyard picnics together over the years. "What in the hell have I just done?" he asked himself, hanging his head. He let the tear fall from his face and into the sink.

•••

# CHAPTER 40

Steve's night went by pretty uneventfully, yet he was exhausted from his mind racing. He tried hard to make sense of Sarah's moods, but he kept coming up blank with no answers and no real solutions, at least not above the obvious.

At 4:05 a.m., Steve awoke when Marcus came in from his watch. Marcus had relieved Steve's watch at midnight. They were on a four-hour rotation. Steve dragged himself out of bed, stretched, and quickly noticed that Sarah was already up too, and not in her sleeping bag. Steve was glad. Maybe they could have a chance to talk some more before they headed out. More time passed and there was still no sign of Sarah returning. Steve assumed that she went to relieve herself, but he'd been awake for 10 or so minutes now and had expected Sarah to return. Steve was now concerned for her safety and decided to go looking for her. He grabbed his blade and walked outside. Marcus followed him out the door on his way to the truck.

"Have you seen Sarah, Marcus?" Steve inquired.

Marcus replied, "No, not yet this morning. The only one who came out of that cabin door, besides you, was Eli. Do you realize how many trips that old man takes to use the bathroom in the middle of the night? It's a wonder he gets any sleep at all."

"Yeah, I've noticed. Sucks getting old, but what about Sarah?"

"What about her?"

"Have you seen her?"

"No. Do you mean she's not here?"

"No, Marcus, she's not. She must have snuck out in the middle of the night. Maybe while you were making your rounds."

"Or you," Marcus replied with no hesitation. He didn't want to be blamed for her disappearance if, in fact, she was truly gone.

"Or me. Sorry, I'm not trying to blame you, Marcus. I just want to know where she is," Steve said worriedly.

"I understand, but I haven't seen her."

Dave appeared from out of nowhere, arms stretched to their capacity, back curved, mouth wide open in the biggest of yawns. "What's up, guys?" he moaned. Marcus and Steve stared back at him. Dave looked down to his fly and checked his zipper. "What?"

"Looking for Sarah. Have you seen her?" asked Steve.

"No, why? Is she gone?"

"You're quick in the morning, Dave," Steve replied.

"Sorry, I haven't had my coffee yet."

"Christ, where in the hell did she go? Tell me Jamie is still here," Steve stated.

"Yeah, she's here," answered Eli, now awake helping Linda roll up sleeping bags, getting things ready to go.

Dave went out to the post and looked around through his binoculars. He could see the whole camp from there, as well as the town below. "Marcus, Steve, you better come here and take look at this." It was just light enough to see down the mountainside.

"Sarah?" Steve said as he took off in Dave's direction.

"No, sorry Steve, not Sarah. There's movement coming out of the Bear Creek." He handed Steve the binoculars.

"Oh my gosh. It's started. Walkers, by the thousands, mixed with survivors trying to escape the city."

"We have to go!" Dave blurted.

"Go? We can't leave. What about Sarah?" Steve asked anxiously.

"She left by her own will, Steve. She knew we were leaving at first light. She obviously didn't want to go."

"Sarah! Sarah!" Steve cupped his mouth with his hands and shouted in all directions as he walked the perimeter of the camp. "Saraaaaah!"

Shrubbery rustled a few feet from Steve. He gripped his blade tighter. "Sarah?" he said in an unsure voice. Just then, like a bolt of lighting, a deer bounded up and ran away. Steve jumped in his tracks and grabbed his chest to catch his breath. He continued searching.

"Steve, keep it down, man. You're going have every zom in sight up here."

"They're going to be here anyway, Dave. I have to find her."

"We are leaving in five, Steve," Dave yelled.

Steve didn't turn and showed no sign of responding. He just continued his search at breakneck speed. He refused to leave Sarah behind.

Minutes later, Dave appeared again. "We're ready, Steve. Are you coming?"

"Dave, we can't just leave her. I should have talked to her last night but you ... damn you."

"How was I to know she was going to take off, Steve? You know how far we have to go and the short time we have to get there. Who knows what we're up against? If we stay any longer, we're going to be up against things we can't handle."

"Then go. Take Jamie and Eli with you and go. Leave me my bike. I'm going to find Sarah or I'll die trying."

"I understand." Dave handed him a 9 mm handgun and a box of 100 rounds. "Good luck, Steve," he said, hesitating. "Steve, there's something you should know. It's possible that Sarah went looking for her dad. It's all she's talked about lately. In fact, one day while you were missing, a couple of bounty hunters showed up at camp offering their services. Sarah showed a lot of interest in them and what they

304

do but couldn't afford their price. She may have gone searching for them."

Steve just looked on, all ears.

"They said they operate a farm east of town, just over the bridge. Walker, I believe they said. She's really worried about her dad, Steve. She may be desperate."

"Thanks, Dave. That's good to know." He paused and thought to himself. *I wish I would have known that last night.* He decided not to argue with Dave about it. "Good luck to you and the gang. Take care of them, and I'll catch up to you down the road. With Sarah." They shook hands, but for some reason Dave didn't think that would ever happen, and deep down, neither did Steve.

The gang loaded Sarah's car and Steve's truck and ironically left without their respective owners. They slowly pulled out of camp and down the hillside with Steve trailing behind on his bike. The car and truck turned right at the bottom of the hill where the road made a T. It was there that Steve diverted, making a left back into town.

Steve swerved around and weaved in and out of hundreds, if not thousands, of people leaving town. It was like going the wrong way down a one-way street during rush hour. The people were making a beeline out of Bear Creek, hunted down by zombies. Steve clubbed a few zoms down along the way, saving who he could for whatever short time they had left. Most were sure to fall victim, as they appeared to be very unprepared and inadequately armed for the ongoing events. Some were swinging golf clubs, ladies swinging their purses. They all tried their very best to get away with whatever possessions they had left. Unfortunately, their very best would fall far short of victory.

Dogs, cats, rabbits, and ferrets were running alongside their respective owners. Their loyalty was unbelievable. Family dogs turned on the "turned," doing their best to protect their masters and biting the ankles of the undead. There were a lot of teeth showing and a lot of growling going on from the dogs and from the zoms. All in all, the dogs only tripped the zoms up, slowed them down at best, having little to no long-term effects on the zombies. They didn't feel pain. The dogs could bite them all they wanted. Unfortunately, it only hurt the dogs and their respective families, as down the road some of the same dogs, now infected with the zombies' blood, would eventually and accidentally infect their owners during playtime. As for the other animals, they feared for their lives and ran away from anything or anyone that chased them.

The town was in complete chaos. People were running every which way, bumping into one other and tripping each other up, making them easy pickings to be preyed upon. Even the zoms looked confused as to which person to follow and which person to bite. There were so many to choose from. A buffet mixed with Americans, Mexicans, Chinese, and even a few visiting from Thailand, running everywhere, giving the zoms quite a choice of cuisines depending on their taste. They would follow one person for a while only to turn and follow another when one came even closer. The zoms really didn't care; they just wanted a bite to eat.

Out of nowhere, an alarm sounded all across town. Sirens mounted high on poles, used to alert the town of tornados and inclement weather, all went off at once. Every siren in Bear Creek was blaring so loud it made it very difficult to think. Most zoms stopped in their tracks, some in mid-bite, as if the sound had clutched their minds, or whatever they had left. People covered their ears and at the same time checked their watches, only to find out that it wasn't 1:00 p.m. in the afternoon, and it wasn't the first Saturday of the month either – the time and day the alert system was normally tested to make sure they functioned properly in case of a weather emergency. This confused the people to no end.

Veterans of war started to freak out as the familiar sound brought back memories of air raids. They were similar to those heard on the TV show M.A.S.H., five seconds after Radar announced "incoming." Only here, no one knew what was coming. Everyone looked to the skies, but they were clear of clouds, only streaked with smoke. Past the smoke was nothing but blue sky. It certainly showed no signs of inclement weather, let alone a tornado. According to the leaflet, they still had more than four days left before the bombs were to be dropped.

So what was going on?

"Air raid!" a large man shouted out at the top of his lungs with no need for a bullhorn.

People feared the worst and started looking for planes in the sky. Some people ran for cover, burrowing themselves in ditches, and hiding under overpasses, in storm drains, and in vacant buildings and cars. These people were some of the first to be taken down by the hungry as they took advantage of the ones who reacted foolishly and didn't keep their heads about them.

Running into empty buildings that weren't scouted out beforehand was a very foolish thing to do. Some zombies still followed, paying little attention to the ambient noise, especially when food was in plain sight, and had a feeding frenzy on the distracted. Other zoms stopped what they were doing and followed the noise like they were in a trance.

Maybe something had happened. Maybe the pamphlet had a typo and gave the wrong date for the bombing. It couldn't possibly be today, people thought. If so, literally no one would have had a chance to get to the safe zones, but no one doubted that it could happen. Crazier things had been happening for days. After the military fiasco, they wouldn't put it past the government to screw them all.

People panicked. Some couldn't take it anymore. Gunshots were fired and heard throughout the town; more now than ever before. Only this time, some of the bullets weren't intended for zoms. Some were taking down innocent people as fights erupted out of nowhere, from being pushed and shoved in directions they didn't want to go. Some people were even begging to be shot. A shot to the head had to be better than being blown up by a bomb or eaten by a zom. When the guns were almost empty, those carrying them always seemed to have one bullet left for themselves, unless they had lost count.

The sirens caused so much confusion that the people

didn't know what to do or which way to go. They panicked like never before. They were frightened of the unknown but more afraid of each other. They were more afraid of the big bomb than the zombies themselves.

Little did they know that the sirens were just a ploy, a decoy used to draw the zombies away from the survivors so more would have a chance to escape. Unfortunately, no one knew about this plan. There was nothing on the pamphlets that fell from the heavens that said anything about it. Who would have known? The chief of police would have known something, for sure. That's who took it upon himself to throw the switch up on the wall, after watching countless people trying to flee the town only to be taken down by the zoms right in front of his own eyes. There were just too many to help. Throwing that one little switch set off every civil defense siren across Bear Creek, sending more than 100 decibels of continuous noise 30 feet above everyone's heads. It was the only thing the chief could think of that would have an effect on everything and everyone within earshot.

The plan seemed to have backfired at first, but seriously, not many had a chance anyway. People were being taken down by the zoms by the hundreds. Those who kept their heads, and used them, survived and benefited the most from this spontaneous act. Most of the zoms were attracted to the noise and moved in herds toward the tornado sirens and gathered beneath the poles.

Word got out across the Internet, so this technique could be used across the country. After several more closed-door meetings at Mt Hope, it was also decided that these poles would be the precise spots where the bombs would be dropped for more effective kills.

•••

The zoms went in one direction while Steve rode in another, searching every ditch and every alley for Sarah as he passed by. There were still no signs of her. It was like she had vanished into thin air. It was deja vu all over again for Steve. It seemed like he had just found her, and now was searching for her again. Steve knew the chances were getting slimmer by the minute of finding her. She could have up to a four-hour head start on him for all he knew, and she could have covered a lot of ground in four hours, unless she'd been trapped somewhere like he had in the Dumpster. Not that Steve hoped for her to be trapped, but was hoping for a miracle, a sign of some sort telling him which way to go. She could be just about anywhere in this town. Maybe even dead – or worse, turned into one of them. Then what? Could Steve face her? Could he put her out of her misery if need be? Steve shivered at the thought.

The first place Steve would look was Sarah's home. He knew she still lived with her dad, and, lucky for Steve, he had taken her home from the bar on the back of his bike the first time they had met. She had been at the bar with a friend, but her friend had ditched her and left with someone else that night and had taken the keys to the car with her. Steve, being the Good Samaritan, offered her a ride home. It was pure coincidence that they had ended up in the backseat of her car the following night. It usually didn't take Steve that long.

Sarah, on foot, may still have been on her way to her

dad's. Steve rode hard and fast through town. He swerved in and out of zoms, attracting the attention of some unintentionally and pulling them away from the sirens to the sound of his bike. They were quickly shaken off and fell back as Steve pulled away. The zoms then returned to the noise coming from the poles.

Steve rode right past the garage where he worked, coming to a slow rolling stop a block away. He looked back over his shoulder. His mind raced as he thought of Bob. Not only had Bob been his boss, but he had also been a good friend and had always been there for Steve.

"I can't leave him like that," he said to himself as he turned the bike around and drove back to the garage. He pulled into an open bay and looked around. He grabbed a few things off the workbench and stuffed them in a pouch on the bike. The place was empty. The military had taken just about everything when they left. Spare parts, oil, and most of the tools were gone. The last time he'd seen Bob was out back in the yard when his former boss had chased him out of there. *Maybe he's still there*, he thought, and moved to the back door. *Or maybe he's with the rest of them under the poles.*

Steve slowly pulled the back door open. It opened with a haunting moan. It startled Steve, which took a lot by now. He looked to the left, tightening his grip on the blade, then looked quickly to the right, and finally behind. He thought it might have been Bob moaning nearby; it sounded close. Seeing nothing, he checked the door and gently swung it back and forth. It moaned in both directions. Pulling it toward him made the same haunting moan as before. He paused, waited for his heart rate to slow, and then opened the door and stepped outside. He walked to the edge of the covered porch and quickly scanned the area.

The porch was a hoarder's dream – piles and stacks of car parts tossed in every direction, stacked high to look somewhat organized but failing miserably. There were plenty of places in there to hide, but zoms didn't hide. What would they hide from? They just existed. They just stood around, aimlessly wandering until they saw something good to eat, so Steve didn't bother searching every little crevice. He was sure that Bob would just show up, probably sooner than later. He hoped, away. Little did Steve know that Bob was standing on the opposite side of a refrigerator, just to the left of the doorway.

The refrigerator was filled with beer, pop, and a couple of quarts of semi-fresh nightcrawlers. Bob liked to fish in the man-made pond out back. Steve fished with him on occasion and helped keep the pond stocked so Bob would never run out of fish to catch.

While Steve scanned the grounds, Bob sniffed the air. A familiar scent filled his nostrils and his fogged-over eyes opened wide. Steve was standing no more than 15 feet away. Bob shambled his way, arms swaying left then right as he struggled to keep balance. Bob's left leg had been mangled from falling debris landing on him, pinning him to the ground. Helpless, a zom had chewed on his exposed arm, gnawing it to the bone and infecting him with the virus. Army personnel freed him not knowing he was infected at the time.

Steve didn't hear Bob creep up on him. The siren blared just two blocks away, which was probably why Bob never bothered to follow the noise. Bob was almost upon Steve and reached out for the collar of his shirt, hoping for a bite of his shoulder, but at the same moment, Steve stepped off the shaded patio, out into the hot sun.

Steve started walking out in the yard, cutter at the ready, swinging it back and forth, pretending to be swinging at zoms. Bob silently followed close behind. The warmth from the sun fell on Steve's shoulders, then moved down his back, across his buttocks, and crept down his legs, as he left the shade of the covered porch. He cast a long shadow before him as he walked. He followed his shadow a few more steps then noticed the shadow became two. Steve gripped his blade tighter, feeling the handle through his leather gloves, and without hesitation he spun his weight on his heels in the loose gravel to come face to face with his good friend and boss, Bob.

Bob looked worse than when Steve had seen him just a few days before. He was thinner, as if he hadn't had enough to eat lately. Open sores spread across Bob's face, exposing his jawbone and rows of blood-stained teeth. Bob looked at Steve with the same concerned eyes he always had. Steve read more into them this time. He thought Bob looked concerned that he couldn't do what he'd come there to do, possibly afraid that Steve would leave him once again. Without putting him out of his misery.

Steve lifted his blade, then brought it back to his side in remorse. He looked to the ground and shook his head.

What Steve really saw was his own reflection, doubt that he could do it himself. Bob paused and tilted his head from side to side, which could have been mistaken for emotion, or maybe Steve was reading too much into that as well. Steve searched his mind for any excuse not to do it.

"I'll get you help, Bob," Steve said, shuffling backward as Bob advanced. Bob tilted his head the other way. It appeared to Steve that Bob was actually listening, but that wasn't the case. Bob had suffered nerve damage to his neck, which made him tilt and sway from side to side, at times with a jerk. Bob reached for Steve again. Steve raised his cutter once more and swung the blade wide, decapitating Bob with one smooth swipe. Steve wiped the blade clean on Bob's coveralls as he lay on the ground dead. Blood pooled where his head should have been.

*1955 Chevy. Bob's favorite truck,* Steve thought as he dragged Bob's body into the cab. He then walked back and picked up Bob's head and carefully set it in the truck as well. He said his goodbyes.

"Thanks for all the good times, Bob. Sorry it had to end this way, but I'm sure that's what you wanted me to do." Steve locked the door with the palm of his hand before slamming the door shut. He left, hanging his head while looking at his cutter. He took a deep breath. When facing the ground, he noticed for the first time a half-dozen or so dead birds scattered all about and backtracked to the back door, trying hard not to step on them.

Steve hopped on his bike and raced through town. The roads were terrible to ride on. They'd been broken up by the military's heavy equipment passing through. Their treads tore the asphalt apart like cheese in a grater, with potholes and loose rock everywhere. Steve loved his crotch rocket almost as much as his GTO, but at times like this, he really would have preferred a dirt bike.

*Just two more blocks,* Steve thought as his back wheel slid out from underneath him. He regained control and motored down another block, pulling down Sarah's street.

Sarah's house was a small bungalow on the north side of town. It was adjacent to a small park. Steve pulled into the park and parked his bike behind a Dumpster. He looked around the Dumpster back toward the house. It was quiet. No sign of Sarah that he could see.

Sarah had left the camp on her own and probably didn't want to be found, so Steve could have ridden right past her without even seeing her. If she was in hiding, Steve was screwed. He would never find her. Not in time, anyway. Sarah could also be a zom by now, and Steve could have driven right on by without even recognizing her, possibly even clubbing her down without even knowing it. She would have blended in with the rest. Steve hoped that neither was the case.

The neighborhood was quiet. The sirens could be heard off in the distance, which meant he was far enough away that there still could be a lot of zombies in the area. He walked around a couple of dead ones lying motionless in the street. One was a civilian, the other a soldier. Steve ran to the house and looked in the windows, hoping to see Sarah or possibly her dad. He saw neither. From the backyard, Steve looked in the kitchen window. Still nothing. From the patio door, Steve could see a man inside, bearded, heavily armed, looking around the house. Possibly a looter. Strapped to a chair was Sarah's dad. Steve watched curiously. The man pulled a camera from his coat pocket and took several shots of Sarah's dad and then left through the front door.

Steve's eyes lit up. "Bounty hunter?" Steve recalled his earlier conversation with Dave. "That's where she is," Steve said to himself and ran back to his bike, being careful not to be seen. Instead of following the armed man, Steve knew right where to go and purposely went in the opposite direction. The bounty hunter heard the bike and turned just as Steve drove away.

Steve ditched his bike under a bridge and followed the creek bank. He kept low to the ground and out of sight as much as he could. He figured he had about 45 minutes before that bounty hunter arrived, provided the bounty hunter stayed on foot and didn't have a car stashed somewhere. Steve would have more time if the bounty hunter stayed on foot and ran into trouble along the way. Zoms would surely slow him down a little, and there were plenty of them between Sarah's home and the Walker farm.

Steve snuck up to the farm and hid behind whatever he could find: trees, rocks, shrubs, whatever he could fit his body behind. While hiding behind a tree, Steve scanned the area. *Nothing but a typical farmhouse*, he thought. There was nothing special about it. It looked like hundreds of others in the area. Now Steve started to doubt himself. *Maybe it's the wrong farm.* He hoped he was at the right place. Seeing no one around, Steve continued to sneak up to the house. He looked in the windows as he worked his way around to the backside. Still no one. It appeared to be vacant. He checked the doors. Locked. That was unusual being this far outside of town. Most people left their doors unlocked out here. Or maybe this farm's occupants had something to hide. Maybe he had the right place after all. Maybe the occupants were just gone. He looked up at the top of the barn. The shingles were multicolored and spelled out the name "Walker" in large letters. It was the right place, all right. Sarah had to be here somewhere, he was sure of it. There was an outside entrance to a storm shelter in the back with large wooden doors that looked like they hadn't been painted in years. They matched the house well. As Steve walked past them, he could have sworn he'd heard voices, followed by slaps, then screams. It was her. It had to be Sarah.

"What the hell?" Steve said to himself as he watched through a small cellar window. Curtains were pulled almost closed, but there was just enough room for Steve to see what he needed to.

•••

# CHAPTER 41

News of the potential bombings on U.S. soil spread across the Internet like lightning in a storm.

**Blogger Post:** I know we can't live forever but geezzzz, is this really the way it's going to happen? It's either get bit, get eaten, starve, freeze or get blown up, or all of the above! Are they seriously thinking of using nuclear bombs on our own soil?

**Comment:** Afraid so, Bud. I'm sitting in my bomb shelter right now but afraid I may be too close to the drop zone to survive. It was built back in the 40s. You know, when threats of world wars were at their peak. Everyone and their brother built one of these. I think it's more of a fallout shelter, now that I sit here and look at it. Not sure it's dug deep enough or built strong enough, to tell you the truth. Oh well, we shall see. ~ Bruce

**Comment:** Good luck, Bruce. You're probably better off there than where I'm going. I'm packing up my laptop, clothes, food, and about 1000 rounds of ammo. I'm bugging out of here. Getting the hell out of Dodge.

**Comment:** What I don't understand is why is this small town targeted for a drop zone. Shouldn't they be dropping on the big cities, with more population, more zoms. ~ Jennifer

**Comment:** Rest assured, Jen, they will be dropping there too. We're the lucky ones. We're too small for nukes. The big cities are too big not to use them. They just don't realize it yet. They think the virus was started here. Had something to do with the accident with the lab downtown. They just want to make sure the virus dies here, as well. They might nuke us just in case. You never know.

**Comment:** Lucky us.

**Comment:** Fuck us. If I ever find out who caused that accident, he's a dead man!

**Comment:** Yeah, if he's not dead already. He's probably shambling around the town laughing at his handy work, asshole.

**Comment:** The last I heard the girl (Jane Doe) just lost control and slammed into the building. She ended up dying at Atlanta General a day or two later. Then all hell broke loose. No one even knew her name.

**Comment:** I heard other stories about these damn birds spreading this virus like the bird flu, started somewhere in South America.

**Comment:** I didn't hear about that. I knew the birds where spreading something ever since they started falling from the sky, but I thought the first case started in Atlanta.

**Comment:** It started with Jane Doe. She died in Atlanta but it had something to do with the accident at the lab here.

**Comment:** Oh, who the hell knows? We're never going to learn what really happened anyway. I'm sure the government will have it all under wraps when all is said and done. Like the post says, we're all going to die, how it happens, where it happens, and when it happens is the question of the hour.

•••

# CHAPTER 42

Steve didn't see anyone but Sarah as he peered through the cellar window of the old farmhouse. She was practically dangling from the ceiling, her hands bound at the wrist with thick rope looping through a hole in the joists where the ceiling tiles had been removed. Her toes barely touched the floor, giving her arms a little relief every now and then when she could manage. By the looks of her, she wasn't managing too well.

Sarah hung there lifeless without a stitch of clothing on. Steve had an idea of how she was paying the bounty hunters for their services. Steve felt terrible to think that killing her father meant that much to her, for her to give her body to two complete strangers to do who-knows-what with.

Nevertheless, Steve had to get her out of there. He tapped on the window to get her attention. She didn't even move. Her back was turned, and her body wasn't responsive to the noise at all. He tried several more times, each time a bit louder. Still no response.

"Dammit, Sarah, wake up," Steve said quietly in frustration. Steve opened the outside cellar door. The rusty hinges creaked and moaned ever inch of the way. "Well, if someone else is here, they surely heard that," Steve said as he flung them the rest of the way open. The door crashed down on the ground. He no longer cared what sound they made. He rushed down the stairs, blade in hand. At the bottom was a set of French doors. Locked. The width of his blade was just slender enough to slither through, releasing the lock. He pushed the doors open wide and stood with his weapon at the ready. To his surprise, no attack came. No one was in the room but Sarah, swinging nude from the ceiling.

Steve ran to Sarah and quickly cut her down and gently helped her to the floor. She was conscious but barely, maybe drugged. It was too hard to tell. Who knew how long she'd been hanging there. Steve lightly slapped at her cheeks, trying to wake her.

"Sarah! Sarah, wake up! We've got to go," he said softly, only getting light moans in return.

Steve looked around for her clothes and found them piled on the sofa across the room. He started dressing her. He tried hard not to look, but with a body like Sarah's it was difficult not to. He pulled her shorts on first, then slipped her top over her head and around her shoulders. Steve's hands accidentally rubbed against her breast while he helped guide her shirt down to her waist. "Sorry," he softly apologized. Then he thought of the other night when no apology would have been needed.

"Dammit, Sarah! Why won't you wake up?" Steve didn't take the time for her bra and panties. "Hope she likes commando-style," he said as he stuffed them down his shirt while he struggled with her sandals.

By this time, Sarah was coming around.

"Sarah?"

"Steve? What's going on? Why are you here?" Her breathing was labored.

"Are you all right?"

"I think so. A little sore, maybe. What's going on?"

"Can you put these on? Quick!" Steve motioned to her sandals.

"Yeah, but …"

"No buts. I'll explain later. We have to go," whispered Steve.

Sarah finished buckling her sandals while she stared down at her wrists. They were really sore, red and bruised. "What the hell? Steve?" She looked down her shirt, then slid her hand down the front of her pants. "Steve! Where are my bra and panties?"

"I said I'll explain later."

A door slammed shut up on the floor above, and footsteps trailed across the hardwood floors. Steve grabbed Sarah's arm and pulled her through the French doors. He gently closed the doors behind them. Sarah pulled her arm away.

"You're hurting me." Steve forgot about her wrists and apologized again. Then he grabbed her arm slightly higher and practically dragged her up the stairs. Remembering the awful sound they made, Steve didn't bother closing those doors. He just took off running, pulling Sarah all the way back to his bike.

"I'm sorry I ran off, Steve," Sarah said as they neared the bike.

Steve turned to face her. "Are you hurt? Did they hurt you?"

"No, I'm fine. Just a little weak. How long was I hanging there?"

"If you don't know, I certainly don't. By the looks of your wrists, quite a while." Steve handed her the helmet. "Hop on."

They both mounted the bike, still in the ditch under the bridge, and heard a man screaming just as Steve turned the key and started the bike. They didn't even look to see who it was. They knew. Steve gunned the throttle and the bike jumped forward, leaping out of the ditch like a bat out of hell.

"Where're you going?" Sarah asked as Steve turned into town.

"To get you safe. Why? What's wrong?" Steve yelled over the engine noise.

"What about the safe zone?"

"Yeah, well, what about your father?"

"He's probably dead, Steve. That was them

326

returning."

"He's not dead, Sarah."

"He's not?"

"You'll see soon enough. Just hang on."

Sarah wrapped her arms around Steve's waist and locked her fingers tight. He gunned the throttle some more and headed into a sea of oncoming people, pets, and zombie traffic. He slalomed his way through the crowd at uncomfortable speeds, but he wasn't about to slow down. Zoms reached for them as they passed by, moaning, hissing.

"Steve stop! You're going too fast. Please slow down!" Sarah begged.

Her request went ignored for at least two or three more blocks, when Steve pulled into the garage where he'd worked. He pulled the bike in the open bay and hit the button on the wall to close the door. Nothing happened. He looked around and noticed the power appeared to be out. He pulled the cord hanging from the garage door, and the door began its journey downward, coming to a crashing halt.

Steve turned to face Sarah while the door made its descent.

"What the hell is going on, chick?" he asked. "Do you have some sort of death wish?" Steve, now in a somewhat safer place realized that he was furious and wanted answers.

Sarah didn't answer and shied away.

"Sarah ... Why? Why did you leave? And why alone?"

Sarah didn't know what to say, and words didn't come easy. "I had to know."

"Know what, Sarah? You could have gotten killed or

worse. They could have raped you and then killed you."
Again, Sarah said nothing and turned away.

"Sarah, did they hurt you?" Steve asked.

"I don't know, Steve. I don't remember much at all. We were just talking."

"Talking? About what?"

"Me, my father, and what had happened. I told them I didn't have any money. Then they offered me a drink, and that's it."

"What's it?"

"That's all I remember. I must have passed out."

"They must have tainted the drink, stripped you, and tied you up after that."

"After, yeah, that's it. I remember one saying they would be back 'after' and work something out." She paused. "I didn't agree to anything, Steve. You have to believe me." She paused, then changed the subject. "Where are my panties?"

"Oh, here." Steve dug deep in his shirt and handed them to her, along with her bra.

"Thanks." She grabbed them, almost embarrassed.

"I didn't look. Well, I tried not to."

"Yeah right, Steve. That's okay. Thanks for coming to my rescue."

"Sure. Did they say they were going to do something?"

"I assume they were going to take care of my father and then come back for me."

"I understand."

"I don't think you do, Steve. I told you I didn't agree to anything."

"Do you think your dad would have wanted you to risk your life checking on him? There's nothing you can do, Sarah. Nothing!"

"I just can't leave him like that, Steve. It's not right. I shouldn't have left him in the first place."

"You did what you had to do, Sarah, what he would have wanted you to do."

"Now what?" she asked with tears in her eyes.

Steve wrapped an arm around her. "Well, now we have less than four days to get about a hundred miles away from here, or we'll be joining the dead ourselves. Your dad is not going to make it out of here, Sarah. The bomb will take care of that."

"What if it doesn't, Steve? What if it just injures him more? I can't let that happen. I need to put him out of his misery."

Steve paced back and forth in frustration, raking his fingers through his hair as he thought. He slammed his fist down hard on the workbench in the back of the shop. "Fine, Sarah. Then we can go?"

"Yes."

"You promise me that you won't give me any flack and we can leave right after we take care of him?"

"Yeah, Steve. I promise. What are we going to do?"

"You're going to do absolutely nothing but stay put. I'll be back."

"You have to take me with you, Steve. I can't just stay

here."

"Yes you can, and you will, even if I have to tie you up." He paused and thought about what he'd just said. "Sorry, it will only take me 45 minutes, an hour tops. Then I'll be back for you."

"Remember what happened the last time you said that, Steve? You never came back."

Steve closed his eyes and took in a deep breath, holding it in for a few seconds before blowing all of the air out of his cheeks as he exhaled. "Fine! You win. Let's go. We are running out of time."

A smile lit across Sarah's face as she raced over to the bike. "I'm ready," she said as she swung her leg over the seat.

Steve sighed and stomped over to manually lift the garage door up. While doing so, he looked out the window and abruptly caught the door and quickly yanked it back to the ground, slowing it so it would hit the floor with a soft bump. "We've got trouble." Little did he know that the door stopped well before hitting the ground. It landed on a legless zom who had crawled his way under at the most opportune time.

Steve lifted the door back up a couple of feet off the zom and jumped on the door using his body weight to help bring the door back down, hoping to crush the zom's skull. But the zom was too far in, and the door only landed on its shoulders, bringing the door to a soft, squishy stop.

The zom reached up at Steve, jaw opened wide, snapping at the air like a crock. Steve grabbed the handle of a four-ton hydraulic jack and cracked the zombie's head wide open with it. While he was doing that, more of them were trying to crawl under the door. He bashed in as many heads as he could, but as soon as he kicked one dead zom away, another would fill the gap. It was only a matter of time before they would all make their way under the door.

More and more gathered outside the door. Bodies pushed on the glass with all their weight, making the door sag in the middle.

"Sarah, get out of here," Steve yelled. "Upstairs! Go! Now!" Steve drew his cutter and started slicing the zoms as they attempted to push their way through, but there were too many.

Steve pulled his 9mm from his belt and started shooting. Most of the bullets hit their targets dead on, while a few went astray, ricocheting off the garage floor and breaking some of the glass windows in the garage door. The walkers quickly filled the holes with their hands, arms, and heads. They stuck themselves in, unable to pull themselves back out. Jagged glass dug its way into the decaying flesh, locking them in a jagged-glass stockade. This ended up being a good thing, as the weight of their bodies hanging there held the door down tight against the zoms laying dead on the floor. The gap between the door and the pavement was dammed up with dead zoms.

The gunshots brought zoms in from blocks away, even pulling a few away from the sirens blaring up on the poles. Soon the garage was swarming with them, trapping Steve and Sarah inside.

Steve stopped shooting to reload his gun and heard a

heart-wrenching scream, then a scuffle, followed by a couple of thuds. He turned just in time to watch Sarah's body tumble lifelessly down the staircase onto the garage floor.

"Sarah!" Steve yelled as he rushed to her side. He held her in his arms at the bottom of the stairway with a strange feeling of being watched. He angled his head to look up the staircase. He couldn't believe what he saw. It was a soldier dressed in full BDUs standing at the top of the stairs with a pistol at his side, but not drawn.

"Hey, asshole, what did you do to Sarah? Jackass! She better be all right or it's you and me."

The soldier just stood there moaning and edging closer to the first step.

"I'm talking to you, bud, get your ass down here and give me a hand, will ya?" Steve got no reply, just a few light moans. Steve took a better look and saw that the soldier was no longer a soldier but a zom in military garb.

The soldier's skin was blemished and grey, covered with open sores. His eyes had no pupils and were solid as a glass marble, milky white, webbed as if they had been cracked hard against cement. His mouth hung open. It exposed a set of carnassials only dentists dreamt of. Steve had never seen such long, jagged teeth on a human being before. But this was no human. It was a wild beast. It panted and growled like a rabid dog, frothing at the mouth.

Steve didn't want to move Sarah in fear of broken bones, but he had no other choice. He couldn't see how the zombie at the top of the stairway could possibly negotiate descending the stairs. Going up, maybe, but doubtful. Down, definitely not. Going downstairs would take far too much coordination.

Deja vu sank in. "Sarah, sweetheart, you have to wake up. Sarah, we have to move! We have to move now!" Steve pleaded, trying hard to coax her into consciousness. The zom's right foot was reaching the ledge of the first step and was about to take the plunge. Steve grabbed Sarah by her shirt collar and pant leg and dragged her across the shop's floor and out of the zombie's path as smoothly as he could. Just then, the zombified soldier came tumbling down, head over heels, arms and legs flailing in the air.

The zom just missed both of them as it landed hard in a clump of flesh and bones. Steve got to his feet, pulled his blade, and swung at the zom now lying on the floor and reaching in his direction. The blade cleanly cut off a hand projecting it 10 feet or more before coming to rest across the room. The fingers were still reaching, opening, then closing, and opening again. With each gesture, the hand crept closer and closer to Steve as if it was walking in his direction on its fingertips.

When the hand got too close, Steve kicked it away, hoping to send it sliding across the room. Steve's boot made good contact, but the hand clamped down around the end of his boot and held on tight. He kicked some more, trying to shake it loose but it seemed the hand tightened its grip even more. He could feel the pressure squeezing his toes as if they were in a vice.

The zom, too made headway, advancing toward Steve. Pulling his body closer, the jaw snapped in Steve's direction like a turtle, but its head was quickly met with Steve's blade crashing down upon its skull, splitting it wide open, brains visible. Black blood and brain matter oozed from the gash in its head, pooling wide on the tiled floor beneath Steve's feet. The hand instantly released its grip as if it were still attached to its body, falling lifelessly into the sea of blood.

Steve took a deep breath and rushed back to Sarah's side. He examined her body for bites and scratches. He found a few scrapes but no bites. *Thank God*, he thought. He didn't know if the scrapes were from falling against the walls, tumbling down the stairs, or from the zombie itself. Sarah moaned softly as she started to regain consciousness but quickly drifted back out again.

Steve was awake all through the night, comforting Sarah as she rested her head on his lap. He covered her with his shirt and stroked her hair and back. Sitting with his back up against the wall, he sat and listened to the moans outside. He didn't take his eyes off the bay door. Not once. Even though the bay door was jammed tight with dead zoms, he never felt comfortable with the door opening like that with all the zoms looming around.

Steve started humming "For What It's Worth" by Buffalo Springfield, to occupy his mind —

*There's somethin' happenin' here*
*What it is ain't exactly clear*
*There's a man with a gun over there*
*Tellin' me, I got to beware*

*I think it's time we stop, children, what's that sound?*
*Everybody look what's going down*

*There's battle lines being drawn*
*Nobody's right if everybody's wrong*
*Young people speakin' their minds*
*Gettin' so much resistance from behind*

*I think it's time we stop, hey, what's that sound?*
*Everybody look what's going down*

*What a field day for the heat*
*(Hmm, hmm, hmm)*
*A thousand people in the street*
*(Hmm, hmm, hmm)*
*Singing songs and carrying signs*
*(Hmm, hmm, hmm)*
*Mostly say, hooray for our side*
*(Hmm, hmm, hmm)*

•••

The only light they had was from the moon. He could barely see it through the glass in the door, as it passed in and out of the smoke trails from the town's fires.

The next day, Sarah was still unconscious, and the zombies were still shambling around outside. They had stopped advancing against the bay door but were still a threat, simply by sheer numbers. Steve continued to sit still, watching Sarah breathe, and whispered to her to wake up. He was worried. Worried about her. Worried about getting out of there. More importantly, he was worried about time. Time was ticking away like a bomb.

One good thing about being so close to the pole with the siren was that they probably wouldn't even realize when the end came, when the bombs went off. They probably wouldn't feel a thing. Sarah moaned.

"Sarah, come on, baby. Wake up, babe. We have to go, baby please." Steve begged, but got no response. Not for hours. Besides, they weren't going to be going anywhere soon. Even if she awoke now, there was little hope of making it to the safety zone before the bombs hit. "Hell, we'd be lucky to get out of here in time," Steve said under his breath. *It's better this way,* he thought. *Better than getting eaten by zombies, anyway. And if she stays unconscious, that would be even better yet.* Steve was giving up. He slid down from the wall, spooned Sarah, and drifted off to sleep.

Steve slept. He slept hard. Sarah, on the other hand, finally awakened. She kept still so she wouldn't wake him. She could see the zoms outside, but she could also hear something else. She could hear a barking in the distance, which was getting closer by the minute. It soon sounded as if it were just outside the building.

"A dog," Sarah said to herself as if it had just registered to her what she was hearing.

"It's a dog, Steve. Wake up, Steve. I hear a dog." The moans were still there as well. "Steve, the zoms, they're going to get the dog. We have to …" Sarah was interrupted by frantic barking that also woke Steve from his deep sleep.

"Sarah, you're awake. How're you feeling?"

"Sore. What about the dog?"

336

"Dog? Sarah, we don't have a dog." Just then, the barking outside registered. "A dog! Stay here, don't move." Steve got to his feet and ran to the window. He watched as a small black and white dog danced around, moving in and out of the crowd of zoms, and doing it with finesse. Zombies tried grabbing the dog from all angles, but none were even close to catching him.

"Sarah, can you walk?" Steve walked back to Sarah and helped her to her feet.

"I don't know, Steve." She stood but favored her right leg. "Yeah, I think so." She applied a little pressure on her foot and fell straight to the floor. "Mmm, maybe not."

"Damn!"

"Sorry, Steve. What's up?"

"That dog. He's a stray. He showed up almost every day at the shop. I would always share my lunch with him. He was nothing but skin and bones when he first came around. You could count every rib. He could be our ticket out of here."

"Sorry." Sarah stared at the floor. "We are going to die here, aren't we Steve?"

"I'll be honest, Sarah, it's not looking good. But I haven't given up all hope yet." Steve looked out the window for the dog. He hoped he could coax the dog inside and possibly use him as a decoy later, but there was no sign of the dog when he looked back out.

"Damn, where did he go?" Steve said.

"The zoms probably got him."

"No, I really don't think so, Sarah. He's a survivor,

like us. He's been through a lot. I think he's all right, probably just moved on. I don't see any of them eating anything right now. They're back to aimless shambling again."

"What are we going to do, Steve?"

"Well, for one thing, we're going to get you well."

"But what about the bombs? Are we going to be all right here?"

"We'll be just fine, Sarah. Don't you worry." Steve held Sarah in his arms while Sarah lay on the floor. He looked at the stairs and thought she would be much more comfortable in the bed upstairs but didn't think he should carry her up there. "Be right back, Sarah," he said as he gently lifted her head off his lap and onto the floor. He ran up the stairs, skipping every other step. Moments later, he was at the top of the staircase about to send a mattress tumbling down, followed by sheets, blankets, and pillows. He took a moment to make the bed up on the floor and helped Sarah onto it.

"Thanks, Steve." She said a short prayer and drifted off to sleep.

Steve, on the other hand, couldn't sleep. He had far too much on his mind. *What am I going to do? Think, dammit!*

Time was running short, and for the life of him, Steve couldn't remember how many days it had been since he'd left camp, since he'd picked up the flier in the city. *It's been two days – no, three – since we left camp. That leaves … not enough time to get to the safe zone, that's what it leaves.* He thought, feeling hopeless to say the least, but he decided not to tell

Sarah. She'd been through enough. She would never know what hit her. Sarah slept the rest of the day and another full night.

*Wait a minute.* He paused, thinking to himself. *I remember a rich guy who brought his BMW in for needless repairs all the time. He always talked about 'the end of the world' and how it would be soon. He was big on prepping. If I can find his home, maybe, just maybe, he has a bomb shelter he wouldn't mind sharing.* Sarah awoke.

"I'll be right back, Sarah."

"Where are you going?"

"I have to find an invoice."

"An invoice? Steve is that really necessary? Now?"

Steve explained the idea to Sarah. "Do you really think he will let us in? What does he do?"

"Don't know, Sarah, but I'm afraid we are running out of options. He was some sort of doctor, if I remember right. He knows me quite well and is a pretty darn good tipper."

It wasn't long before Steve came out from the office with an invoice in his hand and a smile on his face – a rarity nowadays.

"You found it?" Sarah asked, smiling back.

"Yes, and …" he paused. "Dammit, no." His smile flipped upside down.

"Well, what do you mean? You either did or you didn't."

"We are going to have to do a little research on him, I'm afraid. All I have is a phone number, no address. I know he's not too far from here. I see him driving around town all the time."

Sarah got her cell phone out and searched online. Surprisingly the cell service was still up. When trying to place calls, a fast busy signal indicated that all circuits were busy, but she was still able to get online. "It says here he worked out of Atlanta General, Steve."

"Really? Damn, I hope he didn't have to work the day everything went down."

"Checking." She tapped through a few screens and found a page dedicated to all who died at the hospital during the siege. "Shit. He's dead."

"Dammit! Keep searching. We need that address."

"Do you have his plate number?"

"Yeah, why?"

"Well, let's just say I've looked over Daddy's shoulder more than a few times when he was logging in to Central." Sarah's father was retired from the police force.

"Sarah," Steve said with disapproval in his voice. "You're frickin' awesome!"

"How else could I check out who was safe to date around here?"

"You didn't ..."

"Yeah, I did. Your record wasn't the cleanest, by the way, but what the hell. Sometimes you have to give people a chance, right?" Steve just smiled.

"Give me a minute and get something to write with, will ya?" Sarah asked.

By the time Steve came back with a pencil and paper,

Sarah was reading off an address. Steve quickly jotted it down. "Let's hope this is his main address and not a small office."

"Already checked that out, Steve. MapQuested it. It's in a residential area about 14 miles from here."

"You're awesome again, Sarah."

Steve made a splint for Sarah's leg using a wooden yardstick and a lot of duct tape. He also grabbed a push broom and cut it to length for a crutch. It worked. She could at least get around a little, and the bristles from the broom added some comfort. She was able to get out of bed and walk to the bathroom on her own with the splint on, so that was an improvement.

They both were awakened early the next morning by more barking. "Sarah." Steve paused. "Are you awake, Sarah? Hear that?" asked Steve.

"Yeah, sounds like he's back."

"Now's our chance. We may not get another. Do you feel up to it?"

"No, but we must."

"You can do it, Sarah. I know you can."

They quickly climbed out of bed. Sarah hopped around collecting her things and stuffing them in a pack. Steve prepared the bike.

"How are we going to get out, Steve? The back is full of zoms, too."

Steve positioned the bike as far back as he could and pointed it in the direction of one of the bay doors. All the zoms piled at the door were dead, and when the time was right, he planned on plowing straight through.

"Where's the dog? Do you see him?" Sarah asked.

"The barking is coming from over there." Steve pointed to the right. "But it's getting louder, so he's getting closer. Look there!" Steve pointed his cutter straight in front of the doors.

"Where, Steve? I don't see him. There're too many of them."

"Look between their legs. There, over there." Sure enough, the black and white dog was back, antagonizing the zoms like it was a game he was playing. A risky one, one he couldn't afford to loose.

"That one almost got him, Steve. Oh my gosh, I can't look. He's trapped."

"He's not trapped, Sarah, look. It looks like he's trying to corral them together like sheep. This is amazing." The dog continued his magic, getting the attention of more zoms by the minute. Soon all attention was on the border collie. With every roaming pass the dog made in front of the zoms, he led them that much further away from the building. Back and forth he would go, zig then zag, in and out of the zoms' reach, barking all the way.

"They are following his sound," Steve said.

"How did a dog figure that out, Steve?"

"He's a smart dog, and it looks like he's returning a favor."

The border collie clearly knew what he was doing. Steve and Sarah couldn't believe what had just happened. "Who sent the dog here?" Sarah wondered. No one knew they were here. "It's like my prayer was answered. God certainly works in mysterious ways," said Sarah.

Steve quietly and slowly pushed the bay door up. It was heavy with all the dead zoms hanging through the broken glass, but as it lifted off the ground the zombies shed their excess weight leaving body parts dangling behind. Skin stretched to their limits snapping like rubber-bands as strips of flesh hung like curtains from the broken glass stockades.

The dog led the pack of zoms away from the doors as if it were trained to do just that. As soon as the zombies had strayed far enough from the door, Steve started the bike's motor. The noise from the bike brought the attention of a couple of stragglers in the back of the group who slowly swung their frail bodies around in their direction. Steve was not concerned with two or three zoms.

"Hang on!" Steve hollered as he gunned the throttle. The tires spun on the slippery shop floor. The bike's tires cried out a razor-sharp squeal before it gripped the floor, thrusting the bike forward. They hit the pile of dead zoms hard, throwing the front tire in the air. Steve hit the gas and pulled up on the handlebars. The back tire hit the dead zom's skull hard, which forced the front tire to crash down on the dead. He gunned the throttle again and they both held on for dear life. Like a bull in the rodeo, the bike bucked wildly out of control, somehow coming to rest on flat pavement. Steve had no idea how, but he managed to ride it out, without dumping the bike. Once clear, he hightailed it out of the parking lot, leaving the mob of zoms behind.

"Wait, Steve. What about the dog?"

"He'll be fine, Sarah. He obviously knows what he's doing."

Sarah looked back over her shoulder to see if she could see the dog. Her view was somewhat blocked by a wall of zombies, some heading in their direction while the majority of them were still following the dog. She mouthed the words, "Thank you," knowing very well the dog wouldn't hear or understand her, but somehow Sarah felt comfort thinking that the message would somehow be conveyed.

A moment later, the dog appeared out in the open and looked her way. Seeing that they were safely away, the dog hightailed it out of there himself, leaving the zombies to shamble in it's dust.

"He took off. He just took off. He looked at us, then took off."

"He did his job, Sarah."

Steve motored away, putting some distance between them and the walking dead. Before he knew it, he was pulling down Sarah's street.

"Are you up for this?" Steve asked. Sarah was a little confused. She didn't even recognize the street where she'd grown up and lived for 30-odd years. It had changed so much after the military had gone through.

"They certainly didn't clean up their mess when the left, did they?" Sarah really wasn't questioning anybody. "I'm as ready as I will ever be, Steve."

"Wait here. Let me check it out first." Steve dismounted the bike. He'd hidden it behind the Dumpster at the park across the street again. He stayed low to the ground and made his way up to Sarah's house. Steve, unusually nervous, didn't know what to expect or how Sarah was going to react, but it had to be done and it had to be done quickly. They were out of time. They had to get clear of this town in less than two days.

Steve reached the house and looked in the windows. Sarah's dad was still tied to the chair in the middle of the room. His head swayed back and forth, jaws snapping at the air.

*Still alive. Damn,* Steve thought aloud. He had hoped that the bounty hunters had finished him off. It would have saved him from doing it himself. *Sarah's going to hate me forever.*

He didn't see anyone else around. It was quiet, almost too quiet. Steve considered just going in and finishing this, but he didn't want Sarah to be mad, so he waved her in.

Sarah limped her way across the street and arrived at Steve's side. "What do you want to do, Sarah?" he asked. "Your father is in the living room tied to a chair. Do you want me to go in and take care of this? Because, if you do, I have no problem with it. I'll go in and be back out in three minutes. Then we can be on our way."

"I have to do it, Steve."

"Oh no, Sarah, you don't have to do this. No one is expecting you to do this. Your father wouldn't want you to. Let me do it, Sarah. I promise I'll do it right. It will be quick, and he won't even know it happened."

"No, Steve, it has to be me. I would want him to do it to me if I'd turned."

345

"Minutes ago, you were okay with complete strangers doing it. Now?"

"That was then; this is now. I can't ask you to do this, Steve. I don't want to think of this every time I look at you."

Steve reached for Sarah and gave her a hug. While they hugged, Sarah noticed Steve's blade lying on the ground beside him. She reached down for it, and when the hug broke apart, Sarah pushed Steve away. Off guard, which was unusual for him, he landed on his ass.

Sarah with a sudden rush of adrenalin, and forgetting that her leg was on splints, made a bee-line to the front door of the house with Steve's blade in her hand. Steve, surprised by Sarah's sudden burst, could do nothing to stop her. He got to his feet just when he heard the front door crash open.

Sarah kicked at the door, blade in hand, ready to do what she went there to do. After weeks of mental preparation, she now stood just eight feet away from her father and just two feet away from the barrel of an M-4 assault rifle pointed straight at her.

"Well, well, well. If it isn't Sarah! I thought you might show up here," the man with the gun said. It was one of the bounty hunters.

Steve stopped dead in his tracks, back hugging the wall as soon as he'd heard the man's voice.

Startled, Sarah let out a little yelp.

"I believe you owe me something."

"I owe you nothing. You didn't do the job!"

"I didn't? Oh, minor detail." He turned the M-4 toward her father moaning in the chair and pulled the trigger, sending a series of bullets his way. The bullets entered the back of her father's skull, exiting out the front, taking most of his face with it. Blood and brain matter splattered the opposite wall.

"You asshole!" she screamed, charging him with the blade swinging, blocking the rifle from taking aim at her.

Steve heard the shots and barged through the front door, his 9 mm drawn. Sarah had the man pinned up against the wall with the blade. She was too close for the bounty hunter to bring the M-4 around to shoot her, but Steve wasn't. Sarah, covering most of the bounty hunter's body with her own, left Steve with only one option. A headshot. He took it.

The M-4 dropped to the floor as the man's body fell limp, sliding down the wall and leaving a streak of blood behind. Sarah turned and saw Steve standing there with the 9 mm pointed in her direction, smoke still curling from the barrel.

"Are you frickin' crazy?" she asked.

"A little."

Steve holstered the gun. Sarah dropped the blade to the floor and ran to her father's side. Steve met her there, blocking her from touching him. He held her tight.

"I'm so sorry, Sarah," he said while comforting her as best he could. He paused a moment, staring down at his blade on the floor. "Sarah, I don't mean to rush you, but we really need to go."

"Just a couple more minutes, please," she asked.

"I'm sorry, Sarah, but weren't there two bounty

hunters? We don't know where the second bounty hunter is. We have to go now."

"I love you, Daddy," she mouthed to her father and broke away from Steve. "Let's go," she said, picking the blade up off the floor.

"Um."

"What?"

Steve held out his hand. "The blade?"

"Oh, all right." Sarah handed Steve the blade and picked up the M-4. "This is better anyway."

Steve just smiled. "It looks good on you too." He bent down and grabbed the spare clips that were attached to the bounty hunter's belt, along with a pack that the man had been carrying.

•••

# CHAPTER 43

**Blog Post**

"Is this the end of times?"

The black plague strikes again with the Sign of the Beast. In the year 1346, the Black Plague (Bubonic) spread across the Earth, killing more than 43 million people worldwide in just a few years. That all started 666 years ago, a familiar number to both Christians and non.

It's baaaack! And it's time it finished what it had started.

It may not be labeled "the Bubonic Plague" this time, but what a coincidence folks – 666, the Sign of the Beast. Could this be it? Could this really be the end of times?

According to what I'm seeing right now out my upstairs window, it may be. I'm watching an older man, probably in his mid to late 70s, preaching high above a crowded street below. He's standing inside a cherry picker, in a bucket raised 40 feet in the air. He's preaching the end of times, and he appears to have a following.

Down below, standing in the crowd, is a tall man in a tie-dyed shirt. He's sporting a tall rainbow Afro and carrying a large "peace" sign over his head. There are others with signs, as well. Some say "repent" and "Jesus Saves," and a few just have the number 666 painted on them.

In the distance, I can see more people coming to join the group. Except when they get closer, I can see that they aren't people at all. They are zombies, a group of maybe 20 or so shambling in the crowd's direction.

Why isn't anyone moving? Why are they just standing there? I opened my window and yelled out to the crowd. I warned them the zombies are coming and, in fact, they were almost upon them, but no one moved. I know they could hear me, but they still didn't move. Then the group starts singing. It is a familiar church hymn, "When we all get to Heaven, what a day of rejoicing that will be; when we all see Jesus, we'll sing and shout the victory." Oh, this isn't right, folks. What are you doing? "Run," I scream, but they don't listen. They're only listening to the old man up high, not God, but the man in the bucket. The zombies came and they picked them off one by one. People in the group didn't run, they didn't scream, and they didn't even fight back. They just kept singing, and when the song was finished, so were they.

The old man in the bucket showed no remorse, he did nothing to stop the madness. He just continued to preach his sermon from high above.

The zombies were having a feast out my front window. It's like the people just gave up or maybe gave in to their faith. It reminded me so much of Jim Jones and his followers, years ago.

It was very disturbing, to say the least, and maybe they were right. Maybe it is the end days. It certainly was for them.

Until next time, people ... If there is one!

•••

# CHAPTER 44

Lucky for Steve and Sarah, people generally didn't enter homes occupied by zombies. Sarah's home was one of them and, therefore, was never looted. All of its contents were where they had been the day she'd last left for work. That morning, she'd never looked back.

Sarah hobbled to her room on one foot. "Sarah, where are you going?" Steve asked. "We have to go!"

"Let me grab a few things," she hollered from down the hallway.

Sarah hopped room to room and filled a couple of pillowcases with food, medicine, and some personal items, including some family photos from her bedroom. She also grabbed some of her favorite clothes, undergarments, and her

Kindle. Sarah loved to read.

Steve helped Sarah with the pillowcases and secured them to the bike. He then helped her onto the back of the bike. She wrapped her arms around Steve's waist, and they were en route to his place. He hoped to do the same there – retrieve any items they could take with them.

Steve's home, unlike Sarah's, had been broken into, but it looked as though the looters hadn't finished the job. They might have been interrupted or moved on to bigger and better things. Most everything was still intact, just spread everywhere as if the looters had been looking for something in particular.

A thought quickly came to Steve's mind. "Oh no," he said when he noticed keys were missing from the key holder in the kitchen. Steve's heart sank instantly in his chest. He ran to the garage. Sure enough, Steve's prize possession was gone. Someone had stolen his GTO, the car he had spent years refurbishing, painstakingly restoring every piece to factory condition. Steve fell to his knees with tears in his eyes. "Why?"

Sarah limped up behind Steve and tried to comfort him. While doing so, she panned across the room and admired her surroundings. Like most of his female companions, Sarah had never been to Steve's home, and her eyes took in as much as they could.

*So this is Steve,* she thought as she broadened her view into 360 degrees, turning her head almost like an owl.

Steve's garage was not only his garage, but it also served as his living room and workout room. A couch backed up to the drive, facing a wall where a large flat-screen TV had once been mounted. A large bracket and some wires dangled where the TV had once hung. That's all that was left. His bathroom jutted off from there, leaving his kitchen and bedroom as separate spaces.

"Nice place, Steve. It's very ... unique. I've never seen a layout like it. It reminds me of a TV show back in the '70s. I can't remember the name."

"Vega$, starring Robert Urich as Dan Tanna," Steve replied.

"Yeah, that's it!"

"I get that all the time, but thanks. Trust me, it looks a whole lot better with my GTO parked in the middle of it. At least they closed the garage door when they left so zoms wouldn't get in." Steve was grateful for that.

Pressed for time, Steve forced his emotions back where they came from. "Sarah, grab anything you think we'll need and pack it. Only the necessities though, OK?"

Steve started gathering a few things himself and stuffed a large duffle bag with a handgun – a small backup 9 mm pistol – a couple of knives, a pistol crossbow, ammo, arrows, a machete, a couple of shirts, a pair of binoculars, a pair of jeans, socks, underwear, and his laptop computer. *Everything else can stay,* he thought. Sarah helped herself to some personal-hygiene items, then raided the kitchen. Steve was the king of junk food – chips of all kinds, cookies, and Sarah's favorite, Hostess Twinkies®. She grabbed what she had room for while wondering how Steve kept himself fit. She filled a couple of army-surplus canteens with water. They had taken the canteens off a couple of downed soldiers lying in the streets. Sad, but the soldiers no longer had any use for them.

Sarah couldn't help but notice Steve's extensive book collection as she walked past a pair of bookcases. She hadn't pictured him as the reading type. *Finally, something in common besides sex.* She smiled thinking about it. She took note of some of the titles by snapping a couple of close-up pictures with her phone. At the last minute, she grabbed three thick books off his nightstand and stuffed them in a fanny pack and strapped it on. *Hmm ... probably hasn't finished reading these yet.*

The bike was finally loaded. A large duffle bag stuffed full of supplies and weapons draped over the handlebars and came to rest over the windshield. Steve quickly installed a hard case that mounted to the top of the rear fender for more storage. Sarah stocked it mostly with kitchen items. She slipped the straps to the backpack over the rear of the hard case, opposite the tailpipe. It made for a makeshift, single-sided rear saddlebag. Steve outfitted himself in some leather riding gear: jacket, gloves, leg guards, elbow pads, and a helmet, and told Sarah to do the same.

Steve also took a little time to modify the bat and cutter blade with leather straps. Finally, he retired the cutter arm to the duffle bag, exchanging if for the machete.

Steve swung the machete around to get a feel for it. The weight and balance was quite a bit different from the cutter arm. *Much lighter. Smooth. It glides through the air.* He ran his thumb along the blade. *Sharp. Nice.*

*Next stop, hopefully the doctor's place about fourteen miles outside of town.* They both mounted the bike.

"Hold on, Sarah. I'll only be a second." Steve quickly dismounted and ran back into the kitchen, closing the door behind him. A few seconds later, he was back on the bike. "You ready? We need to get going," Steve said loudly over the roar of the bike's motor.

Sarah nodded while strapping her helmet on. "Ready."

"It's going to be a rough ride, you know."

"I know. We can do it." Sarah gave him a kiss for luck.

Before exiting his home, Steve had looked out the front windows and had seen a half-dozen zombies shambling toward his driveway. He lifted the garage door with one hand, never leaving the bike. He backed the bike up with his legs. The zombies turned and started shambling his way. Steve revved the motor a couple of times. The zoms began to filter into the garage one by one. Steve handed Sarah the bat and strapped the machete around his wrist and let it dangle alongside the bike.

Two zoms were almost upon them. Steve gunned the throttle and released the clutch. The back tire spun wildly, creating a high screeching sound before the tire gripped the smooth surface. The bike jumped forward and passed by them in seconds.

"It's all yours," Steve said as he left his home, motoring down the driveway without shutting the garage door behind them. Sarah managed to club one zombie down with the bat as they left.

Steve didn't look back until they reached the end of his street and were clear of imminent danger. He stopped the bike and looked back at his home, a good block away. Sarah hugged him from behind, resting her chin on the back of his shoulder, thinking it was going to be another sentimental moment. Besides seeing him teary-eyed at the loss of his car, she had never seen that side of him before. Her assumption couldn't have been more wrong.

Out of nowhere, Steve said, "Adios." It was just before his house exploded into a million pieces. A ball of flame projected 60 feet into the air, blowing the roof completely off the house and taking the nearby zoms with it. Sarah jumped and gasped before seeing a smile appear on Steve's face.

-

Riding through Bear Creek was like riding through a ghost town. Most of the houses were left empty, some burning to the ground and the streets were relatively clear of people. The rubble left behind from the military made most of the roads impassable by car and difficult, at best, by bike. The overpasses and bridges had long since been taken out in the military's efforts to trap the dead within. The majority of the zombies still hung around the poles with the sirens. That helped make some travel possible, keeping the majority of them spellbound.

Gunfire could still be heard throughout the town, echoing off the buildings and through the alleyways. It was hard to judge how far off they really were or the direction they came from.

Sarah became Steve's eyes, while Steve mainly concentrated on the road immediately before them. He avoided the debris and potholes as best he could. Some potholes were big enough to swallow the whole bike with them on it, and then some. Needless to say, travel was tedious, but Sarah was quick to point out people, zombies, and trouble. Not necessarily in that order.

"Five zoms at two o'clock. Three Peeps left at seven," were just a couple of the commands Steve readily heard over his shoulder. "Peeps" meant people of undetermined disposition, friendly or foe. If she knew which, she would just skip to a more accurate account. Most peeps, when seen, just turned their backs and dove for cover, likewise not knowing Steve and Sarah's intentions. Given a choice, Steve would trust a zombie over any foe any day. Zoms were predictable; foes could be deceptive.

"Two zombies, one o'clock," Sarah called out into Steve's right ear. Steve glanced up from the road just long enough to see the zombies' locations and assess his options. There were no other clear paths to take, so he and Sarah would have to take them out and go through.

Steve motored along. "Bowling, split right," he yelled back to Sarah, which meant Steve was going to drive between the two targets. Sarah got ready. Steve switched hands and gripped the handle to the machete with his left hand. He drove the bike between them. He swung the machete, making contact and decapitating one of them. The zom fell to the ground. Sarah swung the bat at the zom on the right, but her swing came up short, almost throwing her off the bike from the momentum. Steve reached back and grabbed her leg.

"Sorry, missed," she said.

"That's all right, Sarah. We don't need to kill all of them. The bombs will take care of that. We just need to plow through."

Up ahead stood a lone zom, standing right in the middle of the path. There was no good way around him. A large pile of debris lay to the left and a hole large enough to swallow a bus to the right. Looking down into the pit, Steve saw more zoms, trapped like ants in an ant trap, desperately trying to climb their way out but failing miserably.

Steve could see the large zom, panting like a dog in the middle of the path, from nearly two blocks away. Steve stopped the bike and grabbed the pistol-grip crossbow from his bag. He loaded it with an arrow and placed the other arrows nearby. He checked his holstered handgun for ammo. Another group of zombies lingered farther up the road and off to the right. Steve didn't want to make any noise or he would have just shot the damn thing in the road with the handgun. This one was much too large to risk going up against face to face on the bike.

Steve got the bike rolling with minimal sound and rode within 20 feet of the large zombie, who stomped closer as the bike approached. His moaning was nothing but a deep growl, a rattling noise within his throat. Steve pulled in the clutch and glided in, 15 feet away, then 10 feet.

"Shoot it!" yelled Sarah. At eight feet, Steve aimed the crossbow at its head. At five feet, he pulled the trigger. He didn't want to miss. The arrow struck the front of the zom's forehead, stopping with its point sticking out the back. The zombie didn't know what had hit him. It just stood there dazed, rocking back and forth on the balls of his feet, then fell flat on his back. His head hit the pavement hard enough to send the arrow back though his frontal lobe again. Steve slammed on the brakes to avoid rolling over the body. He dismounted the bike to retrieve his arrow and stepped on the zombie's head to pull the arrow completely out. He then dragged the carcass off the path to the edge of the nearby pit. Steve kicked the body over the edge. The large zombie rolled downhill like a huge boulder, knocking several zoms over as it reached the bottom of the giant ant slope.

Steve turned to Sarah. "We have company."

The group of zoms heard the big fellow fall and was now interested in what was going on. They started shambling Steve's way.

Steve remounted his bike and off they went, well before the mob arrived. One mile down the road, Sarah spotted a group of armed men at the corner. "Foe left!" she yelled.

Steve slowed the bike and looked for another route. Avoiding trouble was the key now, anything to better their chances of finding that doctor's home in time.

The gunmen saw Steve and spread out in flanking positions. "Shit! This is bad," Steve said as he turned his bike and jumped on the throttle. "Ambush! Get your head down!" Gunfire rained down upon them, peppering the ground and striking the bike several times.

"Ahhh! I'm hit," screamed Sarah, holding her side. The bullet nearly knocking Sarah off the bike, but she held on. Steve could feel more weight on his back as Sarah fell against him.

"How bad? You all right?" Winded she didn't answer. "Hang on!" Steve felt her fingers grip him tighter around his waist, so he knew she was still with him and responsive, but he also felt she was favoring one side and he feared she might fall off the bike.

"Hang in there, Sarah. Safety ahead." Steve had no idea if there was safety ahead or not. All he could see in front of him were bumps in the broken-up road, bumps he tried even harder now to avoid.

As soon as Steve felt he was far enough away from those thugs, he found an open garage door to pull into. Steve grabbed a blanket out of the duffle bag, spread it on the floor, and eased Sarah down off the bike and laid her on it. He closed the garage door and locked it.

Looking back, he saw that Sarah was still conscious, but she was holding her right side in pain. "Sarah, where? How bad?" He pulled her hand away. "No blood. Good, right?" Steve looked at her back. "No exit wound. That's bad, right?"

"Right," she answered.

"Right? Right what? To the first or to the exit wound? Come on, Sarah, help me out here. You're the nurse."

"Right, as in I'm all right, Steve."

"You're all right? That's great but your ..."

Sarah interrupted, "I'm all right, just had the wind

knocked out of me. I wasn't shot."

"But …"

"Here." She handed Steve the fanny pack she had been wearing around her waist.

"What's this?" Steve saw a bullet hole in the side of it. He opened the pack and pulled out the trilogy of *Fifty Shades of Grey* paperbacks. A large hole had been punched through the first book, and most of the way through the second lay a bullet from a 45mm gun. "I told you only the necessities."

"They obviously were necessary for protection. Sorry about your books, though. I didn't know you were into that type of thing." She chuckled then grabbed her side. "Oh, that hurt. Don't make me laugh; it hurts."

"Hmm, hurts so good, eh?"

She slapped Steve in the arm. "Stop it."

"You're going to be sore for a while, and I'm afraid that's going to leave a mark. We're going to bed down here for tonight. It's getting late, and besides, those thugs are out there, probably looking for us."

"Steve, no, we haven't the time."

"You need to rest. We have at least another day to travel, maybe more. I figure we only have another eight miles to go. We'll leave before sunup while the thugs are asleep."

Steve got up and checked the doors.

"Steve, sorry about your books, but I have them on my Kindle so you can still read them."

"Funny, Sarah. Really funny."

-

"Steve, Steve wake up," Sarah whispered, nudging

him. "Steve."

"What is it? What?"

"Shhhhhh, we overslept. I hear voices."

"They have to be around here somewhere. I want that bike! Are you sure you shot her?" said a voice coming from outside.

"Yeah, I'm sure. I saw her grab her side."

"Because I don't see any blood trail."

"Maybe her clothes soaked it up, boss. She was wearing leather."

"Believe me, I know what that hot bitch was wearing. Find them!"

"Shit!" Steve whispered.

"What do we do, Steve? They're going to find us and kill us."

"Shhhhh, it will be all right. Don't panic." Steve looked around the garage. "Think, dammit, think," he said to himself.

Steve looked to the rafters and told Sarah to hide up there. She struggled to climb up the ladder with her bad ankle, but with a lot of grunting, she made it. She sat up on some plywood that was sitting across the joists.

"Now what?" she asked.

"I don't know. Just hang in there for a second."

"Shouldn't I be armed?"

Steve grabbed her 9 mm that she had been carrying and a couple of clips and handed them up to her. "Do you know ..."

"Yes," she interrupted. "I shot with my father at the

range quite a bit." Steve grabbed his handgun out of the bag and threw some clips into his pocket as well.

"They're coming up the drive, Steve. I hear them." Steve ran to the door, then back to the wall, pistol ready. The handle to the garage door moved back and forth.

"It's locked," announced one of the voices outside.

"Check the service door. Oh, never mind, I got it." Seconds later, someone was at the service door trying the knob. "I know you're in there. Do yourself and your little chick friend a favor and open the fuckin' door."

Steve held a finger to his lips while he faced Sarah's direction. Sarah nodded, confirming she understood. *There is no way they could know for sure we're here,* Steve thought.

"I'll count to ten. Then I'm kicking the door in. One, two ..."

Steve looked at Sarah and shook his head. She nodded back again.

Steve holstered his pistol and grabbed the machete. He widened his stance at the door, ready for it to open.

"... three, four ..."

"Hey, boss?" It was a voice coming from out at the street. "I think I found something. There's blood over here. I told you I shot her. Look, like it's headed that way."

"Great! Let's get that son of a bitch."

Sarah and Steve heard the stranger's footsteps walking away from the door and down the drive.

Steve exhaled in relief. They both kept perfectly still for the minutes that followed.

Five minutes passed and no sound came from outside.

Steve finally took a deep breath. Sarah followed suit, except her deep breath brought tears to her eyes. She grabbed at her side and applied pressure to the pain.

"Can you make it down?" Steve asked. She moved to the ladder, holding her side tight as she took the first step. Steve grabbed hold of her leg. "I gotcha, easy now."

Sarah moved very slowly, taking one rung at a time. Her legs shook like a leaf. With Steve's help, she finally made it down in one piece. She turned around and sat on a stack of tires.

"Let me have a look." Steve pulled Sarah's hand away from her side. She lifted her shirt, exposing a very dark bruise in the shape of a perfect rectangle, the size of a paperback.

"How does it look?" she asked.

"Well, to be honest, it's not fifty but it's a good thirty shades of grey." Steve smiled and got slapped again as Sarah doubled over in pain laughing.

"Shhhhhhhh," Steve said quietly "We don't know where those thugs are. "Shhhhh."

Steve helped Sarah tape her side up with duct tape. With plenty more riding to do, they tried to dress the bruise as securely as they could.

"How's that?" Steve asked. "Walk around a bit."

Sarah walked the length the garage and back again. "So far, so good." She smiled.

"I love your smile, Sarah," Steve said. "We have to move. Are you up for it?"

"Oohrah!"

"That's my soldier. I'm going to look around outside.

Don't worry, I will be right back." Steve emphasized the word *will*, and grabbed his machete, checked his holster, and took his crossbow with him. He stepped out the side service door. Nothing so far, so he walked around the house and down to the road. *Good, no sign of them anywhere,* he thought. He walked back to the garage, and within a couple of minutes, the garage door began to open and Steve and Sarah were back on the road again.

Steve steered the bike back the way they had come. That road was the only way to get where they were going without having to do a lot of backtracking – time they couldn't afford to waste.

"Steve, shouldn't we go a different way? This is where those thugs were."

"They seemed like drifters to me, Sarah. The kind who don't stay in any one place very long. I don't think they'll be there, and besides, this is our quickest route."

Steve was right. The thugs weren't there. The streets were pretty clear, and as long as he and Sarah stayed clear of the poles with the sirens, zombies became fewer and farther between the closer they got to the edge of town.

"Steve, zoms left, ten o'clock," barked Sarah. The announcement startled Steve. It'd been quiet for the past two miles, and he was in the middle of maneuvering the bike through a lot of loose debris and chunks of asphalt. The military's tanks had just crushed the road beneath them as they'd made their way across town, leaving nothing but rubble behind.

The front tire of the bike shifted and sank deep in the

gravel, forcing the handlebars to the left. Steve gave it some gas and pulled up on them hard. The bike spun its back tire. It too dug in deep, catching something. Something solid. The thrust lifted the front tire up in the air and jetted it forward. Sarah was thrown against the hard case mounted on the rear fender. Her back smacked hard, temporarily knocking the wind from her. Steve's arms were stretched out to their limits, hanging on for dear life until the bike settled down like it had a mind of its own. It slammed down hard again in the gravel, bucked, and stalled.

Sarah grabbed her side in pain.

"You OK back there?"

"Fine. Let's get us out of here," she said winded.

This little fiasco sent the bike and its riders dangerously close to a small mob of zoms. Steve had no choice but to draw his pistol and take down as many as he could. Sarah joined in, hitting one zombie with every three or four shots fired. Steve hardly missed and had already reloaded with a new clip.

"Shoot the head!" Steve yelled.

"I'm trying."

Steve looked down and saw his tires buried in the debris. The bike was too heavy.

"Get off the bike and run behind those rocks over there." Steve pointed. "I'll pick you up over there." He paused to fire a few more rounds.

Sarah, with a strange look on her face, didn't want to leave Steve's side. Even though they were in a pickle, she still felt some comfort being with him. But she also trusted Steve's judgment and followed his orders.

"Sarah, wait!" She slid in the loose gravel to a stop. "Come back." Steve shot a couple more zombies while he waited for Sarah's return. "Take the duffle bag. It's too heavy." Sarah struggled to lift the bag from the handlebars and dragged it with her. The bag probably weighed as much as she did, soaking wet.

Once Steve saw she was far enough out, he started the bike and began walking it out of the debris.

Halfway to Sarah's destination, she looked back and saw Steve in trouble. She dropped the duffle bag to the ground. The zoms were practically on top of him. She grabbed her pistol and fired a couple of rounds. To her surprise, she hit the two zombies closest to Steve. They dropped to the ground. Steve looked to see where those rounds were coming from and saw Sarah 35 feet away with her gun pointed in his direction.

"Shit!" he said as he ducked down as low as he could. Sarah squeezed off a couple more rounds, which emptied the gun of ammunition, locking the slide in the open position. "Dammit!" she yelled, reaching for another clip. Her hand came up empty. She noticed Steve was fumbling, trying to hold the bike upright and keep moving forward while loading bullets into a new clip. The bike stopped and bucked, stalling again and knocking the clip from Steve's hand. Bullets scattered on the ground. The last remaining zombie took advantage of the situation and attacked. Steve did everything he could to hold his attacker at arm's length.

The zom's jaw snapped at him as he struggled to keep

it away. Still straddling the bike, Steve had no leverage. It was only a matter of time before the zombie would overpower him. Sarah had to do something, but her gun was empty. She wasn't strong enough to load a clip with her fingers. She always used a loader when she had shot with her dad. She looked down at the duffle bag near her feet. Her bat was sticking out. She reached down to grab it when she noticed the handle of the pistol crossbow. She pulled it out of the bag. It was already loaded. She found the safety and flicked it off. She aimed it at the zombie that was now leaning over Steve, biting at the air between them. Steve leaned backward over his seat, trying desperately to hold the zom back with all his strength. He was bent like a pretzel. He looked back at Sarah upside-down, while battling the zom. Steve's eyes widened, focusing on what Sarah was doing.

"Oh no, no, no! Sarah, no!"

Just then, the zombie's head snapped backward. Steve looked up and saw a small arrow buried deep in the zom's forehead. It fell limp on top of him. He rolled it to its side, dumping the zom to the ground and dumping the bike.

Still wide-eyed, Steve stared at Sarah, having a hard time believing what he had just witnessed. Sarah shrugged her shoulders and smiled.

Steve finally freed himself from the bike and circled around to pick Sarah up. They hugged and passionately kissed. "Thank you," Steve said. "But, please, don't ever point a weapon at me ever again." He smiled. "Come on, we're almost there."

Steve and Sarah finally reached the doctor's home. A locked gate guarded the drive. Steve was surprised the gate still had power, as none of the other homes nearby appeared to have electricity. *Generators,* he thought. He walked up to the cameras and rang the buzzer. No one answered.

"Oh great, we've come all this way and no one's home," said Sarah. "They've gone."

"I don't think so. Preppers don't leave their homes in times of crisis. This is what they live for. I'm sure someone is here, just not the doctor. The family's just not answering, that's all. They don't know me from Adam."

Steve pulled the work order slip from his pocket. He noticed some numbers on the bottom of the page. Before today, he'd had no clue what they meant. He had a clue now. *Maybe it's the combination to the touch pad.*

The doc and Bob, Steve's now-deceased boss, were good friends. Bob had delivered the doc's car to his home a few times after Steve had worked on it.

Sure enough, the numbers worked and the gates swung wide. Steve pulled the bike inside, and the gates automatically closed behind them.

The driveway was long and curved. It took them up to a circle drive in front of a modest mansion. To Steve and Sarah, there was nothing modest about it. The place was massive, considering other homes in the surrounding area.

Steve rang the doorbell. Still no one answered, but he didn't really expect anyone to. He expected to see guards rounding the corner with guns drawn, or at least guard dogs. Luckily for them, neither showed.

"This is really weird," Steve said.

"Maybe they're at their other home?" Sarah replied back.

"*Other?*"

"Yeah, don't rich people have more than one place?"

"Well, probably, but maybe not all of them. Let's hope the shelter is at this one."

"Don't you think they'd probably have one at both? I mean, really, who knows where you'll be when all hell breaks loose."

"Good point." They walked around back. Steve checked doors and windows along the way.

*Hmmm, maybe Sarah's right. It does look empty, but someone had to start the generators or at least keep them filled with fuel.*

The backyard was gorgeous. In that idyllic setting, no one would have ever known the problems going on in the outside world. A multi-level cobble-stoned patio wrapped the backside of the house. A beautiful gazebo stood just outside what appeared to be the maid's quarters. What looked like an Olympic-sized swimming pool sat in the middle of the yard with an unusual cover.

Steve sat down on some patio furniture and Sarah followed.

"What's up, Steve? I can see your mind turning. Is this it?"

Steve leaned back in his chair and avoided the question. "Doesn't it make you wonder, Sarah?"

"Wonder? Wonder what?"

"How the good people live. This is great. This is Heaven. Heaven on Earth."

"Steve, have you lost your marbles? Did you forget about the bombs? Where's the shelter? What are we going to do?" Sarah started to panic. "I didn't come all this way to die here, Steve."

*What a way to go,* Steve thought. "Enjoy a few minutes, will you? Let me think. Why don't you take a dip in the pool and cool down?"

"Swimming? You want me to go swimming? You're unbelievable!"

"What do you want from me, Sarah? I did the best I could. You're the one who took off, not me. We could be safe with the others right now, but no, you had to go see if dear ol' Dad was all right. Well, he's all right now, isn't he? He's better off than we are."

Sarah walked up to Steve and slapped him hard across the cheek. Steve just looked to the ground, rubbing his cheek and chin. He said and did nothing for quite some time. The silence between them was palpable.

Then, out of nowhere, Steve spoke.

"If you were a bomb shelter, where would you be, Sarah?"

"Games, Steve? Really? We're going to die here, you ass."

"I'm serious. Think, Sarah. It's here. I know it's here somewhere. That's all he talked about."

"All I see is a damn swimming pool, Steve."

"Me too. Let's have a look."

"I'm not going near that pool with you, so don't even think about it. Don't you dare touch me either."

"I won't throw you in, Sarah."

"Yeah, right."

They walked closer. "No, really I won't."

"Promise?"

"I won't throw you in because it's not really a pool. It looks like a pool, but it's not." Steve looked to the right side of the pool and noticed a couple of pipes sticking out from the ground.

"Steve, you've lost your mind."

"No, no, wait. Come here. Look." Steve grabbed her hand and walked down the brick steps to the pool. "It's a mirage. It's just painted to look like a pool. This guy's good. He's disguised it so rebels couldn't find it. Look for a door."

The door was actually easy to find. It was part of the pump house, a domed room made of cement and reinforced by metal, which housed a pump for a real swimming pool. Inside were wide steps leading downward.

"Wait, let's get our things first. We could be walking into a trap," Steve said.

Steve ran around the front of the building and pushed his bike to the back. There was just enough room inside the pump house for it. Steve grabbed some gear and checked his gun for ammo. He added a few more rounds to replace some that had been spent and holstered it. He carried his crossbow up front and grabbed his machete. Sarah, for the first time since leaving her house, grabbed the M-4 assault rifle. She then checked her pistol and grabbed the bat.

They walked inside, Steve first and Sarah following close behind.

Inside, the shelter stunk. It stunk like rotted meat. It stunk like the Dumpster Steve had been trapped in. They left the door ajar to help air it out. It was dark inside. The doorway was the only light source. Steve's flashlight provided the rest of the light, but he used it sparingly. He didn't know how long the batteries would last. The cement walls were lined with shelves – shelf after shelf as far as the flashlight's beam would illuminate.

The shelves were stocked with food, mostly canned goods of all varieties. There were gallons upon gallons of bottled water, as well as blankets, sheets, and pillows. Some of the shelves swung down to form chairs, benches, and even cots. Whoever designed this fortress had plans of staying here for a while. Steve explored more while Sarah rested her ankle on the steps leading inside.

Steve found boxes, tubs, and bags filled with all types of survival equipment and supplies.

"Find any air fresheners, Steve?" Sarah asked somewhat sarcastically.

"No, not yet. But I'm sure they're here somewhere."

"Keep looking, please. This place is rank." She paused, hearing a noise. "What was that?"

"It's all right, Sarah, it's just me. I just kicked over a box," Steve replied in a cheerful mood. The supplies he found were enough to last for months, if not years.

It wasn't all that good, though. It was certainly not as good as Steve thought. He soon found something that was very disturbing.

"What the hell is this place?" he asked himself. Just then, Steve's feet were taken out from underneath him. "Whoa! Shit!" He found himself sliding down a very slippery slope – a slope leading to where, he didn't know. It was darker than pitch.

The slope was slick as ice, coated with what looked like streaks of dried blood. Steve caught himself on some shelving before sliding all the way down. His flashlight wasn't so lucky. It didn't stop until it hit bottom several feet away.

"Steve? Are you all right?" Sarah stood at the top of the slope with a battery- powered lantern she'd found on a shelf.

"I'm fine. Sarah, I told you to stay put. Now keep off that ankle. Okay?"

"I heard you fall. I just wanted to make sure you were all right. Is that blood?" she said as she shined the lantern closer to the ground, illuminating black streaks of blood fading off to nowhere. The light on the lantern wasn't bright enough to reach the bottom, but she could see the flashlight lighting up part of the floor. "Steve, that's blood."

"Yes, I know, Sarah. It's blood."

"What is this place?"

"Well, what it looks like to me is that this was an in-ground swimming pool at one time – a very large one. It was one they had dug deeper with reinforced walls, converting it into a bomb shelter. This must be the slope to the deep end. Deeper than I've ever seen."

"Steve, get up here. Get up here now!"

"What is it, Sarah? What?"

"Just get up here! Now!"

Steve heard panic in Sarah's voice and started to pull himself up. He struggled with his footing and slipped on the blood on the floor. He managed to grab hold of some shelving and pulled himself up to the top.

"What is it? You see something?"

"Something's moving down there, Steve." Sarah pointed to the bottom of the pool. "See that?" A shadow moved in front of the flashlight.

"Hmm, I don't know, Sarah. The flashlight's probably just going dim or rocking back and forth. The batteries may be dying. Who knows? It's all right. How you feeling?" The light at the bottom flickered again before going completely out. "See? The batteries just died. Now come on, let's get you off your feet." Steve wrapped his arm around Sarah and guided her back to the stairs. Steve helped her sit down.

"Mmmm."

"Are you all right?"

"Fine, thanks."

"That's quite a moan for being fine. Where's it hurt?"

"I didn't moan, Steve. That wasn't me. I thought it was you. It came from your direction."

Steve grabbed the lantern and shined it back in the direction they'd come from. He held his blade at the ready. "That wasn't me either. Something's in here with us."

"I told you I saw something."

"Did you see any flashlights on any of these shelves?"

Steve asked, seeing nothing with the light from the lantern.

"I don't know. I got that one from over there." She pointed to the left. "Where're you going?"

"To check for flashlights."

"You're not leaving me here. I'm going with you."

"Sarah, I will just be over there." They both heard another moan. This time they both agreed that it was coming from the deep end of the pool. Sarah jumped to her feet and was hanging onto Steve's arm in no time at all.

Steve found a box of flashlights and batteries. He loaded one up. He pressed the button, but the light didn't work. He took the batteries back out to make sure he'd inserted them correctly. Sure enough, he had. He smacked the light against the palm of his hand. The light came on just as he and Sarah heard another moan. He grabbed another flashlight and fresh batteries and handed them to Sarah. Steve made his way through the maze of shelving back to the deep end.

"Steve, no, let's just go."

"Go where, Sarah? The bombs will be going off soon. This is our best and only chance of surviving."

"I have a bad feeling about this."

"Yeah, me too. Stay here."

"I'm going with you."

The flashlight at the bottom of the deep end was on again, but only briefly. Sarah was right. There was something down there. Steve caught the silhouette image of a person. Something or someone just walked in front of the light. Steve shined his light down to the bottom, illuminating the very thing he feared – a zombie.

This one had been a little boy. He was dressed in shredded, blood-soaked jeans and a T-shirt. He peered up at Steve and hissed. Steve looked around at the floor. It was covered with dried blood, which appeared to be coming from the left side. A body lay there with its torso ripped apart. Its insides where spread open like a dressed deer. It looked female and older than the boy, possibly the child's mother. She probably hadn't had the heart to kill her own child and fell victim to him instead.

"We have to get that thing out of here. Find some good, strong rope, will ya, Sarah?"

"I saw some. I'll get it."

Sarah returned less than a minute later with about a hundred feet of rope. "Okay, now what?"

Steve tied the rope around his waist.

"What are you doing?"

"I'm going down there to take care of things."

"Can't you do that from here?"

"Well, I could, Sarah, but I'd rather not waste a bullet on something I can handle with a blade."

"Use an arrow, Steve. We can retrieve that."

"All right, fair enough." Steve aimed the crossbow and fired. "There, happy? Now will you lower me down?"

Sarah grabbed the other end of the rope, and Steve began his descent.

"You got me?"

"Yeah, all set."

She lowered Steve to the bottom. Steve hadn't

traveled more than a couple of feet when down he went, falling the rest of the way. Sarah hadn't been able to hold on, and the rope just slipped through her fingers. Steve slid to the bottom. Sarah stomped on the rope to stop it, but it was too late. Steve was already at the bottom.

"Are you okay?"

Steve picked up the flashlight and shined it at the boy. "I'm fine. He's dead."

"Now what?"

"Throw me a blanket and the other end of the rope." She did, tossing the other end down, forgetting that she needed to hang onto the middle. The whole rope slipped to Steve's feet.

"Really?"

"Sorry, I accidentally let go. Steve shook his head and chuckled under his breath. He then wrapped the bodies in the blanket and tied it up at both ends. "One zombie burrito to go," he said. He then threw his end of the rope up to Sarah.

"Great catch, Sarah."

"Thanks, here you go." Sarah threw another rope down. Steve tied it around his waist.

"OK, pull me up." Steve only took a few steps when he fell and slid back down, almost taking Sarah with him. "Uh, better yet, tie it to something secure. I'll pull myself up."

Sarah secured the rope to a pole in the center of the room. Steve climbed the bloody slope. When reaching the top, they both pulled the bodies up to discard them. Sarah found some bleach and poured it everywhere and mopped up what she could see. The slope was more manageable now that the blood was gone. Steve dragged the zoms out back and hoisted them over the fence.

When Steve came back in, he looked around for a few minutes more. In the corner he found a writing desk and lots of paper and books on a shelf. In the desk drawer was something more interesting: paperwork and a journal left by the doctor who had lived there. Inside the journal were newspaper and magazine clippings. Written inside the journal were dates and doctors' names. Some dated back to the early 1800s.

In fact, there were several pages of names. Beside each name read the words, "Cure for cancer found." Each entry included dates – date of birth and date of the cure, followed closely by the date of death.

Steve scanned the list of names. On the sixth page, he came across the last entry on the list. It was the owner of the bomb shelter they were standing in. Next to his name were his date of birth and the date that he was cured, which was January 2012. The date of death was still blank. After that was just one word – "seed" – followed by a phrase in quotes: "you know what happens next …"

Flashes of current events played in Steve's mind. First were the headlines that graced every newspaper and blog across the country, reading, "Cure for Cancer Found!" Then came visions of the book he had just flipped through. His mind scrolled through the pages of names and cures with dates going back to the early 1800s. Pictures of zombies then filled his mind. Next was the phrase, "You know what happens next …" Then came the National Guard and the burning of Atlanta General. "You know what happens next ..." Atlanta General, the army pulling into Bear Creek, the pamphlets falling from the sky, and tweets and Facebook posts about the cure. And all of those names in the book ... "You know what happens next ..." Sarah began reading the lists of deceased from Atlanta General and about the hospital burning to the ground. Steve's mind raced with images until they all fit together like a puzzle.

"My God," Steve whispered. "There's been a cure for cancer for centuries. They just didn't want us to know."

"They? Who are they, Steve?"

"Don't know yet, Sarah." Steve looked down at a symbol from one of the magazine clippings. It was a drawing of the infamous cancer ribbon, only this one had a pair of scissors cutting through it. Below it was the name, "Ribbon Cutters," and the slogan, "Save the World."

"That's interesting," Steve said, mostly to himself. "I bet the pharmaceutical companies have something to do with it, and I wouldn't doubt that our government is somehow behind the cover-up as well."

"Am I understanding this right, Steve? All of these people found cures for cancer and were killed before the news leaked out? These people, the 'Ribbon Cutters?' They believe ..."

Steve interrupted, "That the world is a better place *with* cancer than it would be *without*."

"That's absurd."

"Maybe, but they have a lot of research behind it, it looks like. Look at all these statistics." Steve flipped through pages and pages of graphs, charts, and figures, showing scenarios and predictions of what would happen if a cure were to be found. "Wow," Steve said. "Sure looks convincing." Steve closed the notebook and stuck it in the desk drawer.

Steve looked up on a shelf above the desk and saw several Mason jars. Each jar was filled with seeds, some much larger than others.

"Those must be the seeds he's talking about. What do you think they are, Sarah?"

Sarah grabs a jar off the shelf and shines a light on it. "Well, these look kind of like pits, from avocados." She sets the jar down and replaces it with another, as for these... She examines it closer, turning the jar in every direction. "I bet these are from the Graviola tree."

"Wow, how did you know that? I've never heard of it."

"From the label on the bottom of the jar, see." She turns the bottom of the jar towards Steve.

"Nice."

"But, Steve, what if after the bombs fall, there are no more of these trees?"

Steve opened one of the jars and dumped a few pits in his hand and held them out to Sarah. "We'll grow more."

•••

# CHAPTER 45

"What's the meaning of this interruption?" asked the president of the United States during a very important meeting with his advisors and the secretary of defense.

"Mr. President, sorry for the interruption, but there is someone at the gate insisting to be let in. He claims to be the infamous professor from Bear Creek," said a guard through the intercom system at Mt. Hope.

"Professor? The professor or just another person claiming to be the professor and trying to get some protection?"

"He's claiming to be the original, sir. He has ID. It's confirmed. He heard the CDC has been looking for him. He says he would like to tell you everything he knows," stated the guard at the gate.

The president just stared at the secretary of defense, waiting for a response. He received a nod.

"Well, let him in. What do we have to lose at this point!" the president declared.

"Aye, sir." Outside, the gates opened, and three secret service agents escorted the professor via motorized cart. They pulled up to the cave in front of the massive 18-foot doors. The doors didn't open. Instead, the smaller service door, about the size of a single garage door, opened along the adjacent wall. The driver had swiped his ID card, and the door automatically opened. The electronic car, no more than a modified golf cart but sure to have had an enormous price tag, rushed through the doors. The two agents in the cart held their badges up as they passed even more security agents inside. They continued through many hallways and corridors throughout the mountainside. The driver continuously rode the brake, as the cart seemed to be traveling in a downward descent. After several minutes, the cart finally came to a screeching stop in front of a large elevator. They drove the cart in, swiped their cards again and entered some numbers on the touch pad. The elevator started its descent. How far down it was going, the professor didn't know. The door slid open, and the driver drove forward, down even more hallways. The cart finally slid to a stop, sliding a few inches on the tile surface in front of a conference room door, which was also heavily guarded. The light above the door to the room was flashing red, indicating the nation's security level. The panel included four other colored indicators: green, at the bottom, signaled a low danger of attack; blue, general risk; yellow, elevated or significant risk; orange, high risk. Red, at the top, indicated a severe threat level. Since the inception of the color-coded system, the nation had never been above yellow.

While the president was waiting for the professor to arrive, he summoned the CDC officials to join the meeting. The president was in a rather heated discussion with them when the conference room door quietly swung open. The president, the CIA, nor the people from the CDC, heard the professor enter the room. The professor just stood there and listened.

"So let me get this straight. This virus, which spread across the states in a matter of only a couple of days, has no cure or antidote?"

"Sorry, Mr. President. It's still too soon. We just don't have enough data yet."

"Who is responsible for this outbreak?" the president asked. "Terrorists?"

"No one has come forward, sir."

"If you are looking for someone to blame, you can start with the girl who crashed her car into my lab, but from what I hear, she is dead, so I think you probably will have to blame the monster who created this germ somewhere down in South America. I'm presuming that he is dead as well."

"Professor Campbell, I presume?" the president asked in his best Henry Morton Stanley impersonation.

"Yes, Mr. President. Professor Simon P. Campbell, at your service, sir."

"Professor, thank you for coming. Did I understand you correctly? What you're saying is that this was a terrorist attack?"

"Please, call me Simon. I'm officially retired."

"Very well, Simon."

"Terrorist attack, sir? No, I'm not saying that at all. An act of terror, possibly."

"What is the difference, professor? I'm sorry, Simon."

"Well, in the eyes of some, absolutely nothing. But unfortunately, the word 'terrorist' in most eyes usually means an attack from a Middle-Eastern country. This may not be the case, and I would hate for that kind of rumor to enter global circulation."

"Then what are you saying, Simon?"

"I'm saying that the germ or virus was, for the most part, a natural mutation until it was tampered with by someone for an unknown reason."

"Well, what good reason could there be to tamper with such a thing that could have catastrophic consequences, such as what we are dealing with?"

"Well, it's very common in this line of work, sir. Some do it to get a jump on the 'What if?' scenario. They like to learn as much about the virus and what it could possibly mutate to, to help find a cure or antidote. Sometimes it takes a considerable amount of time to find a cure, so the first thing to do is try to isolate the problem before it spreads. This, I see, you've tried but failed."

"Go on," said the president.

"Second is to find out what we could be up against by

the time a cure could be found. Stopping the virus rarely occurs in its original condition, but more into the mutation process. It gives us more evidence of the direction it's going so we can stop it before it gets there. Or ..." Simon paused. "It could have just been a mistake."

"A mistake? Do you honestly believe that this was just an error, professor?" the secretary of defense inquired.

"Sir, it doesn't matter what I believe. It's here, no matter what the reason, but my professional approach would be to look at the strain that the tampering was excessive and if it was probably done to cause some sort of terror."

"Military?" asked the president.

"You would know that more than I, sir."

The president looked toward the secretary of defense. He shrugged. "Not that I'm aware of, sir. We're looking into it now." He motioned to an agent standing beside him. The agent shook his head in the affirmative and immediately left the room.

"Well, would you be interested in telling us what you do know, Simon?"

"I'd be happy to, Mr. President."

Simon took the floor and stood behind the pulpit, in front of the top officials of the United States, Homeland Security, CDC, CIA, every branch of the armed services, and the president himself. He began to tell them everything he knew about the virus.

"The virus is nothing more than a very sophisticated cancer." The word 'cancer' alone perked up the ears of many in the room. "It's a very aggressive one, I might add. It's one that attacks, flanks the brain." He nodded to the military personnel in the room. He pushed his glasses back onto his nose and continued. "The cancer flanks left and right, and just at the right moment. It's usually right before death that it rushes the brain. For you football enthusiasts, it's an all-out blitz. It attacks the brain from all sides. It creates an unbearable fever, ultimately cooking the brain from the inside out."

"How is it transferred, doc?" asked a voice from the crowd.

"I was getting to that. On contact, usually by bite or deep scratches, these aggressive cells are transferred from the infected to the uninfected. If the uninfected, now infected, gets away before he or she is eaten alive, the cancer cells quickly start their journey toward the brain. Once reaching the brain, the cells rapidly grow and go straight to work, shutting down all unnecessary organs and only leaving the organs necessary for survival. It then begins eating away at the brain, leaving only the brain stem active. Your frontal and cranial membranes are mostly gone, and all that is left are the very basics of body movement and the incredible urge to eat and spread this deadly virus, but mainly to eat. I should say that they are not vegetarians.

"The spread of the virus is secondary. In fact, it wouldn't spread human-to-human if no one got away. They would just become food and be eaten alive.

"Time of transformation will vary depending on where you are bitten and how badly. It will range from twenty minutes to three days after the initial bite or scratch. It will start as a typical infection, feeling severely hot and giving the victim, at minimum, a low-grade fever. The use of heavy antibiotics will temporarily slow the processes down and relieve some of the pain. However, the outcome is unavoidable. The fever will gradually worsen, frying whatever's left of the brain, and you will die.

"Reanimation occurs shortly after, in seconds or sometimes minutes. Since the walking corpse is still essentially a corpse, it literally feels no pain. It's dead. You can't hurt it anymore than it already is. To kill it once and for all would mean severe head trauma or decapitation. Bashing in the skull with blunt force is effective but requires close encounters, which are risky at best. A simple headshot, practically with any-caliber gun should do the trick, and it is the safest way, provided it's a clean enough shot. Grazing the head will only change the appearance and will have no other effect.

"I should tell you that if your friends or family become infected, do not try to save them. They can't be saved. Get as far away from them as you can, because the closer a person is to them, the more likely it is that they will become their next meal. Trying to save them is futile, as there is no known cure at this time. It's either them or you. Both cannot coexist."

Hands were raised throughout the room. "Professor, sir are you saying that if our own families gets infected, we should kill them?"

Someone else spoke up. "Yeah, it sounds like that's our only choice – kill our own families. You have to be kidding me, right?"

"I'm not at all insinuating that you should kill anyone, infected or not. As of right now, it is still illegal to kill anyone, through mercy or otherwise. What I'm saying is that once the transformation occurs, it will either be them or you. You will have to make that choice. You have the right to protect yourself, and I only suggest that you exercise that right," replied the professor.

A man stood up in the back row, introducing himself as a news reporter. "How did this get started, sir?"

"Sorry for the interruption, professor, but a better question would be, 'how the hell did a reporter get in here?' Guards, please escort this gentleman out of this room and into solitary confinement immediately, and do not let him talk to anyone," said the director of homeland security, as he watched a couple of armed guards take control of the situation. "Christ, if this gets out to the main public, all chaos will erupt."

The president interrupted. "Chaos has already erupted, and the professor hasn't told us much of anything that most people haven't already experienced. Please continue, Simon."

"I really don't have much more to add," he related.

"I don't mean to sound like I'm questioning your integrity, sir, but how do you know all of this? Did you have these zombies in your lab?"

The professor hesitated and avoided the directness of the question. "I was able to obtain blood samples from an infected victim and performed weeks of lab tests on everything from rats and ferrets to chimpanzees. I was trying to find a serum up until someone drove their car through my lab. Then ..." He paused. "By that time, it was too late. Damage was done, contamination occurred, and the virus leaked out."

"Why didn't you go to the CDC, sir?"

"With all due respect to the CDC, I worked there for many years. In fact, I'm retired from there, but I'm sure you already know that. I know the procedures there all too well. Like all governmental agencies, there is too much red tape, too many meetings, too many breaks, and way too many chiefs. There plainly wasn't enough time.

"The virus didn't just leak from my office, sir. It was running rampant in South America long before, and it was only a matter of time before it reached us. I was trying desperately to find a solution before that happened. Then someone decided to make a drive-through out of my lab, accelerating things a bit out of my control.

"In summary, the germ in question evolved naturally, with one exception. There was a line in the DNA strain that was manmade. Someone developed a super cell from the common bird flu strain, solely intending to be passed to us from birds all over the world. This strain is a little more unique in that mammals can also carry the germ as well. Although it may have started as a type of influenza, it has been altered to a fast-growing cancer cell that attacks the brain at an incredible rate. That is all I know at this time."

Hands again raised throughout the room. Professor Campbell selected someone in the back row who asked, "You mean to tell us that we now can catch cancer like the common cold? That's absurd!"

"It may be absurd, sir, but it certainly looks as if that's what's happening. Except it isn't exactly airborne – at least not yet. It is transferred through a bite or a transfer of bodily fluids through sex or through blood, possibly through an open wound."

"So you are saying it can't be caught just by breathing in the same air space?"

"Yes, you can leave your Hazmat outfits in the bags for now. I'm not saying that it can't mutate in that direction, but for now, it's safe to breathe."

"Well, that's a relief," the man said sarcastically with a fake sigh.

"If I could only get to my lab, I could probably save the CDC months of work toward a cure, or at least a solution for this deadly disease."

The president's ears perked up.

A man in uniform looked at his watch and quickly spoke. "Mr. President, Bear Creek is scheduled to be bombed in fifteen minutes, sir."

"Professor, I'm afraid your lab is only a mile or so away from one of the drop zones. The chance that there will be anything left is very slim to none," said the secretary of defense.

"So sorry to hear that. That's very bad news indeed," said the professor.

"Can I ask what your building was made of, sir?"

"The building is made of bricks and mortar, except for the gaping hole the car left behind, which I assume is now plywood."

"Still, even with brick, it probably will not be standing, and the radiation …"

"Radiation?" the professor questioned.

"Yes, Simon, in some of the more populated areas."

"Bear Creek wasn't populated?"

"In your case, Simon, radiation will be used in your town to kill off any chance of the virus surviving the blast. It started there, after all."

"You're using nukes on US soil?" Simon asked.

"In some places, we really have no choice." Just then, the ground shook like an earthquake. "There went Atlanta, right there."

"You can't be serious, Mr. President." The professor searched for an answer. The president hung his head. "Oh yes, while everyone here is all warm and cozy, people are dying out there."

"They were dying before the bombs were dropped, and you're warm and cozy as well, Simon," said the secretary of defense.

Infuriated by the comment, the professor launched himself toward the man, only to be held back by the Secret Service agents.

"I don't think you want to do that, Simon. I'm surprised you're still alive."

"We're all lucky to be alive right now." The professor shook off the guards, assuring them that he was all right." He paused a moment before saying, "There is still a chance. I kept a lot of samples in the basement in locked freezers. If we get a hold of some of those samples, it could help the CDC tremendously."

"It's true, sir, if there is any chance that some of those samples are still obtainable, we need to get them," said the CDC official.

"Sir, according to my reports, Bear Creek hasn't been hit yet but is scheduled for noon for a five-ton hit, one-point-seven miles from his lab. Its 11:42 right now, sir. You could abort the mission or at least postpone it. Wind direction is to the east. It's possible that radiation levels are sustainable for short periods of time in this location."

"Abort the mission!" the president ordered.

"Aye, aye, sir." The general got on his phone, hit speed-dial, and barked out an order himself. "Abort Bear Creek. I repeat, abort Bear Creek!"

"Aye, aye, sir. Bear Creek, abort mission," a small voice replied through the speaker for all to hear.

"There you have it. Get the professor to his lab and bring back all the samples he's got."

"There are risks?"

"There are always risks, sir. Bombs have been dropped in nearby cities already, including Atlanta. It was nuclear, sir. The wind could easily carry the radiation cloud over Bear Creek. As of now, the wind is blowing to the south, but just a slight shift in the wind could be detrimental to the mission. It may be sustainable for short periods of time."

"Mr. President, I'm seventy-nine years old. If I make it, I make it. If not, there's not much left of me for the world anyway."

"There's a Blackhawk standing by, sir."

"Take a team and get him where he needs to be."

Bombs went off across the nation, some standard, some nuclear. The nuclear radiation fields made communication sketchy at best. It seemed to be interfering with contacting the bomber headed for Bear Creek. They were getting no response. They tried the fighter jets escorting the bomber; still no response.

"Do whatever it takes to stop that bomber! Even if it means shooting it out of the sky."

"Sir, you want us to shoot down one of our own, over our own land?"

"'Want,' General? Hell no! But if it's our only chance to get a cure, then yes, by all means." Then the president quoted Spock's famous quote from Star Trek, "General, I shouldn't have to remind you but, 'the needs of the many outweigh the needs of the few or the one.'"

"Aye, sir. I understand our mission. I was a 'Trekkie' once too."

The Blackhawk helicopter was loaded with supplies and raced off with the elderly professor and a handful of heavily armed personnel. The chopper tried to chase the bomber down, but the bomber was getting close to the drop zone, and there was not enough time for the Blackhawk to intercept. This was known, well before the chopper had lifted off, by the people at the command center. Two F-16 fighter jets were dispatched from Jefferson Airport minutes after the chopper had lifted off, heading in that direction at breakneck speed.

"This is Whiskey Alpha Sierra Delta Charlie 1, calling bomber en route to Bear Creek, over." The pilot of the F-16 was never given the call sign of the bomber en route. This information probably would have come in handy, but the pilot never got it, so he did the best he could to raise the bomber on the radio. The pilot repeated his call. "This is Whiskey Alpha Sierra Delta Charlie 1, calling the bomber en route to Bear Creak. Do you read? Over."

He repeated the call over and over but received no response. His signal was being blocked. FInally the pilot tried to raise communication with his wingman flying just yards away. No reply from him either. The pilot scanned the radio frequencies, but no voices came back; just dead air, static. They were flying through the radiation cloud, and it blocked all communications and was making their instruments go haywire. They had no clue how fast they were going or at what altitude they were flying. They were flying by the seat of their pants. They could easily miss their targeted location or even fly into the ass-end of the bomber itself. The bomber could also miss his target, as well. The only way to stop the bomber now would be to fly up to it and use hand signals, or shoot it out of the sky by line of sight. Needless to say, the message was never delivered.

"Bombs away."

•••

# CHAPTER 46

Steve and Sarah sat just outside the pump house door on the lower level of the cobblestone patio.

"Can I ask you a question, Steve?"

"Sure, what's on your mind?"

"Why?"

"Why, what, Sarah?"

"Why do you think this is all happening? Why now? Why this?"

"I don't know the answer to that, Sarah. All I know is, why not? We live in a very corrupt world. That book we just looked through really has me baffled. If nothing else, history has taught us that when the world gets so far out of control, the world knows how to correct itself and usually takes drastic measures to do so, so life can begin all over again. We just have to survive so we can enjoy the next time around, I guess.

"So you believe God did this?"

"After reading that journal, I don't know what to believe. But if we ever do find out, I bet corruption had something to do with it."

Steve was drawing in the sand on the patio, sand that ants had left behind when building their homes. Steve had always been fascinated by ants and watched them for hours as a kid. He always thought it was the neatest thing that they knew danger was in the air long before any other creature. They knew just when to run for cover right before a storm. It was no different now. He'd been watching the ants build their homes on the cobblestone patio ever since he had sat down on the stairway. *They're so strong,* Steve thought as he watched.

"So, it's about that time, isn't it?" Sarah asked.

"Not sure." Steve looked to the sun. It looks like it's around noon to me. I'm sure we will hear the bombers coming."

"Shouldn't we be in the shelter, seeing what we have and what we don't?

"I've seen enough. I'm sure we will have plenty of time to see more. I want to enjoy the last little bit of time we have above the ground."

"Sounds good to me, Steve." Sarah scooted closer and snuggled. Steve wrapped his arms around her and continued to watch the ants in action.

"Look, they're building more houses with not a care

in the world. They're oblivious to what's going on, aren't they?" Sarah asked.

"Sometimes that's not a bad thing, Sarah."

Steve watched the ants even closer. They all started to filter into their little holes, one by one, in a quick but orderly fashion. Steve's eyes widened. "Get inside, Sarah. Get inside now!"

Steve stood up and pulled Sarah toward the door. "What, Steve? I don't hear anything. Just a little longer."

"Sorry, Sarah. Now!" Steve pulled her all the way in the door and locked it behind them. "Go, go, go," he said, hurrying her down the stairs.

"Steve, you're scaring me."

"Sorry, Sarah. There's no time. Get down and cover your head."

The ground shook like an earthquake of the highest magnitude, knocking Steve clean off his feet. The whole shelter shook and rumbled for minutes. Canned goods and supplies fell from the shelves. Sarah screamed and screamed; she screamed for comfort, she screamed for Steve, but Steve didn't come running this time. Steve wasn't there like he had been in the past. It was pitch-dark, and Sarah had no clue where Steve had gone.

The ground finally stopped shaking, and Sarah continued to call out Steve's name, this time whimpering more than panicking. "Steve, where are you? Steve, are you here?" She called out in complete darkness over and over again but got no answer at all. The shelter was in shambles, but Sarah managed to crawl out from under the shelf she'd hidden under and found a flashlight. She looked around. Steve was near, nearer than she thought, but he was knocked out cold.

Steve had gotten knocked off his feet. He'd hit his head hard against the tiled floor. Sarah didn't notice at first glance, but Steve's hair was hiding a good-sized puddle of blood, which helped soak a lot of it up, preventing it from spreading much further.

"Steve! Oh, Steve." She put her hand around his head to lift it up off the hard floor. She was going to tuck a pillow underneath for comfort until she saw the blood. The blood was trickling out of a gash on the back of his head. She got a towel and applied pressure to his head to stop the bleeding and used another to tie around his forehead. She didn't want to move him, so she managed to push blankets and pillows under him. There wasn't much more she could do. She got water and gauze from the first-aid kit and some Motrin to give him when he regained consciousness, if he regained consciousness. Being a nurse, Sarah knew the dangers.

The only thing she could do now was wait. She let him rest awhile and lay down beside him, holding his hand. She started to talk in whispers to him, as he lay there unconscious.

•••

CHAPTER 47

All those in the Blackhawk helicopter could do was watch as the bay doors of the bomber opened up and out rolled the bombs. They watched, almost in shock, as the bombs fell to the Earth.

"Oh my God ... there are people down there," the professor said, pointing out the side window as the chopper veered away to avoid the shockwave from the bombs' blasts. Below, they saw a crowd of thousands formed underneath a pole that a held a siren. "They need our help!"

"Those aren't people, sir," said one of the chopper's crewmen. Those are zombies, and besides, there's not a damn thing we could have done anyway. Impact in five, four, three, two, one." They all listened to the countdown as if they were watching the ball drop on New Year's Eve. "Ka-boom," he added.

The blast sent shockwaves far out in all directions. The passengers inside the Blackhawk hung on tight, but they still found the need to rubberneck to see what kind of damage was left behind.

A cloud of smoke and dust shot straight up into the sky and mushroomed. Those aboard the helicopter couldn't yet see through the debris and dust to determine anything at this point. The professor stared out with a blank look on his face, not believing what had just happened, even though he had just witnessed it himself with his own two eyes.

The shockwave hit the Blackhawk like a ton of bricks, much harder than the pilot had anticipated. The chopper shook violently, sending it twirling away from the blast zone and toward the ground. The pilot's evasive maneuvering hadn't been enough.

"We are going down folks. Hold on to your ass," the pilot barked out. He tried hard to regain control, but it was no use. The tail rotor had been blown completely off, sailing away in the breeze. There was nothing more to do but hang on for dear life.

The shockwave sent everyone and everything that wasn't tied down crashing against everything and anything that was. The chopper's windows were blown out, sending shards of glass everywhere. Surrounded by shattering glass, the pilot's body caught as many as it could handle, killing him before the Blackhawk even hit the ground. The ride seemed to last forever for everyone onboard, swaying right, then left, up, and, within seconds, down.

The helicopter hit hard, its tail slapping the ground, sending the rest of the ship flopping on the ground like a fish out of water. The rotor blades dug deep into the ground, sending rocks, dirt, metal, and gravel in all directions. The blades twisted into crumpled metal like a spent pop can inserted into a crusher. Finally, what was left of the Blackhawk came to rest in a cloud of dust, and smoke.

Sadly, the pilot and three of the six soldiers aboard didn't make it out of the wreck alive. Another soldier, while still alive, didn't look like he'd last for long. The chopper itself would never see the tops of trees ever again.

-

The survivors were pretty banged up. Two had been thrown several yards away from the wreckage. They were the lucky ones, walking away with just a few bruises and one with a broken arm. The professor was still strapped in his harness inside the wreckage and was bleeding badly. His head had been split open from flying debris and glass. The soldiers rushed to the chopper to assist the survivors. Then they ran for cover, carrying the seriously injured with them. They saw fire and rubble everywhere they looked, not just from the wreckage but also from the blast of the bombs miles away.

-

The dust didn't settle for days, and when it did, it was replaced by falling ash. Visibility was no more than 20-30 feet at best. The soldiers gathered as much equipment from the wreckage as they could, especially masks, which became a necessity because of the dust and smoke that swirled though the air like a giant Dust Devil. The only thing they could see was devastation.

*No one could survive this,* one soldier thought to himself. But he thought wrong. They soon found others.

The soldiers, dressed in standard BDUs, were now equipped with gas masks. The air was too thick to breathe, and they used them to protect themselves from the dust, smoke, and falling ash, hoping to God that there was no radiation present. They weren't prepared for radiation, and they had no way of detecting it, as most of their equipment was destroyed in the crash.

The team crouched low to the ground near the remnants of a nearby brick building. They set up a triage area beneath several silver tarps. They attached the tarps to a wall, creating a lean-to. The tarps helped keep most of dust and ash away while the soldiers dressed the wounds of those who were injured. The tarps were silver in color to reflect the sun so they wouldn't bake to death underneath, but the sun would never be an issue for them. The temperature was fairly warm for now but in days to come it would plummet, since the sun would be blocked by smoke and ash for a very long time. The buildings were unrecognizable, even to the locals, if there were any remaining. The professor was still too shaken to tell his companions where they might be, and the soldiers had no clue. None had even heard of Bear Creek until a few weeks ago.

The last visible landmark any of them saw had been the pole with the siren blaring from its top with hundreds, possibly thousands, of zoms gathered below. The chopper crew had no clue how far away or in what direction that was, but they assumed it would be several miles to the southeast. Twirling uncontrollably in mid-air had made each of them a bit disoriented.

They rested, patched what wounds they could patch, and waited. There wasn't much they could do with the fellow soldier who was in critical condition. He was sure to die, but when, no one knew. They couldn't leave him behind to die alone, or could they? They had some tough decisions to make. They also had a mission to complete.

Waiting for someone to die was a helpless feeling. The medic in the group hadn't survived the crash. No one else knew beyond the basics of medicine. Morphine was given for pain, and, despite the odds, the soldier hung on. He was clearly a fighter in a hopeless situation.

They needed to find the small lab and obtain what the professor needed, what the CDC needed, what everybody would need. But they couldn't just leave a dying soldier alone, and they couldn't take him with them. Hours passed, and the patient was still breathing on his own. They gave him more morphine for the pain.

The longer they waited, the longer they chanced radiation exposure. They were out of time. They have to get back to the mission at hand. The professor finally came around and was ready to find out where the hell they were. The dying soldier shouldn't be moved, so someone had to stay behind. They had already risked moving him from the chopper to their current location, but they really had no choice. The soldier with his arm in a sling volunteered to stay behind, leaving the other to escort the professor to his lab.

"You go with the professor, find what you need, and come back for me – us. I'm not much good to you anyway with a broken arm. I'll stay and look after him." He nodded to the soldier lying in critical condition on the ground.

"Very well. We'll be back as soon as we can. Hang tight." With that said, the soldier looked at the compass dangling from his uniform. He wiped the dirt from the glass and tapped on it with his fingernail. The hands just spun.

"Must be broken," he said in disgust, as he led Professor Campbell around the damaged building in, what he guessed, was an easterly direction.

The building wasn't just damaged. The wall they were using for protection happened to be the only part of the building that was left standing. The rest was gone, like it had never been there. The soldier and the professor were puzzled by what they saw, or, rather, by what they didn't see. They had expected damage, yes, but to see nothing at all, not even rubble left behind, gave the two a new level of worry.

As they rounded the corner of what used to be a building, a large group of people appeared out of the dirty ash. Row by row, they appeared out of nowhere. With each new row, the first became more and more visible. The group could easily have been mistaken for anyone, as they looked like the victims at Ground Zero when the two World Trade Center towers fell on Sept. 11, 2001. They were covered from head to toe with dust, dirt, and ash. It was hard enough to tell man from woman, let alone to distinguish between races. They were moving closer and closer to the helicopter crash site. The soldier with the broken arm heard gravel being kicked underfoot and footsteps getting louder and louder. He grabbed his rifle and looked out from behind the tarps, but he couldn't see a thing; the dust and the ash were just too thick. He called out for the other soldier and the professor but received no response. He ducked back into the makeshift tent when he thought he heard the dying soldier let out a moan. He quickly tended to the soldier, making sure he wasn't in pain. Another morphine injection was in hand. The man lay motionless, his chest no longer heaving for air.

Bracing himself with his one good arm, the other soldier laid an ear on his critically injured comrade's chest. "Shallow breaths," he said to himself. "There's no way that moan came from him." Hearing footsteps just outside the tarps, he opened the flap. "Boy, am I glad to see you guys," he said to the approaching group, thinking a search party had finally arrived. But this was no search party. He had come face-to-face with a mob of soot-covered zombies. They were the ugliest things he'd ever seen. He had no time to react, and with one arm in a sling what could he do? They were too close for him to even raise his rifle. The mob pushed its way in, and the soldier was quickly overcome. He fought back, but there were just too many. The one-armed soldier screamed for help and screamed in pain as the zoms choked down strips of his flesh ripped from his body. The dying soldier who lay motionless on the ground became their dessert.

The professor and the soldier who accompanied him, a mere 100 yards away, didn't hear a sound. Needless to say the soldier's screams for help went unanswered.

•••

Simon and the soldier were making pretty good time. The professor was able to recognize a few of the streets and got his bearings fairly quickly.

"Just a few more blocks that way," Simon said, almost out of breath and stumbling straight ahead. Walking around in the ash was like walking in drifts of snow. It was tiring and had taken a toll on the old man.

"Are you OK, sir?" Asked the soldier.

"I'll make it."

The soldier looked around at the homes in the area. They were demolished, completely leveled. A couple more blocks weren't going to be much different. He hoped he was wrong, but for now he had concerns for the mission's success. Lives had been spent, blood had been spilt; he hoped it all wasn't for naught.

Walking in ankle-deep ash, soot, dirt, and everything else the bombs tossed up reduced visibility to next-to-nothing making two blocks seem like two miles.

Detouring around fallen debris, burning trees, and buildings didn't bother them nearly as much as tripping over dead bodies covered in ash. They could never get used to that, and it was too common of an occurrence.

The professor stumbled for the thousandth time. "What was that? You all right?" the soldier asked.

"Yeah, I'm fine. Just a boot from another dead body," the professor said, almost falling on his face.

The soldier took him by the arm, and they trudged

on.

As they walked away, the boot the professor had just kicked in the ash moved. Then the body's arms moved as well. Like an angel in the snow, it created its own design. A moment later, the body sat up. Dust and ash dumped from the body as it rose to its feet. It sniffed the air and shambled close behind the soldier and professor with outstretched arms, reaching to appease its appetite.

"I think it's right up here," the professor said as he pointed out into oblivion.

"How can you tell, sir?"

"Over there was a donut shop," the professor pointed. "The cops always hung out there. I picked up a cappuccino there just about every morning. Seven a.m., sharp. See, there is a piece of the sign right there." He nodded to the ground. Sure enough, part of a sign protruded from the ash. Most of it was burned and unreadable, the fire smothered out by the ash itself. "That means my lab should be right over there." The professor pointed to his left where he could faintly see the foundation of a brick building.

The soldier and professor walked to the center of the street, facing where the small lab once sat. Most of the lab was gone. A few bricks remained. Small smoldering fires lit their path.

"Sorry, doc," said the soldier. "Now what?"

"There's a basement here somewhere. We must find it. I kept the samples in the freezer down there."

"Lead the way."

The professor headed over to where the stairs had

411

once been. The staircase was full of rubble blocking the way. They both started clearing out the debris until there was enough room for one to squeeze through. The professor started to climb down when he heard the soldier clear his throat.

"Yes …?" The professor said, as he paused and turned to face the soldier.

"With all due respect, sir, I should be the one to go first to check it out."

The professor climbed back out of the hole. "Very well. You have no argument from me." The professor motioned toward the hole. "Be my guest." The soldier started his downward climb, with the flashlight at the end of his M-4 in the "on" position. "Be careful."

"I will, sir. Thanks," the soldier answered, looking back at Professor Campbell. The soldier's eyes widened as he reached for his 45 ACP and aimed it toward the professor. In such tight quarters swinging the M-4 around in time was out of the question.

"Hey, hey there. Put that down," the professor requested. Just then, the soldier fired off two consecutive shots. The professor felt the heat of two rounds sail past his cheek and heard the soft, moist thud of the rounds impacting into a skull. A trickle of blood filled the hole that the first bullet made. The second bullet missed its target, sailing high above. Blood dripped down the zombie's forehead. The professor jumped, looked over his shoulder and watched the zom fall to the ground, sending ashes flying in the air.

"Holy shit!" he cried out.

"Sorry sir," the soldier said with a quiver in his voice.

"'Sorry,' my ass. That was loud!"

"Be grateful you heard it, sir. You won't hear the one that takes you down."

"Where in the hell did he come from?" the professor inquired. "The bomb, it didn't kill them?"

"Not all of them, sir. I'm sure some survived, but I'm sure it thinned the herd considerably." He paused and looked around for more. "Come on," he said, motioning with a quick head jerk. He saw all was clear, at least as far as he could see, which wasn't very far. For all they knew, an army of zoms could have been standing 30 feet away, and he and the professor wouldn't have even seen them.

•••

## CHAPTER 48

The pilots of the F-16 fighter jets had watched the chopper go down over the burning land and notified headquarters as soon as they returned. They reported that they hadn't seen any survivors, but they also said that they could hardly see anything. They had thought survivors were unlikely, considering the way the Blackhawk had tumbled from the sky.

"Get those two in for briefing right away," the president ordered.

"Aye, aye, sir."

The two pilots landed at Jefferson Airport and were rushed to a chopper, which carried them to Mt. Hope.

"First of all, let us thank you both for your service.

We deeply regret that the bombings could not have been stopped. We know you did all you could under the circumstances, but we must ask you both a few questions."

The two pilots stood at attention, nervous as hell. Being in the presence of the commander in chief after a failed mission scared them both half to death.

"These questions are directed to either one of you, and please feel free to answer at will."

The pilots nodded, sweat rolling down their faces.

"The chopper, you say, went down, but you saw nothing? Please explain."

One of the pilots spoke. "Sir, the air was thick with smoke, dust, and debris. I saw it spinning wildly out of control and vanish into the debris cloud. Seconds later, a smaller debris cloud burst through right above the spot where they went down."

"Did you see smoke?"

"Yes, sir. Smoke, dust, even flames."

"Then there was an explosion?"

"If there was, sir, it was muffled by the debris. But yes, more than likely, sir."

"Did either of you turn and go back?"

"We did, sir, but we still couldn't see anything."

"Why didn't you shoot it down?"

"Sir?"

"The bomber. You had orders to shoot it down."

One pilot did all the talking, while the other just stood at attention, looking straight ahead.

"Sir, we lost all instruments while flying over Atlanta.

We were flying by line of sight only, sir."

"You couldn't shoot it down by sight, pilot?"

The other pilot finally spoke up. "With all due respect, sir, we were flying by the seat of our pants up there. We had no radio communications, no instruments to tell us how fast or how high we were flying, sir. Things happen pretty fast at nine hundred miles per hour. The fact is that we got there too late. We ended up about ten miles south of where we should have been when the bombs started falling out of the ass-end of the plane as we approached, sir."

"Thank you, gentlemen, for your service to your country. That's all for now."

The pilots were dismissed and escorted from the room, the heavily guarded door closing behind them.

"Your thoughts, Mr. President?"

"We need confirmation. There could be survivors. We need to know if that professor is alive or if the mission was scrubbed. How long before the dust settles for a safe landing? Can we air-drop in?"

"Not safe either way, sir. An air-drop through a fallout cloud, is just suicidal. The paratroopers would be dead before hitting the ground. Flying in? Who knows what we would be landing on or in. Maybe in a week, sir."

"A week?"

"Sir, we could drive there quicker."

"Very well. Take a unit for search and rescue."

"Leaving in forty-five minutes, sir." The ground crew packed its rigs and was off in less than a half-hour.

●●●

The search team pulled into Bear Creek and located the crash site, but there were no signs of any survivors. They found tarps rigged into some kind of lean-to, ripped to shreds with some remains of two victims scattered beneath. Who the two victims were, only a dentist with proper records would be able to tell. There was a lot of blood and many human tracks in the dirt and ash, which led every which way. The team found signs of a lot of scuffling around, as if they had been left by a mob of zoms dragging their limbs.

"The tracks lead everywhere," a soldier hollered.

"Keep your voice down, soldier."

"Sorry, sir."

"Follow them until you find ones that look natural."

"Sir?"

"The tracks – find the professor's!"

"Sir, how do we know that some of those pieces in there weren't the professor's?"

"They were soldiers. They would die before they would let anything happen to the professor."

"Right, sir." The soldier looked to the ground and followed the tracks with his flashlight.

Minutes had passed when the sergeant in command saw flashing lights from a flashlight, signaling that one of his men had found something. The sarge and two other soldiers headed that way.

"Whataya got, soldier?"

"Look, sir. Two tracks walking off straight in that direction." He shined the light east. "Doesn't look like shamblers, sir. The tracks are pretty clean and straight."

"Good work, soldier. Let's follow them." The search team headed off on foot.

"Look here, sir. Now there're three. What gives? It's like the third came out of nowhere. Pilot maybe? Maybe he got thrown from the chopper and landed here?"

"Not likely. Besides, there were three bodies burned up in the wreckage. Two were believed to be the pilots, since they were still strapped into their seats. This was probably a shambler just lying in the road until something good passed by. We need to hurry."

Boots hit the ground double-time. They followed the tracks for what seemed like miles.

•••

"What do you see?" the professor asked.

"All clear, Doc. Come on down. Get what you need, and let's get the hell out of here."

The professor cleared the bottom step and was amazed at how everything looked. There were just a few things out of place. Books had been knocked off the shelf. That was about the extent of the damage below. He opened the freezer and noticed the light was not on. "Oh, no …" he said as he felt the side of a container. "Still cold, good." He grabbed a Styrofoam cooler and laid a partially frozen ice pack from the freezer in it, along with a few samples. Got it. Let's go."

The soldier was busy looking around the labs basement. There were cages everywhere. Most were empty, but some still contained animals: snakes, mice, and rats mostly. All were dead from what he could see. He heard a

419

noise coming from behind a locked door. "Doc?" he called out. "What's behind the door, Doc?"

"More specimens."

"Live ones?"

"Yes, for now."

"Are you just going to let them starve, sir?"

"Well, there is something back there that would be very valuable to the CDC." He paused. "But that would be impossible to take back."

"What? What would be impossible? What do you have back there?"

"Live specimens. A captured zom and some chimps."

"You have a live zom back there?"

"The last time I checked, yes. She was indeed alive."

"A female? You've kept a female zombie back there?"

"Well, it's not what you think."

"Open the door, professor."

"I don't take orders from you."

The soldier turned the gun on the professor. "No, you don't, but I have my orders, and they are to bring back anything that I feel may be needed. You said yourself that it would be valuable, so open the damn door!"

The professor ignored the order and started for the stairs when he heard a gunshot. The soldier had shot the padlock off the door.

"What the …? Do you have any idea what's in that room, or what the world could be exposed to if it gets out?"

"No, sir, I don't, but now that the door is open, show me."

The professor headed toward the door. "Let me go on record as telling you that this could be a big mistake." He opened the door and let him in.

Inside were more specimens in cages. Some were rabid, some sleeping, possibly even dead, but there was one in particular that gained the soldier's interest. A very large cage stood in the back of the room. It was covered by a tarp.

"Don't get too close," the professor warned, but the soldier continued anyway. He poked his rife under the tarp and started to lift it up. Inside was a little girl, her skin too deteriorated to determine her age.

"What in the hell do you have going on here?" barked the soldier. "Are you all right, little one?"

"That little girl you call 'Little One' would love to bite your head off if given a chance. She's infected."

"Who is she?"

"Well, she did work for me until she cut herself. She changed into one of them a short time after. She gave me permission to study her and do whatever it took to find a cure. Here it is in black and white, with her signature at the bottom." The professor dug a copy of the signed paper from the drawer and handed it to the soldier.

"You're one sick bastard, aren't you?" the soldier asked, not really expecting an answer.

"In a way, but things have to be done, and she was willing to do it. In the name of *research*, of course."

"Research? This can't be legal! Look at her. She's an innocent little girl."

"You know, I'm not sure if it's legal or not, but she's

far from innocent and may have been the only chance we had to find a cure for this. We must go. The CDC is waiting."

The soldier grabbed onto the cage, trying to figure out how they were to take her with them.

"I wouldn't do that if I were ... Ah, too late."

Within a microsecond, the girl bolted to her feet and bit one of the soldier's fingers completely off.

"Oh, now look what you've done. I told you not to get too close. We couldn't take her anyway. I couldn't risk moving her."

"I've never seen one move that fast. She bit me! My finger, it's gone!" the soldier cried, dropping his rifle and holding his bloody hand with his other.

"I see that." The professor opened a cabinet door and shook a couple of pills from a bottle. "Here, take these. It will help ease the pain a little."

"Thanks." The soldier paused to dress the wound. He then looked up to the professor, wide-eyed. "Am I going to turn into one of them—them things out there?" he asked as his voice shook.

"Oh, no, I'm afraid not." A sigh of relief fell over the soldier. "You're more than likely going to turn into something like her." The professor nodded in the little girl's direction.

"Like her? What do you mean, like her?" The professor handed him a bottle of water from the fridge to wash down the pills.

"Well, my friend, I've been studying her for quite some time. She used to be one of them but not anymore."

"You found a cure?"

"No, not exactly. She's more of a supermodel, let's say."

"I don't get it."

The professor bent down and handed the soldier a towel. "Apply pressure," he said while sliding his rifle out of the way. "It's quite common to have to enhance a virus to see what it can become, see what it mutates into, before you can find something to stop it. She's that."

"She's … she's what?"

"The virus can easily adapt and mutate its carrier into something like her over a period of time. That's why it's very important to destroy the virus at all cost, right now, while they are just walkers, shamblers, zombies, or flesh junkies – whatever you want to call them. Within time, the virus will mutate into a super-zombie, one that has superior strength and can run. Now that would be very difficult to stop."

"You created a monster!"

"In a way. It's just a prototype and will eventually create itself. Like I said, in a matter of time."

The soldier's blood had now soaked through the rag and was pooling on the floor. The professor backed away, making sure to step around the puddle.

"So now what? Am I going to die?"

The professor glanced at the door, thinking that it might be time to make his exit.

"Well, this has certainly changed things, hasn't it? I sure wish you would have listened to me about opening that door and not getting too close." The professor opened a drawer and reached inside.

"There's got to be something you can do."

"Sure there is. Don't worry. I have it all under control." The professor turned, pointing a 9 mm pistol at the soldier, catching him completely off guard.

"Wait a minute, you don't have to do that," he cried out, glancing at his M-4 rifle that lay on the floor.

"I wouldn't even think about what you're thinking right now." In the professor's left hand was another padlock. He walked closer to the door, kicking the rifle out to an adjacent room. "Your 45? Two fingers, please. Oh, I'm sorry, use your left hand, you seem to be missing one on your right."

"You're an ass." The soldier grabbed his gun dropping it to the floor.

"A little help."

The soldier aggressively kicked the gun across the floor. "You can't just leave me here!"

"Oh, yes I can, and I must. What you have can't ever be let out of this room." With that said, Simon stepped out and padlocked the door behind him. The soldier's screams fell silent as soon as the door shut tight.

Simon grabbed the cooler and made his way up the staircase. On his way up, gunfire erupted at ground level. Simon stopped in his tracks, midway up the stairs. The fighting went on for quite some time and sounded like a war zone. The ground shook above as dust and ash floated down from the ceiling. The professor backed his way down the stairs and sought out cover. He stood in the doorway of a closet and waited.

The gunfire gained intensity. The screaming was muffled but audible enough to make out at times. The troops were in trouble. The mass of zombies was too much for them. Loss of men was imminent. The professor could hear one screaming in agony. He pictured in his mind what the poor lad was going through. Then ... "Soldier, no! No grena–" The order was covered by a blast. The soldier, overtaken by zoms, was being eaten alive. Swarms of zoms were upon them all. He reached for his belt and pulled two grenades, pulling the pins with his teeth, and waited.

The grenades exploded, shaking the ground and knocking the professor off his feet. The cooler he was carrying went airborne, crashing up against a file cabinet not too far from him. The impact broke open the case, and the contents spilled to the ground. Debris fell all around as if the ceiling was coming down on him. The staircase collapsed, caving in from all directions.

•••

## CHAPTER 49

"Steve, you have to wake up. Steve! You can't leave me like this. I don't know what to do. Please, Steve, please wake up. Tell me everything is going to be all right. I can't do this without you, Steve. I need you. I love you, Steve." Sarah stayed by his side. She couldn't wipe the image of blood pooling beneath Steve's head from her mind.

Just then, Steve started breathing on his own. Lights on the wall began flashing as if generators had kicked on automatically. Steve's heart rate increased on the monitor. Nurses came rushing into the room and started unplugging him from machines that helped him breathe. Steve started coming around and mumbled a few words.

"Don't try to talk, honey. Not until we get that tube

out of your throat." She looked to another nurse standing in the doorway. "Get his doctor, stat," she ordered.

"What's going on?" Sarah questioned. She knew she just wanted conformation.

"Looks like your husband is coming out of his coma."

Sarah gave a heavy sigh as tears ran down her face.

The doctors walked in and took a quick look at Steve, then looked at Sarah with a smile.

Steve drifted in and out of consciousness for several hours. Sarah never left his side.

She heard a slight moan and then another as Steve slowly became conscious again, still holding Sarah's hand. He looked around the room and tried to speak.

"Where am I?" he moaned painfully.

"I'm right here, Steve," Sarah replied.

"Sarah, where's 'here'?" he asks again.

"You're in the hospital. You passed out."

"Passed out? Doing what? What are we doing here? It's ..."

"It's what, Steve? Don't you remember what the doctor told you?"

He thought, not saying a word.

"About the cancer, Steve?" asked Sarah.

"Cancer ..." He paused and thought some more, struggling to recall. "Yes, I do. I remember it all. And, Sarah?"

"Yes, Steve?"

"Everything's going to be all right," Steve said thinking back to the dream he'd just awakened up from – a dream that seemed so damned real. He smiled.

The door pushed open and in walked the doctor to check on Steve. He was dressed up like a zombie for the Halloween party that was taking place after his shift. Steve's eyes widened.

"Are you all right, Steve?" the doc asked. "You look like you've just seen a ghost."

Sarah drove Steve home from the hospital two days later. It was a very quiet ride, as it seemed Steve was preoccupied in thought. Sarah didn't want to pry but broke down and asked anyway. "Steve, are you all right?"

Steve hesitated, ignoring the question as he noticed a Walmart coming up ahead. "Can you pull in there, please? I want to get something."

Sarah slowed the car and entered the parking lot. "I'll get it, Steve. What do you need?"

Steve got out of the car. "I'm all right, Sarah. I'll only be a minute." Moments later, he returned with a grocery sack in hand. He climbed back in the car. They drove off.

They drove past the donut shop on the left and a small private lab on the right along the way. Steve noticed the lab was all boarded up. "What the hell happened there?" he asked.

"A young girl didn't make the curve and crashed into the building the day before your doctor's appointment. You don't remember? You're the one who told me about it."

Steve appeared to be lost in deep thought. "Oh, yeah. Yeah, I remember now," he replied, pulling an item from the grocery bag. He looked it over and tossed it in the air a few times, catching it in the same hand. Then he took a big bite out of the green avocado, chewed, and swallowed it down. He pulled another from the bag and offered it to Sarah. She refused with a head-shake and a disgusted grin.

"Ewww."

"To each his own." Steve took another big bite.

•••

Steve had only been home from the hospital a couple of days when a taxi pulled up his drive. Only the driver got out of the checkered car, as there were no passengers. The man strode up the walk and rang the doorbell twice. Without hesitation, he also gave the door a couple of taps with his knuckles. He had a clipboard in one hand and a small package tucked under his arm when Steve answered the door.

"Steve?" the driver questioned. "Steve Gable?"

*Oh this can't be good*, Steve thought. "Yeah, that's me," he answered.

"Please sign here." The driver pointed to a line on the sheet of paper held on by a clip.

"What's this all about?" Steve asked as he signed.

"I just deliver them, sir."

Steve looked past the driver to the cab sitting in his driveway. He wondered, *Who the hell would send a package via taxi?*

"Thank you," Steve said while handing the driver back his pen.

"You're welcome, sir. Have a good day." The driver turned and walked back to the cab.

"Uh, excuse me, sir?" Steve hollered to the driver

before he reached his car.

"Yeah?"

"There's no return address on this. Do you happen to know who the sender is, by any chance?"

The driver looked down at his clipboard. "Hmm," he said. "No, sorry Steve. There's nothing here."

"OK, thanks."

Steve set the mysterious package on the kitchen table and tried not to give two shits about it by continuing on with his daily duties.

Steve tried to keep his mind off that package, but every time he passed by, he had to force himself to look away. He felt a connection to this package, yet he had a very odd feeling about it, as if something just wasn't right, almost as if he were afraid to open it. The package must have sat there for hours before curiosity got the best of him. He opened it.

Inside the package was a DVD and nothing more, no note, not even a label. He inserted the DVD into the player, and hit "play." It was the security video from the lab.

"What the hell?" he said as he sat back in his chair. Steve watched it from beginning to the end not just once, but multiple times. The tape clearly showed a maroon Monte Carlo jumping a curb, deflecting off a pole, and hitting the building. Each time the file ended, the final frame appeared to show a very blurry back end of a bright yellow crotch rocket motorcycle.

"Oh my God."

Dumbfounded, Steve sat on his couch and flicked on the news. He watched as the anchor announced that someone had created a "super-flu" with mutations of the avian flu, and was now considering publishing the results and directions online. Steve couldn't believe what he was hearing. "No!" he yelled. "They can't do that. Someone has to do something about this."

And do something about it, Steve certainly did.

The end.

www.ingramcontent.com/pod-product-compliance
Lightning Source LLC
Chambersburg PA
CBHW070348260626
47161CB00001B/66